HUNTING AND HERBALISM

BOOK FOUR

HUNTING AND HERBALISM

BOOK FOUR

Leif Roder
aka Synonymoose

Podium

Cover design by Art of Neight

ISBN: 979-8-3470-1138-4

Published in 2025 by Podium Publishing
www.podiumentertainment.com

HUNTING AND HERBALISM

BOOK FOUR

CHAPTER ONE

Transformation

Zalia
Two months after the invasion's end

Zalia stood in the throne room of the capital of Endaria. With her was her best friend and giant snow cat, Boreal; her partner, Ember; their adopted child, Aylie; and her glimmering starlight puppy, Lumin. Soon after the final fight here in the capital, Zalia had gone back to the Grove she had created to reunite with her family. The past two months had been some of the most relaxing since her first arrival in this world. Sure, they had needed to kill the odd demon or help a refugee or two, but compared to the past, it was nothing.

That was until a shared friend of Zalia and Ember, Lady Indis, had sent word that she wanted them to come meet her in the capital.

While Zalia had been relaxing, she knew that Indis had been hard at work. The army had taken over the capital as their base of operations, with Indis as the main civilian leader amongst their group. The capital was quite different from the last time Zalia had been there due to their hard work. The walls had been shored up, the complex and powerful enchantments of the capital fixed, and ranging squads sent out.

Refugees started flowing to the city from all over the land once word had spread. Some of those who had left Endaria and gone to the desert to the south had even come back once they heard that the capital had been freed. There was nothing like the smell of opportunity to bring desperate souls to your doorstep. Those who came now and worked towards the repair of the capital and the surrounding lands would have ample opportunity to advance in the world, should they have the courage to take it. Whether that was through hard work or not-so-moral methods was anyone's guess.

Zalia was not one of those people.

She had no aspirations to become a leader of the kingdom or be in power over others. All she wanted was to spend a little time relaxing with her family before everything went to hell again.

That was why she was so confused as they stood in front of Indis, Generals Faian and Ballast, as well as various other advisors and administrative types while Indis spoke.

"—as well as your help in bringing the Ascendant Nateysta to help us, then fighting in the final battles of the invasion. The generals and I have agreed that you should be commended for your actions. As the current council of Endaria, we grant you Et's Way and its attached lands for you and your line. You shall be given the title of lady and appointed as nobility of Endaria."

Zalia's first thought was to turn about and leave. Her second was to yell at Indis for being stupid. She resisted both of those thoughts, not wanting to act rashly.

Once, Zalia might have had no idea as to what was happening when confronted by this but she had since learnt a lot about dealing with people, Lady Leyra Indis especially so.

She knew that the only reason Indis was doing this was because she wanted to keep Zalia close by. The woman would use each and every opportunity she could to further her own standing and ability to control others. However, Zalia wasn't as naive as she had been when first meeting the woman.

That wasn't to say she actually hated the idea of having the town as her own. She wanted to stay close to the city anyway, since Ember would want to live near others and so that Aylie might have the chance to make other friends her own age. Friends that were people, not baby Ascendant gods. Not that there was anything wrong with having baby Ascendant gods as friends; they could be quite nice to have around.

"Alright, I accept."

She couldn't care less about the title. Having a nice piece of land that she could return to nature and live in would be nice, though.

With her easy acceptance, Indis looked a little worried, as if she had been expecting Zalia to put up a fight. Ever the actor though, she continued onwards without disruption.

"Excellent. We would usually hold a feast for such an occasion, but since food is at quite a shortage at the moment we will forgo that particular custom. Again, thank you for your service to the kingdom, Lady Zalia."

With that, Zalia finally gave in to her initial reaction and turned around and left, her family following.

As soon as they had left the keep, Ember bumped her shoulder into Zalia.

"*Lady* Zalia, why exactly did you accept? You do realise she is trying to manipulate you again right?"

Zalia looked at Ember with mischief filling her eyes.

"Of course, and I'm about to make her regret doing that, I think. Also, you know that makes you a lady too?"

Ember scrunched up her face, obviously disliking it as much as Zalia did. If she was able to do what she wanted to with the town, though, it would be well worth it.

It was less than two days' travel from the capital to Et's Way when their travelling group consisted of only five people, all of whom were quite quick on their feet—or could ride on the backs of the others who were quick on their feet, in Aylie's case.

The town of Et's Way was completely abandoned. What had once been a thriving mercantile town of tens of thousands was now an empty walled husk. Zalia didn't plan on trying to repopulate it, rather, she wanted to do what nature often did with such places and reclaim it. She had two abilities perfect for that.

Profile - Zalia Taori
Health - Excellent
Mana - Full
Stamina - Full
Class One - Hunter - Bronze 4
Linked Attributes - Strength, Dexterity
Active Skills
Kill Shot - Bronze 5
Hunter's Mark - Bronze 8
Fight or Flight - Bronze 6
Passive Skills
Hunter's Sight - Bronze 4
Survivalist - Bronze 11
Class Two - Herbalist - Bronze 3
Linked Attributes - Vitality, Resilience
Active Skills
Flora Identification - Bronze 4
Preparation - Bronze 7
Druid Grove - Bronze 4
Passive Skills
Harvester - Bronze 3
Herbal Magic - Bronze 11
Unity Class - Druid - Bronze 8
Linked Attributes - Wisdom, Intellect
Active Skills
Nature's Wrath - Bronze 9
Protection of the Wilds - Bronze 8
Passive skills

> **Healing Presence - Silver 1**
> **General Passives**
> **Heat Resistance - Bronze 11**
> **Cold Resistance - Bronze 11**
> **Aura Observation - Bronze 1**
> **Enhanced Vision - Bronze 1**
> **Poison Resistance - Iron 7**
> **Mobility - Bronze 9**
> **Stealth - Bronze 11**
> **Trapper - Bronze 11**
> **Teaching - Iron 19**
> **Flight - Iron 18**
> **Physical Resistance - Bronze 11**
> **Mental Resistance - Bronze 11**
> **Weapon Proficiencies**
> **Bow - Bronze 7**
> **Sword - Bronze 6**
> **Throwing Knives - Tin 17**
> **Bonded Items**
> **Druidic bow, Blessed by Starlight (Blessed Heirloom) - Deeply bonded Bronze rank.**
> **Druidic Armour, Blessed by Nature (Blessed Heirloom) - Deeply bonded Bronze rank.**
> **Ethereal Vault Gauntlet (Heirloom) - Deeply bonded Bronze rank.**

Both Healing Presence and Druid Grove would be perfect for the task; one helped nature regrow for kilometres around Zalia and the other could transform an area to become her Druid Grove, a beautiful protected piece of nature.

She hadn't advanced the rank of her abilities much since the final fight at the capital, a memory that still sent shivers down her spine—countless undead, powerful demons, and the two Ascendants that had been warring above it all.

Rather than hold back Healing Presence as she usually did around towns and cities, she allowed it to be free, sweeping over Et's Way.

It started slowly at first, as they walked through the gate into the town. Grass started poking up through the pavers, little Manifest vine buds opened and started growing up the sides of buildings, and saplings began to push onwards towards the sky.

They took a trip around the edge of the town, looking through the windows of houses and walking down the slowly degrading paths. They were all silent, even little Lumin, the quiet feeling . . . right, like it was respectful to those who had died here.

After doing a lap of the town, they started circling inwards towards the centre. The slow growth began to overcome the buildings of Et's Way, the grass cracking apart the pavers and forming soft, smooth walkways interspersed with flat stones, vines covering up houses with large leaves, and trees growing above them, forming a shadowed canopy above.

At the centre of town stood the statehouse, the same one that they had made plans in two months ago, just before the battle for the capital. It stood much as it had, though it was also being buried beneath the nature that was growing over the entire town.

When they reached the town centre and Zalia walked into the statehouse, the slow growth of Et's Way exploded into movement as she activated Druid Grove.

Active 3 - Druid Grove - spell - targeted - realm.
Tin - You may place herbs in stasis. Additionally, you are able to establish a small Druid Grove.
Iron - Herbs in stasis may now be put into a spacial storage. Plants and friendly creatures within your Druid Grove are constantly affected by the base effect of Healing Presence separate from your aura.
Bronze - The spacial storage effect of this ability is now linked with Ethereal Vault Gauntlet, creating one larger space. This space is considered part of your Druid Grove.

Druid Grove Added Effects
Healing Presence.
Druid Grove Base Effects
The protective energy of your Druid Grove extends to ward off harmful magical influences and creatures, providing an added layer of defence to those within its bounds.
Your Druid Grove changes with the seasons, adapting its flora and effects accordingly. In spring, it might emphasise growth, while in winter, it offers protection from the cold.
Your Druid Grove becomes a haven not only for plants but also for animals. Creatures within the Grove may form a bond with you, aiding you in various ways.
Mana - Low / N/A
Cd - N/A / N/A

The wooden beams of the statehouse came alive once more and sprouted roots, spreading outwards. They grew upwards and formed together over the roof, creating a huge tree with multiple trunks and branches that reached above the statehouse.

Similar transformations spread out from the centre of the town, completing its transformation from a ghost town to a lush forested glade built over its empty shell.

CHAPTER TWO

Nature's Reclaim

Zalia
Two weeks later

Zalia strolled through Et's Way, chewing at her lip, deep in thought. She'd been thinking about renaming the town to something else, something more fitting to its new appearance and purpose. Previously, it had been a main commercial stop between the majority of the kingdom and the capital just a few days west of it. Somehow, she doubted that it would ever serve that purpose again.

It was unfortunate that she was only able to create one Druid Grove. Something surprising to her, however, was what she had found when she had made a little trip to the old war camp.

She'd gone alone just to check up on the old farmer Mate and his few. Strangely, she found that the plant and animal life that had thrived within the old Grove was still there. Sure, he had mentioned that the crops were no longer growing as quickly and the effects of her Grove were certainly gone, but the animals were still helping out the farmers, and it seemed a beautiful little ecosystem had formed.

That helped settle Zalia a bit, as she'd feared the Grove was manipulating the animals to act that way somehow. Instead, it seemed like it had given them a place where they felt safe and shown them how they could interact with each other and the people living there. In addition, Ro's brief appearance had caused some of the animals in the old Grove to start worshipping him as well. She had caught the large feline that guarded the place dropping off a few shiny bits of foil at the altar, though she had no idea where from. Where Ro had been for the past few months, she had no idea. Shortly after the fight at the capital, he had flown off with the remains of the thousand-eyed one. Wherever he was, she was sure he was okay; it wasn't like there was much in the world that could threaten him.

With her mind settled and knowing that both Ro and the farmers would be okay, she had returned to her family and new Grove.

It felt a little weird to still call the place Et's Way. It just didn't feel right for what had become their new home, a lush forest built overtop an abandoned town. She had briefly considered calling it Et's Grove instead but didn't like keeping the original name as part of it. That was mostly because she had no idea who Et was or what they had done to have the town named after them. Deciding she needed to find *that* out before she changed the name, just in case they were someone important to the Endarians, she had invited Indis and the generals to come to see what she had done with the place.

In a way, it was her own message back to Indis. Indis could try to manipulate Zalia, twist her words and actions to keep her close and doing what she wanted her to do. She could try, but Zalia wasn't going to just roll over and accept it. Indis wanted to give her the town as a way of saddling her with some sort of responsibility within the kingdom to ensure she wouldn't go wandering and never come back.

Well, Zalia was going to do what she wanted with the town, then.

She was expecting them to arrive within a few hours, having received confirmation of their departure almost two days ago.

They had reached out to Indis and the generals through Aylie, of all people. Using her ability called Dreamweave, Aylie was able to bring both Zalia and General Faian into the same dream. Or, it might have been better described as showing each person the same dream and sharing the reactions they each had to what the other said in their own separate but identical dreams. Zalia wasn't even quite sure exactly how Aylie managed it, but it had been amazing to experience either way.

It was an ability that Aylie had been experimenting with more and more as of recently. Mostly, Ember and Aylie worked together on that ability, as Zalia didn't exactly sleep very often. They were probably back at the statehouse at that moment, playing around with Aylie's abilities and working them towards leveling up. Zalia expected a few of her abilities to start ranking up to Iron rank any day now.

Lumin was another matter entirely. She wasn't exactly sure if they would rank up in the same way everyone else did, due to the Ascendant affix that came after their Tin rank designation.

Zalia had been feeling out the limits of her own abilities as well, such as they were. In doing so, she had made a discovery about Healing Presence.

While the range of its effects greatly outpaced what she could usually perceive through her normal senses, as well as the magical ones, she couldn't see what it affected. At least, not in a way that could be considered seeing.

She had noticed it a couple of weeks back, a sense on the edge of her mind. It felt like her power was a part of the land as much as it was a part of herself, meaning that while she couldn't see everywhere it affected, she *could* feel it. She could sense the lay of the land, not to an exact, but more a vague, blurry image of it. In addition, she could feel when that land was being affected by some kind of magic.

That was how she sensed Indis and the generals coming.

They must have had an earth mage with them that was flattening out the land in front of them to provide easy, sure footing on their horseback journey to her town. It was something that she had seen the army do a lot of the time, though usually there were quite a few of them that also returned the land to normal behind them so as to eliminate any tracks they might leave.

Zalia strolled towards the front gate, eating some kind of nuts she had found growing on trees that had popped up in the main street. They were nice, kind of like almonds. When she reached the gate, she sat on a nearby piece of broken stone fence, one leg over the other.

She didn't have to wait long, soon seeing five figures riding down the road from the capital.

Once they were close enough that Zalia could see them, she allowed herself some slight satisfaction at seeing the disgruntled expression Indis held. She was looking at the new and improved town behind Zalia, her annoyance more than obvious.

They trotted up on their horses, everyone except Indis dismounting as they walked up to Zalia. She popped another of the almond things in her mouth, enjoying the satisfying crunchiness of it.

"Hello."

Faian nodded, gently patting the neck of her horse.

"Hey, love what you've done with the place."

Zalia smiled.

"Well, come on in, then."

She stood up and started walking at a casual pace into the town.

"How are things in the capital, anyway? Last I heard, you were all much too busy to be coming all the way out here."

"We certainly are too busy, but—" Indis started, speaking from where she sat atop her horse. "But, we can make time for one of the people that was majorly responsible for the current free state of Endaria, despite not being from here," Faian finished for her.

Zalia could hear Indis's teeth grinding in frustration. They had obviously had this argument already. Zalia didn't envy Faian having to deal with the woman on a daily basis, but if anyone could, she was the one.

"Good to hear. I actually wanted to know some of the history about this town you saddled me with. Who or what is Et?"

General Ballast was there too, along with Faian's advisor, Ryn, and a mage she vaguely recognised from the army. Ballast was looking around at the overgrown town with an air of approval similar to Faian's. Indis, on the other hand, was looking more and more annoyed.

Faian was the first to answer.

"Well, I don't know the full history, though Lady Indis might, but from what I remember, Et was a high-ranked merchant, one of very few in history. He was the founder of this town."

Zalia looked to Indis, who nodded in agreement.

"That's about all I know as well. He was the reason the town ended up so large, from what I know, though how he did that, I'm not sure."

General Ballast let out a deep chuckle. "Aha! Finally, something I know more about than you two! Et was no merchant, he was a scientist at heart. Sure, he excelled in mercantile business, but I happen to know that the only reason he did this was to set Et's Way up as a major trading post in the kingdom! Why, you might ask? Well, it's simple. He did so because the lazy man didn't want to have to go anywhere to buy his materials! Why go to them when they can come to you? Well, that and the fact he ended up with enough money to do as much of the said buying as he could wish for."

Zalia frowned. "So, to put it simply, a somewhat greedy man basically made the town and named it after himself?"

Ballast laughed again, much louder. "Ha! Greedy. No, the only thing that man was greedy for was knowledge. He was an inventor!"

Zalia hummed in thought as they arrived at the statehouse. The tree was fully grown now, with a huge canopy reaching out over the town. Leaves gently floated down amongst warm floating lights.

"Well, it doesn't particularly sound like anyone would mind my renaming this place, then. Welcome to Nature's Reclaim."

CHAPTER THREE

Fireside

Zalia
Nine months after the invasion's end

Zalia walked through Nature's Reclaim with her family, the five of them enjoying the sunny day. She was ahead of the rest of them, eyes closed and face raised towards the warm rays of sunlight.

When she opened her eyes, Ember was standing in front of her, but something was wrong. The flesh was melting from her face, revealing a grinning skeleton beneath. Zalia spun around to see the fur and skin sloughing off Boreal like she was melting in the sun. Aylie was curled up on the ground, turning to dust.

She turned back around and grabbed Ember's hand, holding it tight.

"No, no, no, no. Please, not you, not them."

With a single blink, Ember was back to normal. She heard giggling behind her and turned to see Aylie rolling on the floor laughing, trying to push away Lumin, who was intent on licking her face. Boreal was standing over both of them with her signature look of disapproval.

"Come on, darling, it's time to wake up."

She turned back around and Ember was smiling at her warmly, a deep love in her eyes.

"What?"

"Wake *up.*"

Zalia opened her eyes with a start, looking around in confusion. She was in their living room in the statehouse, head in Ember's lap as her partner gently stroked her hair. Aylie and Lumin were sitting by the crackling hearth, keeping warm in the winter cold. Boreal was stretched out cozily just beneath the couch that Zalia and Ember were on, the firelight reflecting off her mottled white fur.

She'd been having a nightmare, and not the first since the battle for the capital. Her subconscious continued to think about her family being turned undead, even when she tried to avoid doing so whenever she was awake. Luckily, her daughter was capable of manipulating dreams.

"Thank you, Aylie."

The girl, still very quiet for her age, gave Zalia a gentle nod and turned back to watch the fire in the hearth. The inside of the statehouse had been significantly changed by the creation of the Grove. It had reformed to reflect Zalia's needs, as well as those of her family. It had rooms for her and Ember, as well as Aylie. In addition, it had a few different living spaces. They were currently in a room with a comfortable, soft, leaf-padded couch and a beautifully carved stone hearth depicting Boreal, the stars, and flames frozen in time, which Zalia thought represented Ember—the hearth had become their favourite place once winter had rolled in.

She had missed the middle of the previous winter during her time in Cormaine. It had become her favourite time of year already, with light snowfalls that covered the land, dulling down any sounds. Many animals went to ground or huddled quietly in nests, making it the most quiet time of year. Zalia loved that more than anything else. She had been tempted to go north and see Glemp, to see what it was like up there at this time of year, if it was covered in snow all year long as it seemed to be.

When she had first thought about that, it hadn't made a whole lot of sense to her. Why was it that the season for snow was so short down here, yet year-round in the north?

Then she had remembered how she could create little ecosystem rituals, living rituals, using plants. They would help maintain the environment they lived in just as it maintained them. Here, where there was magic, the way nature worked wasn't entirely the same. It could be snowy year-round to the north because it was the plant's magic that maintained that.

It made her wonder how hard it would be to affect the seasons herself. Could she make it some kind of fake winter in Nature's Reclaim *all* of the time? She was tempted to try but didn't because, well, it didn't seem natural. Even if what was "natural" was something entirely different in this world.

"What are you thinking about?"

Zalia looked up at Ember, who was watching her. "Just thinking about how different nature is in this world."

Ember poked her in the forehead. "You know, you've spoken around the subject a few times, mentioning bits and pieces, but I don't think you've ever told me where you come from."

Zalia fought away the offending finger with a gentle smack, frowning a little. "I guess I never have, probably because I don't like talking *or* thinking about it."

Ember stayed silent, watching her with those warm, caring eyes.

"But, I suppose I could tell you a little bit." She sat up, trying not to smile at how excited Ember looked. "Well, where do I start?"

"How about with your world?" Ember suggested.

Zalia chewed at her lip, thinking.

"Ok, my world. It is much, much further ahead of this one technologically. There are things that they have figured out how to do there that I couldn't even begin to explain to you, there's just nothing like it here. There was no magic there though, none at all. People were just people, animals were just animals. The problem that the mixture of these two things created is that the technology had far exceeded what any animal was capable of. Nature began to disappear from the world, piece by piece, as the population of humans in the world grew and grew. You would have hated it there, I think."

Ember tilted her head, looking confused.

"What do you mean by technology?"

Zalia looked around the room, trying to find something so that she could explain.

"Hmm. People learned how to create things that were capable of feats more powerful than magic yet available to anyone. Imagine if anyone and everyone in Endaria had Bronze rank magic, or the ability to talk to anyone else in the world, or . . . they could travel at extremely fast speeds and all they needed was a key to do it. I'm not explaining it very well, but in essence, they learned to make things that had the potential to make everyone's lives better, yet more often than not, these things were used to harm or take advantage of others."

Ember pulled her in again, laying her head down on Zalia's shoulder. "I can see why you hated it."

"I didn't love it, no. But that isn't why I don't like thinking about that place. No, that is because of my parents. They were, for lack of better words, crazy. In my world, there are religions and gods too, but not in the way you have them here. The gods there aren't really ones you can meet, at least as far as I knew about. They also don't manage the people who follow their teachings. Because of that, many extremist groups exist across the world, ones that take things too far, or do horrible, horrible things in the name of those 'gods.' My parents were a part of one such group and I did *not* like it. They . . . hurt me in ways that only a parent can. When I was twenty, I up and left without a word and never spoke to them again. I moved away from where they lived, to a far, remote place of the world. Somewhere they wouldn't find me, a small piece of nature I hoped would survive the plague that was humanity, at least until I died."

Ember took her hand. "And then, you lived there for a while until one day you arrived in Endaria?"

"Yep, that about sums it up. It was a pretty hard first year, learning what to do and what not to do. There were a few close calls, but I made it through, with each year becoming easier than the last. Then yeah, I got sucked up by some portal that dragged me here. I've got barely any idea how that happened still, though my best guess is it was the Astar."

Ember squeezed her hand.

"I'm sorry you had to go through that."

Zalia shrugged gently so as not to disturb Ember too much. "It's alright. It was a long time ago, and I had a long time after it alone to think about why they did what they did. I think deep down they were really just scared, scared of dying, scared of confronting the world if there wasn't some mysterious god up there with a 'plan' for everything. I can understand that. I just couldn't deal with how it made them act."

Ember lifted her head up and nodded. "I can see that. Thank you for telling me."

Zalia hugged her closer. "Thank you for listening."

She hadn't missed that both Aylie and Boreal had been listening closely as well, her two children that she had saved after their own mothers had died. It hadn't occurred to her before, but maybe she had felt the need to care for them because her own mother had never really cared for *her*. She didn't want anyone to have the childhood that she'd had. Like the childhood that Ember had as an orphan.

"How are you doing, Aylie?"

Zalia had noticed that Aylie had gone still.

"Yes, Astral Walker just reached Bronze!" she exclaimed.

Zalia jumped up from her seat in excitement. It was Aylie's first Bronze ability, a long time coming since she had reached Iron some eight months ago.

"Well then, show us what it does!"

A list of Aylie's abilities popped up.

Druid

Active Skills

Active 1 - Plant Manipulation - spell - targeted.

Tin - You are able to manipulate plants within a small distance from yourself.

Iron - The range of this ability increases, and you are able to manipulate the shape of the plant's spirit as well.

Active 2 - Nature's Wrath - spell - area.

Tin - You invoke the wrath of nature. Nearby enemies are bound by vines, sinking sand, or other area-related hazards. Enemies are also subjected to a damage-over-time effect relevant to biome that lasts until the restraint has ended. The damage-over-time effect deals moderate damage per second.

Iron - When used, Nature's Wrath now summons two short-lived allies of nature. The allies are one rank lower than this ability. The allies are of a type based on the surrounding environment.

Active 3 - Worldweave - spell - varies. (Previously Dreamweave)

Tin - You may weave the dreams of creatures that are asleep. The more

familiar you are with the creature, the further away you may use this. Additionally, these dreams can have an effect on the target's real body.

Iron - If the target of this ability is tired but not asleep, you may weave a waking dream that has only minor effects on them.

Passive Skills

Passive 1 - Healing Presence - passive - aura.

Tin - Your very presence grants life to all around you. You, nearby allies, and any flora and fauna you so choose within your aura are affected by a heal-over-time effect. The heal-over-time effect heals for low health every second.

Iron - Healing Presence now heals the most grave injuries first, and you may focus it onto a single target, increasing that target's healing while reducing the healing other targets receive.

Passive 2 - Spiritual Connection - passive - enhancement.

Tin - You have a strong spiritual connection to the world. You are able to interact with the spirits and souls of creatures and plants alike, living or deceased.

Iron - When interacting with spirits and souls, you are able to discern things about them that others would not. This can include things such as lies the target tells themselves, wounds to the soul, and other similar things.

Starlight Priestess

Active Skills

Active 1 - Starfall - spell – area.

Tin - You may cause stars to fall in target area, dealing a high amount of damage to enemies in the area.

Iron - Stricken enemies are temporarily blinded and inflicted with a starlight fire.

Active 2 - Starlit Portal - spell - target.

Tin - You may teleport a short distance

Iron - You may create a portal that travels a long distance. You and one other creature are able to step through it.

Passive Skills

Passive 1 - Astral Walker - passive - enhancement.

Tin - Part of your soul walks the astral plane, allowing you insights into otherwise invisible or unknowable things.

Iron - You are able to see into the astral plane.

Bronze - You begin to touch the astral plane.

"Ok, now what does that mean?"

CHAPTER FOUR

Towards Silver

Zalia

With the rank up from Tin to Iron, Aylie's Astral Walker ability had allowed her to see into the astral plane. This had manifested in a few different ways, from her being able to see when people were talking through mental communication, to being able to see bonds between people and between people and their heirlooms. It hadn't been particularly useful as of yet, but with the rank up from Iron to Bronze, that changed.

Zalia tried again to talk mentally to Ember, but once again, Aylie reached out with her hand as if catching something. Ember shook her head.

"Well, that's . . . scary. Should we try bonds now?"

Ember looked concerned. "Zalia, I don't know if that's a good idea."

"Maybe not, but I think Aylie should understand what her abilities are capable of so that she can avoid doing anything dangerous or harmful to others."

Ember didn't look convinced.

"We won't do it without your permission."

Ember eventually nodded, so Zalia nodded to Aylie.

"Alright, just reach out and touch it if you can. Don't pull on it or anything just yet."

Aylie tentatively reached her hand out and poked at the air, and Zalia felt a little vibration across her bond with Ember, like it was a suspended string someone had just plucked.

It was weird.

"I can feel . . . something."

As Aylie reached out and touched it again, Zalia sent a pulse of thought down the bond. Aylie yanked her hand back like she'd been bit.

"Ow."

Ember raised an eyebrow at Zalia and she just shrugged.

"Ow? What did it feel like?"

Aylie looked up at the sky for a little while.

"Like . . . pain but not in my body. Pain in my soul?"

Zalia nodded. She'd felt that kind of thing before, usually when using a passive ability too much. Holding back the Ascendant's aura and sprinting for days using Mobility were the two that came immediately to mind.

"Right, so be careful of touching other people's bonds. That kind of pain is weird, hard to measure. I don't know if it's dangerous or not. Ro would know."

They played around with it a little more, finding that Aylie was able to read their emotions through the bonds. Kind of. She described it as trying to read someone's emotions except in another language. It soothed Zalia's fears about the abilities a little, though she was sure that as Aylie ranked up more, it would become more of an issue.

While Aylie had ranked up a lot, Zalia also had a few things to look at. Survivalist had reached Silver. That meant that six other abilities had also done so. In addition, Teaching and Flight had both reached Bronze as well.

Profile - Zalia Taori

Health - Excellent

Mana - Full

Stamina - Full

Class One - Hunter - Bronze 7

Linked attributes - Strength, Dexterity

Active Skills

Kill Shot - Bronze 8

Hunter's Mark - Bronze 13

Fight or Flight - Bronze 14

Passive Skills

Hunter's Sight - Bronze 7

Survivalist - Silver 1

Class Two - Herbalist - Bronze 7

Linked Attributes - Vitality, Resilience

Active Skills

Flora Identification - Bronze 7

Preparation - Bronze 14

Druid Grove - Bronze 9

Passive Skills

Harvester - Bronze 11

Herbal Magic - Bronze 18

Unity Class - Druid - Bronze 10

Linked Attributes - Wisdom, Intellect
Active Skills
Nature's Wrath - Bronze 11
Protection of the Wilds - Bronze 10
Passive Skills
Healing Presence - Silver 1
General Passives
Heat Resistance - Silver 1
Cold Resistance - Silver 1
Aura Observation - Bronze 16
Enhanced Vision - Bronze 18
Poison Resistance - Iron 7
Mobility - Bronze 15
Stealth - Silver 1
Trapper - Silver 1
Teaching - Bronze 6
Flight - Bronze 9
Physical Resistance - Silver 1
Mental Resistance - Silver 1
Weapon Proficiencies
Bow - Bronze 14
Sword - Bronze 12
Throwing Knives - Tin 17
Bonded Items
Druidic Bow, Blessed by Starlight (Blessed Heirloom) - Deeply bonded
Bronze rank.
Duskwraith Armour (Heirloom) - Bonded Iron rank.
Ethereal Vault Gauntlet (Heirloom) - Deeply bonded Bronze rank.
Passive 2 - Survivalist - passive - body enhancement.
Tin - The body of a hunter shall not fail easily. Gain the Heat Resistance
and Cold Resistance passive skills. They level alongside this ability. You
are able to survive with less nutrition.
Iron - Gain the Stealth and Trapper passive skills. These also level along-
side this ability. You require less sleep.
Bronze - Gain the Physical Resistance and Mental Resistance passive
skills. They level alongside this ability. You are able to survive with
less air.
Silver - Your aging slows. You do not require nutrition. You do not
require sleep. You do not need to breathe.

The Silver rank abilities were . . . ridiculous. No food, water, sleep, air or anything, really. She didn't need any of it. That also extended to Boreal, who shared

her Survivalist passive, something that Ember didn't get despite having a similar bond. Zalia thought it had something to do with the fact that she and Boreal had started with a Beast bond, not an emotional one.

Heat Resistance - passive.
Tin - You take reduced damage from high temperatures and heat-related magics.
Iron - You may manipulate fire and heat to a minor degree.
Bronze - You are able to channel heat from the environment to minorly boost yourself or allies.
Silver - Your ability to manipulate fire and heat is increased. Additionally, you may alter your form to take on a fiery visage.
Cold Resistance - passive.
Tin - You take reduced damage from low temperatures and cold-related magics.
Iron - You may manipulate ice and snow to a minor degree.
Bronze - You are able to channel cold from the environment to minorly heal yourself or allies.
Silver - Your ability to manipulate ice and snow is increased. Additionally, you may alter your form to take on a frozen visage.
Physical Resistance - passive.
Tin - You receive reduced damage and effects from physical attacks and physical-related magics.
Iron - You may manipulate earth and stone to a minor degree.
Bronze - You become harder to move by force.
Silver - Your ability to manipulate earth and stone is increased. You may alter your form to take on a stony visage.

Heat Resistance, Cold Resistance, and Physical Resistance all had very similar upgrades. Each of them increased how well she could manipulate the elements, as well as allowing her to take on their form a little bit. She was a little scared about trying them out initially but enjoyed it once she did.

The heat visage made her flicker with flames and made her body a little bit more . . . malleable. It wasn't exactly useful because she could already walk through most things with the ability her armour granted her, but it was still fun.

The cold visage did exactly the opposite. It made her look kind of like Boreal. She had icy shards growing off her shoulders and back, and her body became tough like ice.

The stony visage she hated. It made her skin crack in a way that reminded her of the obsidian demon, as well as making her body tough as the cold visage did. She stayed far away from that one after she'd used it the first time.

> **Stealth - passive.**
> **Tin - Normal vision and sight-based skills and abilities have a harder time seeing you.**
> **Iron - Other senses are also inhibited and you blend with your surroundings.**
> **Bronze - When still, you become invisible to the eye, only becoming visible again when you move. Certain perception types can see through this.**
> **Silver - You may now remain invisible when moving. This invisibility is more resistant to alternative types of perception.**
> **Trapper - passive.**
> **Tin - Your traps are magically hidden from sight.**
> **Iron - Your traps are magically enhanced.**
> **Bronze - You are able to magically fabricate basic traps you have been able to make before in an instant without materials. You are limited in how often this ability may be used.**
> **Silver - The strength of all traps are significantly increased. Additionally, you may create up to ten traps that remain permanently. These will also rearm themselves soon after being triggered.**

Both Stealth and Trapper passives had interesting and useful upgrades. Zalia had already scared Ember multiple times with her invisibility, though she still hadn't managed to sneak up on Boreal. She and her vibration vision were just too damn perceptive.

Zalia had also already laid those ten traps around Nature's Reclaim, knowing that they wouldn't trigger on any of her friends or family.

> **Mental Resistance - passive.**
> **Tin - You receive reduced damage and effects from mental attacks and mind-related magics.**
> **Iron - You may perform minor telekinetic feats.**
> **Bronze - You may mentally communicate with creatures capable of understanding language.**
> **Silver - The power of your telekinesis is increased. You are able to create invisible surfaces only you can touch with this ability.**

The final ability ranked up by Survivalist, Mental Resistance, allowed her to push off pretty much anywhere she wanted. If she stumbled, which she never did anymore anyway, she could just catch the air. She could even walk into the sky on invisible footholds, making that part of Mobility useless.

> **Teaching - passive.**
> **Tin - You gain a better understanding of what methods of teaching will work with certain people, scaling with the level and rank of this ability.**

> **Iron - When teaching someone, they have an easier time grasping concepts that you explain, scaling with the level and rank of this ability. You are also able to convey simple concepts even when there is a language barrier.**
> **Bronze - Attempting to teach someone about something you aren't fully educated in will give you insights into the subject, allowing you to learn even as you teach others.**

The Teaching passive had helped her *a lot* in trying to figure out Aylie's powers, as strange and hard to grasp as they were.

> **Flight - passive.**
> **Tin - Your manoeuvrability is increased and your air resistance is reduced while in flight. This scales based on the rank and level of this passive.**
> **Iron - Your ability to perceive your surroundings while flying becomes exceptional. You can spot distant details and potential threats with remarkable clarity, allowing you to anticipate and counteract aerial assaults effectively, as well as see threats on the ground.**
> **Bronze - All flight-based abilities are easier and cheaper to maintain. This effect increases based on how many allies you also give flight to.**

Her final rank up over the past months was Flight, a very nice addition that she wished she'd had earlier when they were travelling all across Endaria.

Both Ember and Boreal had also ranked up an ability or two each, but Zalia only had so many rank-ups, as Survivalist pulled six other passives along with it.

Not needing to sleep had been weird the past few weeks. While she didn't *have* to, she still could do so if she wanted. Falling asleep in Ember's lap had been a conscious choice; for some reason it was something she was able to do whenever she wanted now. Sleep was now a switch she could flick on and off, rather than a life necessity.

Recently, Zalia had been feeling more and more comfortable where she was. Thoughts of getting revenge on the Astar had faded far into the back of her mind, and thoughts of reclaiming Cormaine had faded even more so. Without constant danger, pain, or people dragging her into conflicts, she was getting more and more happy to just sit around with her family all day.

CHAPTER FIVE

Frozen

Lumin
Two years after the invasion's end

Little Lumin stalked down the hallway, trying to keep the pads of their paws quiet on the soft leaf-littered floor. The prey Lumin stalked was powerful, stealthy, strong, perceptive. The prey could perhaps be considered one of the hardest things to sneak up on when it came down to it.

Still, Lumin tried their best.

Then, they saw it. A flicker of movement, fur swishing. It was only a brief moment in time, a dashing figure flying past a doorway.

Lumin gave chase, sprinting after their fleeing prey. It was quick, almost quicker than they were. Almost.

Lumin reached the prey, pounced, and chomped onto its tail with as much force as they could muster. But it wasn't enough.

They looked up into the cold eyes of the prey they had been stalking, prey no longer. No, this was a predator.

Boreal

Boreal whapped Lumin across the head with a paw, gentle yet firm in its meaning.

"Stop biting my tail, idiot."

She was getting tired of the puppy trying to hunt her like she couldn't see their glowing, starry form from a mile away. It didn't seem like Aylie was going to teach Lumin how to hunt properly and Zalia hadn't been on a hunt in a long time. Boreal missed those days, when they would work together to make a kill so that they might eat for the day. Not that either of them needed to eat anymore.

Still, things were tasty, and learning how everything tasted was *important* to a happy life. Boreal knew that, even if Zalia didn't.

Peering down at Lumin, she decided that it was up to her. The others wouldn't teach them this important life skill, so she would have to do it. Oh, the cruelty of adulthood, to deal with youngsters like this one. But Zalia had done it for her with no complaint, so she would continue on with that tradition.

Boreal snuck away from the others, easily managing the feat now that they had grown so lax. Aylie was growing up now, almost as tall as Zalia, taller than Ember already. Boreal had a feeling that she would outgrow Zalia soon. After all, Aylie was what, two years old or so?

By Boreal's reckoning, Zalia had found her six months before they had found Aylie. That meant that if Boreal was eight months and two years old, Aylie was only two years and two months old. Yes, two years and two months. That made sense. Boreal had no idea how old Zalia was, but she must be quite old indeed, ancient even, for how knowledgeable about things she was. Maybe Zalia had already tasted everything, and that was why she didn't ask the right questions. Boreal wondered if she would ever taste everything like Zalia had, and what questions would be on her mind when that time came.

Boreal knew that the other animals in the Grove were off-limits. Zalia didn't need to tell her that, she could feel it from her power. The Grove wouldn't let them harm each other here. Not that Boreal wanted to, as most of the animals in the Grove were quite nice once you got to know them.

No, Boreal had a better idea anyway.

Recently, she had been catching the odd demon here and there. Nothing bad enough to tell Zalia about just yet, since they couldn't get into the Grove, but she wanted to find out where they were coming from. She knew from the past that they made nests in the ground where they caught nearby animals and created new demons. Well, she would just have to stalk one back to the nest.

Lumin followed her, of course, as they left the statehouse, then the town completely. The last little Tin rank demon she had squashed had been in the same direction the sun awoke from. She probably should have told Zalia where they were going, but she had just reached Silver rank recently, before Zalia as well, and wanted to test out her new ability. Her final ability to reach Silver was Frost Adaption, which had become Embodiment of Frost.

Passive 1 - Embodiment of Frost - passive - body enhancement.
Tin - You have incredible resilience towards snowy and icy terrain and environments. This includes ignoring the majority of cold and cold-based magic damage and walking easily on ice and snow.
Iron - You have a passive healing effect based on how cold the temperature is.
Bronze - The passive healing effect is increased. Additionally, you may now receive a small amount of nourishment from cold temperatures,

> reducing your need to eat. Finally, you may emit an icy aura that creates a severely chilled area around you.
> Silver - The icy aura around you enhances Frostbite effects. If you die, it triggers "Frozen In Time."
> Frozen In Time - Your body is encased in a near-indestructible icy coffin within which all time is frozen. Nine days from when this is triggered, you are released from the coffin, fully healed.

She liked the sound of Frozen In Time, it sounded comfortable. Plus, she could probably sleep that whole time as well, not worried about being pounced on by the little glowing wolf.

Thinking about the glowing wolf, she had the ability to help with that now too.

> Active 2 - Blending Shadows - spell - channelled - body enhancement.
> Tin - You are able to blend into shadows, using their darkness to hide yourself.
> Iron - When blended in a shadow you can move directly into a nearby shadow as you move.
> Bronze - While blending into a shadow, you can now manipulate the shadows around you. This enables you to stretch or extend shadows and creates shadowy movements that mimic your shape.
> Silver - You may extend this ability to hide nearby allies. The shadowy movements that mimic your shape are more defined and can inflict wounds with strength similar to your own.

Extending the shadows around Lumin, she was able to stop the glowing as they both padded into the forest that had popped up around Nature's Reclaim. With Zalia living there, the land had become a densely packed forest, extending for kilometres, and it was almost hard to move through, even for Boreal. Almost.

She found the body of the demon she had killed a few days ago and started tracking where it had come from. Lumin at least looked like they were trying to copy what she was doing.

Thanks to her ability Feline Eyes, she saw the entrance to the cave that she might have otherwise missed.

> Passive 2 - Feline Eyes - passive - body enhancement.
> Tin - The sharpness of your vision is dramatically increased.
> Iron - When activated, you may see heat in addition to your normal vision.
> Bronze - You are now able to see vibrations in the air and ground around you to a much more significant degree.
> Silver - Your gaze inflicts terror on those it is focused on. You can see invisible creatures.

This demon den felt different. They had magic that was making the entrance invisible, so there must be some strong demon in there. Perfect for the hunt.

She prowled up to the entrance, sneaking inside with Lumin by her side. They were trying to be as stealthy as she was but didn't quite manage to be silent despite her aid. That was fine, Lumin was still learning after all.

There was one little Tin rank demon standing close to the entrance of the cave, and Boreal fixed her gaze on it. The demon froze, then ice crackled along its body as Predator and Partner activated.

> **Active 3 - Predator and Partner - spell – targeted.**
> **Tin - You can use your cuteness to make others less aggressive towards you. Alternatively, you may instil a primal terror instead.**
> **Iron - You're able to slightly affect the actions others take in regards to you. Additionally, you can cause others' bodies to betray them, causing them to freeze or run in terror.**
> **Bronze - You become the embodiment of fear in the animal kingdom, radiating an aura of dominance and terror that can influence even the most ferocious of beasts. Wild animals will instinctively avoid confrontation with you, and you can call upon them to aid you in times of need. Additionally, particularly cowardly enemies may turn on their allies when confronted by your presence in battle.**
> **Silver - Enemies that are scared of you are frozen, literally. They are inflicted with Frostbite and cannot move.**

The ice spread slowly, covering up the sides of the demon until it was fully encased. There, it died a silent, suffocated death.

Boreal knew that there were usually Bronze rank demons defending these dens but that would be easy for her to take on. There wasn't much they could do against her, especially if she inflicted them with terror.

They crept past the dead Tin ranker and into the main chamber, where there were dozens of newly hatched demons. Just as she thought, there were two Bronze rank ones in the centre, looking somewhat at peace. She recognised them as the shapeshifting type.

Power built along the length of her legs, the glow building in her crystalline shards dulled and hidden away by Blending Shadows.

She pounced.

> **Active 1 - Cryokinetic Pounce - spell - body enhancement.**
> **Tin - When charged, pouncing on something will cause it to be coated with a layer of ice and snow.**
> **Iron - When charged, your pounce will have greatly increased strength and weight behind it.**

> **Bronze - When charged, your pounce will now grant you a body-tight magical icy shield that will protect you from one attack, no matter its strength. This can only trigger once every so often.**
> **Silver - The icy shell can now resist two attacks and negates momentum. When landing, the layer of ice and snow created is significantly larger, as well as applying Frostbite.**

When she landed on the two Bronze rankers, she unleashed her aura of terror from Predator and Partner, as well as her aura of ice from Embodiment of Frost. In an instant, the room was flash-frozen.

Everything in the room was still, frozen in time by her powers as the demons succumbed to the cold. She could feel the fear coming from the shapeshifters in front of her, their eyes frozen wide open. Slowly, everything in the room succumbed to the ice and died, their den a scene frozen forever.

She turned about and trotted past Lumin, out of the cave.

"That is how it's done."

CHAPTER SIX

I'm Going on an Adventure

Zalia
Three years after the invasion's end

It was on a beautiful autumn day that Zalia prepared to leave Nature's Reclaim to travel across Endaria once again. Since they had settled into their comfortable, relaxed life within the Grove, Zalia had taken to travelling three or four times a year, just by herself. She loved her family more than anything but in her heart, she would always be introverted. Sometimes, she just needed to spend some time alone, to recharge.

This had become especially true now that Aylie was fifteen. She had grown out of her silent stage, becoming more and more outspoken as the events of the past faded into memory. There were still hard times for her when the trauma of the invasion made getting out of bed impossible, or put her on a hair's breadth from an emotional breakdown. Even with Ember's emotional healing ability, Zalia guessed that it would always be something that affected Aylie like that. It was simply too big a piece of her life.

Aylie had listened to Zalia's every word like a devoted worshipper since she had saved her from the demon that had killed her family and fully intended to kill her. Those times seemed to be a thing of the past however, as the teenager quickly grew both in height and power, and she felt the need to start taking more and more control of her life. That might have been something caused by the powerlessness she must have felt when losing her family, or it was just a natural part of growing up, but Zalia was thoroughly exhausted by it. She had to tiptoe around every conversation, to not cause *another* argument. Ember, of course, managed it with apparent ease.

It was for this reason that Zalia was going on her fourth trip this year. Usually, she went up to the north to see Glemp, Zen, and Zen's family, to make sure they were okay and doing well. The two groups there had formed quite a nice relationship, working together towards survival. Zen and his people taught the Heat and Stone denizens about their "modern" construction and farming techniques, while they learnt about nature and the spirits in return.

This time, Zalia felt like going somewhere different. When she had returned from Cormaine, it had been to an expansive desert to the south of the kingdom. She had met a woman there, Sazcha. The woman had been stuck on top of a rocky outcropping surrounded by some type of underground wyrm that would wait for travellers to walk overtop of them before striking. Since Zalia had not seen another person in a long while, she'd had a short conversation with Sazcha before saving her from her predicament.

Zalia wanted to go and see what life was like for those people, whether they lived in cities, roving tribes, or even alone. It was another way of living that she was keen to learn about. They might even be powerful allies in the times to come if they were forged into powerful people by the hard life they lived. She suspected it might be so.

She was a little upset that Boreal wouldn't be coming with her this time. Her fluffy companion had grown more and more independent over the last years, taking to her own adventures. She had once been gone for a month before coming back with a scar across her cheekbone and a new heirloom item called "Crown of Frozen Terror."

> **Crown of Frozen Terror (Heirloom) - Bonded Silver rank.**
> **Tin - Cowardly enemies are more likely to freeze in terror at seeing you.**
> **Iron - Even enemies stronger of the mind have reduced reaction speed and movements while they are aware of your presence.**
> **Bronze - Enemies that cannot see you but are aware of your presence will hear whispering footsteps, brushing fur, and other sounds that distract from your real location.**
> **Silver - The effects of Predator and Partner and Embodiment of Frost are made significantly more powerful.**

Zalia had no idea where Boreal had gotten it from, nor would she even give a hint as to where she had been. The item was a cold, frozen crown that looked to be made of the same material as the icy spikes protruding from Boreal's shoulders, spine, and tail. It was a half-crown, jagged and sharp, form fit to sit between Boreal's ears on her head, yet floating ever so slightly.

While Zalia was yet to rank up any of her heirlooms to Silver, Aylie had finally managed to bond with the staff that they had taken from the body of the Silver rank illusionist demon they had killed in Ostoss. Upon bonding, it had changed itself to suit Aylie, something that Zalia's own heirlooms only seemed to do when blessed or deeply bonded. She had a suspicion it had to do with Aylie's astral connection.

Starlight Priestess's Druidic Staff (Heirloom) - Bonded Silver rank.
Tin - You can draw upon the light of the stars to emit a brilliant light from the staff.
Iron - All Druidic and Star-based abilities are enhanced when cast through this staff.
Bronze - When calling down Starfall, you may take extra time to cast the spell using the staff as a focus to call down a second wave.
Silver - Using the staff as a focus, you may concentrate to form a deeper connection with the astral and spiritual worlds for a time. This allows your perception and effect on those worlds to be deepened.

They were all there to see her off, Aylie with her gently glowing wooden staff, Boreal with her crown, and Ember with her radiant smile. Lumin was there as well, of course, frolicking with the grass off to the side. Zalia had a feeling that it would take a long, long time for the pup to regain their previous power.

Zalia herself had a big decision to make. Now that she had reached Silver rank, her Druid Grove ability had a new effect that she would need to consider strongly.

Active 3 - Druid Grove - spell - targeted – realm.
Tin - You may place herbs in stasis. Additionally, you are able to establish a small Druid Grove.
Iron - Herbs in stasis may now be put into a spacial storage. Plants and friendly creatures within your Druid Grove are constantly affected by the base effect of Healing Presence separate from your aura.
Bronze - The spacial storage effect of this ability is now linked with Ethereal Vault Gauntlet, creating one larger space. This space is considered part of your Druid Grove.
Silver - Druid Groves are now only possible to remove with an extensive on-site ritual. You may have two Druid Groves. Your Groves are now managed by three ancients. These are the ancients of War, Life, and Wisdom.
Ancient of War: The Ancient of War is represented by a feline. This ancient's purpose is to look after the defence of the Grove.
Ancient of Life: The Ancient of Life is represented by a tree. This ancient's purpose is to look after all living things within the Grove.
Ancient of Wisdom: The Ancient of Wisdom is represented by a crow. This ancient's purpose is to consider the future of the Grove.
Your Druid Groves are now linked together with a portal located in the Ancient Hall, allowing free travel between them.

> **Druid Grove Added Effects**
> **Healing Presence.**
> **Grove Portals.**
> **The Three Ancients.**
> **Druid Grove Base Effects**
> **The protective energy of your Druid Grove extends to ward off harmful magical influences and creatures, providing an added layer of defence to those within its bounds.**
> **Your Druid Grove changes with the seasons, adapting its flora and effects accordingly. In spring, it might emphasise growth, while in winter, it offers protection from the cold.**
> **Your Druid Grove becomes a haven not only for plants but also for animals. Creatures within the Grove may form a bond with you, aiding you in various ways.**
> **Mana - Low / N/A**
> **Cooldown - N/A / N/A**

The ancients were a calming presence for Zalia, now that she knew the Grove would be looked after while she wasn't there.

The Ancient of War was the same plains cat that had been there in her first Grove in Endaria. The one that had made quick friends with Boreal. It had apparently been offered a place as the protective ancient within her Grove and accepted upon the rise of that ability to Silver rank. She often saw it prowling around the perimeter of the Grove, now Silver rank itself, and wondered what kind of powers it had.

The Ancient of Life was the large tree at the centre of the Grove. It was . . . awakened, kind of. She had tried a few times to talk to it and had only once managed to receive words back. What the tree was actually doing, she had no idea.

The final Ancient, the Ancient of Wisdom, was a crow that looked exactly like the first form of Ro-ak, the one she had met before knowing he was a god. It lived in the house with them under the tree, often saying things that made no sense until a few days later. It was like having an oracle that could see the future but only spoke in a broken language that it was trying to use to make riddles.

So far, Zalia had found the ancients to be a little underwhelming in what they could do, but figured in a hundred years, or a thousand, they might be incredible to have around. That was, if she lived that long. Which was something she was considering now that it was a possibility. Something that she still hadn't quite wrapped her head around.

Going by the previous ranks of Survivalist—which went from reducing her requirements to eat, sleep, and breathe to eliminating them—the fact that at Silver rank it reduced the speed at which she aged might mean aging would be eliminated entirely at Emerald or Diamond rank.

The more important part of the ability was that she could now create two Groves. She had wanted to put one up with Glemp and his people but decided against it. The mountain was quite close to her current Grove, relative to the size of the world, so she wanted to make one farther away. Another reason she was going to the southern desert.

With a few final goodbye hugs and kisses, she left her family in the Grove, flying up into the sky and accelerating towards the south.

CHAPTER SEVEN

Ulzahar

Zalia

Zalia landed gently on the rocky outcropping where she had last seen Sazcha. Taking in a deep lungful of dry desert air, she looked around for any signs of life. Her vague goal was to find any kind of civilisation out here, learn something about them, and if the opportunity arose, find some new herbs to take home. Mainly, though, she wanted to find somewhere that she could set up her second Grove.

She really wanted to explore further east as well, towards where the Astar kingdom existed. That would be a dangerous trip, however, not something to be taken lightly. It would be best if she took someone with her when trying to go there.

From her vantage atop the outcropping, the world looked like an endless sea of dune waves stretching across the horizon. She remembered the direction that Sazcha had gone, yet there was nothing to be seen. From where she was, at least.

She took flight again, coasting through the sky on eddies of wind given life by the heat of the desert. The endless nothing ahead and behind her was surprisingly refreshing, all of her concerns for the future and memories of the past seeming small in comparison to the ever-rolling dunes.

Her reverie was broken by the sight of two figures trudging through the desert. It was a person followed by a large, flat creature leashed by a strip of leather which she only barely spotted. From the air, Zalia could see that the person was armed with the same type of spear that Sazcha had: a body-height length of wood topped with a slightly curved spearhead. Without any reason not to go talk to them, she dropped down from the sky towards them.

The figure below must have seen her shadow as she spiralled down from the sky, as they turned about to look up into the sky, holding their spear at the ready.

Without her feline backup, Zalia decided to land a healthy distance away. A healthy distance being exactly more than a spear-length away.

Having fully accepted the farmer look, she must have seemed quite strange dropping from the sky with her straw hat, suspender overalls, flannel shirt, solid work boots, and large magical wings made of wispy cloud. She bungled the landing a little, sending sand spraying all over the place and most annoyingly, into her shoes. She took a moment to stand up straight, brush herself off, and inspect the fellow in front of her.

He was very tall, somewhere over the six-foot mark, wearing long strips of sun-bleached cloth wrapped around his entire body save the face. There, he had a type of crystal fashioned into a face covering that completely enclosed his face from top to bottom. He kind of looked like an astronaut if the astronaut's suit wasn't airtight and had a spear. And a weird lizard thing.

The leashed animal he was travelling with was huge, only reaching his waist, yet thirteen or fourteen feet long. It had six legs stretching outwards from its body like a skink's would, and two bulbous eyes covered by protective, clear eyelids. It was also covered in sand-coloured scales that she guessed would be hard as stone.

"What do you want, *farmer*."

He said it like an insult, spitting the word as if being a farmer were a sin.

"Okay, firstly I'm not a farmer. Secondly, I just wanted to ask you if there were any . . . cities or anything nearby. I'm not super clued in to how you guys live out here."

? - Bronze rank.
? - Bronze rank.

She was settled in, knowing they were only Bronze rank, while she was now Silver. Remembering the fights she'd had with Silver rankers as a Bronze, she didn't like the man and lizard's chances if they did decide to attack.

He squinted his eyes, obviously suspicious of her. She wondered if having a more powerful stranger drop down on you alone in the middle of the desert was commonly a sign that you were about to lose your belongings and possibly life out here. Personally, she would be suspicious and a little worried if she were in his position too. Also, what did this guy have against farmers?

"Where are you from then, not-farmer?"

She gave him her best I'm-not-here-to-kill-you smile.

"Endaria! I have a friend living out here, Sazcha. I'm trying to find her since it's been a while and thought to look for the closest city. Have you heard of her?"

He shook his head warily.

"No, but there is only the one city. The magnificent wandering city of Ulzahar."

Zalia tapped her fingers lightly on her leg as she considered.

"So it's like, a city built on the back of something? Like a giant tortoise or . . . a beetle?"

He looked at her strangely, relaxing a little as she remained unthreatening.

"On a *what*? No, the city itself moves."

"Oh."

She stood there looking at him for a moment before he sighed.

"Fine, if it gets you to go away, the city should be somewhere in that direction," he said, gesturing vaguely south-southwest.

She gave him another smile. "Wonderful! Thank you for your help. Do you want anything? Maybe a nice wooden carving or something?"

He looked at her dumbfounded, so in response, she summoned her chunk of wood. With quick movements of her hands that were totally unnecessary, she used Preparation and Healing Presence to grow and cut off a piece of wood. The larger chunk vanished and within a few moments, she had a wooden figurine that looked a perfect image of the man's lizard pet.

Active 2 - Natural Matter Alteration- spell - targeted.
Tin - The careful preparation of herbs, poisonous or healing, can enhance their effects. You may magically dry, cut, or otherwise prepare various foods, herbs, and other similar items that are plant-based.
Iron - Natural Matter Alteration can now be used to magically harvest plants. All bonuses from harvesting manually are still applied. You may also dry, cut, or otherwise prepare foods that are not plant-based.
Bronze - You may harvest entire plants in their healthy form to be transplanted later. These can be stored directly in your Stasis ability or bonded item Ethereal Vault Gauntlet under those abilities' normal conditions.
Silver - You are able to control the shape of natural matter such as wood, stone, and dirt with perfect precision. The range and amount of matter you are able to manipulate at once with this ability increases based on your rank.
Mana - Very, very low.
Cooldown - N/A

It had been her final ability to rank to Silver, having been overtaken by Flora Identification in the last few weeks as she spent a few months walking around looking at plants—something that Ember insisted most people don't do. Zalia didn't believe her though, because who *wouldn't* walk around looking at plants for months?

The desert man was staring at her still, as she stood there holding out the wooden lizard.

". . . No?"

He hesitantly stepped forward to take the lizard. "Thanks?"

Zalia gave him a final big smile as she handed it over before a single powerful wingbeat took her soaring into the sky. A few more and she was gliding through the air across the desert once more.

She'd been feeling great since coming on this trip. Travelling around was made significantly sweeter by the presence of her wings and the fact that the majority of the wildlife was unable to harm her anymore. When she had been back on her own world living in the snow she had enjoyed exploring around her little wooden hut as much as she was able, but the constant danger of the million ways she could die kept her from feeling as free as she did now.

Down below, she saw a withered little bush that she wanted to identify. She landed in a much quicker manner than before, dropping from the sky and hitting the ground with an explosion of sand. A quick bit of wind magic using Zephyr threw the sand away from her this time.

She stared down at the withered bush, proud of its stubborn will to live in such a lifeless place. It wasn't even anything special, a rankless plant that managed to survive out here.

With a touch, she was able to tell that it had no cultural significance or use in cooking, magic or otherwise. However, she also received brief flashes of vision, depicting the long and arduous life of the plant. Events of import in the life of the plant. Dropped here as a seed by an animal. Lying dormant for years before a single life-saving rain drenched the desert. A water reservoir forming underneath it due to the rain, allowing it to grow. Living off that reservoir for a long time, growing tall and strong through the months before that reservoir ran out. Reducing in size, withering and dying down until it lay dormant once more, waiting for that next life-saving rain.

She let out a small gasp, blinking quickly as the visions faded away. Using Water Lily Petals, she cast a small ritual to create a localised rain just above the plant, allowing Healing Presence to nurse the withered shrub back to life. Once she thought the reservoir was filled once more, she gently stroked the new leaves on the shrub and flew off once more.

The visions were a benefit of Flora Identification's Silver rank.

> **Active 1 - Flora Identification - spell - targeted.**
> **Tin - Poison, cure, or food, you'll know. You may identify whether the targeted flora is poisonous, helpful, nutritious, or all of the above.**
> **Iron - You may now identify what elements different flora contain.**
> **Bronze - Your ability to identify flora extends to understanding their role within ecosystems, including their interactions with other plants and animals, aiding in ecological preservation efforts. Additionally, you gain knowledge about the historical uses and significance of the identified**

flora, allowing you to uncover hidden cultural or magical insights related to them.
Silver - You are now able to tell the life cycle of identified flora. When identifying a plant, you are given flashes of the plant's life.

With it, she had seen the life cycle of many different plants, giving her a deeper understanding of the natural world around her. The most interesting plants to see the life of were the most ancient ones. The trees that were hundreds of years old had seen Zalia's current lifespan many times over. She even wanted to return to Cormaine, just to see the life of that Living Trapvine that had protected Ro's power for so long.

A few days later, she finally found the city. It had taken quite some flying back and forth, speaking to the odd desert dweller here and there before she saw it.

From what she could tell, the desert people lived as free as could be, venturing into the rolling wasteland on their own or in small groups to hunt for food and literally anything else of interest. The magnificent wandering city of Ulzahar lived up to its name in a spectacular manner. It was a complex of hundreds of buildings, sprawled across a large section of flat sandstone. The huge sandstone block itself was half suspended in the air by some type of magic, carving a path through the sand.

Zalia stared at it in wonder, trying to figure out how exactly the thing had been created. Even Matthias, the only other sand mage she had known, couldn't have managed something like this. That either meant these people lived in a more tight-knit community than she realised, or a really powerful mage had created it. That meant this thing might be really important.

She flew towards it with many questions on her mind.

CHAPTER EIGHT

Sazcha

Zalia

Before talking to anyone, Zalia wandered through the streets of the moving city called Ulzahar. She'd had her aura ability, Healing Presence, restrained since entering the desert, since she had no idea what kind of effect it would have. Revitalising the entire landscape and returning it to a forest *sounded* good to her, but it was also unnatural and disturbing to whatever life did live in the desert.

The city itself wasn't anything like those in Endaria. While there were beautifully shaped buildings of stone and wood that looked like they had been grown into houses rather than built, these looked more like sand had built up from storms over time to create a wind-blown structure. They were oddly formed, some with jagged edges and others smoother than she thought possible, as if polished. Each building was different from the others, but they all held a similarity in that they were made from sandstone and sandstone alone. No other materials were used in their construction, no wood or normal stone; not even dirt or mud.

The people there were much like the few travellers she had encountered: wrapped up in cloth, much of it the same sun-bleached white. There was some variance in that within the more central areas of Ulzahar, however. It looked like the people there spent the majority of their time within the city, some having stalls that sold pieces of different animals or artifacts. What surprised her the most was the average rank of a person here. The people wearing sun-bleached cloth all seemed to be Silver or Gold rank with few exceptions. The stall owners and others wearing more colourful clothing, as well as the younger population, were lower-ranked, sitting at Bronze for the most part.

It made sense to Zalia, as these people must live in a kill-or-be-killed manner with the environment around them. Being higher-ranked, many of the desert dwellers would have anti-aging abilities, as well as potentially needing much less water and food, like she did. It was almost a given if you thought about how scarce any resource other than sand was. She also thought they weren't hunted by the Astar after reaching too high a rank, considering how many high-ranked people were just walking the streets going about their day. There must be Emerald or even Diamond rank people around if these were the norm.

Where the Endarians were numerous, low-ranked, and spread across many cities and towns, the people of the desert were longer-lived, lesser in number, and much more powerful. It brought up memories of being taught evolution in school back when she was a kid. If a species lived in a hostile environment, they tended towards longer lives with traits that made them much harder to kill. Alternately, if a species lived in a bountiful and safe environment, they tended towards shorter lives and traits that allowed for quicker reproduction.

It was very interesting to her to see evolution displayed so starkly, not through the separation of species but through the evolution of their society and magic level.

After an hour of wandering about, getting odd looks from some of the locals, and losing herself in the city, Zalia decided it was time to try talking to some people. There were a few specific questions she wanted answered: Are there any other cities out here? What is on the other side of the desert? Where is Sazcha? Most importantly, is there any oasis of any kind within the desert?

The desert people were such a small community, maybe a thousand people at the most, which was why she wasn't surprised to find someone who knew Sazcha so quickly. It was also partially thanks to Hunter's Sight's Silver rank effect.

Passive 1 - Hunter's Sight - passive - body enhancement.
Tin - The hunter tracks their prey. You can track creatures more easily. When tracking, you learn very basic information such as number of legs, number of creatures, and general size of creatures.
Iron - You now learn how long ago a creature left tracks and may apply a Hunter's Mark if tracking it for more than an hour.
Bronze - You are now able to discern finer details from tracking your prey. These details include things such as maturity stage, general health, and even the individual who left the tracks if they are known to you. Additionally, you gain an innate sense of direction.
Silver - When you know the target you are tracking, you are able to see who or what that target has interacted with in the past seven days even if tracks are not present.

With Sazcha in mind as her target, Zalia noticed that many of the people around her lit up immediately, along with various doors and roads. She stepped up to a nearby vendor who was glowing to her sight.

"Have you seen Sazcha?"

He glanced up at her, looking annoyed that she wasn't there to buy some of the ancient pieces of pottery he was selling labelled as "Pottery from the ancient civilisation of Yi'thar."

"And why do you want to know where Sazcha is, Endarian?"

"I met her a few years ago and saved her life, I want to see how she's doing."

He regarded her strangely, a look of reverence passing over his face at her words.

"What is your name?"

Zalia furrowed her brow.

"Zalia."

He nodded, then walked from behind his stall and gestured for her to follow.

"Come, I will show you to her."

She glanced at his now empty stall, items still laid out on a cloth atop its surface.

"You aren't worried about . . ."

He glanced back.

"What, thieves? No, we have honour here."

She wanted to object, but followed him anyway. Without any other information about the woman, this was her best chance at the moment. She wasn't trusting him blindly, though. Even if the vendor was only Bronze rank, the average rank in this city meant it wouldn't take much for him to lead her into a trap.

"Where are we going?"

He slowed down a little so she could catch up, then pointed to the city outskirts.

"Sazcha is using one of the rooms on the edge at the moment. You are lucky to have gotten here at the right time, she usually only stays here for a few days before heading off into the deserts again."

"Oh, you know her personally, then? Is that how you know about me saving her?"

He grunted in amusement.

"Of course I know her. Everyone knows everyone here. But no, she didn't tell me about that personally. We take a life debt very seriously here, with each debt owed by who to who being writ down in the records. Each day, any new debts are shown in the hall. I remember yours since it was a name I had not seen before."

"And how do you know I am who I say I am?"

The vendor stepped aside for a Gold ranker before replying. "I don't, but she will."

He pointed to a building further down the road; a figure was leaning against one of its walls. Sazcha.

"If you're lying, she'll kick your ass."

Sazcha looked up at them as she noticed the vendor pointing. A series of expressions passed over her face starting at surprised, moving through concerned and ending on mildly annoyed.

The vendor left them to it, going back towards the centre of the city. Zalia closed the distance between herself and Sazcha.

"Hey!"

Sazcha looked her up and down.

"Hello. Come to cash in the debt I owe you, I see."

Zalia held up a single finger.

"Actually, no, it didn't start that way. I came here to learn about your people and find you again. I *happened* to learn about this whole debt thing from that vendor back there. If you're willing to help me out with why I came to find you though, I'll consider it repaid."

Sazcha pursed her lips, thinking.

"Alright, I'll bite. I *was* going to go find the ruins that vendor got his pottery fragments from but it's always best to be rid of your debts when they come calling. What do you want?"

Zalia clapped her hands, rubbing them together with excitement.

"Alright! So, I want to know a few things, then I want to find a place. Which would you prefer to do first?"

"Well, it depends. What kind of place are you looking to find and what kind of things are you hoping to know?"

Zalia tapped her fingers rapidly on her leg. "Ok so, I've got this . . . thing I want to set up, but I need a relatively nice place out here to do it in. Well, I guess I don't necessarily need a nice place first, but I'd like one. I suppose I'm looking for an oasis or something like that, one that people aren't too attached to. As for the things I want to know, I'd love to know how far the desert goes and what's on the other side. I'm also here to learn about your people but I can do that along the way."

Sazcha eyed her.

"You know, maybe we can both get what we want here. The place I was about to head out to is an old, old temple dedicated to some god that no one remembers, once a part of the great civilisation of Yi'thar, if that vendor is to be believed. People say that the place is haunted, that those who are unwary will be killed entering its premises. Now, I know that all sounds pretty bad, *but* it's surrounded by a nice copse of trees and a deep reservoir. What say we go there, I'll tell you what I know about the other side of the desert, split whatever is inside the temple fifty-fifty, then call it a done deal? It'll be safer with two of us."

Zalia watched the woman closely, trying to judge if she was trying to trick her somehow. She hadn't given Zalia any reason to distrust her so far, nor had she last time they had met. Sazcha had been Iron rank then, but now boasted a powerful Silver rank. It seemed life in the desert was just as dangerous as Zalia's normally unusual life was. She wasn't worried about being able to defeat Sazcha in a fight if it came to that, as unlikely as she thought that would be. The only concern was being led into a trap or being taken by surprise. She had to be a little more careful out here alone, without Boreal by her side. Of course, she still had extremely powerful healing, anti-death ability, and protective abilities such as Protection of the Wilds.

Active 2 - Protection of the wilds - spell - area - counter execute.
Tin - You call upon the protection of the wilds. You and nearby allies are protected by a biome-specific shield and are subject to a moderate heal-over-time effect. The heal-over-time heals exponentially more based on how low the target's health is and remains until the shield is broken.
Iron - Protection of the Wilds now has a more ethereal and moving visage. You and Allies within a shield created by this ability may still see and move as normal. Additionally, you may enhance this ability with a single effect replicable by the Iron rank ability of Herbal Magic.
Bronze - Upon activating Protection of the Wilds, you and your allies within the shields are not only healed over time, but the healing effect becomes more potent as the shield absorbs damage. The shield's resilience increases with the amount of healing it provides, creating a symbiotic relationship between protection and restoration.
Silver - The shield created by Protection of the Wilds now stores all damage it takes, releasing a single powerful attack focused on who or what broke it. The nature of this attack is based on what type of damage is done to the shield.
Mana - Very high mana.
Cooldown - 6 hours.

The rank-up effect was representative of her often using the ability not as a tool to heal up from a dangerous wound, but to give her the room to ignore incoming attacks and launch her own, carefree.

"Alright, I'm down for it. When do you want to head out?"

Sazcha gave her a broad, almost predatory smile.

"Right away, if you're ready."

Zalia felt that the woman had somehow gained more out of this than she had. She wasn't bothered by that one bit.

CHAPTER NINE

Pyramid

Zalia

Zalia slowed to a hover, again, as Sazcha dropped down to the sand.

"Do you really have to land every time you check we're headed in the right direction?" she called down.

Sazcha looked up, then shaded her eyes against the sun, panning around.

"Yes, the dunes can't guide me from up there."

It hadn't taken Sazcha long to adapt to the flight, yet for some reason she was unable to guide them unless landed. While Sazcha wouldn't tell her why, Zalia guessed it was one of her abilities. In fact, despite seeing a lot of high-ranked people, she hadn't seen any flying. She would have guessed it would be extremely common, making the traversal of the desert much easier. Sazcha didn't have anything *against* flying or she wouldn't be doing it, so Zalia doubted it was a cultural thing.

She tried discerning where they were from her position in the sky, but the desert all looked the same as it had the day before and the day before that. Landing next to Sazcha, she tried to figure out what exactly the woman was seeing that she was not.

"How . . . are you determining where we're going?"

Sazcha glanced at her, then went back to what she was doing.

"It's complicated."

Zalia waited.

With a sigh, Sazcha looked back at her. "I know where we are by how the dunes form. Even though the dunes might all look the same to you, there is a chaos to the order that you can use to differentiate between one place and another."

Zalia stared blankly, not understanding a word.

"Come here and look over there."

She stepped over and looked towards where Sazcha was pointing.

"Um . . . what am I looking at?"

Sazcha shook her head, muttering. "Look. Dunes form in waves perpendicular to the wind. The small section of land between the desert and the sea west of Endaria, north of us, is a plain. Winds are always blowing off the sea into the desert, causing the dunes to build in a certain pattern. If you use that, plus the location of the sun, you can figure out where we are."

Zalia stared at her. Whoever had figured that out and passed it down to Sazcha must have been incredibly intelligent. She knew that the hot air created in the desert would rise, pulling in the cooler air from the sea and surrounding land but using that and the formation of the dunes to determine one's location was incredible, something she never would have come up with.

Granted, the method wasn't perfect and by no means accurate, but when you were in a desert filled with a whole lot of nothing, you didn't have to aim for your destination with any amount of exactness unless it was hidden.

"Ok, I get it, kind of. So is that how you all navigate the desert, then?"

Sazcha scoffed. "What? No, only this part. The dunes tell a different story wherever you go."

Zalia rolled her eyes. "You've got some kind of ability that helps you read the dunes though, don't you? Something that you need to be landed to use."

Sazcha looked down from the sky, checking the dunes once more. "Ah, this way."

She took off into the sky once more.

With a sigh, Zalia followed.

Zalia and Sazcha stood atop a dune looking over a single structure. It was made of huge, roughly shaped sandstone blocks forming a pyramid that was missing a wall. It was hollow, with a wide set of stairs leading down into the ground and out of sight. Chiseled into the sandstone blocks were images of sandstorms, many with people fleeing from them.

Around the pyramid were two dozen trees that reminded Zalia of palm trees, only these had branches that stabbed diagonally into the sky, rather than large arching leaves. On the side of the pyramid with the opening, in the centre of the trees sat a small, calm pool of turquoise water.

"Well, that is pretty much exactly what I asked for."

Sazcha laid a hand on her shoulder in a friendly manner.

"I thought it might be."

Zalia took another look at the markings on the sandstone blocks.

"Now I probably should have asked this before, but *how* haunted is this place exactly?"

She wasn't exactly prepared to fight spirits, though she was certain that her sword and bow would be able to harm them with their starlight powers. If that failed, she could always use Manifest to cast spiritual rituals. Her preference would be to make peace with any possible spirits though, as they might prove valuable to Aylie in the use of her Spiritual Connection ability.

"Well, if the person I spoke to is to be believed, which they should be, there are a few Bronze ranked spirits on the first few floors of the place, with Silvers appearing further down. The guy I spoke to, who was a contact of that vendor, never got to the bottom. Said something warned him away from going down any further."

Zalia nodded a few times.

"Okay, sure. Don't go too deep and we should be fine."

Sazcha peered at her.

"I usually wouldn't do this but before we go in, it's best we share what our skill sets are." She gestured to her long bladed spear. "I am a Fighter class, with Sand Magic as a specialisation. I mostly do melee combat with disabling abilities related to my Sand Magic and a little bit of minor healing." She sighed. "And yes, an ability that helps me navigate."

Zalia pointed at Sazcha.

"Ha! I knew it wasn't just you looking at the dunes."

"All of us learn to navigate by the dunes before we ge—"

"And are any of your abilities capable of hitting something incorporeal?"

Sazcha sighed. "Kind of. I can enhance my weapon with magic, which usually hits most things."

Even if it didn't, Zalia thought she *might* be able to cast some kind of weapon enhancement ritual.

"Alright, sounds good. I'm a Hunter, Herbalist, and Druid. Focus on hunting things down, ritual magic, and powerful long cooldown abilities. Usually use a bow, but can use a sword when necessary. I've got a lot of healing and good defensive abilities. Here, these are the three that are probably most important for you to know about."

She shared the descriptions of Healing Presence, Nature's Wrath, and Protection of the Wilds with her.

Active 1 - Nature's Wrath - spell - area.

Tin - You invoke the wrath of nature. Nearby enemies are bound by vines, sinking sand, or other area-related hazards. Enemies are also subjected to a damage-over-time effect relevant to biome that lasts until the restraint has ended. The damage-over-time effect deals moderate damage per second.

Iron - When used, Nature's Wrath now summons two short-lived allies of nature. The allies are one rank lower than this ability. The allies are of a type based on the surrounding environment.

Bronze - Upon using Nature's Wrath, you gain temporary control over

**the natural elements within the area. You can manipulate the environ-
ment to your advantage, causing vines to entangle enemies, rocks to rise
as barriers, or water to surge forth and sweep foes away.**

**Silver - The mana drain from continued use of Nature's Wrath is reduced.
The range and ability to manipulate the elements from this ability is
increased greatly. You now summon five elemental allies instead of two.
The Tin rank effect no longer restrains enemies in place, instead dragging them all towards each other.**

Mana - Extreme mana.

Cooldown - 6 hours.

Sazcha frowned. "Hunter, Herbalist . . . and Druid? What!? Three? Is that something that you Endarians can do somehow?"

Zalia shook her head. "No, just me. Still haven't figured out why or how it happened yet, though I do have some clues."

"That should help, having three classes must be great, assuming you get just as many abilities per class. These abilities look very strong as well. How are you against spirits?"

Zalia stepped off the top of the dune and started floating down towards the pyramid. "I'll manage!" she called back.

CHAPTER TEN

Spiritual Unrest

Zalia

Zalia knelt by a palm tree, inspecting it. With a touch, she received flashes of images lost to time as the desert transformed around the tree, pond, and pyramid. The dunes around shifted and moved, some building and others being worn down. Just as Sazcha had said, though, they always formed facing in the same direction.

She was pulled from the flashing images as they ended, met with a little notification.

Woody Palm - Unranked.
These trees grow by small pools formed across the northern edge of the desert. They are seen as signs of safety, leading the way for thirsty desert dwellers.

"Alright, I'm ready to go in."

Sazcha was waiting nearby, watching as Zalia inspected the trees and pool. There wasn't anything growing or living in the turquoise water, just the trees nearby.

They walked up to the pyramid, Zalia summoning her sword as Sazcha cast a spell. A swirling mini-storm of sand floated up and wrapped around her blade, some of the grains of sand glowing as they heated up.

"You have two heirlooms?" Sazcha asked, glancing from her glove to her sword.

"Three," Zalia corrected, summoning her armour as well.

Sazcha stared at her, wide-eyed. "Where did you find so many? Who are you?"

Zalia shrugged. "I just kind of stumbled across them. One was given to me and the other two I found in an abandoned city filled with undead in another world."

Sazcha stared at her in confusion for so long, Zalia wondered if her translation power had broken. "I—" Sazcha shook her head. "Never mind, let's go."

They moved down the wide stairway leading into the darkness, both at the ready.

The stairway slowly narrowed until it stopped at a doorway, the arch of which was covered in more depictions of sandstorms; this time they had some human features like eyes, or were shaped in a vaguely humanoid manner. She wondered if this old civilisation had worshipped the sandstorms or if she had discovered what might be another nature spirit.

They walked through the arch and into pitch darkness, Zalia able to see by her many forms of vision and Sazcha by her warmly glowing sand embers. Past the arch was a complex, with corridors and doorways set into walls.

"Want to head deeper straight away?" Zalia asked in a whisper.

Sazcha nodded and they walked forward, coming to a T intersection. To the right was another corridor and to the left, a set of stairs spiralling down with a single glowing spirit stood at its top.

Disturbed Spirit - Bronze rank.

Zalia glanced at Sazcha and she gestured as if to say, "All yours."

Zalia stepped around the corner and walked towards the spirit, weapon stored away and hands held in a placating gesture. The spirit was an amorphous torso with a head and two limbs that could be called arms, though there were no hands present. The head had two eyes and no other shape or form.

"Hello, spirit, I see you've been disturbed by something. Do you need help?"

The spirit turned ever so slightly to look at her and an opening formed where its mouth would have been if it were a person. A quiet whispering echoed around the halls, saying something she couldn't understand.

She furrowed her brow, trying to decipher its whisperings.

"I'm sorry, I don't understand. Is there something you could show me?"

The whisperings grew louder, angrier.

She took a step back, hands still held open in front of her.

"Woah, okay. Please don't attack me."

The spirit must not have understood her either because the moment she spoke, it attacked.

Her blade was in her hand before it reached her, the spirit floating towards her at speed. It had one arm reaching out towards her head, which she immediately slashed at.

The blade passed straight through, leaving a burning blue gash. The whispering turned to a high-pitched scream as it flinched away from her. With the strike, Hunter's Mark was applied.

Active 2 - Hunter's Mark - spell - targeted - channel.
Tin - Marked by the hunter, there is no escape. This ability marks a creature you can see. Marked creature takes a small amount of extra damage when damaged by you. You know the general direction of the marked enemy. Marking a second creature removes the first mark.
Iron - You may apply Hunter's Mark to three creatures at once.
Bronze - The three-creature limit increases to ten, and a small amount of damage a marked creature takes is applied to other marked creatures as well.
Silver - Any damaging ability or attack now applies Hunter's Mark. When applied this way, the mark does not count towards the mark limit.
Marked creatures are more susceptible to controlling effects such as restraint and are slowed.
Mana - Very low/second
Cooldown - N/A

The blue starlit fire burned through its arm, severing it in moments. Zalia took a step forward and cut upwards with her blade, setting the spirit alight down the length of its entire body. The scream withered out and died, just as the spirit did.

She turned back to Sazcha, sword still held overhead.

"Well, they're pretty easy to kill at least."

Sazcha snorted in amusement.

"Easier to kill than to make conversation with apparently."

Down the stairway, Zalia saw something glowing. She prepared her sword, thinking it was another spirit at first. Looking closer though, she could see that it wasn't a spirit at all, rather a little ethereal root sprouting from between the sandstone brickwork.

Sazcha stepped past her and down the stairway to touch the root but her hand passed right through it.

"Damn," she muttered.

Zalia stepped up and nudged her aside.

"Watch and learn."

She opened her vault door and stepped inside, letting Sazcha stare in wonder at the beautifully decorated sandstone arch that had appeared out of nowhere. Walking to the back, she collected a little wooden bowl of paste, something she had discovered with Ember all those years ago.

Manifest Paste (Potent) - Silver rank.
Capable of solidifying incorporeal beings.

Turning about and leaving the vault, stepping around the gawking Sazcha, she applied some of the paste to the root and found that it went on as if the root were entirely solid. Once that was done, she checked it with Flora Identification.

Hundreds of years flashed by in an instant, each image the same as the last. It had been here . . . forever, and the only image that was different was one of a man wandering down the steps, some pottery fragments sticking out of his bag.

> **Soulroot - Iron rank - Use in rituals to add an element of Soul.**
> **This root forms in places of spiritual unrest, often accompanied by various disrupted and enraged spirits. The cause of these kinds of places is extremely varied.**

She used Natural Matter Alteration to harvest the root, sending it straight to her vault, the process enhanced by her passive, Harvester.

> **Passive 1 - Harvester - passive - skill enhancement.**
> **Tin - The herbalist harvests herbs and other flora, with which they do what they will. You gain an instinctual understanding of how to harvest flora of your rank and lower. When harvesting flora of your rank or lower it has increased potency.**
> **Iron - You are able to sense nearby herbs and flora of a type you have already harvested before.**
> **Bronze - Plants you harvest of a rank lower than yours are granted additional potency to match your rank. Additionally, plants that are transplanted by you have increased resiliency.**
> **Silver - Once you have harvested a plant, other plants of that type communicate with you. The information these plants communicate with you is dependent on their nature but will often be things such as insights into the health of the environment or a source of corruption, as well as potential dangers.**

Immediately, her perception of the underground complex was widened. She could sense more and more of the Soulroot growing further down, and a sense of both danger and corruption was emanating from the bottom floor. It was obvious that it was the bottom floor, as there were no more of the plants growing below that point.

She could feel it, the sense being communicated to her by the plant. A powerful presence, the source of the spiritual unrest.

This felt like something that she was better equipped to handle than almost anyone else, considering the amount of time she had spent around Ascendant beings and other shades and souls, as well as trying to teach Aylie about her own soul and astral related powers. Hell, she had revived a god, how hard could it be to fix a little spiritual unrest?

They descended further, finding the place emptied of anything valuable. She had a feeling that the guy who had been here before them must have cleared out the first few floors. As such, they agreed to find the quickest way down to the point where they could find Silver rank spirits.

While the Bronze ones were easy for the two of them to take out, as both of their weapons were equally effective, the Silvers were much harder.

Once again, Zalia tried to talk to the spirits.

"Please, I want to help. Why are you attacking us? I can stop whatever this is that is causing your pain."

Once more, her pleading didn't work.

A more effective weapon she had found to fight against the spirits was soulfire. Using Flame-root and Soulroot, she cast a ritual that burned through the spirits in moments. With Hunter's Mark cast on ten different spirits, the soulfire also appeared on all ten.

Passive 2 - Herbal Magic - passive - varied.
Tin - Minor herbal-based rituals are a keystone of magical herbalists. You gain an instinctual understanding of herbal rituals of your rank or lower. Herbal Magic you use of your rank and lower has slightly increased potency.
Iron - You may emulate the effects of herbs you have used in rituals of a rank lower than this ability.
Bronze - When applying a herbal ritual effect to a target marked by Hunter's Mark, all other marked targets are also affected. In addition, you are able to combine certain herbs to gain a new base effect.
Silver - Your living rituals become almost indistinguishable from natural magic. The scale of your ritual magic expands, allowing you to now perform significantly larger and longer rituals.

The spirits dissipated with hissing whispering sounds, their anger dissipating in her soulfire.

They were four floors down now, and Zalia could feel the cause of the spiritual unrest was on the next. Sazcha was starting to look unsettled and Zalia knew why. Where the Soulroot did not inform her, her magical senses did. Whatever it was that was on the next floor, it was Ascendant rank. It was easily distinguishable as such, yet the power radiating from it might have been something of Gold rank, like it was diminished or lessened in some way.

"I can see why that other guy didn't go further down," Sazcha said.

They stood before the stairs down to the next floor, both of them hesitant.

Sucking in her fear, Zalia took the first step down the stairs.

CHAPTER ELEVEN

Spirit

Zalia

As they stepped into the room at the bottom of the stairs, Zalia was taken aback by its contents. It was a lab, a rectangular room filled with tables covered in various scientific instruments that she didn't recognise. The source of the Ascendant aura was a giant sphere in the centre of the space. It was made of hundreds of rings, each bigger than the last and each spinning on a different axis. Something at the centre of the sphere was glowing with a golden light that only escaped through a gap in the rings once every few seconds. In the irregular flashes of light, a single Gold rank spirit could be seen. The only reason they didn't immediately leave the room was that Zalia's soulfire was able to take out the Silver ranked spirits in seconds.

Sazcha immediately prepared herself for a fight, spear enhanced by her swirling molten sand.

Zalia did the same, holding her sword up. Despite having seen them, it wasn't yet attacking, so Zalia tried once again to talk to it.

"Hey, I know you're angry because of . . . whatever this spinning orb is, but please, let us help."

The spirit looked at them, opening its mouth in a silent scream.

"Oh, for fuck's sake."

The silence was broken by an ear-splitting sound so loud it burst her eardrums. She held her hands to her ears as the silence returned to her and blood dribbled out.

While Healing Presence worked on repairing her wound, Zalia cast the ritual of soulfire, lighting the spirit up in a ghostly flickering flame that worked hard to eat at its being. Sazcha, quicker on the beat than Zalia was, had already dashed up to the being and was slashing through it with her spear. The spirit ignored the fire and the spear, then punched Sazcha with lightning speed.

A scream left Sazcha as a ghostly afterimage pushed out of her body, flying backwards. Her physical body followed quickly, snapping back together with it. The spirit had tried to punch her soul out of her body.

As Sazcha lay panting, arching her back in pain, Zalia shot four, then five arrows through the spirit. Each left a glowing line that burned at it from the inside. It was beginning to look tattered at the edges, like a piece of parchment left sitting in dust too long.

It floated towards her and Zalia activated Protection of the Wilds, using Soulroot as the enhancing herb for the ability. At first, nothing seemed to happen and Zalia was worried that the spirit had somehow countered her ability. Then she felt, rather than saw, that the shield was indeed in place over both herself and Sazcha. The woman began to recover, the healing and protection of the ability now both altered to affect the soul.

The spirit tried to do to Zalia what it had done to Sazcha, punching at her with a single powerful strike. Zalia felt the impact on her shield; cracks formed across its entire surface. It wouldn't take another hit.

She shot with her bow point-blank, using the little boost of speed and invisibility to try to get away from it. Unfortunately, it didn't seem like the thing saw using any type of normal sight. Another quick punch made her shield explode, and a spike of energy with power equal to two of the spirit's punches returned right back at it. Half of its torso and one arm were blown away by the strike yet it seemed unfazed, still approaching Zalia.

She activated Fight or Flight as the spirit suddenly sped up towards her.

Active 3 - Fight or Flight - spell - cleanse - body enhancement.
Tin - Choose one:
When used, your perception increases greatly for five seconds.
Remove all slowing and restraining effects, and prevent further slowing and restraining effects for the next five seconds.
Iron - Option one now grants the ability to sense if you're going to be hit by an attack and where the attack is coming from within the duration.
Option two now grants you increased speed and dexterity.
Bronze - Fight or Flight now grants both options at once rather than having to choose between them.
Silver - Your body now temporarily adapts to the danger when this ability is used. In addition, your Strength, Dexterity, Vitality, and Resilience all increase for the duration of the ability.
Mana - Medium.
Cooldown - 1 minute.

She felt her body surge with power even as time seemed to slow. The attacks of the spirit were no longer untraceable as she dodged its next strike and her body had fundamentally changed somehow so that it could resist the spirit's soul attacks better. Her bow turned to sword and she struck out at the spirit at every opportunity she could get.

It just wasn't enough.

Zalia might have been quick and able to see where the spirit would attack, but after using her teleport to dodge the previous attack, the thing spun around and dashed at her, managing to grab onto her with a sweeping arm.

She felt it latch onto her soul and pull.

The pain was excruciating as she saw her own ghostly afterimage being ripped from her body. She fought with everything she had, casting a Soulroot major Dodge-vine minor ritual to increase her resistance to the attack. Her attacks didn't stop even as the pain increased, her sword swiping through the tattered and torn spirit as quickly as she was able.

Her attacks slowed as her consciousness began to fade, but then Sazcha was there, striking through the spirit with her spear in precise, quick attacks.

All the damage they had done to it soon added up as the strength of its pulling lessened. Zalia fought even harder, pulling on an invisible string between her soul and body to pull herself back together.

Just before she lost consciousness, Zalia used Hunter's Mark on the spinning sphere and gave the spirit a final stab empowered by Kill Shot.

Active 1 - Kill Shot - spell - targeted - execute.
Tin - Enhance an attack, go for the kill. This ability deals a tiny amount of damage. The damage of this ability scales exponentially with the target's missing health.
Iron - Kill Shot deals increased damage based on how many separate effects you have active on the creature.
Bronze - Kill Shot gains Enhanced Shot. You are able to infuse arrows with an element your Herbal Magic ability can create, or execute a Kill Shot, putting this ability on cooldown for thirty seconds.
Silver - If Kill Shot kills the target, excess damage is transferred to the nearest target marked by Hunter's Mark. Enhanced Shot becomes Enhanced Attack with the element infusion working on any weapon you have a proficiency with.
Mana - High.
Cooldown - 30 seconds.

The spirit, which was so close to dying that it had almost entirely faded away, evaporated. The overkill damage done by Kill Shot bounced towards the sphere and Zalia passed out.

* * *

Zalia woke up what felt like seconds later but must have been quite some time. She was propped up against the wall with Sazcha nearby inspecting the sphere. A cough racked her body, followed by a few more. Everything hurt in that weird way it tended to when she overstrained with passive abilities. Using a Frozen Heart major and Soulroot minor ritual, she applied a healing spell to her soul. The strain and strange pain began to fade away.

"I guess I owe you a debt now."

Sazcha looked at her and cocked her head in confusion.

"You owe me? Why? You're the one that took its attention away from me after it smacked my soul out of my body with that first hit."

Zalia held a finger up.

"But, you wouldn't have come down here if I didn't take the first step, then you did enough damage to it that my spell could finish it off before the thing killed me . . . or rip my soul out or something."

Sazcha shrugged.

"Alright, I can see your side of it if you insist. But remember we don't take these debts lightly."

Zalia gave her a weak smile.

"I know."

It might have been a bad idea for her to insist on the debt like that but it was for a good reason, or so Zalia thought. She wanted to make allies with the desert people, and it seemed like honouring their way of life might be a good way to begin going about it. Yes, she would have to pay out that debt when Sazcha came calling, but it gave her reason for a continued presence amongst their community in future. She would need their goodwill if they were going to be alright with her setting up a Grove in their desert.

"You chipped one of the spinning rings. Mind clueing me in as to why you did that?"

Zalia looked back up at her and the sphere. "Oh, because I think I figured out what exactly is in that thing."

Sazcha turned to look at her again. "And what is that?"

"A god of nature, an Ascendant like the others, possibly the god of the desert. Trapped here in this sphere somehow."

CHAPTER TWELVE

Freeing the Storm

Zalia

Sazcha stared down at Zalia from where she stood next to the many-ringed sphere.

"And you thought it was a good idea to break the cage holding that thing, why exactly? If it is some god like you say, we don't know it wouldn't just kill us the second we let it free. Did you not see all the pictures of storms chasing people engraved on this pyramid?"

Zalia stood up, groaning at how sore she felt. Not sore in her muscles or bones, but her very soul. "I did and we don't know, that's true. A simple fact remains, though, and it's that this god does not belong here, it should not be trapped in this sphere. The nature gods might seem purposeless and vacant, but I know that they serve a very important purpose. I know it is not evil, just as I know it isn't good either. It simply is nature, the nature of the desert."

Sazcha crossed her arms, remaining unconvinced. "Sure, but I'm not letting you break that thing free until you tell me how exactly you know it is what you say it is. How do you know it's one of these nature gods you talk of?"

Zalia walked over to the sphere and held her hand over it. Floating along the line of power that was the Ascendant aura was a . . . nature. As Nateysta had once explained it, the aura of an Ascendant was not the same as a normal person's, it was their very being. What escaped only once every few seconds was the desert, the dunes, the hot breeze that flowed above it, the beating sun, the freezing nights, and the desert storms. To Zalia, it was clear as day that whatever lay in this sphere could be nothing else, and she had been around enough Ascendants to know.

"Can't you feel it? To me, it feels like the desert itself resides in this sphere."

Sazcha put her hand up next to Zalia's, trying to feel what she felt. After a minute she furrowed her brow.

"Kind of? All I get is a sense of . . . home."

"And home to you is?"

Sazcha sighed. "Alright, point taken. Fuck it, why not? What could go wrong?"

Zalia put a supportive hand on her shoulder. "That's the spirit!"

Sazcha glared at her.

Zalia smiled. "Get it? Spirit?"

Sazcha continued glaring.

"Anyways, let's open this."

She considered how she could go about actually doing that. Destroying it carelessly was certainly an option but Zalia checked around for some kind of manual first.

The lab itself was filled with old and dusty equipment, vials, and books. The one that drew Zalia's attention the most was a journal of a sort that logged the scientist's path to discovery written by none other than Et, most likely *the* Et that founded Et's Way. What he had been doing out here she had no idea, until she read through some of the journal, that was.

The man had learned of the Ascendant nature spirits that existed all across the world and had gone in search of one. He had found this pyramid that had been ancient even then. According to his research it was an old building, dedicated to the desert spirit, that had been built by its worshippers. He had used its connection to the desert spirit to draw it to him and capture it in this prototype device. Unfortunately, it had gone wrong, and some of the spirit's aura was still able to escape by the slight miscalculation he had made. Zalia thought that was the brief flashes of light that escaped every now and then; it made sense.

As she was reading that, Sazcha was searching over the rest of the room. She slapped her hand on the page lightly. "Ha! Knew it. Here, come read this."

Sazcha took the book from her and started reading while Zalia went back over to the sphere. She was tempted to try jamming her sword into the rings, which could force them to stop. Or, you know, break her sword. She really didn't want that to happen, and something capable of containing an Ascendant might actually be able to do that too.

"Alright, you were right, then. How do you want to break this thing?"

Zalia was barely able to track the ring that had been chipped by her first attack. That had been as strong an attack as she was able to do in one strike; its power was massively increased by the exponential damage it did depending on the target's missing health.

"I was thinking 'violently disassemble' is a better way to describe it."

Sazcha rolled her eyes.

"Ok, fine. How do you want to violently disassemble this thing?"

Zalia pointed to the missing chip. Tried to, at least.

"I think we could just break a single ring at a time until the god is able to escape on its own. No need to destroy the entire sphere."

Sazcha nodded in agreement. "Alright, how you want to go about this?"

Zalia summoned her sword and instead of trying to jam the blade between the spinning rings, she slashed at it.

The blade bounced off with a deep vibrating hum.

"Well that didn't work."

"Apparently not."

Remembering the only way she was able to damage the obsidian skin demon when she had been Bronze rank, Zalia turned to Sazcha. "Try to hit me and let me parry it."

Sazcha stared at her. "What? Why?"

"It's an ability I have, just do it."

Sazcha struck at her and Zalia stepped to the side and into the strike, letting the haft of the spear slide down the blade of her sword. Using the strength from pushing against the spear and the increased power from parrying, she continued moving the blade in a glowing arc overhead to her side, hitting the sphere. It struck the outer ring, the one with a chip in it, and a whole section of that ring broke off, got caught in the lower spinning rings, and was flung across the room at speed, embedding itself into the wall.

Now unstable, the outer ring slowly dropped, grinding against the next ring a few times before its edge got caught, and the entire ring exploded into several pieces, all of which were flung across the room. One cut a slice across Zalia's bracer as she raised her arm to block it.

The desperation and thirst for freedom coming from the trapped god was now easily readable in the room as its power was able to escape a little more. Hidden in the aura was also a little ray of hope.

"Alright, that worked even if it was a little dangerous."

"Next then?"

Zalia nodded.

"Next."

They got into stance, and with another series of moves Zalia struck again.

Each of the next rings took three of four hits to chip or crack, with the next strike often enough to shatter a piece off of it. Breaking the symmetry of the rings seemed to be enough for them to become unstable and shatter the rest of themselves on their own.

Each time a ring broke, Zalia sheltered any exposed flesh of which there wasn't a lot due to her armour, and Sazcha would shelter behind Zalia.

As the regular humming vibration of metal striking metal sank Zalia into a rhythm, she started thinking about Hidey. The poor soul was still locked inside the cube that was his prison, not free despite the invasion being over.

Clang.

She had been thinking about how to find his true name so that she might free him and be safe in the knowledge that there was nothing anyone else could do to turn him against her ever again. Juniper would know, her soul was floating around somewhere in Cormaine. Zalia hadn't been thinking about it then, but if she had simply used Juniper's name to get her to reveal Hidey's, she would have had it by now. There had been too many other things on her mind at the time though and she hadn't realised.

Clang.

Another ring shattered, and the intermittent light from the sphere became steadier, now shining for longer than it was hidden away. The aura got stronger with each broken ring.

They would find a way to get back to Cormaine eventually. In fact, Zalia wouldn't be surprised if Ro was out there doing just that right now. She hadn't spoken to him for a long time and had started to wonder where he had gone.

Clang.

He was safe out there, she was sure, perhaps making his own connections with the other gods of nature and trying to get their assistance with destroying the demons and taking back Cormaine. It was a sister world to their own, after all.

Clang.

Three more strikes, and the next ring broke. The room was littered with shattered pieces of rings, a few stuck into the walls or ceiling, though many were just lying about.

They both stepped back after the aura of the god got stronger, then didn't stop growing in power. She had a feeling that the sphere had reached the point where it could no longer contain it.

This was the moment of truth, the moment they would find out if this particular Ascendant would be vengeful for the years it spent trapped.

The sphere stretched, the rings warping as the god pushed to escape. Zalia built a wall of stone in front of them just as a few of the rings collided, causing the entire thing to explode. The room was filled with a whirling storm of sand moving so quickly it left little cuts in Zalia's armour and skin.

The god did not speak; the only sounds were that of the storm and the feeling of victory and joy coming from it.

CHAPTER THIRTEEN

Desert Grove

Zalia

The storm slowly faded, and both Zalia and Sazcha's cuts were healed instantly by Healing Presence. As the storm faded, a little notification popped up before the storm disappeared entirely.

> **Scour, the Desert Wind, wishes to grant you a blessing. Do you accept?**

She pushed the stone wall she had built back into the ground and looked around the room. "Huh."

Sazcha glowed with a golden light and Zalia looked over at her to see a sheepish expression on her face. "Did you just accept the blessing *immediately?*"

"I got excited!"

Zalia sighed. She took a few tentative steps and peered up the stairs to the floor above. There was nothing there. "I kind of expected it to at least . . . talk to us."

Sazcha, obviously distracted reading whatever the blessing had given her, only murmured a reply. "Why would you expect that? We freed it, it paid that back with a blessing. Deal done."

"I don't know, all the other ones have spoken with me quite a bit . . . The ones I knew about, at least."

Sazcha murmured a bit, eyes flicking over invisible text.

Zalia sighed again. "Alright, what does it do?"

Sazcha finally looked up. "Well, it's basically a free pass to the entire desert. I could only *dream* about something like this!"

Interested, Zalia considered it. She had taken blessings from many other nature gods before and it hadn't ever gone wrong.

"Accept."

Blessing of Scour, the Desert Storm.
When in the Yi'tharan deserts, you are protected and led to your destinations. This manifests in several different ways:
The deserts seem to shift in a way that naturally leads you to your destination. Follow the dunes and they will guide you.
The desert will periodically bring to the surface long-lost items that will be of use to you.
The desert will warn you of dangers before you stumble into them.

"Wow. Not exactly what I thought with what you said, but I can definitely see it being useful."

Sazcha was looking more and more excited. "I don't think you know what this means for me! Life is going to be so much easier with this. We lose people sometimes, and it's always to a mistake or something overlooked. I would have been one of those losses if it hadn't been for you saving me from that rock outcropping a few years back. The chances of me making it to a rank high enough to survive have just gone up significantly."

That sounded a bit off to Zalia. "Making it to a rank high enough to survive? What does that mean?"

Sazcha waved like it should be obvious. "We're a very small group of people, Zalia, everyone needs to contribute to the city or things fall apart. The choices are contribute or be exiled, and either option means going out to the desert. As you might have noticed, it's not exactly safe out here. Silver brings relative safety, but if I make it to Gold rank, there isn't a lot out here that can kill me then."

Zalia drummed her fingers on her leg, thinking about it. It made a kind of sense, everyone had to pull their weight or there wouldn't be enough to go around. "What about your parents? Surely people normally wouldn't be expected to go about alone at Iron rank like you were that day?"

Sazcha shook her head, face darkening. "Normally, no. My mother died on a trip out to the desert. Surprise attack by a group of sand elementals going wild for some reason. Dad just wasn't ever the same after that day. I've had to look after him ever since." Her face had hardened but a hint of pride was showing through.

"Well, I'm glad you've survived so far, and if this blessing helps you survive further, well, it's a godsend."

Sazcha looked over at where the remains of the sphere lay on the ground, then back at her. "Uh, yes, it *was* a godsend."

Zalia stared blankly for a moment before realising. "Oh, no. Godsend is a turn of phrase where I come fr . . . never mind. We're splitting everything fifty-fifty, right?"

Sazcha nodded, and Zalia headed straight for the sphere's remains. It was a shame the thing had been destroyed because she would have loved to have one, for personal use. The ability to trap a god was no small thing.

Ruffling through the debris, she found something that gave her hope.

God-Trap Core (Constructed Heirloom) - Gold Rank.

"Oh ho ho, I like this."

Sazcha came over to look at it.

"Not super useful, despite its power. You can have it."

Zalia tapped on the metal plating, hearing that it wasn't entirely solid.

"I'll cut you a deal. I'll take this, all of the debris from the rings and the journal and everything else is yours. I was more looking for a location like this than the stuff in it anyway."

Sazcha shrugged, agreeing easily to the request, and Zalia opened her vault to start collecting and storing all the pieces of the sphere. She had to pull a few out of the walls and ceiling but managed to get everything, even the tiny fragments, stored away in one of the vault pockets. Though, she had no idea how it worked, what it was made from, or how to fix it. Hopefully, the remains and the journal would allow someone smarter than her to figure that out, though.

When they were both done, they left the bottom floor and started exploring upwards. There were no more spirits or Soulroot to be found, like Scour being free had dispelled them all. It was interesting to Zalia that the distress of an Ascendant was actually enough to change the environment around them. There were a whole lot of broken and old fragments, all of which Sazcha wanted to take. Zalia even had to store a few of them in her vault for the woman after she was unable to carry any more in her own bag. They used similar spacial bags as the one Zalia had once had here, and while the strength of a Silver ranker was able to carry a lot, there were also a lot of fragments.

When they reached the top, Zalia asked Sazcha to wait for a moment while she created her Grove.

She'd started the preparation for the ability right at the bottom of the pyramid, wanting it to be a part of the Grove, leading all the way up and then circling out around the few trees on the surface. When she went back to the entrance of the pyramid, change exploded across the surface of the desert.

While she couldn't see it, Zalia could feel every change that took place. The very bottom floor of the pyramid was cleaned of dust and cobwebs, the tables were repaired and placed themselves orderly. The floor was covered in soft, comfortable sand and little yellow glowing orbs floated about the space. Similar changes flowed up each floor of the pyramid, creating a complex of rooms fit for all kinds of creatures.

When the changes reached the top, the pyramid itself was wiped of the imagery dedicated to Scour, replaced by starry depictions of Boreal, Ember, Aylie, and the journeys they had all been on. It became a symbol to what they had been through during the war and invasion.

In front of the Pyramid, a section of sand cleared away to reveal a square plot of dirt. From that dirt grew a huge tree of the same species as the others, a leafless palm tree with spiked branches reaching diagonally up into the sky. In the base of that tree a portal arch like Zalia's vault portal opened, and through it she could see the front of the statehouse all the way back in Nature's Reclaim.

All around the pyramid and portal the desert transformed from steep dunes to soft, rolling waves of sand. Multiple pools of clean turquoise water formed all around the place, with many more of the palm trees growing from the ground. Some small, tough shrubs like the one Zalia had saved also grew, transforming the dead desert to a beautiful oasis.

When that was all done, Zalia turned back to Sazcha. "This is where I'll leave you for now. I'll put all of the things you can't carry in a pile within the pyramid's entrance for your return."

Sazcha was still gazing about in wonder at the transformation. "Wow, that is some ability you have there."

Zalia nodded in agreement, waiting.

"Right, yes. I'll see you later, I suppose. How can I find you if I ever need to?"

Zalia gestured to the portal. "You should be able to get back here easily now because of your blessing. If you ever need me, you should be able to find me or someone who knows where I am through there."

Sazcha nodded a few times, then stepped forward, hand outstretched. Zalia shook it.

"Good working with you."

"And you."

Sazcha wandered off, still gazing about the Grove. If she had never left the desert, Zalia thought this might possibly be the most green the woman had ever seen.

Zalia looked about a bit herself, then stepped through the portal to Nature's Reclaim, ready to be with her family again.

CHAPTER FOURTEEN

New Life

Ember
Three years after the invasion's end

Ember walked casually through Zalia's Grove, still a little awed by the whole thing. The fact that her wonderful, beautiful partner was able to create something like this, especially at Silver rank, was a certain sign of her competence as a Druid. People often thought that the power of your abilities came from the luck of the draw, whatever classes you were fortunate enough to get access to before you chose. She had always thought differently, though.

In Ember's opinion, the power of the abilities you developed was entirely based on what you had been through to get them. She knew Zalia had been through a lot to get hers.

Hildebrandt was another example of this, a woman so capable and determined that she had become the strongest person in the kingdom and nigh unkillable. She hoped that Zalia would reach that rank, and she dearly hoped she would be able to keep up.

Ember had reached Silver rank a few months after Zalia had; the opportunity to level up many of her skills how she usually did was limited by the lack of people around. Not that she hadn't gone on her own journeys across the kingdom to help people, and not that it was an issue anymore.

They'd had a good few years of peace and silence as the rest of the kingdom recovered and rebuilt, but people had eventually started flocking to the Grove once word got around.

As people had started arriving, Zalia had begrudgingly allowed them to live in the town. The only reason she had done so was because of the three ancients who looked after the Grove.

A building near the centre of town had been transformed by the Ancient of Life and the Ancient of Wisdom working together. It had become a temple to Nateysta, the god in whose image the Ancient of Wisdom had been made. That very ancient now stayed in the temple, taking in anyone who needed help or guidance and taking care of their needs with the assistance of the other two ancients.

Thus, a thriving town had been born.

The animals that lived in the town lived there as citizens, with their own jobs, homes, and lives. It was a bit of an adjustment for the newly arriving Endarians but they soon grew used to it.

Ember nodded to Grey, the cat, as she walked down the street, receiving a little purr in return. She plucked a sweet fruit off a nearby tree as she went, on her way to help settle a dispute.

The Ancient of Wisdom had asked her to mediate between a group of farmers who wanted to set up a farm just outside the walls and the giant moles who lived there. It was an excellent distraction for her as she was waiting for Zalia.

The moles were an extremely productive group within Nature's Reclaim, often bringing up raw metals and minerals for everyone's use. They didn't ask anything for it, nor did anyone else ask anything for what they contributed. If you needed something, you simply went to the Ancient of Wisdom and it would make sure it happened.

These newly arrived farmers had been a bit of a problem, however.

They insisted that they deserved more space, materials, and almost everything else than the animals of the Grove did simply because they were human and this was a human kingdom. Well, that kind of mentality had started angering not only the animals but the Bathar that lived with them as well.

For some reason, the Bathar population in the kingdom had surged after the invasion. Ember thought it might have to do with the amount of space they now had since many people had died, but Zalia said it might be because of all the souls she released in Cormaine. Ember didn't question that, as Zalia often had thoughts and ideas seemingly from nowhere that turned out to be right. Kind of like Aylie.

Parenting Aylie had become harder and harder of late, ever since her powers over the astral had reached Bronze rank. Now fifteen, the girl had a tendency to know exactly what you were thinking, often because she could literally see it.

Ember hadn't figured out how to stop her from doing that, though Zalia had somehow managed to block it entirely. Either way, it was hard to make an argument about anything with the girl when she'd just break it down with information pulled from your own brain. Issues for another day.

For now, she had to resolve this dispute.

She had reached the town gates and could hear the arguing already. A few of the farmers were yelling something about this being their land, to which the moles were replying loudly through mental communication that they were here first and the farmers should find some other dirt further out from the town.

She strolled towards them and one of the farmers spotted her.

"Finally! The Ancient of *Wisdom* has finally sent someone to get rid of these pesky moles for us."

Ember scowled at him.

"The fuck is your issue, man?"

The farmer stood silent, mouth agape.

"Good, now stay shut up while I explain something to you. The moles have been here for years and have contributed more to the Grove than you may ever do. They're hardworking, peaceful, and most importantly, mind their own business. You've been angering a lot of people in this town, so you can either figure your shit out and be respectful to the others or take your shit and leave. This is not a place of opportunity, this is a community for those who want to live as equals."

Some of the farmers began to look angry, so Ember soothed their emotions.

Emotional Soothing
Tin - You may heal emotional wounds.
Iron - This healing is applied in a gentler way. This may cause it to take longer, but the resulting healing will be much greater. This is further amplified by your understanding of the emotions within your patient.
Bronze - You can develop a temporary empathic link with another person, allowing you to share their emotional burden. This will allow you to better understand the emotional wound and provide greater care with lesser risk.
Silver - You are able to heal and soothe emotions and emotional trauma in a way that the patient is unaware of. The degree to which you can dull down extreme emotion is significantly increased.

Usually, she tried to avoid using the ability on people unless it was necessary, as messing around with others' emotions without consent was something she considered disrespectful at best and downright intrusive at worst. For these farmers, who had been walking around disrespecting the denizens of Nature's Reclaim, however, she felt no shame in using it.

She watched the anger slowly vanish from their faces, a calm settling over the group. The muttering and yelling stopped as they watched Ember through unsettlingly calm eyes. She let up on the ability, allowing them to feel their own emotions again.

"So, will you be staying here respectfully or leaving for a different town?"

One of them grumbled under his breath.

"What's that, sorry?"

"We'll be respectful," he repeated, louder.

Ember nodded.

"Good, now go to the temple of Nateysta in the town centre and talk to the Ancient of Wisdom there. They will give you what you need to get by. If you continue to disrespect the others in the town, it will be the Ancient of War that comes to deal with you next time."

She pointed back into the town and the grumbling group of seven farmers went through the gates.

Shaking her head at the idiots, she apologised to the moles before going back into the town herself.

After ten minutes of walking about the town, giving respectful nods to people and animals alike, she finally got the mental message she had been waiting for.

"Alright, Ember, you can come see them now."

She rushed back to the statehouse, excitement pulsing through her body. It had been a stressful seven hours of waiting, her nerves so wrecked that Zalia had sent her from the room. Why she was so stressed out, she didn't even know, but now that the message had come, all that stress had faded away.

Rushing through the front door, she ascended the stairs quickly and down a hallway to the new room the Grove had made for them. Going inside, she saw Aylie, Zalia, and Boreal with five new fluffy little kittens.

CHAPTER FIFTEEN

Kittens and Concerns

Ember

Ember rushed over and knelt next to Zalia and the exhausted-looking Boreal. Lumin burst into the room through the door she had forgotten to close. Zalia had to quickly hand Ember a mewling pile of fur and catch Lumin before they annoyed Boreal into smacking them again.

"They're so small!" Aylie exclaimed.

Zalia held firmly without issue onto the wriggling Lumin, her grip like steel. While the bouncy and energetic Lumin was usually a joy to be around, it looked like Zalia really didn't want them annoying Boreal right now. Ember wasn't even sure if even Lumin could keep Boreal awake at that moment, however, as the purring feline slowly nodded off.

The new room the Grove had created for them was a cat's dream. The floor was covered in plush, soft bedding while many thin poles fashioned like tree trunks led up towards the high ceiling. All across the sides of the room and leading up the walls were various paths and bridges, crossing across the room and along the ceiling. All of it was the proper size for a feline of Boreal's size.

It would be heaven for the new kittens, Boreal's kittens, to play around in a safe environment.

Just to be sure, Ember used Triage, her ability that had evolved from Holistic Diagnosis, on them all.

Triage
Tin - You can tell how severely someone is wounded by touching them.
Iron - You're now able to tell by sight rather than touch and can tell where the wound is located.

Bronze - You can tell exactly what the wound is and what it was caused by. Additionally, you're able to tell who is in more need of immediate healing. Silver - Using Triage on a wounded creature temporarily stops bleeding and any other damage-over-time effects, allowing you to heal them without concern.

Happily, they were all safe and sound, healthy as could be. Most importantly, Boreal was fine as well. The constant stream of healing from Zalia during the process had been a comfort for them all.

She put down the kitten next to the other four and wrapped her arms around Zalia, resting her head on her shoulder, Lumin still struggling under their arms.

"She's so grown up now."

Boreal was breathing calmly, her crown still floating ever so slightly above her head. She was huge, reaching up to Ember's shoulders when she stood. Aylie was six feet tall now, so was a bit less dwarfed by the feline than both Zalia and Ember were, but compared to the tiny kitten that had stood on Zalia's shoulders all those years ago, the Boreal before them was massive. Ember still remembered the day Zalia had picked up the icy cold kitten from the mountaintop where her mother had died. Seeing the five kittens, Ember wondered if Boreal had siblings out there somewhere, others that weren't with them at the time or had already left by the time they had gotten there.

There was a wide variety amongst Boreal's kittens, ranging from one that looked like a replica of her to one that looked like a replica of the father, with the other three somewhere between. The Ancient of War, the same plains feline that had protected Zalia's first Grove, was the father. Ember hadn't seen him on her way in but had no doubt he was prowling about protecting the statehouse at that very moment. She also had no doubt he would come in to see them the second Zalia went back outside. For some reason, he thought one of them had to be out there making sure nothing would attack.

"That was an extremely strange experience," Zalia murmured.

Ember lifted her head up, looking at Zalia.

"Oh?"

She waited as Zalia sat silent for a moment, collecting her thoughts, her fingers drumming on her leg now that she had one hand free. Ember loved that about Zalia, how she always thought about what she was going to say just a little longer than most people would.

"Well, I could feel everything through the bond. It was like I was there with her the whole time, sharing the anxiety and excitement, then the pain."

Ember smiled, resting her head on Zalia's shoulder again.

"That's pretty normal, dear, though I'm sure you were sharing those emotions on a deeper level than normal because of the bond you have. I was so anxious you had to kick me out, remember? Though you two have a deeper bond than many ever get, and sharing the pain must have been a strange experience, I'm sure."

Zalia nodded, finally putting Lumin down.

The starlight puppy had not grown even a pinch since they had gotten them. Still small, still Tin rank with an Ascendant affix and still excitable as ever.

Fortunately, once they had gotten over the initial excitement, Lumin was able to calmly greet the new kittens with curiosity rather than explosive energy. Sniffing at the crawling pile of kittens, Lumin got an accidental whack on the nose by the one that was a replica of Boreal.

Laughing at the offended look on Lumin's face, they all watched as the kittens slowly oriented themselves to their new world. Each of them was already Iron rank as Boreal had been when she was born, and Ember wondered what kind of abilities they would have. A mixture of Boreal's and the Ancient of War's was her best guess, but how that would show was entirely unknown to her.

Boreal soon woke up under the gentle healing of the Grove and Zalia alike and proceeded to fuss over her kittens, cleaning them and making sure they were all okay. It didn't matter how many times Zalia and Ember told her they were fine, she had to be sure. None of them expected anything else.

Zalia got up and left so that the Ancient of War could finally come inside. The patter of paws heralded his arrival and he was soon fussing over the kittens and Boreal as well.

Ember watched their happy little family and dragged a complaintive Aylie in for a hug. A few more of her abilities had reached Bronze in the past year yet her progress was slowing down. To advance in rank any further, especially at her young age, would require a lot more dangerous situations than any of them were willing to allow her into. Sure, she could very well handle herself against a lot of enemies now and had shown just that on some of their excursions but she was still too young to be anywhere near anything super dangerous. Eliminating a demon nest under the careful protection and guidance of three Silver rankers was a lot different from going out and doing the same thing alone.

Still, they didn't want to shelter her too much from what was coming. They all knew that war would come again eventually; whether it was started by Endaria or the Astar or even the demons invading again, it would come. None of them had seen Nateysta, Ro-ak, for the past three years and it might even be him that started the next war. Ember had started to worry about where he had gone, but Zalia didn't seem to be concerned at all.

They had recently been talking about making a move to the desert Grove for a few months and exploring it together. Not only would it be good for Aylie's continued progression into Bronze rank, but it would be exciting for Ember too. Despite having lived in Endaria for a much longer time than Zalia, she hadn't ever gone that far south. Sure, she had gone through the portal and had a tour of the place from Zalia, but entering the dunes was something else.

The only reason she had been considering it was the blessing that Zalia had gotten from Scour that allowed her to find her way in the desert, a guarantee that they wouldn't get lost.

Ember often found herself worrying about whether they were raising Aylie right or not. While she could be a bit strange at times due to the abilities she had, Aylie was still a respectful and kind person, someone nice to be around the majority of the time. Sure, they had arguments, but who didn't with their fifteen-year-old teenager?

What Ember worried about the most was the way they were almost subconsciously preparing her for the next war. They both thought of it as a when, not if, and she wasn't sure if that was something healthy to do to the girl. If one did come, they would most certainly be in the middle of it. There was no way either she or Zalia wouldn't fight for the kingdom, and that meant Aylie either needed to be ready and powerful, or left behind. Perhaps it was selfish of them both to think that way when they had Aylie to care for, but Zalia had been the reason they had won the first invasion and might be the reason they won the next. Not through her personal power but through her ability to bring people together.

On the other hand, it might be selfish of them to not help Aylie become more powerful in preparation for the next war when they knew it was coming. If they could get her to a place where she had the power to guide her own life, wasn't that better than the alternative?

She hadn't expected to be so worried about whether she was doing the right thing when she had decided she wanted to be Zalia's partner and raise Aylie together. Maybe that was just a normal part of parenting though. She and Zalia had spoken about this more than a few times, both of them similarly worried about whether they were doing the right thing, but neither of them had ever asked Aylie what she wanted.

Thinking about it, Ember realised more and more that they should do just that. She wasn't a child anymore and would need to start taking over her own life as she became a young adult. Perhaps now was the time to start allowing her to make these kinds of decisions.

CHAPTER SIXTEEN

Meeting the Parents

Zen
Three years after the invasion's end

Zen woke up, stretching as wide as he was able in the little cot he slept in. It was much too small for him but oddly comforting, reminding him of simpler days on the farm with too many family members squished into a tiny house. They could have built a bigger one, but as Grandmother Polina always said, "Living with too little grows *character*, and I would know about growth, I'm a farmer."

He had always complained about it when he was younger, but after coming back from experiencing the wider world, he couldn't help but believe some people needed to have just a little less comfort growing up. There was only so much privilege and entitlement a person could have before it became a little obnoxious.

Life had been good as of late. While still new, things were going well with Mel and he was starting to think that it might be something that could work for them both in the long-term. He hadn't expected to find a partner out here in the frozen north, but things had just evolved ever since she had arrived from the south a few months ago.

The south. It was strange thinking of his old home as the south. All of his life, he had lived in the north with places like the capital being the south. Now the entire kingdom was "the south" to him.

The last time she had been up to see him, Zalia had offered for him and his family to come down and live in the town Indis had given her. He had been tempted; it was a beautiful, nature-filled place where the people and animals of the land lived in harmony, protected by the magic that Zalia had imbued it with. Who wouldn't be tempted with a description like that? After all, it definitely sounded more pleasant than the frozen north. Life there sounded . . . easy.

That had been part of the reason both he and his family had decided against it, though.

Sure, he had given up on the life of an adventurer and member of the Morning's Shade, but that didn't mean he wanted to live an easy and boring life. No, he still wanted a challenge and they had found that here in the north. Learning to farm and live in a place that naturally didn't want you to do either in it had been a fulfilling day-to-day life. Building a friendship with the Born of Heat and Stone people had been an amazing addition to that, though it had turned out to be the easier of the two tasks.

They worked flawlessly with each other, like a hivemind. They basically were one, from what Zalia had told him. While it was a bit harder for them to work in the same way with the humans now living with them, they had taken to it and after the difficult early days, things were good.

His younger cousin Jasper had been working with Glemp quite a lot and under his teaching and guidance, had taken an alchemist class. Glemp loved to talk about how much easier it was to work with Jasper than it had been to work with Zalia, which always got a laugh out of Zen. Having worked with Zalia himself, he tended to agree. Not that he didn't love Zalia and respect her greatly for the things she had done, she just tended to be very strongly inclined towards her decisions with little room for argument. It worked out more often than not but it felt a little like working *for* Zalia, not *with* Zalia.

He groaned a little before throwing himself out of bed. The sun wasn't up yet, but his father had always said getting up before the sun got the work done.

His mother Annette was already up and handed him a bowl of mushrooms, bread, and meat. They traded for the mushrooms from the Heat and Stone denizens, made the bread themselves, and the meat came from hunting parties that were a combination of both their peoples.

After eating, he bid his family a good day and left, walking further up the mountain towards his current project.

While his mother, grandmother, and two younger siblings, Jaz and Harry, worked on the farm below, he and his father had been building a house up the mountain. The houses made for them by the Heat and Stone denizens out of obsidian were nice but just weren't as easy to make comfortable. The colour and hardness of the material made it feel like a bit of a prison no matter how much you decorated.

So, when Zen had gone to his father and told him that he wanted to build a house for himself and his possible future family, he had agreed.

The forest below had been cleared away a bit to accommodate the farming fields, the wood put away in the mountain for future use. Zalia had even used some of her magic to make the fields warmer and protected from the snow, which was a boon for the growth and continued life of the crops. Previously, they had been trying to farm the natural plants in the north—various types of berries, for the most part. With the strange mini-biome Zalia had made, they were able to grow some of the more traditional crops they were used to. Eating bread again was great.

The wood from the clearing had dried out nicely now, with the process sped up a bit by the constant high temperature inside the mountain. It was this wood that he and his dad were using to build the house.

Zen trudged through the snow to the frame of the house, looking over their previous day's work with fresh eyes. His dad had taught him to always check your work the day after and it had saved him more than a few mistakes in the past.

His dad arrived a few minutes later, layered up against the cold. For some reason, he and Grandmother Polina had never developed the Cold Resistance passive that the rest of them had. Zalia had given some explanation about developing passives being harder the older you get when he had asked. He had no idea how she knew that but it did make sense.

"Ready to get to?"

His dad nodded and they started building.

It was later in the day that they finally stopped. They had made good progress that day with the framework all done now. A few more days and they might have some of the walls going up. One of his dad's mates had fashioned the stone floor for them with his stonemason abilities and would come by when they were doing the walls to help. He was a builder with the stonemason specialisation, which made him the perfect man for the job to help finish off everything. While Zen and his dad could build it themselves, the builder would help to properly weatherproof everything so that they didn't have constant drafts blowing through the house. That was especially important when they were living on a frozen mountainside.

Today, Mel was coming over to meet his parents. They had seen each other peripherally a few times but today was the day they would meet properly. His nerves were a little wrecked, but he was certain they would like her. She was honest and hardworking, an earth mage with a landscaper specialisation. It was quite unusual to ever go for a Utility specialisation when choosing a Mage class, yet she had done so. With the specialisation, she obtained Plant Manipulation as well as a skill that made a landscape she created provide benefits as long as it existed. Examples she had given of that were fields that helped plants grow, gardenscapes for houses that radiated calm and happiness, even defensive scapes that provided defensive bonuses to those using them. It was a truly unique class combination that Zen hadn't ever seen before and one he knew his family would love to make use of. Just another piece in his belief that they would like her.

He also thought Mel and Zalia would get along well, which filled him with dread. He loved plants and ritual magic as much as the next guy, but if those two ever got to talking about it, it might be the death of a few hours.

In comfortable silence, Zen and his dad arrived at the family home. They were put to work by Annette as soon as they entered, set to cutting up the few vegetables they had, butchering meat, preparing herbs, and starting the oven fire to bake bread.

Polina was sitting on the couch with baby Ingrid in a cot, simultaneously rocking the cot while crocheting. Jasper would still be with Glemp for a while yet, with the rest of the cousins making themselves scarce for the night and taking his younger siblings with them. Today would just be his parents, grandmother, and the baby Ingrid.

When dinner was almost ready, he quickly washed up and put on his only nice clothes. He made his way down the mountain to where Mel lived, in a smaller one-person house, and knocked on the door. Mel opened it within seconds, wearing her own well-tailored, thick leather coat, with her auburn hair pulled up into a ponytail. She had pleasant features, not stunningly beautiful, but the face of a hardworking woman who spent most of her life in the sun and fields, just like Zen.

"Hey, are you ready?" His nervousness was growing but he tried to contain it.

"Hey, yeah absolutely!" She caught on to how obviously nervous he was. ". . . Are you?"

He nodded a few times, nervously wringing his hands, then forced his hands to stop. "Yes, let's go then!"

They walked up the hill towards his family's home, Mel chatting casually while Zen tried to reciprocate as concerned thoughts rushed around his head.

When they arrived, he opened the door and led the way in. "Everyone, this is Mel. Mel, this is my father, Anton, my mother, Annette, my grandmother, Polina, and my baby cousin, Ingrid."

Mel stood beside him as he made introductions. "Hey, everyone, wonderful to meet you all."

His mother came forward first and gave Mel a big hug. "Come on in, dinner is just ready."

Mel hugged her back. "Smells lovely!"

Zen's worries faded away as an easy conversation sparked up between Mel and his mother, his father chiming in every now and then as he set the table. He wondered why he had even been worried in the first place.

CHAPTER SEVENTEEN

To Act

Lady Indis
Three and a half years after the invasion's end

ndis sat at her desk, finishing off a letter with a flourished signature. She folded it up and sealed it with one of the many magical stamps at her side. This stamp meant the letter could only be opened by key members of the Morning's Shade, more specifically, those whose imprints had been put upon a Morning's Shade signet. She handed the letter off to the messenger who waited by her desk at most hours of the day. He checked the stamp mark and went running.

Taking over the Morning's Shade had not only been easy but one of the best decisions she'd made in her time as a civilian seated to the council. When she had gotten word that Hildebrandt no longer wanted to be their leader, she had very quickly offered herself up as a replacement. As Indis was a member of the order herself and already one of the leaders of the Endarian council, Hildebrandt had agreed.

Before long, she had the organisation assigned as a civilian task force under the jurisdiction of the civilian seated, who just so happened to be herself. In a sweeping move, she had given herself more power and secured her place on the council because people knew that as long as she stayed there, the Morning's Shade would work for them.

The order she had just sent off to them was due to a resurgence of demon dens in the kingdom. It happened every year as winter ended. Animals would leave their winter burrows or hibernation and suddenly the dormant demon dens would have a significantly increased food supply. Their population would increase dramatically, and they would start probing into towns and villages nearby. As such, she sent off almost every team in the Morning's Shade to hunt down and eradicate as many of these dens as they could.

Doing so had a dual purpose for her. Mainly, it would help keep her people safe, but as a bonus, it would build their goodwill towards her as people saw *her* task force roaming around killing the demons that were hounding them. Sure, the military-seated General Faian would be doing the exact same thing, but Indis had made it very clear in the proclamations the council made that the Morning's Shade was under the control of the civilian seated. Which was her.

The way the council worked suited Indis just fine. There were the civilians and military seated to the council, and then there were the civilian and military councils. Each council was built up of eleven members who assigned their respective seated to the council member, those people currently being herself and Faian. Each council group had authority over their own areas of responsibility with some matters that were deemed important enough being ruled over by both councils.

Every member had responsibilities within their own civilian or military council and would bring related issues to be debated and then voted upon, with the seated to the council being the deciding vote in a draw. Members held office for four-year terms, after which a kingdom-wide vote was taken. They had yet to take one of these votes, with the current members having been assigned after the invasion as an emergency matter to get the kingdom back up and running before any more people died. That very vote was six months away now, and Indis had been currying as much favour amongst the people as she could to maintain her position amongst the council.

Most of the other council members had gone home for the day, leaving the castle at the top of the hill in the capital to return to their families down below. Indis sometimes wished she'd had the opportunity to live a life like that.

She stood up from her desk and walked out of the room, nodding to the guard on duty. When her mind was off on a tangent like this, she often found it easier to work through her thoughts on the move. That hadn't been the case a few years ago, but her time as a Morning's Shade member traveling across the country with Zalia, Zen, and Ember had affected her.

The tall, lavish hallways and communal areas of the castle were hauntingly familiar to her. They might be decorated differently, used for a different purpose, and lived in by different people, but they were the same rooms and halls that she had grown up in. She sometimes expected her friend Prince Alistair to walk around the corner and crack some wise joke about one lord or another. He had been the only person who could break the mask she put up so easily and so often.

In her mind, Prince Alistair and King Alistair had been two different people. The man he had become when his father had died and he had taken the throne had not been the same man that had walked these halls with mischievous abandon with her. Both she and Faian had thoroughly searched the castle and capital for any explanation as to what had happened to Alistair to cause him to turn like that, but neither of them had come up with any evidence or leads. One day he had been an energetic, mischievous, charming, and funny prince, the next a cold, calculating thrall of the demons, without any apparent reason.

But that was enough thinking about the past; it was the future she needed to look to.

Despite Zalia having turned Et's Way into some kind of animal haven, something she should have expected, Indis was somewhat happy with how that whole ploy had turned out. The woman was kept close and invested into a part of the kingdom now and that was all she had been working towards. All she had to do to keep up appearances was appear disgruntled every now and then, and Zalia would continue living as she had been.

She had known that first day that keeping Zalia close would yield great results. Someone with three classes was just bound to end up attracting the attention of powerful beings and someone who came into the view of powerful beings was likely to make a few friends amongst them. And she had, thus bringing the salvation of the kingdom.

The concept of power had always been interesting to Indis. Someone such as the king of an entire kingdom like Endaria theoretically had an unimaginable amount of it, yet within the span of a few weeks, that was all gone to a power from another world. Someone like Zalia, on the other hand, was given power by nature of luck or circumstance, a power that couldn't be taken away unless by death. As she advanced in rank, the gap between her and others of her rank would only increase due to the scaling of her abilities.

The power Indis had was different from both of those. She had been neglecting her advancement as a magic user, only having reached Bronze rank as of the year before, some two and a half years after Zalia, Ember, and Zen had. Her power didn't exist in her magic, nor did it exist by luck of circumstance or having it handed down from her parents. The power she had was in her ability to manipulate others into doing what she wanted without them knowing. People thought that made her a bad person, Zalia thought that made her a bad person, but that wasn't true.

At the end of it all, everything she did was for the good of the kingdom and its people. Yes, she had manipulated Zalia into the position she was in now, but that was so the kingdom would remain safe. Yes, she had done things to maintain her position amongst the council as the civilian seated but that was so she could *continue* to keep Endaria safe. And yes, she had lied to friends, allies, and everyone around her, but all of it for the kingdom. If it came to it, she would die for the safety of the kingdom.

That was what Zalia didn't understand about her. She didn't need her to understand, though, as long as Indis, and therefore the kingdom, could continue getting what was needed.

Today she had to make a decision. One she had been putting off for a few months now. Recently, General Faian had been pushing back on a lot of the things Indis had been trying to do. At the start, it had been mildly annoying and just a little amusing. The general was obviously fed up with Indis's ploys and politicking, which she somewhat understood. She thought she knew what was best for the kingdom, just as Indis did; they simply didn't agree with what the other thought was best in all cases. Indis had been willing and able to work with the woman for a long time now, but with the increased aggression of what the general was doing just six months out from the election vote, she would have to start acting now.

As such, she stepped up to the office of one of the other civilian council members and knocked twice politely.

"Come in!"

She opened the door, walked in, and closed it behind her.

"Oh! Civilian-elected Indis, I didn't expect to see you this late at night. How may I help?"

Indis sat down casually in the chair on the other side of the woman's desk and folded one leg over the other. "I've got a proposal for you."

CHAPTER EIGHTEEN

Ro Returns and the Star Falls Clumsily

Aylie
Three years, nine months after the invasion

Aylie watched Ember and Zen speak in hushed tones with the newcomer. While she couldn't hear them with her ears, she was able to see the words coming from their minds, mostly from the newcomer. From what she gathered, they had come here to see Zen and get his help.

Ember had brought her and Lumin here to see Uncle Zen, with Zalia and Boreal unfortunately unable to join them because of issues at home. Ember had offered to cancel the trip, but Zalia had insisted she was fine and they should come along and see Zen anyway. Everything had been as pleasant as usual; both of Zen's parents and his grandmother were sweet, and his younger siblings were as annoying as usual. It was a nice little break from training, though, something her mothers had started ramping up at her insistence.

She had been surprised when they had asked her if she really wanted to train to become someone strong enough to combat the demons directly. If she was sure she didn't want a normal life. Of course she wanted to! Her life hadn't been normal for a long time, and there was no way she would let the demons continue their horrible invasions, not after what they had done to her family. With her decision made, Aylie got to see a side of her mothers that she hadn't before. Usually, they were quite held back with the training they had done over the years, being quietly supportive and letting her explore everything at her own pace. Now, they pushed her limits as much as they could manage without putting her in any serious harm's way.

And she loved it.

It felt good to properly test her limits, to grow her abilities and her mastery of them quicker. For the first time, she felt like she might actually be ready when the next war came.

They hadn't ever spoken to her about that, but she had picked it up from their thoughts. It was always there if she knew where to look, a tag-along riding hidden in the depths of everything else. Not that she could ever read Zalia without her letting down her defences yet.

She tried focusing on the conversation Ember and Zen were having again, more focused on the man they were talking to than either of them. There was something odd about him she couldn't quite place. Thinking of how the next war rode along Ember and Zalia's thoughts, she swore there was something hidden amongst this man's thoughts too. Something sinister.

Tapping her leg repeatedly, she inspected the man closely. He didn't *seem* sinister, or untrustworthy at all. Ember and Zen looked like they trusted him.

The astral was suddenly filled with another presence, one she recognised. She spun around and watched as Nateysta, Zalia's friend Ro-ak, grew from the ground. Roots twisted amongst themselves to form the two trunk-like legs, the body, and the wings of leaves topped by the vine hair of the Ascendant they all called their saviour. She ran forward and embraced him in a big hug.

"What are you doing here! It's been so long!"

"Your growth has not slowed in all that time either, I see."

Aylie pulled away from the soft, leafy crow as the conversation behind them had stopped, the three adults having noticed Ro.

"Ro!? Where in the worlds have you been?"

Ember came marching up, looking annoyed. Not annoyed for her own sake, Aylie could see, but for Zalia's.

"I apologise for my absence these years. The other spirit who lives here and I have been working together to fashion a prison so secure for the thousand-eyed one that it will never escape. Our work is only now finished."

"What, you mean the god in the lava? If you've been here the whole time, why didn't you ever pop out to see us?"

Ro's head cocked. "I have not been *here*, Ember, my essence has been deep in the earth. Forming a permanent cage for an Ascendant is no easy feat." He paused for a moment. "Well, maybe not *permanent*, but such a long time that it is so, even by my perception of time."

Ember crossed her arms. "Still, you could have told us where you were going to be."

Ro's head flicked back and forth a bit like he was trying to decipher the words. "Why? It has not even been a decade."

Ember pressed her face into her palm and took a deep breath. "Right, you should probably go and see Zalia. There's a lot I think she'd like to talk to you about." She thought a moment before adding, "It's good to have you back."

Ro dipped his head. "It is good to be back. I would like to see how this kingdom has advanced in the past four years, you humans might not have much power but you change with incredible speed. If your progress is any basis to go on, Starblessed, I will not be disappointed. I shall speak with the starlight wolf before I go to see Zalia, as I sense them nearby."

With that, Ro took off with a single beat of his wings. He shot off and landed further up the mountain where Lumin was no doubt getting up to no good.

Aylie and Ember turned back to where Zen and the other guy were busy shaking. This had been their first experience with an Ascendant, and a very strong and vocal one at that.

As they started talking and Ember tried to calm the two down, Aylie focused on the man's thoughts again. The sinister undertone to them had disappeared, replaced by something akin to fear. There was no need for such a feeling in relation to Ro, but humans often reacted weirdly when faced with *that* much power.

At the end of the conversation, it was decided that Aylie, Ember, and Lumin would swing past the man's town to try and help them with their demon problem on their way back home. The man said that a team from the Morning's Shade had been sent out to clear it out but they hadn't been able to find it. The demons hadn't attacked during that time, but as soon as the team left, the town was under attack again. Being close to the kingdom's northern border, he had decided to come here for help instead. It was a town Zen had even helped before, some years back when the invasion first happened.

Aylie could read from Ember's mind that she expected it to be a den of the illusionist demons. They were the hardest ones to find, often hidden extremely well and guarded by intelligent demons. It would make sense that such a den wouldn't attack while a strong Morning's Shade team was nearby. Aylie would have believed it if the man didn't still have those hidden sinister under thoughts escaping his mind. If she could only read them, then they would know what was up.

"*This man is not what he seems,*" she sent to Ember.

Ember didn't visibly react, used to Aylie's mental communication. Unlike Zalia, Aylie had developed a way to perform the task through her ability to see and touch the astral rather than an ability that could do it specifically.

"*How so?*" Ember asked back.

Aylie sent a mental shrug. "*He has sinister thoughts hidden in his mind. I believe he means to trick us somehow.*"

Ember smiled and nodded, reassuring the man that it was okay as he thanked them for offering to help. "*Alright, we'll play it safe, then.*"

For the second time in the short conversation, an Ascendant interrupted.

Lumin, now in the body of a young starry wolf, dropped from the sky like a falling star. They landed in a crash, sprawling across the snow, limbs tangled. Lumin had yet to perfect their landings.

Luminescence - Iron rank (Ascendant).

Shaking her head at the silly wolf, she waved goodbye to Zen and followed Ember as she led the man away from the mountain.

CHAPTER NINETEEN

Dreaming of Death

Aylie

Aylie trudged through the snow behind Ember and the man they were following. His name was Ren, a piece of information she had read from his mind about twenty minutes before Ember had remembered to ask.

Their travel time had been cut considerably shorter by Aylie's use of Starlit Portal, and they were due to arrive within the next few minutes.

> **Starlit Portal - spell - target.**
> **Tin - You may teleport a short distance.**
> **Iron - You may create a portal that you and one other creature are able to step through that travels a longer distance.**
> **Bronze - The number of creatures that may step through increases to a total of five, and the distance increases.**

She had been attempting to read Ren's mind the entire time they had been walking and yet still couldn't pull out whatever hidden information resided in there. It was strange, as the man was an open book except for this single thing.

Normally, she would avoid purposefully attempting to read someone's mind like this. It was hard enough in cities to avoid catching stray thoughts from the thousands of people living their lives even when she wasn't focusing on the ability. When she *did* do that, it became hard to determine her own thoughts from those of the people around her.

Out here in the wilds, it was a bit easier. Without many creatures around, the only stray thoughts she caught were the base instinct urges of the animals living in the snow and those were easy enough to ignore.

She knew it was an invasion of privacy to read someone's mind, yet the little sinister *thing* attached to this man's thoughts was too strange not to look into. It felt like something was calling her attention to it with all the strength it had.

The more she looked, the more certain she was that it was a type of demonic influence.

In the almost four years that they had been fighting the demons, during the invasion and after, she hadn't ever felt something like it. Was this a new type they hadn't seen before?

She had told Ember about it, but she hadn't wanted to act on it yet. Ember had confidence that they would be able to deal with whatever it was, seeing as the highest-rank demon they had seen during the invasion had been Silver rank, excluding the thousand-eyed one. While that may not hold true four years down the line, it wasn't an illogical assumption.

Through the trees, Aylie saw a deep red thread of mist floating in the air, twisting. It was like an ethereal thread going from one invisible point to another. She was about to point it out to Ember when Ren turned to them with tears on his face.

"I'm . . . I'm so sorry. The—they threatened my chil—children."

Red threads trailed out of the forest, shifting back and forth like they were searching for something. Ember didn't react to them, watching the man with concern, the scan of her diagnosis ability visible to Aylie.

She spun around, watching the threads behind her inch ever closer. They looked and felt dangerous to her and she didn't want to touch them unless there was no other choice. Starlit Portal was still on cooldown and would be for a while longer. The threads weren't natural in any way, their essence antithetical to the living nature around them. They definitely came from demons.

A ripple in the astral drew her attention back behind her, where Ember stood with a red thread attached to her head. Like they had finally caught a scent, a dozen other threads surged forward and attached themselves to Ember, the woman standing rigid.

Aylie didn't panic, trying to read what was happening. They were under some kind of mind control; the power felt incredibly strong despite being undoubtedly Bronze rank. She wouldn't be able to beat this thing with power directly, she knew that. There was always a way though, and she knew what she needed to do.

Stepping forward, she grabbed one of the red threads in her hand and felt an immediate link to the demon's mind.

> **Active 3 - Worldweave - spell - varies. (Previously Dreamweave)**
> **Tin - You may weave the dreams of creatures that are asleep. The more familiar you are with the creature, the further away you may use this. Additionally, these dreams can have an effect on the target's real body.**
> **Iron - If the target of this ability is tired but not asleep, you may weave a waking dream that has only minor effects on them.**

> **Bronze - You are able to weave waking dreams on any creature, but these dreams may be broken if the dreamer realizes what you are doing.**

She used Worldweave, letting the demon see a simple change to reality when she had grabbed the thread. Rather than it being stuck to her hand, it was stuck to her head, and she was under its control.

The demon accepted the waking dream easily, as it matched the demon's expectations of events better than reality did.

Weaving dreams was a complicated thing. It was easy to get someone to accept the dream if the change you made was small enough, careful enough. Maintaining one, then changing it to suit your needs, was a bit more difficult. If something too outlandish happened, it would snap them out of it. Aylie would have to read the demon's mind so that she could change its reality from what it expected, to what it feared.

She felt a nudge of command come down the thread and she followed it, turning and walking towards the town.

As they walked, she slowly pulled information from the demon's mind through the thread. It had been born here, in a den not too far north of the town. Slowly, it had taken over the people one by one, each controlled mind increasing its power enough that when the remaining third of the town had figured out why people were acting so strangely, it had been strong enough to take them all by force.

Unluckily for the demon, it had missed one person. It had noticed too late, the person too far away by then to be caught. A short time later, the escaped man had come back with a group of mercenaries, ready to eradicate a demon den. However, all they found was a perfectly normal town.

The demon had worked hard, studying the minds of its victims to figure out how they lived, spoke, ate, walked, and all the rest. It had fooled the newly arrived mercenaries into believing the escaped man was crazy and they had left. Little did they know, it had taken the mind of that escaped man before they even stepped into the town.

Then it had run into an issue.

Without more people to control, it was stagnant. If it didn't grow in power, it held no hope of standing up to the other powers of this world. It wouldn't take much for it to be found out, just the right person with the right set of abilities, and when that happened, whatever had defeated the thousand-eyed one would be able to kill it with ease.

So, it had to find more people. Luckily, it had known of a few secluded people in the mountains northeast of the town, thanks to the memories of the townspeople.

Aylie opened her eyes, able to figure out the rest for herself. She had let her body unconsciously follow the commands coming through the thread and found herself in the town now, walking about and performing daily tasks as if nothing was wrong and she had always lived here. Ember was still near her, thankfully.

She knew what its fear was now, the arrival of something too strong for it to handle. Someone like . . . Zalia.

If it was beginning to search through Ember's memories, it would find Zalia there first. It would feel the bond between her and Ember.

A plan in mind, she began weaving the waking dream, manipulating reality for the demon. When the man who had brought them here had turned around with tears in his eyes, Aylie had felt a little slip of control from the demon. She played into that, making the demon believe that the man had escaped control.

A thread became visible, attached to Ren's head. Then, it pulled free and the man had control of his own body once more. He immediately ran, chased by more threads and all of the townspeople.

Aylie laid a little trail of power in the dream, an ability that belonged to someone else, the feeling of the power being that of Zalia's.

It took a while for the demon to notice it but when it did, it went on alert. No, Ren hadn't escaped its control, Ren had been *freed* from its control by another power, one too strong for it. Aylie had that power rip another towns-person from its control, though that person just stood there stunned.

The demon began to panic, searching around for the source of the power, the powerful being that was taking away its control. So Aylie gave it one.

Zalia flew through the sky on wispy wings of air, bow in hand and her mind, as Aylie knew it, impenetrable.

A few abilities from the townspeople flew up to strike the dream-Zalia but were either ignored or blocked with ease. Another person was ripped from the demon's control.

The power of belief was an interesting thing to Aylie, as someone who could control it so viscerally. It wasn't actually her own power taking away control of the people from the demon, it was her power convincing it that it wasn't strong enough to maintain that control in the face of a stronger enemy. The demon's fear become reality.

She began pulling more people from its control, one by one. Each person lost weakened its power even further, its strength drawing in line with Aylie's.

Ember was still nearby, frantically searching for a way to stop the dream-Zalia from taking away its control. Aylie stepped up to her and grabbed one of the threads linking her to the demon and ripped it away. Aylie felt the demon's panic as it realised there was another being here capable of ripping away its con-trol. Yes, that was right, Aylie was more powerful than it and she had been free all along. She pushed that thought into its mind.

Grabbing the rest of the threads, she pulled them free with ease. She held onto them all, following them back to their source. Ember looked around con-fused, then jogged up to Aylie.

"What is going on?"

Aylie gave her an easygoing, confident smile.

"I'm dealing with the problem."

She followed the thread out of the town, continuing to pull townspeople out of the demon's control with the dream-Zalia behind her. She could feel that the demon wasn't focused on Zalia anymore though, no, it was focused on her as she followed its own threads back to where it lived.

They found it, a den opening with hundreds of threads leading out of it, many of them receding back inside. Aylie walked through and into a cave. There was a small demon sitting centrally in the space, curled up and whimpering as she pulled its power and control from it.

Then, she felt bad.

It had only been trying to survive. Yet so had Aylie. When it came to survival, it was either you or them, but that didn't mean she had to feel good *or* bad about it. Zalia had told her that long ago, and she had remembered feeling angry about the words then, yet she thought she understood now.

As more and more of the townspeople were taken from the demon's control, she had it fade into a real dream and the whimpering stopped. Now that it was asleep, she was capable of much stronger effects. In its sleeping dream, she made everything slowly disappear until only the demon remained in the pitch blackness. Then, it popped out of existence.

As that happened, the demon died.

CHAPTER TWENTY

Making the First Move

Zalia
Four years after the invasion

Zalia sat leaning against the base of the Ancient of Life, legs resting up on a root. It was winter, a blanket of snow resting across the Grove, dulling down the sounds from all the animals and people living in it. Despite the surface calm of the Grove, there was an excitement pulsing through the town for multiple reasons.

The results of the elections had been sent across the kingdom, and Zalia had been surprised when she read them. Lady Leyra Indis had failed to get reelected, along with two others, one each from the civilian and military councils. Zalia had no idea how that had come to pass until she spoke to the Ancient of Wisdom about it.

Apparently, there had been rumours spreading about Indis's previous involvement with the now-dead king. The people of Endaria held no love for the former king and her closeness to the man had done her no favours. As such, she had lost the election and was now just a citizen like everyone else.

Zalia didn't think this was something that had happened naturally, rather being a cause of some politicking or the other. If she had to guess, General Faian had wanted to get rid of Indis simply because she was too self-obsessed to realise that what she thought the kingdom needed wasn't always what it *actually* needed.

She admittedly felt a bit bad for Indis, as this was the thing she had been fighting for most of her life. Still, it might bring some perspective and a life lesson to the woman. Hopefully.

It had been stressful to learn of Ember and Aylie's fight in the north, with Aylie having to defeat some kind of mind-controlling demon, saving not only the town it had under its thrall but Ember as well. If she had just been with them, it might not have been an issue at all. Still, she was proud of Aylie. Not so much of Lumin, who hadn't even been there until the demon was killed. What was the point of having an Ascendant follow your loved ones around if they weren't even going to be there when they were in danger?

It had sparked an argument between her and Ember because she had been hard on herself for not being there, while Ember argued that she couldn't always protect them, that they had to hold their own once in a while. Zalia had realised Ember was right, eventually. If she was always protecting them from everything, they wouldn't ever stretch the limits of their powers and grow to a point where they could protect themselves from most things.

Despite all that, life was still good. She had been working with the Ancient of War to devise a method to block teleportation into and out of Nature's Reclaim. This was mostly because she and Ember were getting stronger, and if they were right about the Astar taking any stronger humans and doing . . . who knew what with them, they needed to be prepared for that eventuality. The Astar had already taken her once, after all.

They had come to the conclusion that while she could maintain a certain level of protection using a large Dodge-vine and Adastem ritual, the ritual's adaptive nature meant it wasn't extremely well-protected against any *one* thing in particular. It might block some weaker teleportation but that term could not be used to describe the Astar's.

So she had needed to find some herb with the teleportation or spacial element. Without any confirmation that such a thing even existed.

She had never needed to search for a particular element in an herb before, relying on what she had to get by. To be fair, what she had was quite expansive, covering a lot of different scenarios.

It had been a conversation with Glemp that had found her what she needed.

Years ago, when she had first arrived in this world, she had found a plant called Frozen Time. She had almost forgotten about the thing, having given the only piece she had ever found to Glemp to experiment with. While Glemp still hadn't reached Silver rank, they were close and had learnt a thing or two about the plant since then.

Glemp had learnt that when you reversed the element of time that Frozen Time held, you got Space. So, she had collected some more of the plant from the mountaintop and come home, ready to perform a new ritual.

This was the other reason that the people of Nature's Reclaim were so excited. Zalia had told them all about the ritual she was going to perform today, so they were prepared and aware of its effects. She had been planting Frozen Time all across the town for the past few days, along with making sure Dodge-vines were in the right places for what she had in mind.

Something she had learnt about Herbal Magic a while ago was that she could cast a ritual over the span of a very long time, with the time spent meaning the scale of the ritual could be much larger. She had figured out that it would take her two days to perform this one at the scale she wanted, which was a huge amount of time to invest over the course of which she would need to be standing still.

With a sigh, she stood up and stretched. With a twist of her head, her neck cracked ever so slightly. She wished this slower aging would hurry up and slow it faster.

She had prepared a comfortable little spot outside of her house to perform the ritual. While it looked like a cultivated garden of plants, it was an extremely well-protected place. It was a series of living rituals that had the anti-teleportation ritual, as well as spiritual, physical, and adaptive protection from both perception and attacks. That was on top of the protective effects of the Grove that affected both herself and the plants that made up the living rituals. It was a lot, but well worth it to make sure the investment of time worked out.

There were seventy nodes around the town that made up the pieces of the larger living ritual she was about to perform, and each of those was protected by a similar setup as well as enchanted physical barriers to ensure no one could break the living ritual once it was complete. The ritual would be able to handle the breaking of multiple nodes as long as she replaced them quickly enough but she didn't want to take any risks.

With all that ready, she moved over and sat down in the centre of her setup to begin.

The first step was summoning all the material needed for the ritual using Herbal Magic's Iron rank ability. She had spent time growing all of the Frozen Time she needed due to its lower-rank limitation but hadn't bothered with the Dodge-vine.

Piles and piles of glittering petals made of ice appeared around her, summoned from her spacial storage. They were soon followed by Dodge-vine that was dried and crushed into a rough dust. More and more appeared, all of it Silver rank because of the Bronze rank effect of Harvester.

Twenty hours later, she had finished summoning the Dodge-vine. It was an improvement on the weeks she had spent growing Frozen Time but still a painful amount of mana and time. She could feel the very slight buildup of pain in her soul due to overuse of a passive, but compared to the Gold rank spirit trying to separate her from her own soul, it was nothing.

The piles of Dodge-vine and Frozen Time petals around her lifted up and floated across the town. The few people who had slept and then come back to watch the ritual exclaimed as it happened, excited to see something other than summoning herbs finally happen.

They continued to spread until a haze of herbs lay over Nature's Reclaim, each leaf and piece of dust spinning gently as it floated in place. Then, nothing happened.

Many of the people down the hill were looking around expectantly as if they thought the ritual would go off immediately. Zalia could only wish it were so.

Across the next day and seven hours, Zalia sat in the middle of her living rituals, protected from outside distraction . . . mostly.

She was attacked a few times by miniature fluffy missiles throwing themselves at extremely high speeds towards her shoulders, back, head, and body. This was due to the not-so-small kittens escaping Boreal's careful watch.

They were getting bigger now, nowhere near fully grown, yet large enough to have a bit of momentum behind their pounces. Luckily, Zalia was quite immune to their attacks because of her rank and abilities. She was also used to that kind of behaviour, having raised Boreal herself.

In a way, she was a grandmother to the litter. Where Boreal had to be stern and strict in her mothering, Zalia got to relax and have joyous times with the five, leaving the important stuff to Boreal.

They all had names that Zalia couldn't make with her own voice, all of them different sounds that Boreal could make. They also had names given by Zalia and Boreal together that she could pronounce.

The carbon copy of Boreal was named Frost, both for the abilities she had as well as the colour and body shape that was the heritage of the mountain cats that lived in the north.

The other carbon copy kitten that was the exact same colour and body shape as the father, also known as the Ancient of War, was called Rush. This kitten had a long and lithe body, his fur flat and yellow-gold instead of fluffy and grey as well as missing the distinctive icy spines that Boreal had. This kitten's powers were focused on pure speed, with the force of his attacks being based on the very same thing.

There were three others, all of them with different mixtures of fur colour, body shape, and abilities. Breeze was lithe with flat fur but had Boreal's icy spines along his shoulders, back, and tail. His abilities focused on mobility and dodging rather than speed, as well as many that affected the mobility of his enemies.

The two other girls both had Boreal's fur, one with her stockier, stronger body and the other with the lithe body of the Ancient of War. These two were named Prance and Pounce, for the way they often fought. The two of them had been close since birth, lacking the icy spines of Boreal and the flat, yellow-gold fur of their father. Prance was uniquely gifted at distracting things while Pounce did exceptionally well at taking them down with a single, well-placed strike without being seen.

Often, if one saw Prance hopping around something, catching its attention, that meant Pounce was somewhere near about to strike.

Despite the best efforts of the five, Boreal's constant supervision and Zalia's immunity to such shenanigans outdid them. The ritual built and built, the herbs in the air glowing brighter and brighter over the time of the casting, as mana was poured constantly, if slowly, into it.

Towards the end of the ritual, most of the people of Nature's Reclaim had to wait inside as the sheer brightness of the ritual blinded them.

Finally, with a surging flash, it activated.

CHAPTER TWENTY-ONE

Fear on the Horizon

Zalia

Zalia finished packing away her clean clothes, threw the bag of dried lavender in, and closed the lid on the trunk. She sighed, stretching her arms up and arching her back.

Back in the days when she had been adventuring across Endaria, she'd had one set of clothes that both repaired and cleaned themselves. Now, she had more outfits than she could keep track of. That wasn't because she went out and got them herself but because the people of Nature's Reclaim dropped off food, clothes, and other useful items on a regular basis. It was because of the way that the Ancient of Wisdom ran the town that the people were so happy; they did this of their own free will.

The animals of the town often did the same, but those items were usually a lot less . . . useful. Boreal loved their gifts, though, so it wasn't an issue.

She turned around and went to the door, opening it. To her surprise, all five of Boreal's children were lined up, politely sitting, with Boreal behind them. With a little nudging from Boreal, the five young cats gave a discordant chorus of apologetic meows.

Zalia raised her eyebrow at Boreal.

"*An apology, for disturbing your ritual so much,*" Boreal explained.

Zalia held back her laughter and tried to look serious, nodding as if deep in thought. "Apology accepted."

She reached an arm to her right, picking up a hairbrush she kept there for Boreal's children specifically. An item that brought terror to them.

"Now, run!" she exclaimed evilly, raising it high.

The five young cats scattered, dashing away at their top speeds. Zalia only gave a half-hearted chase, letting them get away.

She put the hairbrush back and started walking towards their home's exit, Boreal following along.

Over the past four years, the armies of Endaria had significantly grown in strength. With the Morning's Shade now a force controlled by the council, many people from around the kingdom, stronger now after surviving the invasion, had joined one group or the other. The continued need to destroy nests of demons had provided a constant stream of experience for both armies; the average level of the Endarian armies was much higher now.

Ro-ak had spoken to her after his return, informing her of the thousand-eyed one's burial. He had also told her that it was almost time for the next war.

She didn't know why or how Ro knew that, but believed him all the same. Anxiety wracked her body every day now; dreading the return of the horrors of war was distracting her mind. It was why she had created the anti-teleportation ritual now of all times. Preparations had to be made.

This ritual wasn't the Grove's only defence, though. She hadn't been lax in the past years, experimenting with her powers as much as possible while bringing some of her passives and weapon proficiencies up to speed.

Profile - Zalia Taori
Health - Excellent
Mana - Full
Stamina - Full
Class One - Hunter - Silver 4
Linked Attributes - Strength, Dexterity
Active Skills
Kill Shot - Silver 4
Hunter's Mark - Silver 5
Fight or Flight - Silver 4
Passive Skills
Hunter's Sight - Silver 6
Survivalist - Silver 8
Class Two - Herbalist - Silver 6
Linked Attributes - Vitality, Resilience
Active Skills
Flora Identification - Silver 6
Natural Matter Alteration - Silver 8
Druid Grove - Silver 9
Passive Skills
Harvester - Silver 8
Herbal Magic - Silver 10

Unity Class - Druid - Silver 5
Linked Attributes - Wisdom, Intellect
Active Skills
Nature's Wrath - Silver 5
Protection of the Wilds - Silver 5
Passive Skills
Healing Presence - Silver 11
General Passives
Heat Resistance - Silver 8
Cold Resistance - Silver 8
Aura Observation - Silver 1 (MAX)
Enhanced Vision - Silver 1 (MAX)
Poison Resistance - Iron 7
Mobility - Silver 10
Stealth - Silver 8
Trapper - Silver 8
Teaching - Silver 1 (MAX)
Flight - Silver 1 (MAX)
Physical Resistance - Silver 8
Mental Resistance - Silver 8
Weapon Proficiencies
Bow - Silver 1 (MAX)
Sword - Silver 1 (MAX)
Throwing Knives - Tin 17
Bonded Items
Druidic bow, Blessed by Starlight (Blessed Heirloom) - Deeply bonded
Bronze rank.
Druidic Armour, Blessed by Nature (Blessed Heirloom) - Deeply bonded
Bronze rank.
Ethereal Vault Gauntlet (Heirloom) - Deeply bonded Bronze rank.
Blessings
Blessing of Scour, the Desert Storm.
Aura Observation – passive.
Tin - You are able to identify what rank a creature is by sight, unless it
has a method of hiding that information.
Iron - You are able to identify a creature's general progress to the next rank.
Bronze - Your strength of observation increases. Fluctuations in the auras
of undisciplined beings can give insights into their emotional state.
Silver - You are able to see the aura of beings in their magic. This allows
you to identify the owner or controller of magics. This is the maximum
level of this passive.
Enhanced Vision - passive.

Tin - You see better in low light areas.

Iron - Your vision is able to pierce magical darkness of the same rank or lower of this ability.

Bronze - You are able to filter out too-bright light to a certain extent, and gain the ability to discern details at greater distances.

Silver - Your vision is no longer dependent on your eyes. This is the maximum level of this passive.

Teaching - passive.

Tin - You gain a better understanding of what methods of teaching will work with certain people, scaling with the level and rank of this ability.

Iron - When teaching someone, they have an easier time grasping concepts that you explain, scaling with the level and rank of this ability. You are also able to convey simple concepts even when there is a language barrier.

Bronze - Attempting to teach someone about something you aren't fully educated in will give you insights into the subject, allowing you to learn even as you teach others.

Silver - You become a master of the craft of teaching. You know what others need to learn even before they do. This is the maximum level of this passive.

Flight - passive.

Tin - Your manoeuvrability is increased and your air resistance is reduced while in flight. This scales based on the rank and level of this passive.

Iron - Your ability to perceive your surroundings while flying becomes exceptional. You can spot distant details and potential threats with remarkable clarity, allowing you to anticipate and counteract aerial assaults effectively as well as see threats on the ground.

Bronze - All flight-based abilities are easier and cheaper to maintain. This effect increases based on how many allies you also give flight to.

Silver - You are an expert in flight and may maintain flight abilities indefinitely. This is the maximum level of this passive.

Mobility - passive.

Tin - Your speed is increased. Your stamina is less affected by movement.

Iron - You may step on air one time before stepping on a solid surface once more.

Bronze - You are able to step on air three times before resetting this ability. Additionally, you may perform a short-range teleport with a long cooldown. Finally, when travelling long distances, you are able to maintain a fast pace while maintaining your stamina indefinitely.

Silver - You can set a point in space over the course of an hour. You may teleport to this point from anywhere with a seven day cooldown.

Bow - Weapon Proficiency

Tin - Arrows shot from a bow you are using have increased speed based on rank and level of this skill.

> **Iron - Arrows shot from a bow you are using have increased penetrative power based on the rank and level of this skill.**
> **Bronze - Bows you use will now shoot entirely silently. Additionally, when you draw the string back, you will gain insights into the weak points of your target.**
> **Silver - You no longer need to hold your bow to shoot it. It floats next you to, acting in accordance with your will. This is the maximum level of this skill.**
> **Sword - Weapon Proficiency**
> **Tin - You can wield a sword faster and hit harder with it based on the rank and level of this skill.**
> **Iron - The durability of a sword wielded by you is increased based on the rank and level of this skill.**
> **Bronze - When you successfully parry, you gain a burst of speed for a short time. Additionally, you can gain slight insights into the movements of your enemies when engaged.**
> **Silver - Your strikes now create slashing winds that may hit targets from afar. These winds are weaker than a normal strike and are blockable. This is the maximum level of this skill.**

The biggest change in her passives was something entirely new to all of her abilities. They were at their limit. The final rank abilities were stronger than was normal for passives, yet she could not rank them up any further.

Because of Flight's Silver rank ability, she always had her wings active these days, folded behind her back but at the ready. She still walked everywhere unless she was really in a hurry and had grown used to the feeling of weightlessness the wings brought. She had also made a few more defences using Herbal Magic, living rituals that she had come up with.

Scattered around Nature's Reclaim were living rituals using Zephyr, Manifest, and a lot of Bitterbalm. These rituals were inactive most of the time, but when activated by the Ancient of War, would summon earth golems around the perimeter that would defend the town. That, along with all the permanent traps she set around the place, provided a good amount of protection.

There were also hundreds of smaller living rituals set and ready outside the walls that would create various effects, from explosions of fire to poisonous living vines to blasting winds. All of these were inactive as well, Zalia not wanting to accidentally blow up or otherwise kill the people of the town. All someone had to do to activate these rituals was remove the Frozen Time that sat at their centre. Anyone could do so, yet only herself, Ember, Aylie, Boreal, and the three ancients protecting the town knew about it. The people of the town knew to avoid any living ritual, and so far, there hadn't been any incidents.

The two of them stepped out of their home and looked out at Nature's

Reclaim. It had grown in population quite a lot since its creation, housing more than five thousand people and animals at last count.

"War is coming again, Boreal, I can feel it."

Boreal said nothing as Zalia turned to look up at the Ancient of Life, a giant tree looming over the entire Grove. It had grown with the town, now standing at over a hundred and fifty metres tall, its base split around the house it sat atop. It had become more and more awake as the years passed, in control of the healing aura permeating the entire town. It had yet to learn to speak but still used its control of the aura to amazing effect, ensuring that the life within the Grove was kept safe.

She looked around the town square, wondering what to do today. Ember and Aylie had gone off for some lunch and she knew that Boreal had plans to go hunting with her children. Similar to Zalia's wish to get Aylie to Silver as quickly as possible, Boreal also wanted to get her own children to Bronze. They were getting there, having started at Iron rank and making quick progress under Boreal's teaching.

Maybe she should check the defences again, to make sure they were in good order. She'd done that only five days ago though, so perhaps it could wait.

She *could* go hunting with Boreal and her children, but it didn't hold any appeal. It wasn't that she didn't want to spend time with them, more that she found no joy in hunting down and killing defenceless animals. She didn't even need to eat anymore, so what was the point?

With Mobility's Silver rank ability, she could teleport back to the Grove in an instant. That meant she could pretty safely travel a much further distance without having to worry about either herself or the Grove being attacked.

She shot off a quick message to Ember through their bond and gave Boreal a quick goodbye hug. In a burst of motion, she took off into the sky to begin the short flight west to the capital. While she wanted to find out what had happened between Indis and Faian, the main reason she was going was to see Hildebrandt. She had a few questions that needed answering.

CHAPTER TWENTY-TWO

Casual Grill Chat

Zalia

Zalia flew in low over the capital, watching the patrolling guards all along the city walls. The capital was a thriving city now because most of the remaining population of Endaria had centralised there after the invasion, for the support of the government more than anything else.

The only other place in Endaria that had kept an even remotely large population had been Ostoss in the north, the town that Zalia had helped defend. The Enchanter there had eventually figured out her anti-demon ritual and incorporated it into his defence, lending the people there safety. Other than those two cities, the final places in the kingdom that had remained populated were the villages far, far north. On the very edges of Endaria, those villages were usually considered the most dangerous parts of the kingdom. That had changed over the course of the invasion, with many people having fled to those villages and only a few of those returning once the invasion was over.

That was all in the past now, though. Sure, the odd demon popped up here and there, but life had gone back to normal. The people of Endaria were tougher than ever, and many of the previously abandoned towns were receiving seeding populations from the capital as people started to look outside its walls for opportunity. For those who put in the hard work, there was limitless land around already-built infrastructure for the taking.

None of those reasons were why Zalia had come to the capital, however. She had come to see Hildebrandt, the most powerful person in the kingdom. Zalia wasn't sure if the entire kingdom's army was capable of beating her in a fight. It was good, then, that Hildebrandt was also one of the most selfless people in the kingdom.

When she had ceded control of the Morning's Shade to the Endarian Council, Hildebrandt hadn't stayed with them as a member also under the council. Instead, she had been living the quiet life in the capital in a nice cozy house towards the upper tiers of the city.

Having seen her approaching the city at speed, a pair of shadowy guards borne on dark wings flew up to meet her. Once they drew closer, Zalia recognised them as the twins, members of the Morning's Shade who now apparently acted as air control for the capital.

They let her pass with a simple nod of greeting, and she dropped down towards the area she knew Hildebrandt to live in.

Zalia had been to her house only once in the past four years, some year and a half after the invasion. It wasn't that she didn't want to see the woman, just that they were so often both busy. That, and the fact that Zalia had to fly a mind-numbing twenty-five hours straight to reach the city, even at her faster speed. She often wished that she could make some portals in a few other places of Endaria as well. Actually, couldn't she just . . .

She shook the thought from her head as she landed, peering up at the compact two-story house surrounded by a neat, little garden with a waist-high fence around it. The building itself was made of giant log posts with plastered walls between them, creating a beautiful, simple cottage in a city filled with wonders of architecture. Unlike most of the buildings in the capital that were essentially grown by magical builders, this one had been built by hand by none other than Hildebrandt herself.

Zalia walked up to the huge, thick wooden door that served as the house's entrance and gave it two solid, satisfying knocks. It wasn't often that a door would handle the unrestrained strength of a Silver ranker, but this house had been built for someone much higher than that.

Her head turned at a called "Over here!" from around the side of the house. She stepped down the two steps and walked over the stepping stones through the garden. While she kept her aura as restrained as possible in cities, she did notice some of the grass growing wildly despite her efforts. She absentmindedly trimmed it all back to normal as she turned the second corner into the backyard.

There was Hildebrandt, in a singlet and shorts that showed off her obscene amount of muscle, whistling away as she cooked some type of meat on a flame grill. The woman picked up another log and chucked it through the hatch into the fire beneath as she turned to look at Zalia.

"Zalia! So nice to see you, it's been a while."

It was odd to see Hildebrandt out of her armour, no shield or mace in sight. When you saw Hildebrandt in battle, it was easy to forget that there was a person under all that power.

"Your garden is lovely as ever, how have you been?" Zalia asked, walking over to give her a big hug.

Hildebrandt returned the hug, one hand still holding a pair of tongs. "Great! I'm still grateful you persuaded me to pick up gardening, I've even managed to develop a passive for it since the last time you were here."

Zalia gave her a warm smile, happy for the woman. The last time she'd been here the house had only just finished being built and the "garden" at the time had looked like a war site. Which it kind of had been. Zalia had convinced her to fix it up rather than leave what remained of the grass to grow in wild patches. She was fond of wild growth but all nature could flourish under a careful eye and a caring hand. Her smile slowly faded as she remembered why she was there.

"What is it?" Hildebrandt asked, seeing her expression change.

Zalia's hand tapped repetitively on her thick pants as she thought. "I wanted to talk to you about Indis, if you know anything. And I wanted some advice."

Hildebrandt nodded but made no move to sit, continuing her cooking. Zalia waited as she finished up with the meat and took a few fruits off a nearby tree, crushing them with ease into two cups. She also brought out another comfortable chair and some fresh bread, setting everything on a table between the two chairs. Only once that was done did Zalia talk.

"How exactly did Indis lose the election?"

Hildebrandt sipped some of the . . . fruit juice before responding.

"You'd have to ask Faian if you want details, but as far as I know, she started plotting to have Faian removed but the general was one step ahead. She got politically outmanoeuvred for once."

Zalia was a little shocked. It appeared Faian had taken to her role quite well, then. "Is she still in the city?"

Hildebrandt shook her head. "No, she left. Don't know where she went, though."

Zalia frowned, worried. She didn't have any warmth for the woman but they had been close once. Endaria and its people had been everything to her, and to be rejected by them . . . well, she probably hadn't taken that well. Maybe she could get Aylie to send a dream message.

"The other thing I'm worried about is the Astar. I know it's been peaceful for a while now but I have this feeling, this fear on the edge of my mind all the time recently. A few months back, Ember and Aylie ran into a new type of demon and I can't help but think the Astar were behind it somehow. I have this . . . I have this certainty in my mind that they're going to attack, and soon. It might be a strike against me, or even against the capital. I'm not sure."

It was Hildebrandt's turn to frown as she inspected Zalia closely. "Where is this feeling coming from?"

Zalia shrugged. "I don't know, but it's got me through more than one bad situation in the past. I trust it."

Hildebrandt looked at her sympathetically. "Are you sure you aren't just so used to watching for danger that you're seeing something that isn't there? Maybe triggered by whatever it is Ember and Aylie ran into?"

Zalia hadn't thought about that. During the invasion and the months leading up to it, she had been so constantly in danger that it had become normal to her. After each fight, there was already another enemy waiting. Maybe the close run-in Ember and Aylie had with the demon had set something off in her, some trauma from the war.

She sighed deeply. "You might be right. I just can't shake the feeling. We know that the Astar have come after powerful Endarians in the past. Matth . . . Matthias still hasn't reappeared. When it comes to the next most powerful people in the kingdom after you, it's the twins, a few of the council members, and my family. I think we should strike before they decide to start up that particular habit again."

Hildebrandt gave her a serious look, apprehension apparent on her face.

"Zalia, I understand your fear, but striking against an enemy whose strength is unknown is a surefire way to start a war we might not be ready for. The kingdom has only just started recovering, properly recovering, from the last one. Don't do anything foolish. If you need some closure about this issue, talk to General Faian while you're here and maybe she can work something out."

Zalia nodded slowly, hearing the logic in her words. She was right that they weren't yet ready for another war. "Alright, I'll talk to Faian later, then."

They chatted idly for the next half hour as they, though it was mostly Hildebrandt, finished eating. Zalia asked about what ranking up as an Emerald ranker was like, and Hildebrandt explained how she had reached a level where she felt no push to reach the next rank. She was essentially unkillable and had all the time in the world to rank up, which made for less of a desperate push to reach the next rank than what Zalia was used to.

Hildebrandt asked after Ember, Aylie, and Boreal, becoming incredibly excited to learn that Boreal now had kittens. She wanted to come for a visit as soon as possible to see them.

Zalia eventually had to leave, knowing that Ember would be waiting for her return. With a wave and a hug goodbye and promises to see each other soon, Zalia started the short flight up to the capital's castle. A short talk with Faian, and then she would return home to test a theory she had come up with to do with her ritual magic. If her idea worked, it might change Endaria forever.

CHAPTER TWENTY-THREE

Now She's Thinking with Portals

Zalia

Zalia waited patiently at the castle gates as the messenger that was posted there ran off to inform General Faian of her arrival. She tapped her finger repetitively on the side of her leg as she stood, trying to be understanding of the precaution. It was entirely fair, as they couldn't exactly allow just anyone to walk around the castle grounds, nor would they have allowed looser safety precautions when it came to specific people.

She felt a brief bit of annoyance as the guard there requested that she cut open her palm to prove she wasn't a shapechanger, but pushed through that feeling with logic once more. Of course they should check.

The messenger returned a few minutes later to tell Zalia that Faian was in a meeting but would be available within the next half hour. She was fine with waiting a little longer as the guard finally let her through to wander the gardens there.

There was an intriguing mystery around the garden in the castle that Zalia always tried to figure out when she was here. Most of the garden was well kept and tended, obviously looked after. However, there was a patch of plants that were dead and even when reinvigorated by her magic, would soon die once more without constant tending.

It was the place where the thousand-eyed one had once rested.

No matter what anyone tried, that piece of land always died soon after being healed or replanted. It was a mystery, though one that only occupied her mind when she was in the capital. Thinking about it, she wondered if Nateysta would be able to remove the tiny slice of permanent corruption now that he was back. Her train of thought trundled onwards towards the God-trap, a giant contraption made of hundreds of spinning rings that had the power to trap an Ascendant being.

When she had returned to Endaria from the adventure that had given her the item, she had wanted to find someone to give it to who could work on repairing the thing. It had escaped her mind for a few weeks, and when she had pulled it out of her storage after that, she had found it already repaired. She hadn't taken into account the self-repairing features of heirloom items. Sure, it was a *constructed* heirloom, not a normal one, but it held the same properties all the same.

The only problem she had now was in figuring out how to use the damn thing.

She hadn't been able to bond to it so far but knew it could take years for that kind of thing to happen. At the very least, she knew it had to be used in a location that was significant to the Ascendant you were trying to trap. If Nateysta hadn't already gone through the trouble of spending *years* creating a prison for the particular Ascendant that had created this dead zone in the castle, she might have considered using it here. Assuming the area of dead life was significant to the thousand-eyed one at all and not just some aftereffect of its existence.

Time flew by as Zalia wandered the gardens and a secretary came to retrieve her, leading her through the castle and towards Faian's office.

The castle had received some major interior alterations; its function as a space for a council of twenty-two rather than a monarchy of one required a much different layout.

When Zalia entered Faian's office, she had to admire the efficiency with which the space was used. The two file cabinets were within easy reach of the desk, with a spare quill and inkwell as well as a stack of sheet paper available on its top. The desk was off to the side, with a comfortable but straight-backed chair sitting in front of it. Most of the rest of the space was taken up by a series of more reclined cushioned chairs around a low, wide table with a spinning centre.

There was also a small glass showcase cabinet holding various military medals belonging to Faian, the majority of them granted by the king that Faian had served as general, King Horum. His son, King Alistair, had been the last king of Endaria and the one that had almost seen to its end. In a way, he *had* seen to its end, as Endaria was no longer a kingdom but a nation free.

General Faian was in her office, sitting in one of the more comfortable seats around the low table, sipping a cup of tea. She dismissed the secretary with a smile and a wave, then gestured for Zalia to be seated. "Tea?"

Zalia nodded her assent and Faian poured out a cup of tea from a teapot for her. Zalia took it with a murmured thanks, taking a small sip. It was minty with a slightly sweet taste that reminded her of honey. Strange, she hadn't ever seen a bee in Endaria.

"To what do I owe the pleasure of this visit?" Faian asked.

Zalia took one more sip, savouring the taste. She might not need to eat or drink but that didn't mean it couldn't be pleasurable. Might as well get straight to business.

"The Astar. I'm worried about what they might be doing. Ember discovered a new type of demon, and with the Astar having been so silent after the invasion, I fear they might be involved in this."

Faian leaned forwards, not immediately dismissing Zalia's fears. A good start. "I see, and has there been any further evidence of Astar involvement other than your suspicions?"

Zalia shook her head.

Faian put down her teacup with a sigh, looking thoughtful. "I believe something does need to be done about the Astar, Zalia, even if it is just to get an explanation. I agree with your suspicions about them, *but* I can't allow a strike against them until we have confirmation of their interference with Endaria. Yes, they did capture and torture you, and yes, you have confirmed them to be working with the demons through that experience but . . . what if that was just a splinter group of the Astar, and they are a more varied people?"

Zalia had already thought about that very thing. She knew all that, yet couldn't shake the feeling that something was going to happen. Something was going to happen and she didn't know what to do to stop it.

"Look, I'm not asking for you to send the army to attack them. All I want is for you to look further into it and . . . well, just be careful."

Faian nodded in agreement.

They spoke a little more in detail about what exactly Faian would do. She agreed to convince the civilian council seated to send a Morning's Shade group to investigate the new demon, as they were much better suited to such a task than the military was. Additionally, she was working on anti-teleportation for the capital as well. Zalia couldn't perform a ritual that large, but Faian was convinced that her people would be able to incorporate it into the city's existing magical defences.

When all was said and done, Zalia activated the Silver rank ability of Mobility and vanished from the capital.

She appeared moments later, just outside the city limits of Nature's Reclaim. The anti-teleportation appeared to be working just fine.

While her mind was on teleportation, her thoughts turned to the idea she'd had back in the capital. When mixed with Bitterbalm, Frozen Time gave the Space element to a ritual. Zalia had used it for the very anti-teleportation that had just stopped her from appearing in the middle of her home and instead placed her outside the city gates.

Well, what if she could set up more portals?

The idea was perhaps an absurd one, but the more she thought about it, the more she wanted to try. It would require the two plants she had just listed, as well as Manifest for its element of physical manifestation, of course. Those three in combination should create a ritual that would create a physical manifestation in a space. It was easy enough to alter the ritual so it would allow for a physical manifestation in a space *of a person*. What she couldn't figure out was how to set the destination.

All of the rituals she had used up to this point had a very specific target area: the very same area that the ritual encompassed. It was easy enough to have the ritual target a person by having them simply stand in it, what she couldn't figure out was how to get it to send that person to somewhere far, far away.

She was still stuck in those thoughts when she arrived back home to find Ember standing there waiting for her, with arms crossed and an expression of annoyance on her face. Uh-oh.

CHAPTER TWENTY-FOUR

Portal

Zalia

A thousand thoughts crossed Zalia's mind as she observed Ember's annoyed expression. Had she done something wrong? Had she forgotten something?

She briefly considered whether it was too late to pretend she was just walking by, but eventually steeled herself and approached.

"Good morning, honey," Zalia said in greeting, keeping a cheery expression.

Ember narrowed her eyes at her, and Zalia waited for it to drop.

"These kittens, Zalia, I swear to the gods!"

Zalia breathed a sigh of relief. "What did they do this time?"

Ember gestured for her to follow and went inside the house.

They walked through the main hall and up the stairs to the second floor. Zalia spotted Boreal in a passing room, pacing back and forth in front of her five kittens, tail flicking aggressively. Whatever they had done must have been pretty bad to make Boreal that angry.

Ember brought her to the kittens' playroom and she walked into a scene akin to that of a town after a tornado had passed through.

Firstly, everything . . . *everything* was soaked in water. There was ice all around the place that was still melting, and many of the bridges and high-up posts had been either shredded to pieces or ripped down from the walls and ceiling. The floor was coated in wet shreds of cloth and wood. They had really done a number on it.

Zalia didn't really think it was as bad as it seemed but wasn't about to say that to Ember. She knew that the room would repair itself slowly, so it wasn't a big deal.

"Well, they appear to be getting a bit restless in the town."

Ember gave her a look that said, "No shit."

"I've been thinking, Boreal wasn't ever this bad. She was a bit of a menace, but most of her childhood was spent wandering the world with you."

Zalia waited for the rest.

"Maybe we should go on a long journey somewhere, take them with us, and show them more of the world. Give them some space to stretch out and explore."

Zalia thought it over. It wasn't a bad idea, and in a world where they were living out in the wild, Boreal's children would begin to stray further away to find territory of their own. Zalia still thought of them as kittens, but in reality, they were getting quite big and very strong. It wouldn't be long before they were Bronze rank, and when that happened, they would be stronger than a good portion of the human race.

They would also level much quicker than a human would, as they just had the one class. Zalia, due to her very late start to magic, had only been able to keep up with Boreal because her abilities ranked up at an increased speed. Boreal would probably pull ahead in rank now that Zalia's ability levelling had slowed down.

"Okay, we can talk about it. I've been thinking of scouting out the Astar lands personally, but we could take all of them and Aylie along with us. With you, me, and Boreal, they would be somewhat safe."

Ember frowned. "Are you sure that is a good idea? I was thinking more along the lines of taking them up to the north to see their homeland, even exploring further than we have gone before. The Astar lands might be a bit too dangerous."

"I'm sure," Zalia said. "Aylie is ready, and this is what we have been preparing her for. She proved her capability against that demon in the north. The more I think about it, the more I realise we don't know *anything* about the Astar. I'm not saying we should attack them by ourselves, but surely we can get some kind of intel. Find one of their towns or . . . anything."

"Okay, well, let me think about it. We'll have to talk to Boreal about it as well—they are her children, after all."

Zalia nodded in agreement, and they both looked back down the hall towards where Boreal and the kittens were. "Speaking of, we should probably go check on them."

They went back to the room and found that the Ancient of War, the kittens' father, was also in the room now. He was trying to calm Boreal down while the five kittens sat nervously.

"Alright, what happened?"

Rush, Breeze, and Prance all started speaking at once, the mental communication soundless yet deafening.

Zalia shook her head, gesturing for them to stop. "Hold on, one at a time, please. Frost, you first."

Frost was the most similar to Boreal, both in appearance and temperament.

"*Well, Pounce and Prance were hunting Breeze, but they couldn't catch him so I tried to freeze them all, but . . . accidentally froze the entire room.*"

She was looking down at her paws, shuffling nervously and Rush, quick as ever, spoke up before the other three.

"*Then they all attacked Frost! So I had to help her fight them.*"

It felt strange how they communicated. Boreal had developed a passive ability that allowed her to speak full sentences and understand language, and not long after that, she had taught her children. It was odd hearing them all talk normally, rather than using short words linked with images that Zalia was used to.

Pounce went on to explain how Prance had gotten in the way of her attack and had been thrown into one of the posts, breaking it. They tried to continue blaming each other and explaining how everything got broken, but Zalia stopped them, knowing enough. The echo chamber of chaos created by five carefree kittens was a dangerous thing. When the five of them were alone, there wasn't anyone to dampen their unbridled violence, which was enhanced with magical abilities and strength, and she had seen how that had turned out.

"*Can I talk with you a minute?*" Zalia sent to Boreal.

Boreal stopped her pacing and walked out of the room with Zalia.

"*I'm sor—*" she started.

Zalia waved her off. "*Nothing that time won't fix, little one. Ember and I think it's time that those five got to see more of the world, explore, make some mistakes, and learn from them. I want to explore some of the Astar lands, and I think all of them coming with would make for a good opportunity. Of course, you, Ember, and Aylie would come along as well.*"

Zalia could tell from Boreal's posture that she was unsure of that idea.

"*Think about it, and talk with the Ancient of War about it too. I've got some other things that I want to do before heading out, anyway.*"

She watched Boreal as she quietly considered, her tail still flicking with annoyance at the kittens. Boreal bowed her head in acknowledgement of the idea, and they went back inside. Zalia squeezed Ember's shoulders to get her attention and whispered, "Where is Aylie? I have an idea she might be able to help with."

Ember turned her head, whispering back, "She's down at the market, practicing blocking out people's thoughts."

"Are you going to be okay with these five?"

Ember reached a hand up to Zalia's and squeezed one of them back, huffing. "These little ones? With ease. Oh, hey, I was going to go for a walk outside the city this evening, you want to join me?"

Zalia gave her a quick kiss. "Of course."

She left the house, feeling just a little bad for the kittens. They were a lot bigger now, sure, but they were also still very young. By Zalia's reckoning, even

Boreal was still young, but the life cycle of cats was much quicker than that of humans. She wondered if the Astar thought something similar about the other races of the world and that's why they seemed to treat them with such neutrality, nothing other than a small race of creatures that died easily, quickly, and often needed to be culled so they didn't grow too annoying.

It didn't take Zalia long to find Aylie in the market, the teenager sitting in her usual spot in the high branches of a tree. Aylie had always loved flying and high places, loved the wind and feeling of freedom that came from them.

She waited at the tree's base, unhurried and not wanting to disturb Aylie's practice. The girl would notice Zalia there eventually, she always did.

Zalia counted to twenty-eight seconds before Aylie's eyes opened, a new record. "You're still getting better!" she called up.

"And you're somehow still getting stealthier," Aylie said at normal volume. She knew Zalia would be able to hear.

Zalia shrugged, watching Aylie jump down some fifteen metres from the tree top. She had to resist the urge to tell Aylie off for the risk. Even if she *had* broken something, they were both Druids with healing abilities. Besides, Zalia herself had tested her limits more than once in much more dangerous ways.

"It's like every time I figure out how to detect that you're there, your magic fixes the hole in your stealth and makes a new one."

Zalia tried to keep an innocent face, but Aylie narrowed her eyes at her.

"Me? Never."

Aylie's eyes narrowed further.

"Okay, yes, I have been doing that. It's a good way for you to learn to perceive all kinds of stealth specialists. All they need is a single tell, one thing to show that they're there and I want you to be able to find those things."

Aylie gave a little sniff of annoyance, then said, "Thanks."

"What for?"

"You're always helping me in little ways like that, it means a lot to me."

Zalia stopped and dragged Aylie into a big hug. "I'll always be here for you, I promised that, remember?"

Aylie nodded and Zalia let her go.

"Now, I actually came here because I have a problem that you might be able to find the solution to."

They stood over a small living ritual outside the city bounds some thirty minutes later. It was the teleportation ritual Zalia had thought of. Just as she had thought, it worked as she wanted . . . kind of.

If she walked into the little barely glowing outline of a portal that hovered above the ritual, she could feel herself being teleported, but all it did was teleport her to the exact place she already was. To Aylie, looking from the outside, it was as if she flickered for a second. There was also what Aylie saw in the astral, but that was something else entirely, something that Aylie couldn't quite explain with words. She had tried to send mental images of what it looked like to Zalia, but she couldn't interpret what she was seeing.

"What did it look like that time?"

"The exact same," Aylie growled.

It was getting a little frustrating, the way the ritual refused to work.

There was another of the same living ritual a bit away, sitting there with a similar faintly glowing outline of a portal. Unfortunately, neither appeared like Aylie's ability did, where you could see the destination through the portal.

"Maybe we've been thinking of this the wrong way." Aylie looked up at her, her hand tapping against the side of her leg repetitively.

Zalia smiled, realising she did the exact same thing. "What do you mean?"

"Well, we've been thinking about this like my portal. I choose a location and it makes a connecting portal from in front of me to there. What if we need to give the rituals something that belongs to something the other ritual has."

The second Aylie said it, Zalia knew she was right. She could make the portals target something that was within themselves but not outside of themselves, so she just had to have them both target something that had a fundamental connection through the astral to whatever the other portal held.

She grabbed Aylie's shoulders. "You're a genius!"

It only took her a moment to come up with something, and she pulled out the gloves of her heirloom armour. She put one in one ritual and one in the other, then remade each living ritual, this time targeting the glove within. When she recast the second ritual, the insides of the portals flickered a little before settling into the view of the other, like doors through space.

"Yes!"

All it had needed was a little input from an astral expert.

CHAPTER TWENTY-FIVE

Act Before Acted Upon

Zalia

After Aylie had left to go see the damage the kittens had done, Zalia stayed around and fiddled with the teleportation ritual a little more. She tried further and further distances until the small ritual no longer functioned, finding it could only work across a couple of kilometres unless she made it larger. That was until she made it to Gold and could raise the rank of all her herbs to Gold as well. *If* she made it to Gold.

As the hours passed, she was more sure of the idea to head into Astar lands. Yes, Hildebrandt and Faian had cautioned her to be wary, but she wasn't going to go in there to start a war. Instead, she wanted to scout them out, try and learn something that could help. With her living rituals being almost imperceptible as anything other than natural, they would be able to set up a little home base that was well hidden somewhere deep in the Astar's territory.

Eventually, she broke down the two living rituals, returned her armour's gauntlets to their place within her storage, and started the walk back to town. The size of the living ritual required to make a portal from Nature's Reclaim to the capital would be quite large; something like a living ritual from Nature's Reclaim to the mountain home of the Born of Heat and Stone people would be massive. It would have to be half the size of the town, at least, which was something that she was capable of now but also something that would take a day or more.

That wasn't to say it wasn't worth doing, just that she had more important things to do right now. Maybe it was something she could come back to down the line as a higher-ranked Druid, or something that might become useful in their stay in the Astar lands. In fact, she had an idea on how to use it there already.

The town of Nature's Reclaim was thriving, with the population having adopted the early ideas of the Ancient of Wisdom. People didn't use coin anymore here, simply trading goods to get what they wanted. Zalia preferred it; she was happy with how respectful people were to each other. She had made it clear in the early days that anyone who was to stay here would have to be good to everyone else.

She nodded to a quokka that waddled past, admiring the leather armour it wore. The cheery smile on its face was in conflict with its muscled body, armour, and Bronze rank in what was obviously a warrior class of some sort.

It was a little strange how classes worked for humans. None of the animal population of Nature's Reclaim had classes as such, even Boreal didn't have one, instead just being titled as a creature type of Mountain Frostfang. It wasn't something she had ever thought about while the war had been going on, but over the past few years, it was something that had interested her more and more.

She had three classes, two normal ones and a unity class, which was something unusual even amongst the already unusual humans. At first, Zalia thought it had to do with humans' normally higher levels of sentience and sapience compared to most other animals but had learned the Bathar, who were on a similar level with those things to humans, also didn't have classes. Instead, they were born with abilities that were already fit for the nature of the person. Or perhaps each Bathar developed into a person that fit their born abilities, it was hard to tell.

This felt like another piece in the ever-expanding puzzle Zalia was trying to figure out, a puzzle for which she had been given neither the image nor border pieces. Perhaps one day, she would find something that would give her a better idea of what exactly caused her to have three classes.

Saying that, she wasn't complaining about it at all. It had certainly been helpful, and she would go so far as to say it had saved her life on more than one occasion, though she couldn't say if she would have taken the same risks without it.

If they did end up going to the Astar lands, she would have loved to take Hildebrandt or Ro-ak with them; either of the powerful allies were capable of killing almost any creature Zalia knew of. With her uniquely powerful tank abilities, Zalia wasn't even sure if Hildebrandt *could* be killed. Surprisingly, out of the people she knew, Aylie had the highest chance of accomplishing that. Though who was to say if Ascendants were capable of making attacks against the soul or not.

Thinking about all of her old friends brought Zalia's mind to Delphi and the collective. Their memories still sat in her storage, centuries of thoughts, foreseen futures, and experiences collected in one big, jumbled mess that she still couldn't make heads or tails of. More than a few times over the past years she had tried to decipher more of the mess and hadn't completely failed. She had gotten flashes of past events, days shared with Delphi in Cormaine, images of people she had never met, and things that she had no idea whether they had happened yet or had happened so long ago as to be unimportant. It all might have meaning if she was able to recall all the memories in their chronological order, but the stored memories of dozens, even hundreds of collective members all pushed into her mind at once was an absolute mess.

She would have sent the memories off to someone more capable if she could, but she wasn't even able to accomplish that. At least in her storage, they would remain untouched by time's inevitable warping of the mind.

There was another item sitting in her storage that had been occupying her mind of late, that being the little pouch containing the ritual Juniper had tried to use to summon demons from Cormaine. At least, that was unless Zalia was right about the ritual Juniper had performed and it was originally intended to drag Juniper to Cormaine where she would die, all as part of the Astar plan.

It might be possible for her to figure out that ritual and use it to her own ends, a way of getting them into Cormaine when the time came. She knew that Ro-ak, Nateysta, wanted to return there to end the demons once and for all. From what they had gathered from the keep in Cormaine, the Bathar had somehow developed a way of moving between the worlds in the ages past, as they had originally come from that world. Perhaps that had been the ability of a single powerful mage, which was not an impossibility.

Lost in thought, Zalia was almost back at the town when she sensed something . . . strange.

From the past hours of staring into portals, she was keyed into that type of magic, her mind having just spent a long time analysing it. When she felt that same type of energy fizzing around her, Zalia acted immediately.

At the same time that she summoned her armour and sword, she cast the very same ritual that stopped teleportation magic in the town. It activated just as an Astar appeared, with one hand reaching out to grab her.

Its hand closed on her shoulder, her ritual stopped it from teleporting away with her, and she severed its arm in a brutal slash. The startled look of surprise on its face, one of the very few times Zalia had seen them make an expression, was wiped off with a well-put and concisely explained fist to the face. The fist was followed by a blade through the chest, which swept upwards as Zalia twisted the blade around, grabbed the blade further down with her hand, and *pushed* it up.

Just like that, the Astar died.

It had been Silver rank, same as her, but was obviously untrained in the art of combat. Zalia, on the other hand, had just had an entire war's worth of trauma, combat experience, and instincts honed through a lifetime as a hunter awakened in a single moment.

A few of the nearby townspeople, animals and humans both, looked over at her startled, but Zalia grabbed the body before it dropped, storing away her blade, then opened the portal to her storage and stomped in there, slamming the body into one of the storage slots.

She left that portal, letting it close before dashing to the town entrance, yelling for everyone to get inside.

Having heard her mental call, all of her family and the Ancient of War were racing to the gates.

She raced through the streets as the town gates closed behind her, the buildings flashing past in a blur as she reached speeds that very few people could achieve. It was less than a minute before she met her family rushing towards the gate, and she swept her gaze over them in a quick examination. It looked like everyone was alright. She would never know if the Astar had tried to take any of them at the same time, because if they had tried, the ritual she had created had stopped them.

A vision flashed through her mind of the Astar capturing her family while she remained the only one free. The vision progressed: her, alone, searching through forests and unknown lands, chasing the bond between herself and her faraway family. Astar dying to her sword one by one, yet her loved ones never recovered.

She gasped as the vision faded away, back to where it was stored in the clump of collective memories.

That was why she had been so on edge about the Astar. *That* was why she had felt the need to set up a zone of anti-teleportation now. She couldn't decipher the collective's memories, many of them memories that had yet to happen, but on some level, she could understand them. Once, she'd had issues with the powers of the collective, their ability to see into the future and know what would happen. She had thought the ability was somehow capable of stripping her freedom of choice. Yet today, it had helped her change a future that she would do anything to avoid.

Ember was examining her, eyes flicking over the blood that coated her gauntlets, its unnatural, shiny darkness.

"The Astar?" she asked.

Zalia nodded. She explained what had just happened, including everything about the collective's memories and the future she had just seen.

At her agreement, the Ancient of War ran off to activate many of the traps around the town, even going so far as to activate the dormant living rituals that awakened earthen guardians around the perimeter.

"I knew they would try something, I just knew it! I couldn't shake the feeling. Gods, it makes sense now."

Ember eyed her. "And going to the Astar lands, you still think we should do that?"

Zalia nodded decisively. "Yes, without a doubt."

Ember gave her silent assent and they both looked to Boreal.

The feline stared at the blood dripping from Zalia's gauntlets then looked up, giving a deep, deep growl of anger. Boreal wanted to draw blood of her own.

CHAPTER TWENTY-SIX

To Be Prepared

Zalia

It was a week after they agreed to leave for the Astar lands that they finally left Nature's Reclaim. There was a lot of preparation they needed to do as town leaders and even further as parents to ensure that nothing went wrong at home or on their journey.

By mutual agreement, Zalia focused on getting what they needed for the journey while Ember worked on everything else.

Ember had messages sent out to Faian and Hildebrandt, letting them know what had happened, where they were going, and why. She made sure to promise that they wouldn't do anything foolish that would start an all-out war. While Zalia thought that was a good thing to promise, in her mind they were *already* at war. They just hadn't realised this was how the Astar waged it.

She also spoke with the Ancient of Wisdom in Nature's Reclaim and made sure they had everything they needed, to which she was assured everything would be fine.

Ember did the same in the other Grove, the one located in the desert south of Endaria. They finally had an Ancient of Wisdom there, it having taken much longer due to the lower animal density in the desert. The Ancient of Wisdom in that Grove was like a fennec fox with fur that shimmered like a mirage, making the fox extremely hard to see.

Few people had decided to move to the desert Grove, preferring Nature's Reclaim due to its less hostile and more beautiful environment. Many did travel through the portal to go there, however, enjoying the deep warmth of the oasis springs.

Zalia had been surprised to find that some dozen desert dwellers from the city of Ulzahar had decided to move to the Grove after Sazcha had told them about it. Many of them said they were tired of the constant struggle for survival that living in Ulzahar entailed, choosing to live in the calmer, more relaxed desert Grove. That wasn't to say they didn't pull their weight, as they were still incredibly hard workers.

While Ember worked on all that, Zalia had been working on getting everything ready for the journey. The preparations for the journey that she had to make looked very different than how one might expect, their needs being wildly off the norm due to the capabilities of their magic.

They didn't need tents or any form of cover, having a perfect place to sleep in Zalia's spacial storage. Neither did they really need to bring any food, though she did pack a good portion of dried nuts, berries, and salted meats in her spacial storage.

No, the majority of her preparation time went into working with Boreal to school the kittens.

She explained to them where they were going and why they were going there, but she made no illusions as to the trip being anything other than dangerous. They were still understandably excited about the trip, and it took Zalia and Boreal the week to get across to them that they would need to be responsible. Attacking the wrong thing or making too much noise at the wrong time could lead to painful consequences. They would need to be on guard, watching for danger, and careful of their every move, constantly.

Zalia knew this was a risk, a big one. She also knew it was a necessary one.

The five needed to learn as soon as possible how the real world was. The brutality of nature, the way the world could beat you down over and over, and it was up to you to pick yourself back up again each time. But, she also didn't want them to have to learn that the way she did.

When she had left home at a young age to live by herself in the wild, frozen north of her world, she had been running from something, looking backwards at what she was trying to escape but not looking forwards to what she would have to survive. That mistake had almost cost her life more than once.

Here, the kittens would experience that, but if it came to it, Zalia, Ember, and Boreal were all around to ensure they didn't pay for a mistake with their lives. There was no reason to allow any of them to die in the process of trying to teach them how to survive.

This wasn't a lesson she had to teach Aylie. No, Aylie had already learnt that lesson at far too young an age in a horrible, scarring way. The only thing Aylie needed was love and support.

There was one other thing that Zalia did during that week of preparation time. The incident outside the city walls had her thinking that while a zone of anti-teleportation was good, it wasn't exactly helpful for anyone outside the town bounds, anyone who, say, was travelling long distances each day in hostile territory.

So she tried making something that was a little more portable.

The result of her efforts was an armband of herb stalks woven together, made from the same herbs that the ritual of anti-teleportation required.

It wasn't active all the time, unfortunately, lying dormant but still useful, as all the wearer had to do to activate it was push a tiny bit of magic into it. This did lead to Zalia learning that this wasn't something that any of the others, even Aylie and Ember, knew how to do. None of them had abilities that needed them to do that, they could simply activate their spells and let them work. The way Herbal Magic worked meant that Zalia instinctively knew how to create and activate rituals by pushing her mana into them.

Everyone else was capable of performing these herbal rituals, they just needed a much, much longer time and a lot of learning to do it. If any of them put in the time to carefully lay out the herbs for a ritual in the right configuration, they could push their mana into it to activate it just as Zalia did. Her advantage was in being able to instinctively create rituals in an instant.

After teaching her whole family how to manipulate their mana in this way, Zalia finally got them all to activate the armbands at least once each.

The armbands were one use each, falling to dust after their power was used. What they did do was provide whoever wore them about thirty seconds of time in which they wouldn't be able to be teleported. That time could be increased by feeding them more mana, but in the event of an Astar attack, Zalia would simply create a larger ritual and feed that for as long as was needed. The mana was used more efficiently that way than if everyone was maintaining their own ritual. It also stopped the Astar teleporting, making them easier to kill.

Aylie made some of her own preparations as well. She had acquired a backpack of the type Zalia had used long ago, an enchanted one that allowed her to store as much as she wanted in it so long as she could still carry the weight of all those items combined. In it, she had stored a tent, some food, an enchanted rock that could be used to create a fire, spare clothes, and even a few potions that would heal or remove disease, sickness, and other ailments.

All of her meticulous preparation, while possibly overeager, made Zalia proud. Aylie wasn't planning to be caught unprepared it seemed.

It made sense for her to keep some things outside of Zalia's storage, as it wasn't certain they would remain together. They might get separated for one reason or another, and in that case, the people who needed to eat might find themselves suddenly without a source of food.

Ember knew how to hunt, even if she wasn't great at it, while the kittens were . . . well, Zalia was sure they would figure it out.

With everything prepared, they set out. Amongst their group were Ember, Zalia, Aylie, Boreal, and her children, Frost, Pounce, Prance, Breeze, and Rush. The only one from amongst their family that didn't join them was Lumin. Instead, Lumin had gone to spend time with Ro-ak, also known as Nateysta.

Apparently, there were some things that he wanted to teach the little Ascendant pup, some things about his powers that the others were too low-rank to yet learn.

Nature's Reclaim was quite central to the kingdom, being right in the middle of the northernmost and southernmost points and just a bit east of the centre, where the capital stood.

Zalia, Ember, Aylie, and Boreal were all used to travelling and soon set into a comfortable, easy pace that their magically enhanced bodies had no trouble with. The kittens, however, soon grew tired. They were the lowest rank in the group and unused to long-distance travelling.

Over the course of the first few days, they had to stop more frequently because of this, but as they were unhurried, Zalia didn't particularly mind.

The kittens slowly grew used to this, but as they did, the others picked up the pace even more.

Zalia had learnt long ago that while it was easy to rely on the strength and endurance you gained from rank, you could become stronger or develop more endurance than someone else of the same rank who didn't train.

It also came down to your natural state of being. She'd learnt that when, as an Iron rank, she could defeat higher-ranked Ironfur rabbits simply because she was so much bigger than them, the same way that Boreal, as a full-grown Bronze rank, was so, so much scarier than a full-grown Bronze rank human.

She wondered if that had something to do with her having three classes, and if it wasn't anything other than where she was from that gave her the advantage.

Had she been alone, or had it just been her and Boreal, she would have travelled all through each night and day without stopping for food or rest. As it was, however, the group stopped often to hunt, rest, and sleep as much as was required.

It was a long journey before they arrived at what the Endarians thought of as the border of their lands between them and the Astar. They stopped there for a time, looking out across a flat marshland filled with flitting insects and the occasional animal roaming through the wet, spongy land. There would undoubtedly be unknown threats lying in wait in the marshes, but Zalia was confident that they would be alright. They might be able to defeat a Gold rank animal if it came to it, as animals usually only had one class and two or three bonded attributes.

After a brief rest, and Ember and the children all eating a bit of food, they set off down the hill and into the marshes.

It stank like rotting things; the insects were trying to figure out some way they could eat the passersby but were failing to do so, thankfully. The ground underfoot wasn't an issue to Zalia, Boreal, or the kittens, but did become so for Aylie and Ember. Boreal fixed that issue by freezing the ground along their path, turning the high-water-content earth under them rock solid.

A few days of travel in the marshes had them used to the tedium, and they had to start eating into the supplies of food that Zalia had brought. While they had seen a few animals from above looking down on the marshes, they had only managed to find one such animal to hunt while down here: a strange, slimy, frog-looking thing that was as large as a horse. Zalia had a feeling that most creatures found ways to hide amongst the still water and spongy earth with skill. She would use Hunter's Sight to find them, if it came to it, but didn't particularly feel like hunting in an area where ambushing creatures may lie in waiting.

Her fears became realised the day after as they travelled.

They were walking through the seemingly endless marshes as they had for the past few days, stepping over the frozen ground towards the horizon, when with a crackling sound the ground under their group exploded upwards.

Everyone was flung into the air, Zalia and two of the kittens going one direction, Ember and Boreal in another, Aylie and two kittens in another, and Pounce in a fourth. The creature that had attacked was a huge earthworm with a gaping, toothless maw. It stood ten metres out of the ground with who knew how much more of it under the ground.

Zalia caught the kittens midair, reorienting herself masterfully, and freezing the ground under her before she landed, dropping Prance and Breeze as she did. Her bow appeared next to her, floating on its own, and she launched herself at the creature, ready to fight.

CHAPTER TWENTY-SEVEN

Swallowed by Fear

Zalia

Commanding her bow with her mind, Zalia saw two glowing arrows flash past her in quick succession while she cast a ritual.

Boreal was first to spring into combat, slashing at the worm with her viciously sharp claws. Immediately, frost began to gather over the slick skin of the worm, ice growing up the length of its body from its base.

??? - Silver rank.

Zalia kept the two kittens behind her, keeping them safe from the creature as her ritual neared completion. She cast Hunter's Mark on her entire family, dropping the Hunter's Mark on the worm from her arrows as the ritual finished. They were all covered in a fiery armour born of her magic, and the worm let out a screech of frustration as Ember cut a gaping slash down its side with her sword.

Aylie grabbed Rush and Frost, running from the worm with them, knowing that the three Silver rankers amongst their ranks would manage.

Unfortunately, none of them were near Pounce.

Still stunned from the ambush, the kitten tried to flee from the worm, but it saw her and the gaping maw came down with a crash, swallowing the kitten whole and continuing down into the ground. They managed to get a few slashing strikes and arrows into the side of the worm that rushed by as it dug into the ground, yet it wasn't enough as a large hollow was made deep into the earth.

Zalia hesitated, staring into the dark depths, but Boreal didn't waste a moment.

She turned to Ember and gestured to the others and Ember nodded in understanding. Then, Zalia chased after Boreal down into the depths.

The creature was quick, burrowing further and further under the ground while Boreal and Zalia half ran, half fell down after it.

Boreal, who was already faster than any of the others and spurred on by the danger to her child, caught up to the worm first. Ice exploded around its tail end as she hit and a deep rumble went through the earth around them. Zalia could feel Healing Presence still healing Pounce deep within the earthworm's stomach and she tried to run faster, knowing there was still time.

The worm burst into a chamber deep in the earth, curling about to face its hunters.

The space was huge, supported by thick pillars of stone, the roof a mess of sharp spikes, while the floor was coated in a thick layer of mud and slime. Nearby was a pile of squirming shapes and it took Zalia a second to realise they were the young of the huge worm in front of them.

Boreal didn't waste a second, pouncing at the creature with fury, striking the side of the adult worm as another patch of ice spread across it.

The creature's mobility was dampened by the hardened sections of ice coating it, but the worm didn't give up. A fresh, slick coating of slime started flowing from the worm, pushing Boreal away and bogging her down.

Zalia stepped in for her friend, bow firing off shot after shot into the creature, leaving glowing arrows embedded in its skin. Those wounds glowed with a spreading pale light that burned away its flesh.

She had to throw herself sideways and use Mobility to step off the air to get additional distance as a burst of acid bile was ejected from the worm, splattering against the stone where she had stood but a moment before and melting through the ground.

Meanwhile, Boreal had freed herself by freezing the slime and manipulating it away from her body. She used the newly solid slime as a footing, launching herself at the worm, and this time managed to land on top of it. She ripped through its flesh with sharp claws and teeth, tearing the creature apart to get to her child.

Zalia felt her anti-death activate and started in alarm, realising it had triggered on Pounce.

They needed to end this quickly.

She finished off the ritual she had been casting, watching the explosion of fire take a chunk out of the worm's side. Her floating bow stopped shooting and changed to a sword that she snatched out of the air. With quick slashes, blades of starry air cut deep into the worm exactly where the explosion had taken a chunk out of it. At the same time, she sprinted up and began hacking through its side in close contact.

The worm struggled, slamming into stone pillars that came crashing down around them. Zalia jolted as a large boulder slammed into her shoulder plate, but she continued attacking, very literally shrugging off the stone.

Counting down the time in her head, she activated Protection of the Wilds just as the anti-death measure from Healing Presence ran out. She enhanced the ability with water, hoping that it would help in diluting the stomach acid of the worm to protect Pounce for just that little bit longer.

The cuts grew deeper and deeper into the creature's flesh as it managed to throw Boreal across the room with its flailing. Focused on her attacks, Zalia didn't react in time as the entire side of the creature swung away, then came speeding back, slapping her across the room in an approximation of what a sack of potatoes being thrown by Hildebrandt would look like.

Her shield protected her, cracking ever so slightly as she was embedded a metre into the wall.

Boreal was already up and dashing across the room, and it took a few moments for Zalia to get herself out of the wall.

Just as Boreal was about to launch yet another attack, there was a dull, exploding sound, and the side of the worm that Zalia had been hacking into burst outwards. Pounce rolled out and Boreal grabbed her by the scruff and sprinted away.

They watched as the worm slowly died, not wanting to get close to the thrashing beast to finish the job. Once it stopped thrashing so much, Zalia used Kill Shot to finish it off. There was no sense in needless suffering.

Boreal sat nearby, fussing over Pounce who looked no worse for wear than she had when being swallowed by the worm in the first place. Zalia knew this was just because of the healing properties of Protection of the Wilds. The poor kitten looked shaken up, her eyes wide.

A rumble spread through the cavern, and Zalia looked up to see a section begin collapsing. She searched around desperately for the exit as another pillar came crashing down.

Off to their left, there was an opening in the stone wall and Zalia ran for it. Boreal followed, carrying Pounce once more.

They made it through the opening just as the cavern behind them collapsed fully, a spray of dust and dirt billowing through after them. Zalia used her minor element manipulation to clear out the air and block the entrance so that none of the dirt or stone could come through.

She looked around the new room they were in and was surprised to find that it wasn't just another cavern, but a room. There were structural supports placed evenly throughout the long and wide room, benches placed in rows facing towards a pedestal at one end. Towards the opposite side of the room there was a single doorway that led out, and the wooden door that had once been in the frame lay rotted on the ground.

Utterly confused as to why there was a building this far underground but convinced they weren't in immediate danger, Zalia turned back to where Boreal and Pounce were lying on the ground. Pounce was slowly recovering as the shock wore off, and Zalia was happy to give them some time.

Using the deep magical bond between herself and Ember, Zalia let the rest of her family still on the surface know that they were okay and would make their way up soon. She received confirmation and a similar message from Ember, a little unrest settling as she learnt that they were all okay too.

While Pounce recovered, Zalia walked over to the doorway and peered out. There was a long hallway leading off into the darkness, far enough that her magical vision couldn't see the end of it. It didn't seem populated with anything, so she turned back to Boreal and Pounce.

"Hey, there's nothing out this way, but it might be a bit of a walk so let's get started, alright?"

Boreal stood and carefully helped Pounce to her feet, letting the younger cat lean against her leg.

They followed Zalia as she left that room and began the walk down the hallway.

The architecture wasn't anything that Zalia recognised. Where Endarian buildings all looked like they were grown from the materials used by magic builders, this place looked constructed by hand. The walls were rough, the marks made by some type of chisel or another finer stone-hewing tool. Still, while not perfect, digging out this tunnel must have taken quite some time by hand. Zalia wondered who had built it and why. The room they were in had been some kind of meeting room where announcements would be made, yet it was connected to a single hallway that led for hundreds of metres. Why was it hidden down here?

After a few minutes of walking, they came to a set of stairs that led up to another level. There, they found a circular room with seven alcoves set into the walls. Each of those round alcoves had runes inscribed in the floor, forming what Zalia recognised as rituals. While she didn't have any learnt knowledge of rituals, only what she was given by her ability, they were meant to be portals. Their similarity to her own living ritual portals was undeniable.

She had a look at each ritual and found all of them to be the same, except for a single rune each that was different. The language of magic was strange, being different for each person who used it, yet fit for the same uses. It was as if each person who used it had their own language but could understand most words in everyone else's particular version.

It was this that allowed Zalia to read the rituals, and it was this that allowed her to recognise what the single different runes in each ritual meant. By what was placed around them, she could identify the unique runes in each ritual as . . . something like names.

In the few smaller portals she had made, the target of the ritual had been something that was linked to whatever was the target of the other side. In the case of what had worked for her, it was each of her heirloom armour's gauntlets. It looked like whoever had made these just used a name. A simple but effective solution to the problem, assuming it worked.

She saved a memory of each ritual in her vault, then turned around, looking for an exit. There was none.

Looking at the ritual portals, she realised that there might be another way out.

Reaching towards that magical bond between herself and Ember, she sent a message. *"Can you ask Aylie to try making a portal? She might be able to use our bond to place one side next to me."*

Aylie had an ability that could make a portal, and it had far fewer limitations than Zalia's living ritual ones. She was also capable of touching the astral, which was where the bond between people existed. This unique duo of abilities might make her capable of this feat.

Her theory proved correct as a starlit portal appeared next to her.

CHAPTER TWENTY-EIGHT

Mist

Zalia

Boreal, Pounce, and Zalia appeared on the surface as they stepped through Aylie's portal. It had worked seamlessly, undisturbed by the dormant ritual circles already down there below the surface. There had been something familiar about those rituals down there, yet Zalia couldn't place her finger on it.

Regardless, they were out now and she might have learnt something useful from them. While a terrifying situation for Pounce, it had turned out about as well as it could have.

Zalia smiled as Pounce was, well, pounced upon by her siblings. She was smothered by the four young cats, cleaned and fussed over even more. The five might fight and tussle quite a lot, as siblings often did, but they also loved each other. The loss of one of the five would have changed each of them forever.

She felt sadness at having had to kill the mother worm and was concerned for the young. If the initial cave-in hadn't crushed them, they should be able to escape, considering they were creatures able to live underground. While that was true, she didn't know how old they were or what stage of life they had reached. It might be possible that they would be able to survive, not that she would ever know. They didn't deserve to be killed, but sometimes life dealt an unfair hand.

They dawdled only for a short moment before moving on. They knew now that the humid, musty swampland was filled with more life than the surface showed. If there was one depths-dwelling creature, there may be others. Having seen some creatures moving about when they were above, there were also undoubtedly other things camouflaged amongst the dull greens, greys, and browns of the shrubs, mud, and water.

During the night, they slept safely in Zalia's vault, the only entrance being the small portal that Zalia and Boreal protected whilst the others slept. It was a very rare thing for Zalia to ever sleep anymore and when she did, it was never for more than an hour, at most. Even then, it only happened once every two or more weeks.

The dank swamplands slowly but surely turned into a flat plain, the small sickly-looking shrubs becoming big bushes and tall grass. The younger cats that took after their father more than Boreal rejoiced at the change in scenery, loving the land that was akin to the land that their father came from.

In fact, they saw some other wildcats that looked like the young ones, though both parties avoided each other.

Zalia was beginning to wonder just how far away the Astar lived.

When she had been captured, it hadn't been far from the border of Endaria. It had taken them two weeks to return from that now-ruined castle to the war camp, though half of that time had been within the borders. That ruin would presumably be one of their outermost outposts.

They were now further away from Endaria's border than that ruin, though not by much. She should have perhaps taken them to the ruin to see if there was any sign or hint of the Astar there, but her memories of that place . . . No. No, she wouldn't go back there unless there was no other way.

At the very least, they did have a small hint as to where they were going. When Hildebrandt had freed her, Zalia had managed to affect one of the Astar with Hunter's Mark before they teleported away. She knew the vague direction they had gone before she had dropped the ability and was heading that way now. It would be another few days of walking before they got close to that area, however.

It was two days later that Zalia began to see mountains in the distance, large and looming over the flat plains beneath them. These mountains were huge, taller even than the ones that the Heat and Stone denizens called home. Casting her eye down their range, she couldn't see the end of them, either north or south, and had a feeling that they very well might link up with that very same mountainous terrain in the north.

Fortunately for them, the place Zalia had let go of the Hunter's Mark was before, or at the base of, that range.

It was three or so hours of travel before there was another change in the landscape. A hint of mist appeared, slowly growing thicker and thicker until they couldn't see past a few metres, with normal vision at least. It took Zalia and Boreal a moment to adjust their vision that was based on vibration. The way the mist swirled made each sound and each movement of a body look strange, distorted. They eventually got the hang of it. Their normal vision and heat vision were useless, as was the vision of the rest of their family—Ember and Aylie were latched onto either side of Zalia, barely even able to see where they stepped, while Boreal circled behind and around her children, keeping them roughly in line as they walked.

The mist didn't get any less thick, instead blocking their vision for the next hours of walking. By Zalia's assessment, it would be another two hours before they reached the base of the mountain.

She was about to ask if everyone was okay when a shift in the vibrations within the mist made both her and Boreal stop. The others immediately stopped as well, looking at the two of them in confusion.

Zalia could feel Boreal's aura release, the warm fog around them freezing to a chilling temperature. At the same time, she radiated fear. Zalia had to snap herself out of the effect, and she noticed the others doing the same. While they were all used to Boreal's ability, they still had to adjust when she released it.

The fog around them began to freeze onto surfaces, their skin, clothes and boots, the ground beneath them, and the short grass growing out of it. As the fog thinned ever so slightly, they were able to make out an amorphous shape within it, slowly drifting along.

It didn't react to Boreal's aura, neither did it have ice accumulate on it from the freezing mist. It was incorporeal.

They watched it warily, but the mist creature ignored them, drifting onwards and out of sight. Slowly, they all relaxed as it did, Boreal constraining her auras once more.

Zalia looked over at Ember, who shrugged and gestured to keep walking. She did as suggested, continuing through the mist.

They ran into the odd mist creatures twice more on the way to the base of the mountain and were ignored both times. The second time, they just continued their walking and still, the mist creature paid them no heed.

In time, they reached the base of the mountain and began to climb out of the mist. The air got lighter, easier to see through and easier to breathe. It was refreshing, to be able to use their eyes and lungs as usual, despite needing neither.

Once they were high enough above the mist, they looked back down towards the base of the mountain, searching for any sign of an Astar settlement. Unfortunately, if there was one down there, it wasn't visible from above the mist. Zalia knew it wouldn't be easy yet had hoped all the same.

By agreement, they moved horizontally across the mountain range above the mist until they reached the point where Zalia thought the Hunter's Mark had stopped.

There was still nothing to be seen, so after a short conversation, they agreed to set up a small base. From here, they would spend the next few weeks, or even months, looking for any kind of clue. The mist would slow things down considerably, but Zalia had hopes that they would be able to develop a passive to see through it if they spent a significant amount of time searching for something in it.

Zalia had the best chances of finding something due to Hunter's Sight, which not only allowed her to see anything that the Astar who had tortured her interacted with, but would also allow her to place a Hunter's Mark on anything she tracked for long enough. This meant all they needed to do was find the tracks of an Astar, and she could locate where they were. Next in line would be Aylie, who could see things that others could not. She had a strange perception of reality, perhaps one closer to the true reality due to being able to see and touch the astral, the place where thoughts and magical bonds existed.

First, though, they needed to set up that base.

There was some argument about whether to make it—in the mist or up on the mountain, but eventually, the side in favour of the mist won. While it did have the strange creatures dwelling within it, the mist was too well hidden to pass up, as their base was meant to be out of sight.

Over the next few days, Zalia did most of the initial work.

Using her Natural Matter Alteration ability, she created a large clearing. The small trees, shrubs, and grass within the area were moved to the edges while she worked, out of the way. She lowered the level of the clearing as she flattened it out, pushing the dirt up to the sides to create a small wall of earth with only one dip in it to form an entrance. The larger plant life was placed on top of that wall, with progressively smaller plant life placed lower and lower down to form a block. It would look natural to most, a little clump of plant life that would be easier to walk around than through.

Within the clearing, she used Herbal Magic to create many living rituals.

The first of these was a ritual using Dodge-vine major and Adastem minor to give the clearing protection from different types of perception. The next was the anti-teleportation ritual so that if they *were* found by the Astar, they would still be safe from teleportation.

The next set of living rituals that were placed used Adastem, Dodge-vine, and Soulroot. These created a dormant ritual that, when activated, would create a golem made of whichever material was appropriate that would protect the clearing.

The two final living rituals used the same herbs as the anti-teleportation ritual, the first protecting the area *from* that anti-teleportation, while the second was a living portal ritual. Zalia had an opportunity to test out what she had learnt in that underground structure.

She made the portal ritual normal, but this time, instead of the part of the ritual that allowed it to target something as a bond to the other side of the portal, she replaced that part with the new piece she had taken a memory of, allowing it to use a name.

In place of a name, she just made up a new rune. It had no meaning other than what Zalia wanted it to mean.

That was all the protection she created for the clearing, and once it was done, she dug deep into the ground and made an underground cavern. It wasn't huge, maybe four metres tall and ten wide. At the centre of this cavern, she made a portal ritual the same as the one above. Miraculously, it worked.

She gave a mental thanks to whoever had created that underground structure, the occupants most likely long dead.

With all that done, they all spent some time decorating the inside of the clearing and cavern. The underground bit was a fallback location in case the clearing was found while they created some small hovels up top to live in. Zalia and Ember shared one, and Aylie created her own with Plant Sentience, as it retained its abilities from when it used to be Plant Manipulation. Boreal and the young cats had Zalia make them a small covering, under which they placed a mattress of leaf litter and moss. Altogether, the clearing wasn't super comfortable, but in the short term, it would do.

With their temporary home created, it was time to roam.

CHAPTER TWENTY-NINE

Lessons and Learning

Zalia

It had been two weeks since they had arrived in the misty lands beyond Endaria's border, yet there was still no sign of the Astar. During the trip across the land to get here, the five young cats had been quite exuberant, energetic and joyous. That was, apart from when Pounce had been swallowed by the worm, though their dulled mood from that event hadn't lasted long once they left the swamps.

Over the past two weeks, Zalia, Ember, and Boreal had been taking one or two of the kittens each out into the mist to look for clues pertaining to the whereabouts of the Astar. Four of the five had already developed passive abilities to see better in the mist, with none of the higher-ranked members of the group having acquired one yet. Throughout this time, Zalia had noticed a definite switch in the young cats to a more careful and reserved behaviour. Perhaps the attack by the worm had finally sunk in, or the strangeness and danger of their current surroundings had gotten to them, but whatever it was, they had definitely been calmer, more alert, and a lot quieter.

Each of the three had been teaching the young cats a different skill. Boreal taught them how to sneak and how to fight, as she had the best knowledge when it came to both, especially when you took into account that the others wouldn't even know where to start with how to fight as a cat. Zalia could have taught them stealth, perhaps, but Boreal was just that little bit better.

Zalia taught them some of the finer points of hunting, though the skills were applicable in a much wider range of use cases. It might sound odd to the average person, but she had to teach them how to see properly. Sure, they had quite perceptive eyes naturally, but being able to see something and actually *seeing* it were two different things. One required only sight, while the other required the right skills and mindset to process the information your eyes collected for you.

What that entailed was a proper introduction to tracking others, as well as seeing things from afar. She taught them to see the trails in the nature around them, how different materials from mud to dirt to grass to the plants around them showed that something had moved through. It also included trying to get them to see not only what they were looking at but to process what they saw in their peripheral vision.

This was just a start in the long process of training them, but it would hopefully yield results down the line. Many of them would most likely develop other types of perception as Zalia, Boreal, and Aylie all had. When that happened, this process of learning would begin again, though quicker each time they would have to do it.

Ember taught them the most important lesson of all: compassion, mindfulness, and empathy.

This might have been the hardest of all the lessons as well, as it didn't exactly entail defined and easy-to-follow instructions. For the most part, she tried to get the young cats to think about their actions and the effects they had on others. This could range from something small, like how it made one of their siblings feel when they ganged up on them in a play-fight, to bigger things, like ethical hunting.

When you go about the action of killing a creature for its meat or leather, you can do it in a brutal manner that puts the animal through a huge amount of suffering and fear before the end. You could also do it in a quick, efficient, and instantly lethal manner that leaves the animal without the knowledge that it was even being hunted before it died.

Zalia herself had been a culprit of the former more than a few times, and sometimes it was hard to avoid such things. What Ember tried to teach them was to be mindful of their actions and to treat others in the way they wanted to be treated. Of course, these were lifelong lessons that Zalia, Ember, and Boreal were all still in the process of learning and most likely always would be as well.

While they were all doing their own things, Aylie was focusing on her way of seeing the world.

She found the mist to be strange, unnatural. Zalia agreed with her on this, as the mist had not faded since their arrival there; it was ever-present and too thick to see far in. She was most interested in the strange, amorphous mist creatures that lived within, as while they showed no visible rank or aura, they were an extremely strong presence in the astral.

Most of the time, Aylie resided on top of an old tree stump, shaped into a comfortable seat by Zalia. There, she tried to make contact with the mist creatures, hopeful that if she was successful, they could provide some information as to where the Astar lived. It wasn't a bad idea, and Zalia encouraged her to continue the efforts.

Today, Zalia was going to teach Prance and Pounce a little about how to observe creatures from a distance.

She pushed through the undergrowth with Prance and Pounce by her side, emerging out the top of the blanket of mist and making her way up the mountainside. Pounce was quite formidable in her stealth for her rank, better than Boreal had been at that age, while Prance was still inept at it, managing to trip over or bump into what seemed like every stick, twig, and trunk in the forest. That wasn't to say she wasn't getting better, as she was, but she had a long way to go to reach Pounce's skill, let alone Boreal's.

They made their way up as high as Zalia risked a light touch of snow here and there amongst the rocks, boulders, and grass of the higher mountain. She found a nice covert spot between two particularly big boulders that offered shade and a good hiding place. There, they waited, observing the mist down below.

Zalia was learning from this experience too, and the Silver rank Teaching passive was especially useful. By attempting to teach the young cats how to see into and within the mist, she was learning the best ways to go about it herself.

Over the next few hours in their spot amongst the boulders, Zalia managed to spot three of the mist creatures as they made slight disturbances within the mist in their wanderings, while Pounce and Prance both spotted one each. Unfortunately, they saw no Astar. Zalia held back the frustration, knowing that with time, they would find *something*.

They left their spot there, travelling further out from the little clearing they currently called home. Each day, they tried to range out further and further in hopes of stumbling across something. The one place they hadn't gone very far towards was into the mountains. Zalia wanted to go there eventually with her flight powers but thought it could wait for a bit. For now, there was much space to cover at the base of the mountain, and if she wanted to place a hidden outpost to launch stealth assaults against Endaria, this is where she would put it. Of course, the Astar might not follow any kind of logic that was similar, seeing as they were quite proficient with teleportation abilities.

It was there, a few hours' walk away from the clearing and far up the mountain, that they saw their first hint of the Astar. Well, something more than a hint, really.

Out of the mist, a solitary figure hovered upwards. It hung there for a moment, long, braided hair reaching down to its feet, as a circle of runes appeared beneath it, activating a moment later. The Astar vanished in a brief flash, moving instantly across the world.

Meanwhile, Zalia, Pounce, and Prance were frozen where they stood, thankfully having gone unseen.

With a gesture from Zalia, she and the two cats moved away from where they were and back a bit to a safer location.

She thought for a moment on what to do. On one hand, she wanted to go down there and scout out where the Astar had come from immediately. On the other, she didn't want to do so with the cats following her, nor did she want to send them back to the clearing on their own. While they were out here, the cats had to stay with one of the higher-ranked amongst them at all times.

With a start, Zalia realised she should be able to teleport the little ones out of there. She worked quickly, crafting a ritual circle much larger than usual. The ritual targeted the living one back in the clearing, using the same keyrune as that one did. She knew instinctively that it would work, though the time required was quite significant.

It took half an hour for the materials to be created and then the mana needed to be pushed into the ritual, but once it was done, the entire thing activated with a flash, sending the cats back to the clearing. She had explained what she would be doing to the young ones at the same time she had told Ember through their bond. Her return point for the long-distance teleportation ability of Mobility was set to the clearing, which meant that even if the others were here, it would be safer for her to scout out whatever was down there on her own anyway.

Zalia crept down the mountain and back into the mist, relying on the vibration perception to make her way through it towards where the Astar had risen from. Quicker now that she was alone, Zalia reached it within ten minutes, finding a lot more than she expected.

There was some kind of invisible barrier in the mist that held it back, though the mist collected atop it, creating a squat cylinder of clear space within the mist. In that space sat what she had been looking for.

The Astar outpost she had expected turned out to be a town instead.

There were many squat buildings throughout the space, all of them shaped in that strange geometrical way that the keep she had been imprisoned in had been.

As she watched from the very edge of the mist, Zalia saw not only Astar moving through the town but humans as well. Each and every one of them was miserable, shackled at the ankles, and wearing power-subduing bracelets. The Astar weren't killing off the high-rank humans, they were using them as slaves.

CHAPTER THIRTY

Doubt

Zalia

Zalia crouched just within the mist and stared at all the humans roaming about the town, many of them performing basic labour. A few were carrying sacks or stacks of food, wood, metal, and stone in carts or on their shoulders. Others yet followed after Astar that were presumably their masters, holding things for them. There were so many of them, so many that they outnumbered the Astar floating about by quite a bit.

Even from this distance, she could see that these humans were indeed the powerful of Endaria, not a single person below Silver rank in sight. She was immediately confused by how subservient they all were, backs bent and eyes vacant. What had been done to these people to make them act this way? They had the power-subduing bracelets on but surely they could still overpower a few of the Astar with pure strength alone.

There had been no word, no tales or stories of humans being enslaved by the Astar. She hadn't even heard of people presumed mad rambling about something like this. That meant that, as far as she or the ruling council of Endaria knew, no one had ever escaped and made it back to the kingdom. How was it that this had happened?

She captured a memory of the town, storing it in her vault. For now, she couldn't afford to risk getting any closer. Finding this place was a success in itself and one of the main reasons they had come here. It wasn't time to head back home to Nature's Reclaim just yet though, as there was still much to learn.

Zalia stood up out of the crouch and retreated inside the mist, unsure of what to do next. She started her way back to their temporary home, her sense of direction unaffected by the mist thanks to Hunter's Sight.

They would have to find a way to infiltrate the town to find out more. This seemed like a small outpost of the Astar . . . kingdom? And if they were to truly go to war with them, they would need to find some larger towns. They would need to figure out the military power of the Astar as well, for if they were a race of much higher-ranked people, Endaria wouldn't stand a chance.

An idea came to mind, though perhaps one that was a little risky. Using Natural Matter Alteration, Zalia would be able to make some fake power-subduing bracelets and manacles for her legs. Then, hopefully, she would be able to infiltrate the town and learn a little bit more. Since the power-subduing bracelets would be fake, she could teleport out in an instant if needed. This way, she would be able to pretend to be one of the slaves and walk about a bit, pretending to do some drudgework.

It was risky and the chance of being found out was a real one, but it might be worth it. Of course, she would have to talk to Ember about it first.

Her mind also went to thoughts of breaking out the slaves of the town. Since the proportion of combat-based classes was much higher the higher-ranked you got, it was likely that they would be able to take over the town. Something about them gave her pause though, an oddity in their behaviour. She just couldn't see how the Astar were so comfortable being outnumbered by the human slaves without them having some other type of control over them. She would have to get Aylie within sight of the town so that she might see if there was anything odd in the astral.

The run back home was long but made shorter by Zalia's speed and abilities which made it much easier. When she arrived back at their clearing, Aylie was still meditating on her stump so she let her be. At the entrance to the clearing, however, Ember was waiting . . . patiently.

"You found it!?"

Zalia gave a nod as she moved past into the clearing.

"Oh yeah, and it's *bad*. Where are the others?"

Ember came up behind her, gesturing to the other side of the clearing where Prance and Pounce were animatedly talking with the others.

"They've been talking about your trip with them for hours."

Zalia frowned.

"They didn't even come to the town."

Ember shrugged.

"They got to see an Astar though."

That made Zalia smile. It definitely wasn't something to be excited about but it was something new to the young cats, and so they were.

"Well, we have some decisions to make. Once Aylie is ready for a break, we'll go over everything," she paused for a moment. "We were wrong about one thing Ember. They haven't been killing the humans they've taken. They've been enslaving them and perhaps doing something to their minds. I am going to have to take Aylie to have a look."

Ember looked up sharply.

"Shit, how many were there?"

Zalia shrugged her shoulders.

"I don't know, but a lot. I didn't stay long because I didn't want to be seen."

They stood around for a few more minutes before Aylie walked in. Zalia called over the others, and they all sat for a family meeting, the first in a while.

First, Zalia explained to them what she had seen in the Astar town. After that, she went through her idea for possible infiltration of the town to find out more using fake power-subduing bracelets.

When she was done, there was silence until Aylie spoke up.

"And what if the Astar, as spacial magic experts, find a way to stop you from teleporting out and you get stuck in the town?"

Zalia had no response to that, it was a good point. "I don't know, but I think it's worth it to find out more. Isn't it?"

Ember looked thoughtful but unconvinced, while Boreal's tail was swishing back and forth. Boreal's children sat quietly while they spoke, a strange but pleasant experience.

"I think we need to look further into it," Ember said, "but I also don't think your idea is necessarily a good one on its own. You tend to put yourself into danger while keeping the rest of us at arm's length from that danger at the same time. We decided to come here and learn something about the Astar as a family and we will do it as a family. I know you want us to be safe, but you have to let us help with this."

Zalia opened her mouth to respond but shut it again as she thought. Ember wasn't wrong, she was just used to doing everything on her own, a habitual remnant from her previous life.

"You're right, I know. I hold to the fact that I have the best chance of escape should the person in the town get caught though."

Ember reluctantly nodded. "That is true. I think we should explore some other avenues before we go that far however."

Aylie piped up. "I want to see the town, perhaps I can see something that you cannot. There is something about the mist creatures that is important, I can feel it."

"Alright, we'll all go to see the town first. Then we can make plans for how we will infiltrate the town, agreed?" Zalia asked.

The others nodded.

"Agreed, but we should not do this today. It is almost time for the young ones to sleep and we should think of some other ways to learn more about the town while we are here."

Zalia looked over at the young cats and realised that they did look like they were about to fall asleep. No wonder they were being so respectfully quiet.

They all spent the next half hour trying to figure out how exactly they could infiltrate the town. It was decided that Boreal would go with Zalia, being the stealthiest and fastest amongst them, as she could most likely go unseen in the town. Zalia had not seen any Astar above Silver rank which was promising. If it came to it, she would be able to help Zalia escape.

There were no other ideas on how to get into the town unseen, so they left it at that.

As the others went to sleep, Zalia retreated into her vault where she did some gardening. She loved the simple task. It was not only calming but was helpful down the line for when she performed rituals. While she could create herbs from mana using Herbal Magic, having the ingredients to summon from the vault made them cheaper.

When Ember joined her in the vault, they worked together to make a poultice from Soulroot. They had to apply some Manifest Paste onto it to solidify its form before crushing it down into a gel-like substance. The Manifest Paste had a slight effect on the resulting poultice.

> **Soul Poultice (Potent) - Silver rank.**
> **A dab of this gel poultice applied to the forehead will help a creature descend into a meditative state in which they may dive deeper into their own soul, as well as see into the astral ever so slightly.**

They had been making the poultice for Aylie each night, to help with her exploration of the mist and the creatures within it. While during the day they were both busy, Zalia and Ember took this time before Ember slept to just be with each other. Often, they didn't even speak, simply working efficiently side by side.

Ember would apply the Manifest Paste to the roots and Zalia would use Natural Matter Alteration to turn a lump of stone she kept for this purpose into a mortar and pestle. She would then crush up the roots Ember handed her and store the resulting Soul Poultice in little wooden orbs she sealed up. Aylie could open up these orbs with her own abilities to use it.

Zalia could do all of this herself, probably faster than with Ember there, but it wasn't about that. It was about spending time with her partner.

"Do you think the young ones are alright?" Ember asked, breaking the silence.

Zalia thought for a moment.

"I think so. I know Boreal has been talking to them about what we are doing and why we're here. They were born after the war, so they don't quite understand the things we have been through but I think they're beginning to. I'm starting to doubt whether we should bring them into the next war if it comes, though."

Ember nodded and Zalia could feel that she'd had the same thought.

"I'm not so certain we'll be able to beat the Astar."

Zalia pursed her lips.

"Neither am I."

CHAPTER THIRTY-ONE

Infiltration

Zalia

The next day, they were all travelling towards the Astar town as a group. It was the first time they were all together like that outside of the clearing since coming to these strange misty lands, and despite their individual stealthiness and the obscuring fog, Zalia couldn't help but feel they were much too easy to spot.

While the young cats were still the only ones to acquire a passive that allowed them to see in the mist, Zalia had given Ember and Aylie some Adastem Juice to drink, the tingly liquid making their bodies adapt temporarily. This allowed them to see in the mist, if only for a few metres more.

As they approached the Astar town, Zalia's nerves felt like they were being stretched further and further, like a bowstring about to snap. She was maintaining a ritual across all of her family members that made them more stealthy, yet it would only take one of them being spotted now for things to go terribly. An extended flight back home could prove disastrous if the Astar had any method of seeing or detecting them in the mist.

Instead of focusing on that, Zalia tried to go over the plan again and again in her head. She and Boreal would go into the town and try to learn something about the Astar, with Boreal hiding in the shadows while she pretended to be one of the slaves herself. Ember, Aylie, and the young cats would hide just across the border to the town in the mist, ready to lend help if needed.

That was all, if Aylie didn't see something that warranted a change in plans when they got there.

Zalia had made the fake power-subduing bracelets the night prior as everyone slept, her memory of them from her time as a prisoner stark in her mind. She had also made a pair of manacles for her legs from iron sourced from the ground.

Natural Matter Alteration was becoming quite a useful ability, especially so due to the years of practice she had manipulating things on a finer level. The decision to start doing that long ago was paying off now. That had originally started out as woodworking but the ability had evolved to include all natural matter, which encompassed a very large range of things she had discovered. Iron was one of those. Though it didn't stretch to materials like steel, it could theoretically form naturally, and that realistically happened on such a rare basis that it could be considered a made material.

She tried to distract herself with thoughts of how the abilities decided what was considered "natural matter" while they walked, yet found herself dragged back to reality once they reached the town.

Aylie noticed they were closing in on it first, her ability to see on the astral informing her somehow. She signalled to the others, and they slowed down, approaching at a crawling speed now. The younger cats stuck close to Boreal, while Aylie and Ember stuck close to Zalia.

With a gesture, Zalia told the others to stay back a good distance while she and Aylie moved up to the border of the town and looked through. Aylie stared towards the town, tilting her head in confusion and scrunching up her face as she tried to discern something. Her eyes traced around the odd barrier around the space that kept back the mist, then back to the enslaved humans. Zalia could see anger there in her expression. She felt that emotion mirrored in her own mind.

They didn't know how the Astar rationalised the abducting and enslavement of Endarian people, whether it be through a sense of superiority, them seeing humans as nothing more than animals, or a wrong that the Endarians committed against the Astar long ago—but there was nothing Zalia could think of that justified what they were doing here.

Aylie turned to Zalia and shrugged her shoulders a little. *"There is definitely something strange going on here, something that has been done to those people. I can't figure it out from out here though, so I don't see no reason not to go ahead with the plan."*

Zalia nodded her agreement and they went back to the others.

With some real basic pants, a shirt, and worn workboots that she had in her vault, Zalia looked the part. She had to store away her armband that protected against teleportation, but that wasn't a concern where they were going.

Ember helped her put on the fake bracelets and the manacles, which she would be able to remove using Natural Matter Alteration in an instant if needed, then gave her a passionate kiss.

"Good luck in there, don't take risks, learn what you can, and get out."

Zalia nodded her assent, then stepped away towards the town. She had to remind herself a few times that if things went truly wrong, Aylie would be able to create a portal through her and Ember's bond to bring them both out instantly. That was, if her own teleportation ability failed somehow, in addition to the many other ways of getting out she had planned, slaughtering a bunch of Astar being one of them.

Boreal sat with her as they waited by the border for an opening. She had a sack with her, filled with pieces of chopped wood. She planned to pretend to be carrying it to the home of one of the Astar, as many of the other slaves could be seen doing at that very moment. The only issue was that they didn't leave the bounds of the town, ever, as far as she could see. If she could get into the town without being seen entering, they should be alright.

Deciding against just teleporting in, as Astar could be attuned to that kind of thing, Zalia circled around the edge of the town until she found a section that was less populated. Once there, she waited until there was a break in people and shuffled out to one of the buildings as quickly as she could. She put her back to it and waited, hoping that she hadn't been seen or heard.

There were no shouts of alarm, so she slung the sack of wood over her shoulder and shuffled out from behind the building and into the street, head down and eyes cast to the cobblestones beneath her boots.

Astar floated past to her left and right, yet didn't say a word. She had all of her passives restrained as much as they would go such that she had the appearance of having her abilities subdued and it looked like it was working.

She shuffled past another human and tried to catch their gaze but the man's eyes were empty, soulless like there was nothing inside the body as it shuffled past. Concern filled her as she found similar dead eyes and emotionless expressions amongst the other humans there. With a quick glance around, she tried to find Boreal but couldn't see or hear the feline—a good sign. If she was unable to find her, it was doubtful any of these Astar would be able to either.

The town was larger than it first appeared from the borders, stretching far enough that after a good twenty minutes of walking, she still couldn't see the other side. Over the course of the walk, she made sure to keep her expression as blank as the other humans, eyes down. It was hard to observe the city around her that way, and so she allowed a single passive to function, that passive being Enhanced Vision. With it, she could see all around her, as her vision didn't require her eyes any longer.

Much of the town was the same as she had seen from the border, buildings made of dark stone formed in odd jagged shapes. The cobbled roads seemed entirely aesthetic as the Astar all floated past, some less than half a metre off the ground, others further up in the sky.

The place she was aiming for was a building that loomed over the others some distance from the edge of town. She didn't have anything she was looking for in particular, so it seemed a good place to start.

Towards the presumed centre of town, the density of human slaves was significantly decreased. It appeared to Zalia that only a few were even allowed there, so she avoided going directly to the large building. Instead, she found a secluded alleyway and went down it, allowing herself to relax for just a moment. It was hard to keep the churning anger and confusion at the state of the humans here from reaching her face and body, the blank-slate expression important to her disguise.

She peeked out of the alley and towards the bigger building and observed for some time. The large gateway entrance to the building was filled with passing Astar, as if the structure was a main thoroughfare for the town. There was a constant flashing light that emitted from the structure, and it took Zalia a while to realise that it was the flashing of teleportation. The building must contain a teleportation room, like the one she had found underground. In fact, thinking about it now, it was likely that the underground structure back in the swamp had been built by the Astar. Which other race with an expansive knowledge of spacial magic lived out here?

Deciding that she had seen enough, Zalia turned from the building and resumed her blank expression state as she made her way back to where Ember and the others awaited her. She was mostly certain that the Astar didn't travel via any method other than teleportation between their towns, which provided both an issue and a solution to that very issue. The issue was that there would be no roads or signs of travel between their towns, meaning it would be hard to transport an army from one town to the next should they decide to invade. The simple solution to that, however, was to use the Astar's own teleportation rooms as launch points. There would undoubtedly be protections in place, but they might find a way around that.

On the way back, she was stopped by an Astar, and her heart beat hard in her chest as she looked up at it. A voice pierced her mind.

"Where do you travel, human?"

Luckily, she had seen Astar stop other humans before as well. Following what the other humans had done, she simply pointed in the direction she was going.

The Astar handed off a sack to her and she hefted it over her other shoulder. The Astar turned and moved away, so she grudgingly followed it. It was going in the same direction as her, but had apparently grown tired of carrying its own things.

Adrenaline pulsed through her, a fear of being found out causing an internal struggle so loud she was surprised the Astar couldn't hear it.

The Astar entered a house and gestured to a long central bench within the entrance room. Desperately maintaining her blank composure, she deposited its things there and then left, hoping it wouldn't stop her. She managed to regain some semblance of calm as she was allowed to leave without issue.

Zalia was beginning to think that they had been successful as she reached the edge of town once more, ready to be out of this place. It was then that she noticed a group of Astar moving through the border into the mist. A single sentence came to her mind through the bond with Ember.

"We've been found!"

In an instant, the manacles on her legs were broken apart, the fake bracelets following a moment later. Her armour appeared on her body, and she teleported straight into the mist after the Astar.

It was hard to see what was happening as the vibrations within the mist went crazy. She could see the young cats fleeing in all directions, Aylie and Ember standing their ground against a dozen or so Astar. The bracelets on their arms were active, blocking whatever magic two of the Astar just cast on them.

Zalia's bow appeared next to her, shooting two arrows that took down an Astar each as they pierced through their heads. Ember killed another as her blade slashed through its arm and half its torso. The plants around them came alive under Aylie's control, and two more Astar were torn limb from limb under their strength. Zalia tried to get the zone of anti-teleportation active but was too late, as the spent bracelets didn't protect Ember and Aylie any longer. The two of them vanished a moment before the zone came into effect, trapping the Astar there.

Then Boreal was there, landing amongst the remaining Astar with an explosion of icy fury. Three of the Astar tried to run but were frozen in place as their fear of Boreal overcame them. The four last Astar held their ground, and a barrier appeared around them as they attempted to attack. Zalia felt a warping in the air and threw herself to the side as the very air seemed to rip itself apart where she had stood. Her bow continued shooting, forming a web of cracks in the Astar's shield.

They were outnumbered by the Astar, but only one of them was Silver rank. The shield broke under Boreal's next pounce, another Astar freezing into a statue as its fear got the better of it. The two remaining Astar tried to fight off Boreal using their spacial magic, while Zalia combated the Silver rank one.

She ran towards it, her arrows being displaced as they fired towards her enemy, the spacial magic somehow getting past her ritual. The Astar flickered as it tried to teleport away but failed, and Zalia was upon it. Her sword appeared in hand and she slashed once, twice, cutting a long gash in its torso and removing one of its legs. The physical weakness of the Astar was their downfall as she applied a Hunter's Mark to the two Bronze rank ones that were somehow keeping Boreal frozen. A Kill Shot–enhanced strike felled the Silver rank Astar, and the remaining damage bounced to the two Bronze ones, their bodies exploding into mist under its force.

Zalia looked desperately towards the Astar town where she could feel Ember through their bond. She was still fighting in there, somewhere, with Aylie by her side. She looked to Boreal, and an agreement passed between them. Boreal dashed off to find her children, and Zalia ran back towards the town, terrified and unsure what she could do. It had all gone so wrong.

CHAPTER THIRTY-TWO

Lost Souls

Zalia

Zalia stopped her dash towards the town as she saw multiple more groups of Astar floating towards her. They hadn't seen her yet, as far as she could tell, yet it wouldn't be long before they did.

It was in that moment that she realised she wasn't going to be able to save Ember and Aylie. If they were going to get out, they would have to do it on their own. Zalia was strong, stronger than these Astar who weren't warriors or great fighters, yet she couldn't fight that many of them. Could she?

Most of these newly arriving Astar were only Bronze, easy enough to deal with individually. Together as a unit, however, it was a bit harder. Without using her most powerful magic, that was.

She thought desperately, trying to come up with something, anything that would allow her to save her family. Even if she did defeat all of these new groups of Astar, she couldn't destroy the whole town on her own. And she would need to do that if she were to save Ember and Aylie. She could feel through the bond that they were deep towards the centre, where she had just come from not long ago.

Instead, she ran away from the border, laying out a large anti-teleportation ritual on the ground. She would have to kill these Astar if she were to keep Boreal and the young cats out of their hands as well.

Moments passed, each an eternity as she waited with bated breath. She could see the Astar floating through the mist on invisible waves of magic. There were ten, then fifteen of them. Fortunately for Zalia, while powerful in their use of auras and magic, they were physically weak.

The ritual activated at the same time Zalia used Nature's Wrath.

Thick, sharp vines grew from the ground in an instant, dragging the Astar down to the ground and into a clump of bodies. Five Bronze rank fire elementals appeared, releasing jets of flame into the group of Astar. Zalia used all of her concentration and power to rip a huge boulder of stone from the ground, swinging it from behind, over her head and down on top of the pile of screaming Astar.

The screaming stopped.

She could feel the power flowing through her, the nature around her answering to her call. It told her to go forward, break down those who would wrong her.

At her bidding, the five fire elementals moved through the barrier and into town, sending fireballs before them. They crashed into buildings setting them alight, the force of the attacks strong enough to break the stone. Hopefully, they would cause enough of a distraction that they would be able to get away.

She ran, finding her way towards Boreal through their bond, hoping that she at least had managed to collect the young ones and get them to safety. The misery Zalia felt at how wrong things had gone almost crushed her, but she shoved it away for now. She had to focus.

It only took her two minutes to find Boreal, who was thankfully huddled with her kittens, waiting for her. They joined her in a desperate flight for safety.

Aylie

Aylie woke upon a cold stone table, arms bound. Something was wrong, so very wrong. Her powers were contained, pushed inside and locked. She couldn't breathe properly, the oppression of the bracelets that bound her so strong, sending her back to that time so long ago. It felt like another life, the day she had lost her family, yet the helplessness she felt in that moment drew those memories back to the front of her mind.

That wasn't all. There was something else so fundamentally wrong happening to her. She could feel herself being pulled, hard. She was being pulled, yet her body remained still. It took her a moment to realise it wasn't her body being pulled, but her soul.

She fought against it, yet the magic was so strong, so powerful. It clawed and grabbed until she felt herself floating upwards and away. She looked down and saw herself lying there on the stone table, glassy-eyed with a blank expression. This wasn't right, why was this happening?

As the feet of her soul lost contact with her body, another force grabbed her in its grip and ripped her away. She flew through the wall, floating high above the town before being dumped into the mist-laden forest outside the borders.

She stood, shaking her head, trying to clear the sluggishness of her . . . body. Where was she? Where was Zalia? Where was Ember?

There was a strand attached to her chest, leading away through the mist. She followed it, feeling that it was where she needed to be. The end of that strand was where she belonged, it felt *right*.

After only a few seconds of walking, she slammed into something solid. She looked up and saw the Astar town in front of her. That was right, wasn't she meant to be doing something in there?

She reached a hand up and tried to walk towards the town again, yet something blocked her once more. Why? Why did it block her? She needed to get to where that strand went.

Tapping at it with her hand still, she took a few steps to the left, then tried again. Again, she was blocked. She hit it with her hand and saw a wobble go through the wall. It wasn't a visible wall, more of a . . . spiritual wall. The idea of one, the soul of a wall, there only in spirit.

She hit it again, and it wobbled once more. She hit a final time, as hard as she could, yet the wobble stayed as exactly that. It still didn't let her through.

Turning around, she saw another strand, much smaller and thinner, more translucent. It didn't feel like home, like the place she was meant to be, but it did feel safe. Perhaps she could go to where this one was?

She wandered off, following this new strand. It slowly grew more and more opaque before she found another figure in the mist. It was a woman much shorter than her. She should recognise this woman, shouldn't she?

The figure turned to her, slowly, and looked at her in an odd way. Did the figure recognise her?

It was made of mist, slowly fuzzing at the edges like someone had taken an eraser to it. A name came to her mind. Ember.

Aylie stepped towards the figure and took its hand in her own. Memories flashed through her mind, years spent living with her, one of her mothers. Ember. Yes, this was Ember!

But, it wasn't how she remembered her. Ember wasn't made of mist, she was a living person, vibrant and full of life. What had happened to her?

As she touched Ember's hand, another strand appeared. This time, it reached from Ember's chest and into the mist. It was much, much thicker than the one that linked Aylie to Ember, and the woman looked down at her own chest as it appeared. An expression of longing crossed over her face and she took a step in its direction.

Aylie stopped her and touched the strand. More flashes of memory went through her mind, this time of another woman. Stoic and strong, quiet and independent, a force of nature in this world. Zalia. She remembered Zalia, the one who had saved her from . . . from what? From something, yes, she had saved her. Then, she had become like a mother to her. Perhaps Zalia could help her get through that wall, to where she belonged.

She began following that strand, with Ember following along as well. As they walked, other figures started to appear in the mist as well, people who stood there with blank expressions, staring into nothing. Some of them were fuzzing around the edges like Ember, others had entire limbs missing. Some were amorphous blobs of mist that only had the vague signs of a face. The worst of them were simply eyes whose bodies were indistinguishable from the fog around them.

Aylie felt like there was something important about those figures. They meant something, something important. Didn't they?

Those thoughts escaped her as they found the end of that strand connecting to Ember. A woman was crouched there with a giant mountain cat by her side, five much smaller ones huddled together nearby. This was Zalia and . . .

Aylie tried to open her mouth to speak, yet found no sound or words coming out. She turned to Ember, who stared longingly at Zalia, yet said nothing. Looking back at Zalia, she tried to speak again. Nothing. She stepped closer, trying to get the crouched woman's attention. Zalia glanced at her but looked away quickly as if dismissing her presence. Then she stood and ran off into the mist, the mountain cats following.

She tried to lift a hand to stop the woman, but she was too quick, and Aylie's body was too sluggish. Didn't the woman recognise her?

Zalia

Zalia waited, crouched, as the younger cats caught their breath. They were far enough away now that they weren't in immediate danger of being discovered which was good. It also meant that Zalia's mind was turning towards what had happened.

It had gone so terribly wrong. She should have gone to that town alone, without the others. If she had been by herself, she could have escaped easily enough. If she had been by herself, she wouldn't have been caught.

She glanced up at two of the amorphous mist creatures as one of them floated towards her but dismissed it. They hadn't ever attacked before, and she doubted they would start now. She gestured to the others and they began running again, the journey home a long one. Once they were there, then they could sit and go over what had happened. Hopefully, the young cats would be able to explain how they had been found.

Then, she would have to figure out how they were going to free Aylie and Ember. This town was on the outskirts of the Astar lands, at least she thought they were, so hopefully there wouldn't be many high-rank Astar here. Getting back into the town would be easy enough, as she could sneak in the same way she had before. It would be harder now, as they were probably on high alert, but she was certain she could do it. Then, she would be able to get to where they were being held and free them. At the very least, if they were enslaved like the other humans there were, she would be able to get them out eventually.

Unfortunately, she didn't know if the Astar would be able to get anything out of their minds. That meant they would have to move home to somewhere else. Somewhere closer, perhaps. Once the young ones were safe somewhere, then she and Boreal could sneak in and break the others out.

After that, they would go back to Endaria to bring back the news of what was happening here. Zalia had a feeling that there would be a war between the humans and the Astar soon. A surprise attack launched on this town to free all the slaves would mean a massive influx of high-ranked humans who would hopefully be more than willing to fight the Astar.

As the day wore on, Zalia tried to convince herself that Ember and Aylie would be okay, that she would be able to free them. If she believed anything else, she wouldn't know what to do with herself.

CHAPTER THIRTY-THREE

Broken Barrier

Zalia

Zalia paced back and forth as her magic deconstructed their home base. There was no point leaving it and its defences here to be discovered, as that could allow the Astar to figure out how to take them down safely.

Since Ember and Aylie had been taken, she had been closely observing the bond she shared with her partner. It felt strange, blocked, like the Astar had some kind of magic in the way. She couldn't read Ember's emotions or thoughts through it anymore, and the lack of this ability after so many years of growing used to it brought her pain and anxiety. Ember was still *alive* at least.

Out of the corner of her eye, Zalia watched two of the mist creatures wander about the clearing. There was something off about these two that she couldn't quite put a pin in, an oddity that brought her attention to them. While she was used to ignoring the things by now, they very rarely moved in groups and lingered in the same place even less often.

The plants used in her living rituals vanished one by one into her vault, as the plants that had previously occupied the space moved in and took their original positions. The artificially raised earthen wall surrounding the clearing lowered, and before long, there was no sign of their having lived there. She collected Boreal and the young ones and set off back towards the Astar town.

They wouldn't want to set up too close to the town, as the chances of being discovered now that the Astar knew of their presence were considerably higher. Unfortunately, if they were to save Ember and Aylie, they would have to be near enough to do so. Having to walk or run for hours each way every single time they wanted to scout out or infiltrate the town just wouldn't do.

Both Boreal and Zalia were silent as they walked, the deep magical bond between them describing their respective emotional and mental states better than words could ever manage. Should they have given in to those roiling emotions, they might have rushed in to try to save them right then. Yet logic won out against those urges. The correct path was to plan out their attack, and time it for an appropriate moment with a plan set in stone.

Upon nearing the town, they decided to circle to the other side. It took a while to do so at a distance Zalia deemed safe, but they did eventually find a nice location for a home some forty-five minutes' walk from the town. There, she set up everything as it had been, a well-protected and hidden home with a portal at its centre that led to a cavern deep underground, should they need to retreat.

The younger cats were also silent throughout the whole process of moving, perhaps understanding exactly how badly things had gone. Zalia blamed herself for this. It had been *her* idea that brought them here, *her* plan that had gotten them caught, and *her* incompetence that had meant she couldn't stop them from being taken at the time. This was a large part of the reason she didn't like involving others in dangerous situations. It was okay if she made mistakes when it was just her own life on the line, yet when her mistakes caused the ones she loved to be hurt . . .

Shaking her head, Zalia looked to the others and began planning.

Aylie

Aylie and Ember still floated along in the mist, lost in purpose. They still followed after that thread, the one that attached Ember to the woman she knew to be Zalia. Even when they had caught up to her in that little clearing she had been disassembling, the woman still didn't pay attention to Aylie or Ember. That was odd to her, since she thought that Zalia normally wouldn't have even thought to do something like ignore them.

As she and Ember floated quietly along, visions began to flash through her mind. Strange, jagged shapes of buildings, a sack of firewood, floating people with long hair and depthless eyes. Other people, people she didn't know, shackled and hauling their own goods.

What were these images?

The mist felt comfortable to her, like a safe haven from those jarring images. She didn't like what they told her, what secrets they whispered into her formless mind, what truths they spoke of.

They ran into another spirit, and the three shared looks before silently going their own way. Who were these other spirits? Did they receive these flashes of images too?

She turned to Ember to ask the question, but once more as she tried to speak, nothing came out. Why was that? Shouldn't she be able to communicate these things to her?

The thought escaped her mind, fleeting as every other seemed to be. Was that normal?

That question fled as well. How was she supposed to know the answer anyway?

The only thing that seemed permanent in this place was that thread, connecting her to Ember, then Ember to the distance, far off to where she knew the thread ended, at Zalia.

It was important that they stay close to Zalia, even Aylie's porous mind knew that. It was something fundamentally embedded into her, a truth that came not from that far-off presence that sent her images, but one that came from the soul of her being.

They eventually found Zalia again, setting up a new clearing like the one before. The magic was a stunning display, waves of power flowing this way and that, grasping plants and earth alike, moving them to where they needed to be. The casual strength of the magic was awe-inducing.

There was something she needed to tell this woman, wasn't there? Something important. Something . . .

Aylie looked to Ember, hoping she would remember what it was. Ember's blank eyes stared back at her. Did she remember what . . . what . . . what Aylie needed to remember?

She shook her head in frustration. Why? Why was this happening?

Looking at Zalia again, she raged against her own mind, so elusive as it was. She *would* remember, she *would* keep control over her own thoughts. There was something she could do, wasn't there? Some power she had that would let her communicate. She might not have lungs, a voice box, or a mouth to speak with but she *did* have something else. A power.

A power linked to that distant presence, the one that sent her images. It had something, she was sure of it. But . . . but . . . it wasn't available to her, was it? Why was that?

She pulled and pulled on that distant presence, trying to bring it to her. It moved, a little, but there was something resisting her efforts. An image of bracers, around thin wrists. Her wrists.

With a final pull, she felt something break, a wall somewhere in the distance, a wall that was stopping her from acting, from using her power, from *thinking*.

A flood of memories came to her, precious, beautiful thought and the presence of mind.

> **Congratulations! You have broken through the astral barrier that forms a protective wall between body and mind.**

Power came with that flood of memories, the power that she knew deep within herself, the power that was her own.

"Zalia!"

She screamed that word towards the woman as loudly as she could. Zalia didn't look up.

"Zalia!" she screamed, even louder. She projected it, putting as much effort, as much energy as she could into it.

She looked up.

Aylie waved at her desperately, trying to get her attention. Zalia's brow furrowed as she looked around, an expression of simultaneous hope and devastation on her face.

"Zalia!"

Hands waving, a flood of joy washed through her as Zalia finally looked at her. A booming voice filled her mind.

"Can you hear me?"

Zalia stared at the mist creature, half convinced that she had lost her mind. The two had followed them all the way from the other camp, the same two that had seemed just a little *off.* She swore one of them had called her name, a voice projected into her mind.

They had tried to talk to the mist creatures with mental communication of course, but it had always seemed to scare the things off. It was worth another try though, wasn't it?

"Can you hear me?"

The mist creature flinched like it had been struck hard.

Unlike each other time she had tried to talk to the mist creatures, this time a response came.

"Yo— m . . . lis—en. I—'s . . . e, A—lie."

What?

"M— . . . nd . . . m—er a—e ri . . . —t h—re, can'. . . y—u see—s?"

Zalia shook her head in confusion. *"I don't understand."*

The words were strange, distant like they were whispers brought to her on winds from a far place.

As she spoke to it once more, it flinched again. Were her words hurting it? Perhaps . . .

"What do you want from me?"

She spoke in the mental version of a whisper this time and it didn't flinch. That was one part figured out.

The mist figure pointed at the one next to it.

"M—er, E . . .—er, Em . . .—r, . . .—mb—r, Em—er."

With the word repeated over and over, Zalia finally understood. Ember.

"Ember!? How could that be Ember?"

The part of the mist creature that held its indiscernible eyes nodded vigorously, then pointed at itself.

"*A . . .—ie, Ay . . .—e,—y—ie, . . . yl—e.*"

Zalia understood after the first time. It was Aylie.

She had many questions, but only one was at the forefront of her mind.

"*How? How are you here?*"

She continued speaking in a whisper, not wanting to hurt the mist crea . . . to hurt *Aylie's* mind.

Aylie's form moved in what looked like a shrug, and Zalia began to pace, unsure of what was happening. Memories of the blank-slate expressions of the slaves inside the town came to her mind, closely followed by images of the hundreds of mist creatures she had seen over the weeks. It couldn't be, could it?

Somehow, the Astar had found a way to pull the souls from the slaves they kept, using the powerful bodies of the high-ranked people, yet rendering them nothing more than empty shells. That was . . . that was horrific. It was horrific and it had been done to her *partner* and *daughter*. What was *wrong* with the Astar, what led them to do things like this? How did they justify ripping people's souls out to use their bodies as nothing more than mindless labourers? Zalia would tear them apart for this abomination, this savaging of nature. She didn't know how, but she would find a way.

CHAPTER THIRTY-FOUR

Caught Up by Your Soul

Zalia

Where is your body?" Zalia asked the misty form of her daughter.

Aylie turned and pointed through the mist towards the town. Zalia turned her head to look at Ember and tried to talk to her again, yet Ember only tilted her head in confusion once more. She didn't know exactly why Aylie was able to talk and Ember could not, but she thought it might have something to do with Aylie's astral powers.

"*We . . . an'—g . . . t th . . . o . . . gh the w . . . l.*"

Each time Aylie spoke, she had to repeat herself many times for Zalia to understand. She eventually got "we can't get through the wall" from the whisperings.

So this was how the Astar kept the human population enslaved. They ripped their souls from their bodies and blocked them from reentering the town via some type of impassable wall for the spirits. What was Zalia to do about that?

Her first idea was to make a break in that wall somehow, which would release the entire human population in the city so their souls could get back in. Unfortunately, that might mean a slaughter as the Astar put down the rebelling humans. Perhaps she could perform a simultaneous attack to distract the more combat-oriented Astar while it happened.

She stepped up hesitantly and tried to take Ember's hand but found her own passing straight through it as if she weren't there. The Manifest Paste she had could solidify incorporeal beings but she wasn't ready to risk that just yet. Who knew what consequences solidifying one's soul would have?

"*How can we fix this? Do you have any ideas?*"

Aylie's head slowly shook from side to side. "*Th . . . ki . . . g, ha . . . d.*"

A few repetitions and Zalia discerned the words. "Thinking hard."

Aylie's speech was slowly getting more and more coherent, which was good. Perhaps she was managing to shake whatever effect made her so hard to hear.

Zalia began pacing back and forth, her hand tapping incessantly on her leg as she thought. She had no idea what the long-term ramifications were of someone's soul being detached like this. Hell, she didn't even know if their souls *could* be put back.

She wanted to attack immediately but put that idea aside. At the very least she needed to wait until Nature's Wrath was back up. Then, she could fight.

While she thought, she explained what was happening to Boreal, who tried to brush up against the spirits of their two family members, and failed to do so. It was disheartening to see the sadness in her cold blue eyes.

Zalia had to find a way to break a hole in that wall. That would be the first step in this process, the most important one for sure. As such, she left the clearing and moved towards the town.

It was a long walk, over the course of which Zalia spent a good amount of time thinking about her actions and what she could have done differently. Apart from not coming here in the first place, she didn't see any alternative. It was under Ember's insistence that they had both come on the infiltration, and Zalia wasn't going to try to take her freedom of choice from her.

Her thoughts were still roiling when she arrived at the town, but she put them aside momentarily. Boreal had stayed at the clearing so it was just Zalia and her ghostly family that stood just outside the barrier. Aylie stepped forward and tried to push through in the demonstration but was blocked quite thoroughly by the invisible wall. Zalia waved her hand through, finding nothing stopping it. Strange.

As hard as she looked along the line where the mist stopped, she just couldn't see anything that could explain the phenomenon. There were no enchanted stones or materials that would support the magical effect, not even any visible magical aura as seen by her Aura Observation. This was even stranger, as the ability should have allowed her to see something, anything that denoted where or who the magic came from. The only alternative to all of that was the barrier existed entirely on the astral. It was possible that the magic used to remove Aylie and Ember's souls had somehow thrown them into the astral where usually nothing but bonds and thought existed.

With that in mind, Zalia realised she might have to figure out a way of affecting the astral. If Aylie were capable of using her abilities, she would be able to do it easily. Without her, that was a lot harder.

Her mind immediately went to the herb Manifest. It was capable of making things physically manifest, usually dependent on what other herbs were used in the ritual. Maybe she could find a way to make that target the wall.

It was all theoretical for now, however, as she didn't want to actually do that just yet. She would have to wait for Nature's Wrath to be back up.

Instead, she went back home, reading through the level-ups she had received over the past weeks while she did.

> **Congratulations! Kill Shot has reached Silver 5.**
> **Congratulations! Hunter class has reached Silver 5.**
> **Congratulations! Flora Identification has reached Silver 7.**
> **Congratulations! Druid Grove has reached Silver 10.**
> **Congratulations! Herbalist class has reached Silver 7.**
> **Congratulations! Nature's Wrath has reached Silver 6.**

Her progress was much slower now, thanks to the high rank. Even this much progress over a few weeks was the most she had gotten in a while, with frequent fights and constant new discoveries playing a large role in that.

Looking around her, Zalia wondered if it was best to just try to bring Nateysta here to deal with this problem. Through his use of aura and absurdly strong magic, he might be able to break down the wall and free her family. Something he said when she had left Endaria to come here nagged at her, though. He had said that his ability to contribute was greatly diminished, and she had taken it at face value, simply thinking that now, since the thousand-eyed one had been imprisoned, he felt like he didn't have much to contribute. Now, though, she wondered if it'd had a deeper meaning. He was brought to this world by the power of Balance, a force more powerful than any Ascendant in this world, and perhaps he was held in check by that very same force.

Still, she decided to try to reach out anyway. Just in case.

When she arrived back at the clearing, she brought out the tiny altar she kept in her vault, the one she had taken from Cormaine that was dedicated to her friend Nateysta, also known as Ro-ak. She kept it with her always, both as a keepsake from her time there and as a way of reaching her friend should she need it.

Putting the altar down and kneeling in front of it, she summoned Glowing Cave Mushrooms, ones specifically from the caves in Cormaine that she knew were often used in rituals around Nateysta in the far past. She placed them haphazardly in a circle around herself and the altar before beginning the ritual of communion.

The mushrooms began to glow, bright dust floating away from them as they disintegrated.

"Nateysta, I need your help."

She had to wait for a few minutes, kneeling there with her eyes closed, before a reply came.

"Zalia, what is wrong?"

She breathed a sigh of relief, glad that he would at least be able to talk to her. *"We were seen by the Astar, and Ember and Aylie were caught. Their souls have been separated from their bodies, and now they're blocked from reentering them by a wall that cannot be seen or felt by anyone other than them. Can you help us?"*

Once more, she had to wait.

"I cannot help you, dear friend. I can, however, send you one who may be able to."

The last of the mushrooms burnt away in a flash of light, and Zalia found herself kneeling in darkness once more. All the others waited nearby in anticipation, yet were quickly subdued by Zalia's expression.

She looked around, wondering what exactly he had meant by sending someone who may be able to help. There hadn't been any portal opened or anything of the sort.

"Well, he said he could send someone to help but . . ."

She trailed off as a bright light brought her attention upwards. She saw a pinprick star, shining strong enough to reach them all the way through the mist. She stared at it hopefully, the others looking up to match her gaze.

There, the star grew brighter and brighter until a lone wolf fell down upon them, landing in a stumbling crash.

Zalia stared at Lumin. Lumin stared at her. Then barked quietly, licked her face for good measure, and ran around excitedly greeting everyone.

She stood, trying to get out of licking range and looked at Lumin, then back up at the sky expectantly. Surely Ro hadn't meant *Lumin* might be able to take out the wall, did he?

Thinking that, however, Lumin was different to the last time she had seen them.

Luminescence - Bronze rank (Ascendant).

Being Bronze rank wasn't the only change that had overcome the wolf since leaving with Nateysta. Lumin was also considerably bigger, now matching Boreal in size. Considering Boreal was up to Zalia's shoulders, that made Lumin massive.

Lumin looked at Aylie and Ember with confusion, tilting their head from one side to the other before approaching. They licked Aylie's face and to everyone's surprise, managed to make contact. Lumin could touch them. That meant . . .

Zalia ran up and grabbed Lumin in a big hug, thankful for the wolf's presence. This would make things much easier.

Lumin wagged their tail in happiness, jumping around energetically and almost bowling Zalia over.

"Alright, calm, calm. Stop that . . . stop it!"

After a moment of calming the wolf, she turned to Boreal, who was giving Lumin the stink eye. She did not like Lumin being that big, which was fair, considering how much the wolf liked to play-fight with her.

The young ones, for their part, were extremely excited as well, soon swarming over Lumin and climbing up the wolf's thick fur, causing another bout of excited jumping around. Caught off guard, Zalia tried to get out of the path of the runaway wolf body, but was knocked backwards by an off-kilter spin. She was sent stumbling into Ember, who caught her.

Zalia looked down at the misty hands holding her, then up at the amorphous head of Ember, then over at Lumin. Lumin had done this.

"You beautiful, beautiful wolf."

CHAPTER THIRTY-FIVE

To Anger Nature

Zalia

With Lumin now there, Aylie's voice came through stronger than before, with a clarity to it that gave Zalia a bit of strength.

"*The other spirits look like they are degrading, as if in their extended time in the mist they are dissolving. I fear . . . I fear that the mist is made of other people's souls.*"

That sent a shiver down Zalia's spine as she looked around. How many people had this happened to that it could create such a large area of mist?

"*That's horrible. How many can you see that are still in one piece?*"

Aylie looked around at things that Zalia could not see. "*Many, dozens stand here around us.*"

Zalia looked around but could see nothing. It was chilling. She wondered if Matthias was here somewhere, his soul separated from his body. He had been one of the leaders of the Morning's Shade beside Hidey and Hildebrandt. During her time there, he had been a bit cold and dismissive to her, yet he had fought for his kingdom just as much as the others had. If he was here, she would try to save him too.

She wished that Hidey could have been here with them. He would have been a powerful boon to their cause, especially so when it came to infiltrating the Astar settlement. No one was as sneaky as that shade. It was unfortunate that someone was still out here using his true name to control him.

With Lumin now here, Zalia hoped that they would be able to affect the great wall that blocked the spirits from entering the town. If they could, that would mean freedom for her family.

"*Aylie, I want you to go around and speak to the other souls. Tell them that I plan on breaking a hole in the wall. Hopefully, some of them will understand and be ready for it.*"

The amorphous form of Aylie nodded, painfully slow, before heading off into the mist. Ember followed as well, silently stepping away. Zalia's heart ached at the sight, wishing that she had Ember's warmth and strength to bolster her own.

She turned to Boreal. "One of your abilities lets you get help from wildlife, right?"

Boreal dipped her head, and a little box popped up in Zalia's vision.

> **Active 3 - Predator and Partner - spell - targeted.**
> **Tin - You can use your cuteness to make others less aggressive towards you. Alternatively, you may instil a primal terror instead.**
> **Iron - You're able to slightly affect the actions others take in regards to you. Additionally, you can cause others' bodies to betray them, causing them to freeze or run in terror.**
> **Bronze - You become the embodiment of fear in the animal kingdom, radiating an aura of dominance and terror that can influence even the most ferocious of beasts. Wild animals will instinctively avoid confrontation with you, and you can call upon them to aid you in times of need. Additionally, particularly cowardly enemies may turn on their allies when confronted by your presence in battle.**
> **Silver - Enemies that are scared of you are frozen, literally. They are inflicted with Frostbite and cannot move.**

"Okay, good, can you and the little ones try and find some others to help us? We're going to need every bit of help we can get."

"*Of course, Zalia,*" Boreal replied, before collecting her children and moving off into the mist as well.

That just left Zalia and Lumin.

"And we, litt—large Lumin, are going to find ourselves some help from nature."

Lumin bounced around excitedly, and Zalia gave the wolf a calming pat. They made their way off into the mist towards the town.

When Zalia arrived near, she found a spot nearby but still a good distance out. It was here that she started preparing a ritual.

The day she had entered the kingdom of Endaria, there had been a large battle between the forces of the kingdom and the rebellion. Knight Alara had been leading one side, with the other led by an incompetent leader she had never learnt the name of. In that fight, a huge Gold rank elemental had interrupted the fight, capturing the attention of both sides and leading them to fight together. It had been a true force on the battlefield, unkillable to the point that both armies had to flee.

She wanted to make something like that.

Most rituals she had created that awakened little pieces of nature had been on a really small scale. Little activated living rituals that would create a low-rank elemental to distract the enemies for a while. They weren't particularly powerful; they were weaker than the ones created by Nature's Wrath.

She started off here doing exactly that. Each ritual created a different type of elemental—earth, air, and fire. These were all living rituals, yet to be activated. The elementals that these would create couldn't move far and were all Iron rank despite the fact that magic used to create them was Silver rank.

That wasn't the same for what she started next.

The final ritual Zalia began planning out was huge. It also wasn't a living ritual, it was going to be a one-time ritual instead. That would mean the elemental it created wouldn't be linked to any one location, but it would also last for a much shorter time. That was okay, as all it needed to be was a distraction.

The Silver rank effect of Herbal Magic allowed Zalia to create rituals of a much larger scale than she had been able to previously. The first one of this kind she had done had taken her two days to cast from start to finish—that was the town-wide ritual that stopped teleportation abilities.

This one would take a similar length of time, and Zalia based what she wanted it to do off of an elemental she had seen before.

Years back, when she had still been working as part of the Morning's Shade, Zalia had seen Larel fight one versus one against a huge elemental that had once been a mine. That elemental was an earth and metal one that used lava abilities. It had been powerful, and the only reason Larel was able to defeat the thing was due to her abilities being based around constantly increasing power when used against singular targets.

Larel had been Zalia's rank back then, except with only two classes, not three, and lacked the number of heirlooms that Zalia now had.

The ritual she was creating had many parts. The core of it used a lot of Flame-root to recreate the lava abilities that it would have. Around that core, she placed anti-teleportation measures to stop the Astar from simply removing the elemental from the equation.

Around that was a complex set of addendums made of other herbs, ranging from Manifest to Dodge-vine to Soulroot, all of them a requirement to make this work.

It took her two days to finalise the creation. A lot of that time was spent waiting for mana to recharge so that she could create the herbs required.

During those days, she had to hide to avoid Astar attention—but only twice, thankfully. They missed the large ritual being arrayed in the forest as well, mostly due to how hard it was to see in the mist. Boreal came back and told Zalia of her progress three times, and it looked like they would have the support of the local wildlife as well. Many of the creatures around had stories passed down from prior generations speaking of a time when there was no mist here at all, before the Astar had come.

The wildlife that Boreal had managed to convince included many different species. There were a few other wildcats there, birds of many varieties, and creatures that lived amongst the low-hanging flora of the mist-laden lands. All in all, a few hundred animals answered Boreal's call.

It was a good turnout, much more than Zalia expected, if she were honest. Apparently, the animals of this land hated the Astar as much as Zalia did. They were a cold, cruel people.

During that time, Aylie didn't return to speak with Zalia, but many of the misty souls did gather. More and more appeared from the mist by the day, and those were only the ones that Zalia could see. She imagined that in the astral, there were possibly thousands there waiting. Now all she had to do was make good on her promise.

With the ritual laid out and waiting to be cast, Zalia turned her attention to the wall that blocked the souls from entering. It was their biggest problem, the plan was pointless without a way through for the souls.

At first, Zalia thought about creating a portal that passed through but knew that the Astar would be able to stop something like that with ease. They had shown time and again that they were much more knowledgeable about that kind of thing than Zalia was. Instead, she would have to create a hole in the wall.

With Lumin there, she could indeed feel the wall. It didn't stop her from passing through thankfully, but she could touch it. It was like honey, thick and hard to move through.

Now that everything else was ready, she tried many things to get through the wall. Cutting it with her sword did nothing and neither did any of her magic rituals. Lumin tried to claw and bite at it with no results. Boreal used her icy magic to try and freeze the wall and shatter it, but still nothing.

The answer to their problem came when Aylie returned.

"I can feel something here. The wall is . . . different in Lumin's presence."

The misty form of Aylie floated over to the wall and brushed a hand down it. She was still unable to pass through. Then, Zalia began to see a glow in the misty form of her daughter and stepped closer.

"What are you doing?"

Aylie didn't respond, and Zalia came all the way up to where she stood by the wall.

"Aylie?"

The two eyes that marked where Aylie's face was were glowing too, a bright blue light reminiscent of the stars.

"Go, begin the ritual!"

Zalia didn't question her and turned from the wall, running to where she had laid out the ritual for the larger elemental. It was five minutes from the wall at her top speed.

When she arrived, she stepped straight up to the edge of the ritual and began casting it.

* * *

Boreal watched as Zalia ran off and turned back to the wall. Aylie was glowing even brighter now, so much so that she had to turn away.

With a final flash of light, a piece of the wall must have disappeared because the mist billowed forth towards the town.

Everyone, the wandering souls, the wildlife of the misty forest, Boreal and her children, all stood still. Everyone except Aylie, who took one tentative step over the border and into the Astar town.

Boreal let out a low growl and ran through.

A burst of motion followed from behind as wildlife and souls alike sprinted after her, all intent on one thing.

CHAPTER THIRTY-SIX

Power of the Stars

Boreal

Boreal dashed forwards into the town, her children close behind. They all had new anti-teleportation bracelets made by Zalia and would be safe as long as they were kept close to Boreal.

The alarm must have been raised in the town with the breaking of the wall, as Astar were forming in the air and the edge of the town in waiting. A few barriers went up, and a forceful aura swept over them all. Boreal felt like the door to her soul had been torn open, her very being laid bare before the enemies ahead of her. She could tell that some of the wildlife felt this much more painfully than she did as they stumbled to a stop. Fortunately, these were the lower-ranked ones, mostly Iron ranked.

Boreal reached the town first, an empowered Pounce crashing through a hastily established barrier. The Astar on the other side didn't stand a chance, most of them Bronze ranked, as Boreal crashed through them violently. A slash tore open one's throat; piercing teeth and a strong jaw crushed the spinal cord below the skull of another. Her icy magic tore through three more, freezing them solid and killing them instantly.

Her children followed, Prance distracting one as Pounce crashed into it from behind. Frost followed her example and froze another Astar, who then quickly died to Boreal's powers as well.

Breeze and Rush ran circles around others as they tried to block them in or kill them with space-warping powers.

Boreal saw other wildlife fighting all around. Birds swarmed Astar with sharp pecking beaks, a few going down under dozens of birds each. The other wildcats were all tearing through their own groups of Astar while many of the land animals wielded earth powers that allowed them to pull Astar down from the sky.

It wasn't all a one-sided fight, however.

One of the wildcats was torn in two by a space-warping ability, and some flocks of birds were enclosed by barriers that slowly collapsed in on themselves, crushing the poor things into a paste. A few of the ground creatures were teleported far into the sky, only to drop at much too quick speeds.

The fight had started off well, with many of the Astar being shocked or not ready for the attack.

It was at this turn of the fight that the first humans began to fight back.

Souls had been rushing through the city since the start of the fight, yet now some were finding bodies that belonged to them. Many of these humans were Silver rank, strong enough to tear off the shackles that bound their legs. They were unfortunately unable to break the power-subduing bracelets, but were still strong enough that when they ambushed the Astar around them, they were able to fight back effectively.

Using lengths of wood or stones that they carried, some even swinging the entire sacks themselves, the human slaves turned against their masters and the fight turned chaotic. Where the Astar had been forming a line to fight the wildlife in an orderly manner, the humans waking across the entire town caused mayhem.

Zalia

Zalia stood with eyes closed as she focused. She had no idea how the fight was going so far, but knew that she needed to get help to them as quickly as possible. The ritual in front of her would take precious minutes to activate, she knew that.

At the same time as she spent most of her concentration in a quiet chant to bring this powerful elemental to the battle, she activated the smaller living rituals where she could. She could only do one or two at a time but slowly, these smaller rituals let elementals trickle towards the fight.

Zalia had designed this massive ritual so that it would take less time to activate than the anti-teleportation ritual back at home would have. The limited lifespan of the elemental was the biggest cause of that time reduction, changing it from something that would take hours to mere minutes. It would have been faster again, except Zalia had made it something that was really two rituals in one. The first created the massive elemental, while the other would teleport it straight into the city only a few seconds after it was created.

It took all of her willpower to keep from thinking about her family in danger in the city and remain focused on the ritual. A piece of her mind was reminding her of the promise she made to General Faian not to start a war with the Astar, yet that piece was quieted by the need to save her family. The consequences of this day would be dealt with later.

With a cracking sound, the ritual finally activated. A huge stone arm ripped itself from the ground, followed by another. These two arms pulled a massive twenty-metre-tall elemental from the ground. The thing looked down at Zalia, an intelligence in the two glowing chasms that formed its eyes. She saw it for only a second before it vanished into thin air.

Aylie

Aylie floated through the streets of the Astar town as quickly as her misty body would allow. Ember had separated from her some minutes before, pulled in a different direction than she was. Aylie didn't have time to think about that now, as the thread linking her to that distant location that felt like *home* grew closer and closer.

She could feel it, an escape from the slowness of her mind, the limitations of her body. The way back to how life *should* be. It was so close.

An Astar flashed by in her vision, floating quickly to the edge of town where wildlife and hopefully elementals were fighting other Astar by now. Another misty form merged with a body, and Aylie saw the dead, blank eyes of that person come alive as its expression became frantic and wild. The person tore off their manacles and dashed off quickly, catching the Astar and hitting it with a wild swing to the back of the head. The Astar dropped to the floor like a sack of potatoes, dead.

Aylie saw all of this and more over a few moments, absolute chaos reigning in the once orderly and peaceful Astar town. Through it all, she finally saw . . . herself.

Her body was walking slowly, bound at the legs and carrying a sack slung across her back. Her arms had power-subduing bracelets on them.

She rushed forward and collided with her body.

In a rush, memories came back to her. She opened her eyes to see the town in front of her except . . . different. She felt alive, like she was finally awake after being asleep for so long.

Strangely enough, she could feel her power there, ready to be used, unbound by the bracelets that she wore.

Ignoring the manacles on her legs, she used Starlit Portal to teleport herself to the other side of town, where the battle was warring the hardest. There, wildlife, elementals, and Astar fought in a wild clash as mist poured through the opening in the wall behind her. More and more elementals ran through that wall, flinging fire and earth, while others flew upwards, throwing the airborne Astar around with strong winds.

Her powers still unbound, Aylie summoned her staff and held it tightly, revelling in the sense of power that flowed through her.

She started chanting, the words guttural and harsh, a language that she could not understand, yet knew in her soul. As she did so, the light filtering through the mist above darkened until the entire town was cast in shadow.

No one in the town could see what was happening, but Aylie knew. She was the one who did this.

A few of the Astar looked upwards in confusion but quickly went back to fighting, much of the town lit up by fires being spread by the few fire elementals amongst the wildlife.

Aylie kept chanting.

A huge form glowing a deep red appeared and dropped a few metres, falling on top of a few of the Astar buildings. It was an elemental so much bigger than the others that it caused a momentary stop in the fighting. It opened its mouth with a sharp cracking sound and lava poured forth over a few Astar, bathing the town in light and the screams of the burning.

Aylie kept chanting.

Many Astar swarmed around the bigger elemental, obviously marking the Silver rank as a threat. They chanted in unison, forming a ritual around it that went off. Nothing happened.

The Astar seemed shocked as a long arm swept past and slapped a few of them into the ground with an ear-splitting crack. Whatever they had tried had not worked.

Yet more elementals came from the forests nearby, and Aylie knew that Zalia would soon arrive. Their assault had worked, she was free. Now they just had to find Ember and get as many of the other people out as possible.

Aylie's chant continued.

More and more humans arrived at the edge of the town, some running to join the fight while others fled. Many of them, however, paused behind the lines to try to get the power-subduing bracelets off.

Boreal appeared from the madness and helped one take their bracelets off. Once done, they were able to begin helping others do the same. Apparently, all it took was the help of someone who didn't have the bracelets on themselves.

More and more magic joined the battle as people got their powers back. Some were soldiers, going in and swinging with all their considerably increased strength, as others threw elements that were significantly more powerful than those of the elementals around. Others yet continued to flee, obviously without classes that would help in battle.

Aylie continued her chant.

Zalia appeared above the battle, flying on wide wings of air. Her bow floated next to her, firing off arrow after arrow, each making contact with an Astar head or heart. Zalia hung in the air, unconcerned, casting rituals that started even more fires amongst the Astar buildings. Aylie couldn't see her expression from here, but she could tell that Zalia held no remorse or guilt for what she did. The Astar had done something to her and her people, and this Druid would grant them no mercy.

Aylie watched an arrow strike one Astar, a bolt of power bouncing from it to seven others, killing all of them instantly. Purple fire spread through the town, jumping from building to building, some sparks lighting more Astar on fire.

Finally, Aylie finished her chant.

From the skies above, flashing bolts of light fell. They struck Astar all across the town, impacting with massive force and lighting beautiful ethereal fires. More and more fell, killing hundreds in an instant.

A second wave came, quickly following the first, until the town was alight with the power of the stars.

As the first two waves subsided, miniature undirected meteorites showered the town, smashing through flesh, wood, and stone alike.

Taking a longer time to cast Starfall through the staff, Aylie was able to bring down not one but two showers of the directed stars, each even more powerful because of it.

With her contribution to the fight complete, she ran towards the people who were fleeing the town, hoping to get them organised and out before the Astar could regroup and fight back. They might have taken them by surprise in this storm attack and killed many of them, but she knew that they wouldn't hold this position for long. Even now, the big elemental Zalia had summoned was being torn apart by spacial magic.

Even as she helped the people below, Aylie could see the power building where Zalia flew above it all, and she knew that she wasn't going to let up just yet. They could save many more still.

CHAPTER THIRTY-SEVEN

Storm

Zalia

Zalia floated serenely, letting her power flow through and out of her body as she channelled Nature's Wrath. Around her were five air elementals arrayed like the points of a pentagon, each focusing on its own magic.

Usually, the way Zalia used Nature's Wrath was in an immediate and violent reaction, smashing mana into the ability to destroy whatever was in front of her. This time, however, was like the slow shifting of rocks threatening to fall in a landslide.

The sky darkened as clouds built above her, shifting and growing ever blacker as a thunderstorm built. A bolt of lightning cracked down, hitting an Astar on its short path to the town below, its scorched body tumbling hard onto the pavement just as thick droplets of rain began to fall.

She smiled in satisfaction, watching as the Astar realised what she was doing and began flying up to stop her. It was too late.

Many more cracks of thunder struck as lightning slammed down, each bolt seeking the Astar that flew up to meet her. A few of these bolts even travelled through Zalia herself, but she was unaffected by the magic she controlled. The few drops of rain turned to a downpour, drenching the settlement below and beginning to extinguish the fires raging across the battlefront.

More cracks resounded and more Astar fell. Zalia pushed more and more magic into the storm, letting it build in strength until winds began howling and the rain turned to hail. It was a blinding storm of ice and lightning, each crack signalling the death of another Astar as they desperately tried to reach the source of the magic.

When she started running low on mana—her quite large pool was already low because of the summoning of the elemental—she stopped growing the storm and instead fed it, the torrential flow of mana turning to a trickle.

Flying down, she saw an Astar use an ability that tore a chunk of stone from her large elemental's head. It stumbled around now, blind and missing large pieces of its body, lava dripping to the ground below.

The wildlife that had joined them in this fight had all but retreated, no longer willing to continue the fight. The trick of elementals Zalia had been bringing to the fight had become one large final burst after she had come here, but reinforcements no longer came. The low-ranked elementals stood no chance against the Astar without the support of the wildlife and were dying in droves.

Many of the freed slaves were helping, but the majority of them simply fled from the Astar into the woods beyond, seeking the safety of the mist that now trickled slowly into town.

Boreal was fighting savagely, still tearing many Astar to pieces and freezing others. Aylie acted as a medic, healing the injured now that her single-use ability had been used. Every now and then, she was forced to awaken a plant to distract an Astar as she did so.

Zalia saw this with only a glance, however, as she searched with her eyes and soul for Ember. She could feel where she was through their bond, quickly approaching the battlefront now. She stared and stared until . . . there.

Her wings beat once then folded in as she dropped from the sky at speed towards Ember. She had somehow managed to get her armour on and was glowing with a halo of golden fire, flickering steps of flame following her path. Two Astar were chasing her, but as Zalia watched, Ember turned and stomped her foot. A burst of flame exploded from in front of the two Astar, distracting them. During that short time, Ember had reversed course and now jumped through the fire, slinging powerful, plate-covered fists in their direction. One of the two Astar died with a caved-in head—the other managed to dodge but died moments later with an arrow through its head.

Ember turned sharply to see Zalia coming down, and she could feel the burst of relief that flooded her partner's body.

Zalia only landed for the time it took to pick up Ember before launching into the sky again. There were many other freed slaves still running through the streets, but she would just have to hope that the chaos they had caused would be enough for the majority of them to escape. They couldn't save them all, as much as she wished they could.

In the distance, Zalia could see many more Astar flying in from the large central building in the town. They rose into the sky even as the hail and lightning continued pounding down. It was time to leave.

She sent a mental message to Boreal, telling her to get Aylie and Lumin and get out, then flew to the battlefront, where the chaotic but winning fight had turned into an orderly regroup by the Astar, who pushed the disorganised humans back.

Once they landed behind those retreating lines, it took Zalia a moment to get Ember's power-subduing bracelets off. They both ran in opposite directions down the line in silent agreement, yelling at the still-fighting slaves to get out. It didn't take long, and soon they were all running towards the tree line, the Astar thankfully not giving chase.

That was until hundreds of them appeared in the sky above.

By the time they did, she had met back up with Ember, and she reacted quickly, grabbing her and using Mobility to teleport into the misty tree line. The freed slaves that were lagging behind weren't so lucky, unfortunately.

There was a strange sucking sound as the land, mist, hail, air, and *people* between the town's edge and the tree line simply disappeared. Gone in an instant.

Zalia quickly checked her bond with Boreal and found that she was much further into the forest already, so she put Ember down, and the two of them ran off as quickly as they could manage.

Zalia held Ember close as she cried, painful sobs wracking her body.

They were in her vault back at the clearing, now far enough away from the Astar for Ember to let her guard down. Her experience had been quite different to Aylie's. Where Aylie had maintained some semblance of control and thought, Ember had been an unwilling witness to her soul's wanderings, incapable of proper thought or action. She had described it like having your mind stuck in a cage within a nightmare where rational thought had all but vanished.

For her part, Aylie seemed to be doing alright. The experience seemed to have less of an effect on her; perhaps now that she had the power to actually do something, it made the experience less like an imprisoning of the mind.

Zalia tried to comfort Ember by offering strength and calming words, and she did relax eventually. It was a horrible experience, for sure, but they would be able to overcome it together.

"I remember everything," Ember whispered between deep breaths.

"It's alright, I know."

"No, you don't understand. I remember everything my body did, where it went and what it saw. If I did, many of the others might have as well. They might know things about the Astar."

Zalia pulled away just slightly, enough to look at Ember's face. "They might know how we can fight them, where they live, what other cities look like. That's the first bit of good news we've had from this whole thing."

Ember nodded and Zalia pulled her close again.

It was another five minutes before Ember spoke again.

"Alright, I'm ready to face it."

The "it" Ember referred to was the some two dozen freed slaves waiting in the clearing outside the vault. They were all that Boreal and Zalia had managed to drag along with them in their quick escape. Others undoubtedly wandered the mist, and she did want to try and find more of them, but it would be extremely hard in these conditions. Still, they had to try. The part Ember would play was in trying to help heal people's trauma.

Zalia had tried to dissuade her from that, as she needed to rest, but Ember insisted, saying that helping the others would help her deal with it too. It was hard to argue with that.

After helping her wash up her face a little bit, they both stepped out of the vault to see how the group was doing. There were only a few people who stood strong, waiting patiently for Zalia. Many of them just sat and stared into nothing. They were either broken inside or trying to sift through the possible years of memories that awaited them. Maybe both. Who knew what effect the things they'd been through could have on the soul?

Aylie was nearby, inspecting each person in turn in the way that only she could. If anyone could determine what long-term exposure to soul separation would do, it was Aylie. After doing a round of the group, Aylie activated an ability, and Zalia felt a strong surge of healing spread across the clearing. This healing was different, finding a path deep into the body in a more fundamental way.

> **Tin - Your very presence grants life to all around you. You, nearby allies, and any flora and fauna you so choose within your aura are affected by a heal-over-time effect. The heal-over-time effect heals for low health every second.**
>
> **Iron - Healing Presence now heals the most grave injuries first, and you may focus it onto a single target, increasing that target's healing while reducing the healing other targets receive.**
>
> **Bronze - Healing Presence now attunes to the specific needs of each individual target within your aura. It adjusts its healing output based on the severity of injuries or ailments, offering targeted healing to each person or creature accordingly. You may still change this manually, if desired. Additionally, once every twenty-four hours, you may trigger a Healing Surge.**
>
> **Healing Surge - The power of Healing Presence is increased tenfold and gains the ability to heal the soul. This lasts for one minute.**

Some of the vacant eyes and troubled stares of the people faded away, the combination of Aylie's soul healing and Ember's emotional healing forming a complex net of powerful recovery. Some of the freed slaves blinked repeatedly, like they had only just awoken. Many began talking to each other or staring at Aylie in awe.

Amongst the two dozen freed slaves, there wasn't a Bronze rank person in sight. All of the assembled were Silver, so while the small number of people might not seem strong, this was actually a group of some of the most powerful people in Endaria. Zalia wondered what would happen to the kingdom if she brought back all of the freed slaves, what kind of shift in power would happen.

One man stood up and thanked Aylie with a gesture, one hand forming a fist over his heart. The others began to do so as well, while many also thanked Zalia and Ember in a similar manner. The broken camp had turned into a hive of activity.

Now that people were looking a lot better, Zalia began to ask questions.

Everyone was still trying to sort through their memories of the time in the Astar town, but she did learn some things. For one, the large building in the centre of town was indeed a portal hub. They even had someone who had been through one of those portals, and she spoke of a huge underground cavern supported by jagged, oddly shaped pillars, an entire city built within. There were human slaves there too, though not as many as in this town. By her reckoning, there must have been tens of thousands of Astar living there, if not more than a hundred thousand.

This concerned Zalia deeply. Unless that city was the major city of the Astar, it could mean that they had a population that exceeded the humans by a lot. What if they were advanced enough as a people to have cities containing millions? What could the people of Endaria do about that?

The other thing that concerned her was the possible rank of those people. This town hadn't contained many high-ranked Astar at all, only a couple of Silver ranked among them, while the majority sat at Bronze. It had been a major reason Zalia had been able to take the town as while they were powerful spacial mages, the Astar were physically weak, even when compared to beings of similar rank that hadn't bonded the strength or dexterity attributes.

With these thoughts in the back of her mind, she called all the freed slaves together.

CHAPTER THIRTY-EIGHT

Search and Rescue

Zalia

Alright, everyone! Hello, I'm Zalia. I'm sorry to do this to you so soon after being freed, but we have to get to work immediately while the Astar are still regrouping and putting out the remaining fires in their town. We need to find and bring together the rest of the freed slaves as soon as possible and begin making our way back to Endaria."

There was some mumbling amongst the people and one spoke up.

"How are we meant to find anything in this mist?"

Zalia tapped at her leg in thought, trying to find a good answer to that. The woman wasn't wrong.

"I have a drink that can help your bodies adapt to the environment, if only temporarily. That should help. Otherwise, the young cats here all have developed abilities to see in the mist. Some of you will be able to pair up with one of them and protect them as they search for others. They are trained in tracking, so they should be of good assistance. Aylie and Ember will stay here to greet returning slaves, while Boreal and I shall also head out into the mist to try to find them. Try to keep track of where you are and which direction you walk while out there."

It was a risk, a large one at that. It was quite possible that some of them could get caught out there or even just get lost, but it was also important to find and help as many others as possible. Zalia knew that as Silver rank people, each of them would have a good sense of direction and an incredible memory. That should help in finding their way back at the least.

Each of Boreal's children found themselves a human and wandered off into the mist after a stern word from Boreal. She made it clear that they were to protect her young with their lives or else face the consequences, which would just happen to come in a sharp, quick, and furry manner.

As the unchosen people grumbled and made their own way off into the mist, Zalia gave Ember and Aylie a quick farewell hug and ran off.

It didn't take her long to start finding people.

The first man she found was stumbling over a stretch of rocky ground with vacant eyes, and she quickly stopped him in his tracks. While the others would have to bring stragglers back to camp, Zalia held an advantage.

Using the keyword of the portal back in the clearing as a guide for her magic, she prepared a ritual that teleported the man straight back to camp. Simple and easy as that, she went on her way again.

Over the course of several hours, Zalia tracked down dozens of people. It was easy for her, the tracks left by their mindless wandering easy to see for her trained and enhanced eyes. Each person she found was quickly sent back to camp, where she hoped Ember and Aylie weren't getting too overwhelmed.

After the first few people, Zalia made sure to make her way further out from the camp, as the others would have a harder time bringing these people back. She had a rough idea of how many had escaped the town in the general direction of the camp and would just have to hope that the ones who had fled out other avenues would find their own ways back to the kingdom. It was a long shot for many of them, unfortunately, as it was quite a long journey.

After the first hours, she went back to the clearing to see how everyone was doing, looking through the few rank-ups from the fight while she did.

Congratulations! Hunter's Sight has reached Silver 7.
Congratulations! Herbal Magic has reached Silver 11.
You have fought many battles, each a powerful struggle in its own right.
Throughout many of them, you have worn Druidic Armour, Blessed by Nature.
Congratulations! Druidic Armour, Blessed by Nature (Blessed Heirloom) has ascended to Silver rank!

The final notification had taken Zalia by surprise, as she hadn't felt any changes at all. She was so used to ignoring and dismissing messages during fights so as not to be distracted that she hadn't noticed this one was different.

Druidic Armour, Blessed by Nature (Blessed Heirloom) - Deeply bonded Silver rank.
Tin - Wearing the armour applies Shadows' Veil to you.
Iron – Shadows' Veil gains a new effect called Partial Intangibility.
Bronze - When intangible, you may step through flora to move out of similar flora within a limited range.

> **Silver - Your affinity for ritual magic has made its mark on your armour. You may have three rituals imbued into your armour that are constantly active without any upkeep cost. Changing one of these rituals requires many hours of work.**
>
> **Shadows' Veil - Shadows' Veil suppresses the wearer's aura and magical signature, making it challenging for magical beings or entities with heightened senses to detect their presence.**
>
> **Shadows' Veil now muffles any sound you make while wearing the armour, making your movements silent, even when moving quickly or engaging in combat.**
>
> **Partial Intangibility - Shadows' Veil grants the wearer partial intangibility, allowing them to phase through thin barriers or objects, such as walls, fences, or closed doors, as long as the barriers are not too thick or magically protected.**

She gave an appreciative whistle. Permanently active rituals?

It took her a matter of seconds to decide which ones she would use. With a seemingly inevitable war with the Astar coming up, she would need anti-teleportation protection. If she could design a ritual that didn't stop her own teleportation magic, then she would do that one. The next would have to be the Dodge-vine and Adastem ritual that provided adaptive protection.

Her first thought for the third was to cast the ritual that gave her the wings for flight. Then she realised she could already maintain that ritual on herself indefinitely without mana use, and already did. It would have to be something else then, but what?

Her mind turned to less combat-oriented things. A ritual that enhanced her stealth, perhaps. There was time to think about it, anyways.

For now, she put her armour back into storage, then brought it out in front of herself rather than equip it. She quickly cast the Dodge-vine major and Adastem minor ritual on it and saw the magic imbue itself into the armour. A couple of runes etched themselves into different pieces of the armour, and Zalia admired them closely, recognising them as the runes from the ritual. Could she do this kind of thing without the ability? Enchant items?

It wasn't time to think of that now.

She quickly reequipped the armour, feeling it protect her just a little better now, and checked the description of that last ability again.

> **Silver - Your affinity for ritual magic has made its mark on your armour. You may have three rituals imbued into your armour that are constantly active without any upkeep cost. Changing one of these rituals requires many hours of work.**
>
> **Imbued rituals:**

> **Dodge-vine and Adastem (Adaptive Protection).**
> **None**
> **None**

Excellent.

When she arrived back at the clearing, it was to a scene only slightly less chaotic than she was expecting.

The number of people they had gathered so far spilled out of the too-small space and out, around, and on top of the raised earth wall. Ember was having to walk around the perimeter, making sure none of the more vacant-looking ones didn't wander off again.

Zalia quickly pushed inside and began expanding the walls, lowering them and building new ones further out. It was only minutes before she had a space more than big enough for the odd one hundred and twenty people. Looking through their ranks, Zalia once again saw not a Bronze ranker in sight. There were even two Gold rankers among their number. If they could just get these people back to Endaria, they would undoubtedly be an amazing infusion of strength for the nation.

She wondered how much longer they should try looking for other people. How long could they wait, in reality, before the Astar brought stronger forces to find them? It was a hard decision to make.

Many of the people Zalia had sent back earlier were looking significantly better now, after the ministrations of Ember and Aylie. While it would be another day until Aylie could use her soul-healing magic, the emotional healing and basic healing that Aylie provided were still helpful.

Ember found her shortly after she had extended the walls, questions written across her expression. "Zalia, I agree with what we're doing here, but *how* are we going to feed all these people on the journey back? For that matter, how are we going to keep them all safe?"

Zalia looked around. "Many of them are still capable of fighting. As for the feeding, you have your Universal Wellbeing, remember?"

A light lit up in Ember's eyes. "Oh! I have only ever used it to help towns and such, it completely slipped past me that it would apply here."

Universal Wellbeing was an ability that Ember had developed long ago. Previously called "Help The Needy," the ability was one that she used to provide a community of people with something that they needed. Previous examples of this were repairing buildings, healing wounds, and most importantly, feeding towns. While it could only be used once a day, that would be all they needed to feed these people enough that they could make it back to Endaria, where the council could take over their wellbeing.

Zalia nodded, glad to have helped allay those fears.

"The question on my mind is how long we should wait before leaving. I don't want to be here when the Astar finally decide to come looking. Worse even, if this mist really is made of the souls of enslaved humans, who's to say that it is going to stick around much longer? I'd rather be long gone before we find that out."

Ember nodded, looking worried again.

"Give it another hour, then we should go."

Zalia had been thinking to leave straight away but agreed. She wanted to help these people as much as Ember did, but they did have to be sure not to destroy any chance they had of actually escaping by leaving too late. Being caught on their way back to Endaria could be disastrous, especially if they encountered hundreds of Astar using combined magic to make them all vanish from reality, as they had just done hours earlier.

With a timeline in place, Zalia left the clearing again. There was no time to waste.

She spent the next hour as she had spent the previous few, finding stragglers and teleporting them back to the clearing for Ember and Aylie to look after. The anxiety and pressure of the situation made her stressed, yet she still felt better now than she had when Ember and Aylie had been captured. Nothing could come even close to that feeling.

With the hour done, she went back to the clearing.

Ember had been stopping people from leaving again once they had returned, and they were now all there except for Breeze and the person that he had been with. Great.

Zalia found Ember again.

"Take them and go, Boreal and I will find Breeze."

Ember gave her a nod and started collecting the people together and organising them. She began explaining where they were heading and how they could be found again if people got lost in the mist. Zalia only heard the beginning of the explanation as she and Boreal ran off into the mist once more.

Using Hunter's Sight, Zalia was quickly able to track Breeze down. Glowing bushes, trees, and patches of ground marked where Breeze had been, the tracks obvious to her now that she was on the right path.

Despite that, Boreal saw them before Zalia did.

Breeze was on the ground, writhing in pain as an Astar floated nearby, no expression on their face. There were two more who had the freed slave that had gone with Breeze in a similar pained mess on the floor.

Boreal was upon them in an instant, motherly love turned weapon as she attacked.

The one that was torturing Breeze had the tendons on the back of its legs brutally slashed before Boreal jumped up and grabbed its neck in her powerful jaws. She crunched down and threw the body against a nearby tree where it bent unnaturally around the trunk.

Zalia attacked the other two, arrows peppering holes in one Astar. As she did, the freed slave managed to break free of the remaining Astar's grip and jumped to his feet. He grabbed the Astar's skull as it tried to escape via teleportation magic and slammed it into his knee. Two more slams, and the Astar's head exploded in a gory mess.

While that happened, Zalia scooped up Breeze and began setting up the teleportation ritual. A few minutes later, and they appeared back in the clearing.

She handed off Breeze to the freed slave and gestured for them to chase after the rest of their group while she slowly disassembled the clearing that had been their base.

CHAPTER THIRTY-NINE

To Escape the Mist

Zalia

Zalia chased after the group of freed slaves that her family was taking to safety. Following along behind, she used Natural Matter Alteration to make all signs of their passing vanish. The grass was healed, dirt was flattened back out, sticks and bushes were repaired. It might have been unnecessary but she wanted to give them the best chance at escaping possible. If that meant lagging behind to cover up their escape, so be it.

Once they were out of the mist, she wouldn't do the same. In fact, at that point, they might actually want to be found. Hopefully, their tracks would be visible to other freed slaves they hadn't found who would then be able to follow them. The Astar would see them from up in the sky anyway.

She eventually caught up to the slow-moving group despite her own reduced speed and continued cleaning up after them. Boreal and Breeze were there too, which meant everyone was together again. Now they just had to get back to Endaria. It was going to be a long, long journey.

They didn't stop until many hours later when they arrived at the trailing edge of the unnatural mist. They waited here as Zalia finished up removing their tracks and made camp, if it could be called that. None of them had any bedrolls or tents, not even a backpack in sight.

It was here that Ember used Universal Wellbeing to create a table covered in steaming soup and bread. It wouldn't be anything fancy but definitely a far sight better than what they had most likely been fed as slaves, and infinitely better than the nothing they would have had to eat without her.

While everyone ate, Zalia went from person to person, asking about their stories. If she got answers at all, they were usually brief. From her understanding, many of these people had been slaves for years, decades. Many even named the king of Endaria as being neither King Alistair *or* King Horum, which meant they were from a time before them. They might have been there for hundreds of years.

The other thing she asked about, the more important matter at hand, was what each person was capable of. Three-quarters of the people were fighters of some kind, many being knights or powerful warriors, though there weren't a small number of fighters of the more magical kind as well. Thankfully, there were a few people more like Zalia amongst their number too, people who travelled alone and without contact with the wider world. These people Zalia made good use of, asking them to range a bit further from the group as scouts, which they were more than happy to do. Strangely, they were also the ones who held better control of their mental faculties. Did they have stronger minds or souls as a result of the way they lived their lives?

The other quarter of the people were less warriors and more merchant or craftsman types. The merchants were the travelling kind, capable of defending themselves but not excellent at fighting, while the craftsmen were people who had grown bored of city life and left for outer towns or a holiday from their usual day-to-day experiences. The memories those people had of being taken often lined up with their decisions to do this.

Talking to all these people answered a question that had been hanging over her mind for a while now. How was it that the people of Endaria hadn't noticed that the most powerful members of their nation had been disappearing?

For the warriors, they often spoke of being abducted during battles, taken amongst the chaos of a fight. The merchants spoke of trade routes along dangerous paths, and craftsmen spoke of being taken while leaving to find relaxation or adventure in farther lands. In this way, the Astar had managed to avoid suspicion. People died in battle, sometimes having their bodies completely destroyed, and merchants *did* sometimes die when travelling the more dangerous routes. It happened.

This was perhaps the reason that many Endarians thought that the north was so dangerous, not because it actually was *that* dangerous, but because powerful people who went there often didn't return.

And it was something that had been happening for hundreds of years.

She didn't understand why the bodies of these ancient slaves hadn't deteriorated—some were magic, perhaps. Though many questions had been answered by these people, she began to ponder new ones. Why exactly did the Astar do what they did?

There must have been a reason for it, even if she couldn't yet see it. Was it just so that they had a constant source of cheap labour? She didn't think so.

She had to shake herself from these thoughts as people began to get restless. It was time to move on.

They packed up what meagre things they had—some craftsmen had begun making low-quality weapons from stone and wood for the warriors amongst them, while the more wild types had begun searching the nearby area amongst the plants for anything of use within their environment.

It was approaching nighttime, but none of the group complained as they set off again. All of them were tired, her own family amongst them, but they unanimously agreed that they needed to get further from the Astar than this.

The sun set as they walked, yet they didn't stop until the light from the waning moon vanished over the horizon as well. At that point, it was agreed that they should rest, and everyone collapsed with exhausted sighs. Everyone except Zalia and Boreal, of course.

They wouldn't need sleep nor rest for weeks yet, their bodies maintained entirely by Zalia's passive.

While Zalia was a quarter of the way to Gold rank, Boreal had advanced to almost halfway there from this fight. She wouldn't be surprised if some of her abilities that levelled up quickly advanced to Gold rank soon; her average progress as seen by Aura Observation was held back by the slower ones.

At final count, there were one hundred and fifty-seven people in their group, not including Zalia's family. They hadn't found any more Gold rankers amongst the people brought back in that final hour, so they still only had the two. They were recovering from their experience much quicker than the rest, as both of them were tank types. Thinking about it, Zalia wasn't surprised that it was tank types that often made it to higher ranks than anyone else. Hildebrandt was one of those too. They might not be the strongest in how much damage they could put out, but they sure were damn hard to kill.

While everyone else settled down to sleep, Zalia found a tree to climb that she could use as a good vantage point. She wanted to keep an eye on the entire group, not just watch the sky and surrounding lands for Astar. While they had saved these people, some of them might be the type that would kill or steal for a better chance at survival. Some might even be broken of mind, or have spent so long in servitude to the Astar that they didn't know any other life. She wouldn't have someone sneaking off in the night to tell the Astar where they were.

Fortunately, the night passed without issue and as the next day came, the group rose with the sun.

They continued their journey and as the day progressed, things started to look a bit better. After a good night's sleep, some of the people were looking a lot better than they had the day before. Their eyes were clearer and their steps more confident. The constant emotional healing from Ember was doing wonders, and not too long into the day, Aylie was able to activate her soul healing too. The effect was stunning: the zombie-like blankness of the last remaining members had greatly decreased, though it didn't fade entirely. There was still a shadow in the eyes of some, a trauma and experience that wouldn't ever fully disappear.

The craftsmen amongst the group found a source of iron halfway through this second day, and Zalia watched in awe as they crafted armour and weapons without the use of a forge. At Silver rank, they apparently needed nothing other than their bare hands to create some good quality gear.

The hunters and wilder people amongst the group were outfitted with bows and arrows, and they began to bring back small game from the area. With the leather from those kills, the craftsmen began to make boots, waterskins, and some leather armour for the more agile people. Processes that would normally take weeks if not months were done in an instant with the powers of these high-ranked people.

The fears that she and Ember had at the beginning were proven unfounded as the group of people were more self-sustaining than they realised.

By the end of that first day, they had even begun making tents, and an enchanter amongst the group was enchanting the cloth so that the inside of the tents were significantly larger than the outside.

As they rested for that night, it was to Zalia's astonishment that she kept watch over a proper campsite instead of the group of people sleeping in the dirt that she had seen the night before.

There were fifteen tents, each enchanted to be large enough on the inside that they could hold more than ten people each. They were arrayed in a wide circle around a large campfire tended by a wildman who had a few abilities related to cooking. He had prepared the kills that the others had made during the day, and with the meat from those kills, Ember had been able to use Universal Wellbeing to create some better quality foodstuffs such as salt and spices.

The group was in good spirits that improved even further when a merchant who was also a brewer turned some water from a nearby stream into various alcoholic drinks for the group, with Zalia crafting a few hundred wooden mugs using a mixture of Healing Presence and Natural Matter Alteration.

Be as that it may, spirits weren't high enough, and people were not familiar enough with each other for loud conversation. There was an occasional chuckle here and there as people spoke quietly, but for the most part, people were silent. A few of the more talkative members of the group had begun talking to each other about their experiences as slaves, building bonds over shared adversity.

Zalia was . . . surprised.

She often forgot that while humans as a race fought amongst themselves often and rarely were in agreement, when there was something for them to fight together against they could often throw away those differences and overcome great difficulty. It brought her hope.

That was a strange feeling to her, hope. Even after defeating the demons invading Endaria, her thoughts had turned to the Astar, and even further, to a possible attempt at taking back Cormaine. Both were going to be horrible, hard experiences but if all of humanity could come together and work towards these common goals, then maybe, just maybe, things would be alright.

CHAPTER FORTY

Reclaimed to Nature's Reclaim

Zalia

They were in the marshes now, travelling much like Zalia and her family had when first coming to the Astar town. Across the past two days, she had figured out which other ritual she wanted imbued into her armour and had also created a version of the anti-teleportation ritual that would still allow her to use her own abilities.

The final ritual had been something new. Herbal Magic gave her the ability to combine two herbs to create a new base element, and this was something she rarely ever used, finding it easier to create differences in the ritual formation itself that gave her the effect she wanted. Now, though, she had combined Flame-root and Zephyr, which had the Fire and Air elements, to create a powder with the element of Movement. She combined this new powder and Adastem to create an effect that gave her adaptive movement, meaning it could help her run faster or be more streamlined for quicker flight or swimming. Whichever it did, it would grant her increased mobility while wearing the armour, and that was never a bad thing.

Everything had been running smoothly up to this point—the byproduct of well-fed humans in relatively high spirits. They hadn't even been attacked by any wild creatures, finding that nothing was quite stupid enough to attack such a strong group of people.

It had been great, up until a hundred or so Astar appeared in the sky.

The travelling group reacted quickly, the mages and hunters amongst them throwing magic and shooting arrows into the sky. Zalia's own bow appeared next to her and let off arrow after arrow. The Astar began casting a ritual, all of them working on a single power. Zalia knew what was coming, the people with her knew what was coming.

Unfortunately for the Astar, Zalia had been ready for something like this. She had given each and every one of the people in the group the single-use bracelets that protected against spacial magic. As well as that, she had all the herbs stored in her vault ready for a group-wide protective ritual against the very same thing, which she immediately began to cast upon seeing the Astar.

Her ritual snapped into place moments before theirs went off, and while the air warped a little, the people within its area felt nothing other than a slight tug on their bodies.

Chaos reigned as the Astar panicked.

They were obviously not trained soldiers, more used to abducting people than fighting them. Perhaps they were not used to anyone countering their magic either.

The group of freed slaves were not trained soldiers for the most part either, however.

While many of them stood their ground and shot up at the Astar, the ones who were less used to fighting ran away, scattering in different directions.

Wearing her armour, Zalia felt invincible to the Astar. She teleported up into the sky with them, the wings that gave her flight active as always. Having just appeared in the air, she had to swerve to the side to avoid a hammer flying end over end, barely missing her and slamming into an Astar's face with a crunch. Her bow released a final arrow before it was transformed into a sword already held in Zalia's hand. She slashed in a wide arc and a blade of wind swept forward.

Only the closest Astar was hit, its arm severed. The few behind managed to dodge out of the way, while another destroyed the arc of wind with magic just moments before a ball of fire exploded on their chest, engulfing them.

While they were focusing on the first attack, Zalia had already swept her sword in three more quick, small arcs that eviscerated two of them. She dashed between more Astar, avoiding magic and arrows blasting by from below, marking ten of them with Hunter's Mark. She grabbed one of the marked Astar in a headlock to hold it still while she performed a ritual on it.

Water Lily and Bitterbalm floated about it before the ritual took place. All ten marked Astar slowly died as the water was pulled from their bodies into ten floating spheres. Zalia froze the water, and it dropped down to the ground below.

An Astar wielding twin lithe blades appeared next to her, swinging. She used Fight or Flight, time slowing to her eyes as she reacted, parrying one blade hard enough that the strike from the other blade was put off so that she could dodge out of the way. By the time she recovered, the first blade was already swinging in her direction again as the Astar attacked in a flurry of beautifully methodical strikes.

Taken aback by the nature of this Astar's attacks, Zalia barely held her own, and felt Boreal approaching her position. She took a single moment to look down and saw her bounding up into the sky using the balls of ice as platforms, controlling them with her magic.

Zalia parried another blow, then had to deflect the other blade with her bracer. She kicked out at that moment, making contact with the Astar's chest and flinging them away from her and straight into Boreal's path. She used the Astar as her final stepping stone into the sky, her jaws clamping shut on their skull with a crunching sound. They immediately began to drop from the sky as the sword-wielding Astar died, but Zalia cast a flight ritual on her friend, applying another anti-teleportation ritual to her.

A quick check of her mana saw that it was depleting extremely fast. Maintaining the anti-spacial magic ritual for her allies down below was draining it too fast.

Looking around at how many Astar still stood, Zalia realised that it would run out before they killed them all. They would have casualties soon.

A bright light from below zipped up into the sky, the ball of starlight taking the form of Lumin as they savaged an Astar, changing into a ball of starlight immediately after and dashing over to another target. They were letting off a bright light and powerful heat that blinded Zalia's heat vision so much she had to turn it off. Ethereal fire coated the wolf, little sparks of starlight flickering off to land on Astar, lighting them up as well.

The three of them killed many of the Astar before Zalia's mana dropped low enough that a deep headache throbbed in her skull. She dropped the large ritual below, only barely able to maintain Boreal's flight. The Astar obviously saw this happen as she heard screams and grunts of pain from below.

She swept towards another enemy, missing her strike as they teleported away. It only took seconds for her to reach them again, yet another strike missed as they vanished once more. Strike, teleport, strike, teleport. Growing frustrated, she stopped and switched back to her bow, intending to shoot the Astar before an arrow from below hit it in the head.

Some of the Astar began to retreat, vanishing from the battlefield and not returning. Once a few had gone, the rest began to follow quickly. Within half a minute, all the Astar were either gone or dead.

Zalia went down below to see how the rest of the group was doing and found that they were all in good health. Ember had been down here the whole time, healing as much as possible. That wasn't to say that they came out of the battle unscathed.

Many of the people were missing chunks of clothing where limbs had been destroyed. She saw a few expressions of shock, the memory of pain obviously not yet faded. Once the craftsmen and traders that had run away came back, she also realised that a few members of their group were just . . . missing.

She should have expected it, considering what the Astar had tried to do at the start of the fight.

It took a good half hour for everyone to collect weapons and calm down enough for them to continue on their way. Zalia collected one of the Astar bodies during that time, putting it in her vault.

They had lost fifteen people during the fight, not a large number, but it still had an impact that was felt by the whole group. They couldn't afford to lose more people this way.

Zalia was already back to making more anti-teleportation bracelets for the group, knowing that they had saved them from a potentially crippling fight.

She was concerned about that twin sword fighter that had attacked her. They had been different from the rest of the Astar, obviously well trained with the weapons. Was it possible that the Astar they had been fighting so far were not actually the warriors of their race? What if they were just slave traders, not warriors or powerful mages of any kind? Normal, day-to-day people, so to speak.

It would make sense, as they were much too easy to kill. Looking at the fight they had just had, she could see that. There was no way these were the strongest of their race.

Their journey back to Endaria continued, days filled with muddling their way through the swamp. They were attacked twice more in their time during the swamp, each attack with less Astar, who were holding a sense of . . . desperation to them. They lost another eleven members during those two fights, bringing the total number of people in their group to one hundred and thirty-one.

Once they made it out of the swamps, they were able to relax just a bit. That wasn't to say that they let their guard down, but they were now within the borders of Endaria. It was Zalia's intention to bring the group straight to the capital, but after talking with them over the course of the next few days about what they wanted to do, it came up that Zalia kind of . . . owned a town. A town that had anti-teleportation measures over the entire thing. The group came to the decision that they would rather head there first.

Zalia didn't want to take their freedom of choice from them, and neither would she turn down a good number of high-ranked soldiers, mages, craftsmen, and merchants. The ones that she could see were hard-working and powerful people.

As the members of the group grew more accustomed to each other, they also opened up more about their experiences. Zalia learnt a lot about the Astar during that time, how they lived and what they were like as a people. Much like her experiences of them so far, they were a cold and calculating people, with members of their race that showed compassion or strong emotion often being exiled. That surprised Zalia, as it meant that they weren't that way naturally. Rather, it was an enforced coldness.

She spoke to the member of their group who had been to another Astar city about the Astar there and learnt that, as she thought, the twin sword–wielding Astar hadn't been an outlier by any means. He told Zalia that while the majority of the Astar were Bronze rank with few that ascended to Silver, there were, of course, the powerful few that made it to higher ranks. He had seen a few Emerald rank Astar and a single Diamond rank one over the many years spent in that bigger Astar city.

Zalia wondered then if the real reason the Astar took higher-ranked Endarians was to make sure they didn't grow too powerful. Did the majority of the Astar just not bother ranking up?

They weren't attacked again after entering Endaria's borders, and the day soon came that they arrived at Nature's Reclaim. Everything looked to be at peace in the town, and Zalia revelled in the expressions of joy and relief on the faces of the group she led into the half-forest, half-town. She might have started a war doing what she had done, but it was more than worth it for the people that they had saved.

CHAPTER FORTY-ONE

Good Morning

Zalia

Zalia awoke to soft purring sounds in the comfort of her own home. She had slept for a good half hour, longer than usual these days, and was ready for the coming weeks. The source of the purring was Boreal's children, sleeping in a puddle of fur nearby.

It was the day that Zalia expected the military seated to the council, Faian, as well as General Ballast, and Hildebrandt to arrive at Nature's Reclaim. She had sent for them the day after returning from her trip, knowing that they deserved to be informed of her actions. While she was not under their jurisdiction as such, she did have to live with them, and getting along was good for that continued relationship.

She stepped lithely out of bed, quickly, and more importantly quietly, getting dressed. Ember was still asleep in their bed and would be for many more hours still.

Boreal was awake, overlooking her children, apparently having nothing else to do. Zalia gave her a gentle scratch between the ears as she left the room, hearing another purr join the chorus at the action.

The freed slaves were settling in well, more than happy to contribute to the town in return for housing and food. The Ancient of Wisdom was already finding good use for the skills of the many Silver rankers, sending the mages and warriors to guard the walls and patrol the nearby area, while the craftsmen and merchants were put to work on whatever various tasks needed doing. Their powerful utility would be invaluable within the town, which, for the most part, held people of Bronze and Iron rank.

Zalia had spent a good amount of time thinking about what to do now that the town was running pretty self-sufficiently. In the early days, she had needed to resolve problems between the people and various animals living in the bounds and ensure everyone was properly housed and fed with the support of the Ancient of Wisdom—but that wasn't the case anymore.

The people living there had settled in, now used to their new life intermixing with animals. Where the Ancient of Wisdom had needed guidance when it was young, it now excelled at its tasks, quickly and efficiently allocating resources and labour where they were needed.

The idea to go to the Astar lands had partly been a result of this boredom, in addition to the many other valid reasons for the journey. She probably should have chosen something a little less fragile to spend her days doing, but what was done, was done.

For the first time in a very long time, Zalia didn't have anything to do.

When she had lived in the north of her old world, each day had been filled with the tasks necessary for survival. When she had come to this world, her time had been taken up figuring out what had happened to her and where she was. Once she had sort of figured *that* out, her time had been taken up by the demons' invasion of Endaria. Then had come the administration of Nature's Reclaim.

Now, she *might* have started a war out of boredom.

That was a bit of an overstatement, yet the idea wasn't entirely wrong.

There were definitely advantages they would get from having freed the people they had, however. With their combined knowledge, there was a lot they could learn about the Astar and how they functioned. Something, anything to help in the war that would have come either way.

She walked out of her home and down into the streets of town, nodding to people as she went. Aylie was out here somewhere, practicing her magic, and . . . delving into the astral or something. Zalia had noticed something different about Aylie after her time as a disembodied soul. Something just a little off.

The girl could be anywhere, though, so Zalia settled for a stroll through town.

She took an apple from a nearby stand, smiling at the owner setting it up as she went. Food was free for everyone in Nature's Reclaim, freely available to those who contributed to the town. The occasion in which she would need to remove someone from the town for not pulling their own weight had yet to come, and she hoped it never would. It was another point in humanity's favour, that they were able to live in this way if given the chance.

As she walked through town, she equipped her armour, feeling the increased sense of strength and mobility that came with it. She was greatly enjoying the new permanent rituals that could be imbued into its surface and often wore it just for the feeling, even though it probably scared a good few people, seeing her semi-transparent form walking around the town.

The rank up had been unexpected, as it was the first time any of her heir-looms had ranked up without the blessing of a god. She was looking to rank up the other two soon, if she could, hoping that they would advance to Silver rank now that she had been Silver for a while herself. Not that she could really force or train for that rank up like she could with abilities.

She recognised a few of the freed slaves as she went, a good few of them already awake despite the early hour. It wouldn't have surprised her if a few of them didn't need sleep either.

Most of them had decided to stay in Nature's Reclaim with her for a few different reasons. Some wanted to repay her for saving them, others yet just liked the look of the town. Not all of them decided to stay, however, having family or friends they wanted to find. Those were the ones that had been taken more recently than the others, the ones who still had a chance of finding friends or family. Some of the older slaves had been with the Astar for more than two hundred years—a mindboggling amount of time. Zalia couldn't imagine what it was like for them to come back to their home that wasn't really their home anymore.

Without any sort of destination in mind, Zalia found herself at the building that was both the home of the Ancient of Wisdom and a temple dedicated to Nateysta. Inside, she found many crows hopping around doing their various tasks, with the Ancient of Wisdom talking quietly to some type of lizard. She gave them both a respectful nod as she passed, making her way to one of the many altars bordering the room.

She found herself kneeling and giving prayer at the altar, trying to get in touch with Nateysta, known to her as Ro-ak.

"Hey, bud, I hope you're doing alright wherever you are. Thanks for sending Lumin to help, it got Aylie and Ember out of the Astar's grasp, along with many others. I wanted you to be here today for when Faian and others from the capital come to talk about that very thing. I feel that we'll be planning the future steps in regards to the Astar and know you will have some invaluable insight into the topic."

It only took a moment before Ro-ak replied.

"Zalia of the Druids, it is good to hear your thoughts again. I'm glad that you got them out. Do not worry, I know of this meeting already, I will be there."

She smiled, still finding the experience odd. Back in her old world, she hadn't been a religious person. It was kind of hard not to be in Endaria when the gods replied so . . . directly.

Walking out of the temple, she decided that she really needed to find a hobby. Maybe meditation?

As she pondered, a nearby vine started to wriggle around. It sprouted a branch that grew thicker, spreading out and upwards until the form of her friend, Ro-ak, appeared. It sat still as if it were a plant for just a moment before those infinite, beady black eyes blinked. Then the head turned and looked down at her.

"Hello, Zalia."

She blinked back. "When you said you would be here for the meeting, I kind of expected you to show up when the meeting was happening."

Ro blinked back at her. "The meeting *is* happening, in just a few moments."

Zalia looked around. "The others aren't even here yet."

Ro-ak tilted his head. "They will be, soon."

She sighed. "Ro, are you getting your time mixed up again? You realise they probably won't arrive for a few hours, right?"

Ro's nodded a sort of weird, jerky motion. "Yes, soon."

She gave a louder, more pointed sigh. "Alright, then, come on back to the house before people start to realise who you are."

Ro did join her as they quickly walked back home, and before long, people were starting to recognise Ro, his appearance similar to the various imagery of him around the town.

He had to shrink in size as she brought him through the normal-sized door to her house, guiding him to a sitting room with a fireplace in it. He settled like he was perching on the thick, soft leaf litter coating the floor.

"Ember will wake soon, so I'll be back in a bit. Do you want anything to eat?" Zalia asked.

Ro looked at her curiously.

"Never mind, forgot who I was talking to."

She left and went to their kitchen. It was a small room, both because it didn't need a pantry, fridge, or cooking implements due to its rare use. She had picked up a few things over the course of her walk and took them out now, using Natural Matter Alteration to prepare everything. There were thin slices of meat that she cooked to crunchy perfection using her heat manipulation, along with slices of different fruits that could be found in the town. She had also grabbed some fresh bread and cheese which she added to the plate.

Once everything was ready, she went upstairs to their room, creating a table and chair from the floor. She set the plate down, taking off a few bits of the meat and laying it temptingly near Boreal's children. Using a tiny ritual, she pushed the air around to waft the scent of food towards Ember.

Boreal's children awoke first, pouncing on the freshly cooked meat with abandon, their eyes still barely open. Ember woke not long after, blinking her eyes blearily.

"Hey, good morning."

"Mmmmghhh," Ember groaned as she stretched.

Zalia smiled, still waiting. "Sleep well?"

The resulting groan of protest against the world told her all she needed to know.

"Breakfast is ready when you are, and you should know that Ro appeared a little early for the meeting."

"He's here already?" The words were muffled by a blanket.

"Mhmm."

The young cats began to stretch and yawn, Pounce bapping Prance on the head for getting too close.

It took a few minutes for Ember to gather the energy to get up, and Zalia kept the meat and bread warm for her all the while.

They relaxed together as a family, Aylie coming in with Lumin shortly after Ember had gotten up. It was nice to just be there with them, an experience she had grown used to over the years.

Their morning was interrupted when a knock came at the door an hour later. When Zalia went to open it, she found Faian, General Ballast, and Hildebrandt waiting there.

Faian spoke up first.

"Hello, Zalia, you better have a good explanation for calling us here."

Zalia tapped twice on the doorframe with a knuckle.

"Good morning. Yeah, I do."

s

CHAPTER FORTY-TWO

Breaking News

Zalia

Zalia stood there as Faian, Hildebrandt, and General Ballast all stared at her incredulously.

They were in the living room of her house, Ro-ak also perched nearby. After a short greeting, Zalia had told them what she had done.

"You did *what?*" Faian asked.

She wasn't usually the type to get nervous when confronted, but she had definitely overstepped the original reason she had given for being near the Astar.

"Attacked their town and liberated a bunch of people, mostly because they found and captured Ember and Aylie. I do apologise for being the cause of this in the first place, but I won't apologise for doing what I had to do to save them."

General Ballast looked thoughtful as if considering the implications of the news, while Faian paced with obvious anxiety. Hildebrandt remained calm, a stone wall of a woman as always. She did eye Ro-ak every now and then, however.

"Tell me what you did, *exactly*, please," Faian said, trying to regain a semblance of sanity.

Zalia obligingly went through everything that happened in more detail, explaining the mist, how they had found the town, her infiltration of the place and then the capture of Ember and Aylie. She paused there for a moment, the anger at herself for what happened resurfacing again, before explaining what the mist creatures really were and the attack on the town. The fact that they had freed hundreds of slaves while simultaneously destroying a good portion of the town was the nail in the coffin of peace.

Faian had turned from anxious and angry to concerned, and thoughtful now too. What was done was done, and they needed to plan for the future.

"Okay, that will mean war in no uncertain measure. We are just going to have to figure out how to fight a war against them. It's not going to be like it was with the demons, a close-contact, bloody war. I have a feeling that isn't how the Astar play things."

Both Ballast and Zalia shook their heads, but it was Ro who spoke.

"They do not. You should expect strike teams of small but extremely powerful foes."

Ro was still staring into the fire, not looking at any of them as he spoke.

Zalia looked over at him inquiringly. "How do you know that?"

He finally turned to her. "I have been in talks with the other Ascendant beings here, the ones who remember times long past. Whether you might believe it or not, this is not the first time that events like these have happened. You will not be the only ones fighting a war here. The Astar have many Ascendants of their own who must be combated by the Ascendants of Endaria."

Ballast looked up at Ro. "The Ascendants of Endaria? I wasn't aware we had any."

"You do not. At least, not in the way you might be thinking. The gods of nature who live here are your Ascendants, and though they might be mostly unwilling to act against their nature, they will listen to me."

It was Faian's turn to gain interest in his words. "Why would they do that? Zalia told me that the starlight wolf once tried to get them to act and was unable."

"The starlight wolf is a powerful, guiding aspect of nature, it is true, but the others are powerful aspects of nature too. Scour of the Desert who destroys all unwary life without judgement. It of Heat and Stone, the bringer of heat who will nourish life but burn the unwary. Esser who rides the winds, ever free and never seen. These are the aspects of nature that live in Endaria and the lands surrounding it. The reason they will listen to me, Faian, is that I *am* nature."

Faian nodded slowly, looking like she barely understood but accepting the statement anyway.

Ballast spoke up as Faian considered.

"Alright, then, we go by what the nature bird says. With the Astar's powerful spacial magic, I can see why they would favour small but strong strike forces capable of taking out single targets. Get one or two Diamond rankers, send them on a spree across Endaria killing the leaders and important figures, and you have yourself a kingdom so unstable that it can't wage war any longer. It sounds like a terribly effective tactic, how do we counter it?"

A heavy silence encumbered the room.

"That . . . that's a terrible thought. I'm not even sure my anti-teleportation magic is capable of stopping a Diamond rank Astar. I know they have at least one of those, too."

Faian, who was looking paler by the second, snapped to Zalia, "How do you know that?"

Zalia shrugged. "Well, I did free all of those slaves. Many of them have had their aging stopped somehow and worked under the Astar for hundreds of years. One of the older ones said they had been to a bigger Astar city, perhaps their capital, and saw a Diamond rank Astar there. Just the one."

Faian put a hand to her forehead. "And here I was happy that we finally got the anti-teleportation protection in the capital up and running."

Hildebrandt put a reassuring hand on her shoulder. "Don't fear, that protection *is* important. If there really is a Diamond ranker amongst them, I'm not sure there is anything any of us can do, no matter their powerset. Not even me."

Zalia looked at Ro. "Surely you could stop a Diamond ranker?"

His big, leafy head shook in a jerking motion.

"No, Zalia, I could not. It isn't that I lack the power, it is the rules of interference that block me. In a fight that their Ascendants take part in, yes, I could do this. However, they won't be so stupid as to involve an Ascendant unless necessary as they have more strength in the pre-Ascendant ranks than you do. I could take part in the war with the demons as the thousand-eyed one killed an entire city of your people. This opened up avenues for both my and the starlight wolf's intervention. Here, however, they have only interfered once and I have already reacted to that."

"Why is it that they can interfere first but you cannot?"

"I can, I just choose not to. It is not wise to give your opponent the freedom to interfere as they wish without repercussion when there are other ways to solve the issue."

Zalia frowned. "So how did they interfere already? To do what?"

"To find your family in hiding, Zalia."

Flashes of her family being found by the Astar town went through her mind, the fear and pain of Ember and Aylie being taken. The Astar Ascendants had interfered to do *that*? She had thought Boreal's children had given their location away somehow.

"And you were able to react by sending Lumin to solve the issue."

"Yes."

"I'm confused about these rules. Why is Lumin able to act and not you? Why are there rules to your actions in the first place?"

"You already know the answer to this, I believe. Your wisdom is great enough to see this."

Zalia thought about it, really thought about it, and found she did know.

"Because if Ascendants could freely destroy and create as they wish, to interfere with the lives of the lower-ranked, then they would not be able to live their lives. In a war, Ascendants would just destroy the lower-ranked and nothing and no one would be left to even fight a war over. That's why Lumin is able to do what they want, too. Their power isn't that of other Ascendents anymore and may not be for a long time."

Ro nodded.

Faian spoke up, obviously thinking about other things still. "This is interesting, but there are more important matters to speak of. How do we plan for these supposed Astar strike teams? Other than informing the leaders and influential people to be wary of attacks, what can we *do*?"

Zalia had already been worrying about such things for a long time, ever since learning that it was possible the Astar were ferrying away the powerful people of the kingdom.

"I haven't figured out a good response to it yet. Anti-teleportation, localised *and* personal types, as well as being aware of the danger both help. I've been able to fight off Astar ambushes several times now. These have seemed like the weaker Astar, though, not the type that Ro is warning us of. Perhaps civilians or hopefuls attempting to prove their worth?"

She had rarely seen Faian so troubled, but being a leader of the council put her firmly in the court of the people the Astar would target.

"Well, whatever their skill, the issue is in the time frame with which they can get in and get out."

Ballast tapped his chin thoughtfully. "We should have at least one Silver rank member of the Morning's Shade or army protecting each of the council members at all times, as well as any other particularly important figures. In addition, we need to find a type of magic that each person can use to protect themselves against teleportation. Other than that, there isn't anything else we can do, is there? It's not like we can hide in a clump of fear until it all passes us by."

"I agree on both parts," Faian said.

Zalia pulled something out of her vault and handed it to Faian. One of her anti-teleportation armbands.

"These are a one-use protection against being teleported I designed in the Astar lands. I can mass-produce them since they're pretty easy to grow. Perhaps your enchanters can find a way to design something like this with more traditional materials, maybe even something that can be used more than once?"

Faian took it with thanks, inspecting it closely,

"Well, I don't understand how it works at all, but I'll have some people get on it."

She slipped it onto her arm, then looked up once more.

"Right, well, keep brainstorming on that front, as I'd like some more precautions we can take in regards to the strike forces of Astar. We do need to talk about what we're going to do about potentially striking first and bringing the war to the Astar. We will need to convene the council for this talk, though I would like to have you and Ro there, Zalia. You too, Hildebrandt."

Zalia nodded assent. "I would also recommend bringing a few of the people I freed from the Astar. Their knowledge will be invaluable. Ember, Aylie, and Boreal should come too, they know as much about the Astar as I do."

Faian and Ballast nodded agreement, then turned to Hildebrandt.

"Yeah, yeah, alright. I suppose I can't avoid getting more involved."

Zalia looked at each person in turn, but it seemed everyone had said their part.

"Alright, I guess that's all done then. There are a few of the freed people who don't want to stay here and are looking for family. Since most of the population moved to the capital, I wouldn't be surprised if they were there, if they're still alive. I'm sure these people would go with you and tell you what they know in payment for help finding their friends and family."

"Excellent idea."

Zalia gestured to the door, then tapped Ro on the wing. "I want to talk to you in private if you're happy to stick around for a bit, I'll be back after showing Faian out."

Ro dipped his head slightly, and Zalia led Ballast, Faian, and Hildebrandt to the exit, quickly running upstairs to tell Ember where she was headed before leaving.

She took Faian to the Ancient of Wisdom, who told them which of the freed people wanted to leave. After finding and talking to those people, most of whom agreed to Faian's offer, Zalia showed them to the town exit. Waving farewell to the group, she went back home to find Ro-ak with anger boiling in her veins.

He still stood where he had been, staring vacantly into the fire.

"Tell me, Ro, who the fuck is this Ascendant that would interfere to get my family killed."

CHAPTER FORTY-THREE

Seek Revenge on a God

Zalia

Ro turned to her, his deep, beady eyes filled with thought. "Are you sure you want to know who did this?"

"Yes." She stood, shoulders squared and anger boiling within. They would have succeeded in their stealth mission if it hadn't been for the intervention of whichever Ascendant had revealed them.

"It is the monarch of the Astar. The monarch is not Ascendant but is so close to being so that the rules of Ascendancy apply to them. They tread a thin line in their interventions, creating objects of power and giving information to their lessers that one who has properly ascended could not do. At the same time, I am allowed to tell you of them because of their not-quite-transgressions, yet they gain much. They balance these transgressions in . . . ways that I cannot speak of, yet still end up stronger for doing so."

"The *monarch* of the Astar? Does that mean that they were there that day?"

Ro shook his head. "No, they were not. They are the first in a long, long time to approach Ascendancy, at least from what the others tell me. When a being does this, it begins to form an aspect. For me, it was nature itself. Others you have seen—the stars for the starlight wolf for instance. This being has somehow managed to gain the Astar as their aspect. It gives them leeway that others do not get."

Zalia stared in annoyance. It was kind of hard to get revenge on a near-Ascendant being. "Great, so the Astar are led by, well, a god basically. Wonderful."

"It is not great, no."

"But you will be able to fight them, right?"

Ro paused.

"Perhaps. It depends on the events leading up to what will be the final fight. The monarch's powers are still limited in their form, whereas an Ascended's is unlimited within the realm of their aspect."

"Great," Zalia muttered.

"Do not fear, this is a problem for a later time. For now, you have things to do."

She sighed.

"Yeah, I guess I do."

Ro's form dried and shrivelled until disintegrating into a dust that drifted into the fire, which burnt brighter for just a moment. Used to the way that Ro abandoned his physical form when leaving, she wasn't concerned about the process.

She left the living room and went back upstairs to where her family was still relaxing, comfortable together.

"Hey," she greeted them sullenly.

Ember immediately caught on to her foul mood. "What's wrong? What happened?"

She sighed again. "Oh, just discovered that an Ascendant was the one that gave us away to the Astar, leading to your capture. Thankfully, that allowed Ro to send Lumin to us, which led to your being saved, but it still feels . . . unfair, as stupid as that sounds."

Ember came over and gave her a hug. "Well, at least we know it wasn't anything we did wrong, per se. Just got unlucky."

She hugged Ember back. "That's a good way of thinking about it."

The anger had left her, vanishing along with her sour mood at Ember's hug, a powerful soothing calm flowing over her. They pulled apart as Aylie spoke up

"Alright, so what do we do?"

Zalia tapped her leg, thinking. It was safe inside the town bounds of Nature's Reclaim, excluding the case of a high-rank Astar attacking. There wouldn't be anything they could do in that case anyway, so it wasn't worth taking into account.

"Inside the town is as safe as it gets. We stay here when possible. Outside of the town boundary, we go in groups of two or more at all times. Also, wear the anti-teleportation bands at all times. We're going to be joining the council for a conversation about what happens now, then we'll decide what we're going to do. For now, think about whether you all actually want to join in on this war or not. We all remember what last time was like."

That brought a stillness to everyone except for Boreal's children. They weren't entirely unaware of the possible impacts of such a thing anymore, having experienced true conflict for the first time just recently.

Ember's calming aura spread over everyone and they all relaxed once more.

Boreal looked at her children, concern flashing through the bond Zalia shared with her. She knew exactly what was passing through her friend's mind, as she'd had the same thoughts when bringing Aylie into the war with the demons. Well, the war had come to them, but it had been her choice to keep them all in the kingdom rather than staying in the north or fleeing to the south.

The young ones, though, would have a choice whether they stayed here in safety—even travelling through the portal in the desert might keep them safer—or, they could come with them to the Astar lands to wage war . . . if that's what the council ended up deciding in the end.

Her personal preference would be to get involved, as it wouldn't be fair if she didn't after possibly starting the damn thing, but she'd rather not be a part of the large fights. She would better serve their side of the war by doing other things, like infiltration and targeted attacks.

"Well, I'm getting involved," Aylie said. "They decided they had the right to separate my soul from my body, to separate Ember's soul from her body, to separate thousands of people's souls from their bodies for *hundreds of years*! I can't let that go. This isn't about taking their land or stealing their riches. This is about survival, pure and simple."

Zalia nodded slowly, in agreement with her. She would prefer to keep Aylie, to keep all of them out of it. Realistically, that wouldn't happen.

Lumin stood by her, obviously in agreement with the one who was blessed with the power of the stars. Lumin's power.

"Alright, I won't stop you. We have to be careful about this, though, there are many powers beyond us in this conflict."

They all gave their agreement to that.

"Alright, family meeting adjourned! We'll be setting off to the capital in an hour or two, so everyone get ready to go. All of us should be there for this meeting."

Aylie immediately left the room, and Ember gave Zalia a look. She nodded and went after Aylie, catching her in the entrance to the house.

"Hey, are you doing alright? We haven't really had a chance to talk since getting back."

Aylie searched her eyes for a moment, then looked down at the floor. "Yeah, I'm alright. I won't say it's been easy. I felt so helpless, so . . . violated when they separated my soul. It's unnatural, cruel, and downright evil."

Zalia nodded a few times, standing with open body posture. "I imagine it was. I was pretty scared for you two for a good while there. Hey, you seem different since then. Did something happen to you while you were separated? Why is it that you could talk to me while Ember couldn't?"

Aylie was still looking at the ground, chewing on her lower lip. "I think it was because of my astral ability. Since part of my soul already lives there, maybe it was more used to the experience? Or . . . more capable of existing there, perhaps. I don't think souls are usually meant to be on the astral. They exist somewhere else, the Astar just somehow managed to pull the soul from wherever it usually lives within the body and expel it into the astral."

"That makes sense, I suppose. Was there anything else you noticed while you were there? I can see something about you that lingers, something that Ember or the other freed people don't have."

Aylie shrugged. "Not that I know of."

Zalia kept the frown from her face. Aylie was lying to her, she just didn't know why or what about.

"Alright, if you need to talk about it though, I'm always here, okay?"

Aylie nodded, and Zalia just gave her a single reassuring hug before letting her walk off. She was allowed to have her own secrets, of course, Zalia just wished it didn't worry her so damn much.

Ember found her still standing in the door and grabbed onto her arm, leaning into her.

"She's alright, I think. Hiding something from us, but alright."

"I'm sure she'll tell us if it's important," Ember reassured.

Zalia nodded faintly, still worried. "I know, I just wish that none of this had to happen. I wish the Astar would leave us be, that we could live in peace with them."

She felt Ember's agreement through the bond, louder than words spoken.

"Parenting is hard."

Ember snorted. "Said no one ever," she said sarcastically.

Zalia poked her in the nose for the sarcasm and stood up straight. "Need anything for the trip?"

Ember shook her head.

"Alright, I'm sure Boreal will get the young ones ready, which means we have an hour or two on our hands."

Ember smiled. "That we do."

An hour and a half later, they left Nature's Reclaim with the entire family in tow. Zalia knew the trip would take much longer than it usually did for her, as the slower young ones were with them, but still helped speed up the journey using her flight ability.

Flight - passive.

Tin - Your manoeuvrability is increased and your air resistance is reduced while in flight. This scales based on the rank and level of this passive.

Iron - Your ability to perceive your surroundings while flying becomes exceptional. You can spot distant details and potential threats with remarkable clarity, allowing you to anticipate and counteract aerial assaults effectively as well as see threats on the ground.

Bronze - All flight-based abilities are easier and cheaper to maintain. This effect increases based on how many allies you also give flight to.

Silver - You are an expert in flight and may maintain flight abilities on yourself indefinitely. This is the maximum level of this passive.

With the Bronze rank effect and Silver rank Wisdom, she was able to maintain the flight on the larger number of people for a much longer time than before. She still remembered when they had made that journey up to Glemp's home with just herself, Ember, Aylie, and Boreal. It had been a long trip and was made all the longer by her inability to maintain flight on them all. Now, however, she was able to maintain it on all nine of them for a few hours at a time. They had to walk for ten-to-fifteen-minute stretches while her mana replenished, but it wasn't so bad.

The young ones *loved* flight. Normally super energetic and chaotic, as one might expect, the five small cats zipped around and about the more stable group of adults. They zoomed out and about, flying in closer to land on top of Boreal or Ember for a moment—though never Zalia—before jumping off and dashing away again. They managed to keep this up for hours at a time, their movement powered by Zalia's magic rather than their own bodies.

Despite that, they quickly ran out of energy as the day passed and stopped to rest. Zalia had seen the small forms of Faian and their group below only a few hours into their trip but didn't mind getting there earlier than them. She wanted to go see Larel, hoping that the woman would be in the capital. She hadn't ever properly thanked her for freeing them from the jail years ago, when the kingdom-scale ritual to summon the demons had gone off.

Zalia still had the piece of paper describing Juniper's part of that ritual and was starting to understand it the more she delved into teleportation magic. She had hopes that if she got the chance to study more Astar spacial magic, she might even be able to figure out a way to get to and from Cormaine. It was important to Ro that they get back that world someday, perhaps even reuniting the two sister worlds and giving the Bathar their real home back.

These thoughts made the day-and-a-half journey zip by as they flew and occasionally walked all the way there, with only a single stop to sleep on the way.

Arriving in the capital, she greeted the two Morning's Shade members who came up to identify them, and then flew to the castle at the top, intent on finding Larel.

CHAPTER FORTY-FOUR

Meet and Greet

Zalia

After receiving directions to Larel's location from the civilian seated to the council, it took a while to find the woman. She was still a part of the Morning's Shade, which was now an official policing force under the civilian council's control—the counterpart to the army, which the military half of the council led.

Larel was a Gold rank fist and ice magic fighter. She was one of the only Gold rankers in the organisation, the kingdom, even. With a specialty in ramping damage and quick speed, she was uniquely good at taking down single, slow targets that could take massive amounts of damage. That wasn't to say she wasn't dangerous outside of situations like that, any Gold ranker was. It was more to say that Zalia had seen this woman take down a Gold rank elemental by herself while she was only Silver rank, and that was *not* something anyone could do. Zalia doubted even she would be able to do that.

Being both quick and dangerous, the council often had tasks for her that were on the edges of Endaria. More than anything else, this included taking down high-rank threats that were approaching their borders and protecting the smaller border towns that lived on the edges of their civilisation. Zalia sometimes envied her in the work, until she remembered that she could and often *did* do the same thing.

She had looked for the woman the last few times that she'd come to the capital and was pleasantly surprised to find her in a tavern, one that belonged to a man she remembered. It was Harrick, the Gold rank chef with a brewer specialisation that Ember often went to for drinks during the days spent in the war camp that had been east of Nature's Reclaim. That was now a small town in its own regard, founded by the people who had stayed behind after the army left to reclaim the capital.

"Harrick!" Ember exclaimed, walking past Zalia and giving the man a hug.

"Ho! Ember, good to see your face once more. And Zalia! Our saviour and the hero of Endaria. Is that the ever curious and hungry Boreal I see behind you?"

Zalia stepped aside as Boreal padded up and sat politely in front of the man. Her young ones, however, were not so polite. Seeing Ember hug the man, they approached warily. Smelling the delicious aroma that often followed the Gold rank chef, they swarmed him.

"Oh my, good gods, you've multiplied!"

Zalia chuckled as he desperately searched for something to satiate the hunger shining in the young cats' eyes and turned to search the tavern.

It was much, much larger than the previous establishment the man had owned, which had been a small affair in the war camp. The place held a dozen or so large, round tables each with eight or nine chairs around it. Where the previous tavern he had owned had been mostly empty at the time Zalia had visited, this one was packed. There must have been half the city's Silver rank population in the room, many sitting in big groups with three or four extra chairs from nearby tables pulled over, while there were some more solitary people amongst the crowds.

Zalia spotted the twins, a powerful duo who used combined magic that often hit with a power that was a rank above their own, and gave them a single acknowledging nod.

She also spotted various other Morning's Shade members amongst the people there and realised that in truth, the majority of them were from the organisation.

Harrick moved around behind the island along one edge of the room that served as his bar and found some dried meat snacks for the young cats, and Zalia finally spotted Larel as she came out from a door behind the bar. She quirked her head at the woman, confused as to what she had been doing behind there, until she gave Harrick a hug and a fond kiss.

They were together, apparently.

"Larel! Larel!" Zalia called over the din of the tavern.

She turned towards where Zalia called her name and spotted her, waving as she approached, lithely sidestepping the many cats along her path. "Zalia! Hey, long time no see."

Zalia accepted her proffered hug and followed the woman to a nearby table next to the bar that was mercifully empty. Ember and Aylie joined her while Boreal oversaw the young cats' joint harassment of Harrick.

"I hope you're doing well," Ember said in greeting once they were sat down.

Larel gave a bright smile. "I sure am! Life couldn't be better."

Zalia found it a little strange but mostly cute that the two Gold rankers, probably the only two in the city, had found each other.

"And you?" Larel asked before turning to Aylie. "And Aylie, right? You've grown . . . a lot."

Aylie gave an obliging smile and greeting. "Oh we're doing pretty good, all things considered."

Larel snapped her fingers. "Oh! Right, I did hear you lot were going to find the Astar. How did *that* go?"

Zalia almost winced, watching Aylie to make sure she was okay. The teenager didn't visibly react.

Ember spoke up, answering, "It went . . . terribly in some ways, excellent in others. You'll probably be invited to the meeting when Faian gets back to town. We'll explain then."

Larel nodded, some of the cheerful enthusiasm fading for just a second, showing concern.

"You've been out of town a lot this past year, Larel, what have you been up to?" Zalia asked, changing the subject.

"Oh! Well, this and that. For the most part, I've been dealing with stray elementals that hadn't been destroyed or gone back to sleep after the war. There were quite a few outside our borders that wandered in from time to time, causing trouble. Most recently, though, I've been investigating that demon you lot killed up north, you know, the strange one?"

Ember nodded and Aylie smiled, memories of her victory that day probably flashing through her mind.

"Yeah, weirdest thing. I couldn't figure out how it was killed until Faian told me Aylie had done it with some kind of dream magic. Seems like a strong ability, that one. Anyway, I haven't found any other demons like it since, so I'm hoping it was a one-of-a-kind mutation maybe? It's hard to tell, what with most of the demon dens having been hunted to extinction by now."

Zalia nodded. With the Morning's Shade and the army regularly destroying discovered demon dens, they were getting less and less common. She figured it wouldn't be long until the things were gone from Endaria entirely, with only the odd few outside their borders. They wouldn't survive long out there, though, with how dangerous some of the wildlife got. Hell, the bunnies in the north could probably take out a den with how savagely aggressive they were.

"Sounds fun! You must be travelling nicely along towards Emerald rank doing that kind of thing day in, day out," Zalia replied.

Larel wagged her hand side to side in a "maybe" gesture. "Kind of. Quick for the rank, I suppose, but still taking *forever*. It is going to be a while yet before I catch up to Hildebrandt. Though, with how much time she spends tending her garden and cooking on that barbeque of hers, I think I'll catch up eventually."

Harrick chimed in from the bar, where he was trying to remove Prance from his shoulders. "Nothing wrong with settling in and taking your time with these things, dear."

Larel rolled her eyes but the smile on her face showed that she took it in stride. "Oh, you know me, I couldn't slow down even if I tried. I'm just too quick."

Zalia laughed as Harrick finally managed to lift Prance down, only for Rush to appear on his shoulders, stealing the piece of dried meat from the hand he was holding away from Prance.

"That's a lot of cats, Zalia, how do you deal with it?" Larel asked.

Zalia gestured to Boreal who was looking *tired*. "Seeing Boreal deal with all the things she put me through lends me endless energy."

Larel and Ember laughed, and even Aylie gave a small chuckle.

"I feel for her," Harrick said.

Boreal looked at him approvingly, and as he managed to get Rush down, she lightly bapped Pounce on the head as she tried to jump up to his shoulders too.

With some effort, she managed to herd the five teen cats to the table, under which they proceeded to play-fight. Zalia felt her feet and legs being run into or pounced on with regularity and knew the others were suffering similar fates. Boreal, who was absolutely massive, sat at the table, now taller than any of the sitting people.

Larel leaned sideways to look down at Boreal's claws, then back up and to Zalia. "You know, when you showed up to the Morning's Shade a Tin ranker with a kitten, I really didn't expect you to end up here. I didn't expect to end up here myself either, to be honest."

Zalia shrugged. "Shit happens, I guess. I never properly thanked you for freeing us from the prison that day Larel, so, thank you."

It was Larel's turn to shrug. "You would have done the same, and as a result, you spent a long time down there in Cormaine. Then you came back and proceeded to give us the means to win the war through Nateysta. I think you've repaid my actions many times over."

Zalia was going to protest but Ember nudged her.

"She's right, you know."

Zalia grumbled a bit, but accepted it.

"Alright, alright. Still, you took a risk on freeing us and I'm glad you did."

"So am I," Larel agreed, giving a wide smile.

They spent the next hour talking companionably while the young cats slowly ran out of energy. Eventually, Zalia and her family left Larel there with fond farewells, though they would probably see each other later that day or the next for the meeting anyway.

Zalia took them all up to the keep on top of the hill and was given a space where they could all relax and wait until the meeting happened. It would be another four or five hours until the generals and Hildebrandt made it back, and they had nothing to do until then.

They spent the time productively, Zalia showing the others how she made the anti-teleportation armbands. She wanted to have quite a few of them ready and spent the next hours mass-producing them. These would go to the council, as it was important that they have some type of protection as soon as possible.

The hours passed and Faian, Ballast, and Hildebrandt arrived at the keep, surprised to find Zalia and her family already there and settled in.

They came back an hour later to tell her the meeting would be the following day, so their family was given rooms to sleep in.

The next day came, Zalia having spent the entire night making armbands for the council. Ready for the meeting and ready to finally do something about the Astar, they left the often disruptive younger cats with an aide and made their way to the council chamber. They had seats on the outskirts and settled in for the long haul, hoping that some of the council members would have good ideas for what, exactly, they were meant to do about this.

CHAPTER FORTY-FIVE

Declaration

Zalia

Zalia sat waiting in the council room as murmurs and chatter filled the space. They were waiting for a final civilian member to turn up, as they couldn't be found. She could see that the waiting was making Faian anxious—she probably wanted to get underway as soon as possible.

The council room seemed a lot more packed than she was expecting, with a lot more people fitting into the space than the twenty-two council members. There were various scribes and attendants whose jobs were to record and hold relevant information, or to obtain needed items. In addition to them, there was the group Zalia sat amongst. This seating contained herself, Ember, Aylie, Hildebrandt, Larel, and a dozen or so other people, a large majority of them Bathar. Boreal and Lumin were also nearby, though both were too big to sit in the chairs. She knew that Ro would be joining them once the meeting started as well.

A man came up and said something to Faian, who then gestured to the civilian seated to the council, the counterpart to her own position. They walked over and began whispering back and forth in a quick manner. After a few words, the civilian nodded, and Faian walked over to one of the people at the edge of the room. A few more words were passed before Faian turned to the room, raised her hands, and called for order. After a few seconds, everyone quieted.

"Welcome, everyone, and sorry for the delay. Seated Jish and I have decided that we shall start this emergency meeting without the presence of Councilman Tillman. His associate, Hav, will be filling in for him during this meeting, an accommodation previously agreed to under the rulings of the council, emergency meeting subsection."

No one argued against her proclamation as everyone took their places. There were twenty seats divided into two half-circle sections facing each other towards the centre of the room, with a large circular space in the middle that had a raised platform for speaking members. Behind each set of ten wooden seats was a higher-up stone seat in which Faian and Seated Jish took their places.

As soon as everyone was in their place, Faian stood up and went to the centre of the council members, stepping up on the raised section.

"I have called this emergency meeting after receiving some troubling news from a noble amongst our nation. Zalia, whom all of you know as the woman who was integral in saving Endaria, undertook a journey to the Astar lands. There, she found one of their towns amongst a mist in which hundreds of Endarians were held captive, used as slaves. During this infiltration, members of her family were caught, then promptly freed with . . . due diligence. In this attack on the Astar, many of the other slaves held in that town were freed from their bonds and have been brought back here."

There was a stunned silence amongst the council members as Faian spoke, not even a whisper to be heard.

"The information gathered in this mission has brought upon us questions that require answers. Our main point of talk this day is what we must do in retaliation for the hundreds of years the Astar have been secretly taking away our people, the high-ranked amongst us, for use as labour. We must also discuss how we plan to defend ourselves from such future incursions."

This finally caused an outburst of chatter as council members spoke over one another to ask more of Faian. She waited patiently as they spoke, obviously not of a mind to reward their disorderly manner.

Zalia had expected a disciplined council of members who made their points with order, yet this reminded her more of the type of politics that happened back in her old world.

The abrupt chaos of voices eventually silenced as Faian waited with hands raised.

"Please, we must work through this with order. We shall start with the easier decision. What is it that we shall do about their continued abduction of our people? Zalia is here with us today and can answer some questions and even has something that may help in this regard, if you will allow her to speak?"

Zalia jumped, not realising that Faian had been expecting her to talk in front of the council, but a vote was cast and they agreed to let her speak. Trying to hide her anxiety, she stood and stepped onto the raised section as Faian took her seat once more.

"Um, thank you for letting me speak today."

She looked around at the circle of eyes, swallowing her nervousness.

"The Astar are powerful wielders of spacial magic. Each member of their race is capable of using this type of magic from my experience, which raises both an issue and an obvious path to a solution. My town of Nature's Reclaim and the city we stand in both now have anti-teleportation safeguards in place. This is an important protection but one we will need to implement across Endaria. We should also look to providing individuals with this type of protection."

At this, she took one of the armbands she had been making out of her vault and held it up for everyone to see.

"This is a temporary solution I have designed for the problem, a one-use armband that a wearer can push a little bit of magic into to activate. It stops an instance of teleportation and gives the wearer some time to react to the Astar. Unfortunately, it isn't super effective, as the Astar are quick with their magic. I fear if we rely on these, they shall find a way around them quickly."

As she arrived at the end of her speech, questions began flooding in from the people around her.

"How many of these armbands can you make each day?"

"Who authorised you to go into the Astar lands?"

"How did you free the people from the Astar town?"

"Who gave you the right to start a war on our behalf?"

At that question, Zalia spun to face the speaker. "Start a war? Did you not hear what Faian said? They have been taking the Endarian people for *hundreds of years*. What do you want to do, sit around and wait for them to take you next? What about Hildebrandt or Larel? I might have been the catalyst in this reaction, but as far as anyone knows, they have been treating your nation as cattle since your nation has been around, and will continue to do so as long as we don't do something!"

At the words, Zalia realised how strongly she felt about this. She had been pushing the problem to the back of her mind ever since she had found out about it, not wanting to think about the thousands of people taken by the Astar, even people she knew. Matthias had probably been taken by them, Indis may have been taken by them. Maybe, deep down, she had gone to the Astar lands specifically to bring the problem to the nation's attention, front and centre.

"Before I left to scout the Astar lands, a group of Astar showed up at my town and tried to take me. Two Astar have *already* fucking abducted me once. If you want to ignore the problem and sit here, do so, but I'm not being a part of it."

She left the centre of the chamber and considered leaving the room entirely before taking her seat at the edges.

The council chamber was in silence once more, and Faian took the centre.

"Now that Zalia has shown you a possible path to a defence against the Astar, and perhaps shown you the seriousness of the matter at hand today, we shall move on to the next question at hand. Before we do so, however, I urge you, once this meeting is done, we must find ways to counter the Astar's use of this powerful spacial magic."

Zalia started to regret her outburst, just a little, though not because of the impact it had on the council members. She had just been thinking about how little order and control the members had, as shown by their constant yelling of questions, yet the nervousness and pressure of the situation had gotten to her quickly.

Faian kept speaking.

"Alright, our next point today is to decide whether we should consider this as war and what we should do about the problem. I think we can agree that simply hiding in our cities is not enough."

What followed was a chaotic argument about whether to consider the Astar's actions worthy of war or not. There were people on both the civilian and military sides of the council that argued against considering it war, the years of fighting against the king and the invasion of Endaria still fresh on their minds. Eventually, when arguments began to repeat and no progress was being made, a vote was called. It was close, but it was decided that they were officially at war with the Astar, with eleven for it and nine against. Neither Seated Faian or Seated Jish got votes unless there was a tie.

Zalia could see that they held power in other ways, however. Faian was running this meeting, as she was the one who called it, which meant she got to decide on which matters were voted for and when things would move on. Jish was barely involved in the meeting at all, though, only adding bits and pieces to the conversation.

Once this decision was made, they moved on to what would be done.

Here, Jish started to contribute more, and it was decided that teams from the Morning's Shade would be sent to discover more about the Astar. They now knew where at least one of the Astar towns was and might be able to find more out that way. Faian informed them all that one of the Astar cities was underground, information Zalia had shared with her.

It was also decided that invasion would wait until they gathered more information. They did agree, however, that attacking some of the Astar cities would be needed eventually. Their options to stop the Astar actions were either to destroy them entirely, a course of action that no one seemed particularly enthusiastic about, or to force the Astar into a treaty by way of overwhelming force. The issue was that they didn't know if they would be able to do *either* of those things.

A recess was finally called after what felt like four or five hours to Zalia. Larel immediately sought her out and started hounding her for answers.

"When did this all happen?" she asked.

"A few days ago."

"And—"

Zalia interrupted her with a raised hand. "Larel, please, if you do want to know what happened, both Hildebrandt and Faian know." She saw Faian walking up to them as she said this and turned to greet her.

"Zalia, I'm sorry about that. I appreciate you standing up to talk, anyway."

Zalia shrugged. "Probably should have expected it."

Faian nodded approvingly. "Either way, you're free to go now. There will be a lot of endless arguments now, and I'm sure you have better things to do."

That brought a smile to Zalia's face. She hadn't been looking forward to more of the council meeting. "Thanks, I appreciate it."

"No, thank you."

As Zalia began to walk away with her family, Faian called out.

"Oh, and please don't go starting any more wars, would you?"

Zalia laughed. "Oh, don't worry. I'm quite done causing problems, I think."

At that moment, a bloodied man came to a stumbling stop at the door to the castle, with guards chasing after him.

CHAPTER FORTY-SIX

Towards the Future

Zalia

Zalia reacted immediately, focusing Healing Presence on the man. He stood up a bit straighter but already seemed uninjured.

The guards came running up as Faian raised a hand.

"Don't worry, we will take this from here."

Still alert, Zalia checked the skies and positioned herself close to the rest of her family. Ember stepped forward to check on the man with her Diagnosis ability.

"Who did this to you?"

The man shook as fear passed across his expression. "Th—the Astar, they attacked us. Councilman Tillman, he's . . . he's dead."

Faian stepped forward to grab the man's shoulder. "Dead? How?"

Zalia wanted to interrupt Faian and allow the man some room but his next words stopped her.

"A Gold rank. Appeared next to us and . . . and *slaughtered* them. I . . . I ran. I saw the monster and ran. That's the only reason I survived. Oh gods, I was meant to protect him . . . oh gods. What can I do against something like that?"

He dropped to his knees, tears streaking his face.

Zalia could see Ember's abilities going to work, healing the fresh emotional wound. It would be most effective straight after an event like this, guiding a traumatic memory to a less painful place was easier when it wasn't scarred over by time.

Faian crouched down next to the man and grabbed his face with her hands, careless of the tears and blood mixing there, and raised his eyes to look at her.

"You did good, you hear me? You survived, and you got this to us. We can help. Tell me, where did this happen?"

"I . . . I . . ."

His eyes dropped again, but Faian tightened her grip.

"Where, soldier!?"

He looked up, the firmness of Faian's tone and Ember's emotional healing both helping him work towards his next words. "Outside the city to the north. We . . . we were back from helping a town up north. We were so close to safety . . . so close."

Faian looked at Zalia with a question in her expression.

Zalia nodded. She went and found Hildebrandt, bringing her up to speed on what had just happened as quickly as she could. Hildebrandt agreed to come with, and after giving Ember a promise that she would be safe, Zalia used the flight ritual on Hildebrandt.

They soared out of the city on winds summoned by Zalia to make their journey quicker. She should have guessed that something had happened to the councilman when he hadn't shown for the meeting, but Faian hadn't seemed worried. They had probably been told he left to help whichever town he had gone to up north and hadn't been concerned about it.

This was off for the Astar, a change in how they acted. Usually, they kidnapped the people they targeted, intending to use them as slaves. Killing the councilman was different.

How had that man gotten away?

As it occurred to her that he said a Gold rank Astar had attacked, a thought came to her. The man had somehow escaped from a Gold rank Astar?

"It might be a trap."

She sent the thought to Hildebrandt, who looked at her and nodded.

There were only two reasons they wanted that man to get away. It was either a message to the council of Endaria, or it was a trap for whoever they sent to investigate.

Zalia put her armour on and swerved in the air to give Hildebrandt an anti-teleportation bracelet, though she probably wouldn't need one. It was highly unlikely that anyone would ever get close enough to teleport Hildebrandt, even a Gold ranker.

They flew high, using Zalia's incredible eyesight to scout the ground until she saw a patch of deep red just off to their left. She banked in that direction, Hildebrandt following as she noticed. Zalia's heart beat harder as they dipped from the sky, and the details of what they were about to see became clearer.

She landed amongst what could only be called a massacre.

It wasn't the first time she had seen things like this, but there were a few key differences here. Where an animal might tear something or someone limb from limb in a rough and violent war, the people here looked like they had been carefully chopped into pieces. Each cut that had severed a limb, head or bisected a torso was made with perfecting precision, a clean, smooth slice.

"Fuck." She looked back at Hildebrandt.

"Yeah, that's a pretty good assessment."

They stood in silence for a moment, both still on guard for an attack.

"Which one is the councilman?" Zalia asked, gaze shifting from one mixed body part to the next.

Hildebrandt just shook her head, unsure.

"Should I bury them?" Zalia asked.

"I don't know, can you see anything that might give us a hint to where the Astar went?"

It was Zalia's turn to shake her head. "No, I've never seen one walk on the ground, and even if there were tracks, they would disappear when they teleport away. It's impossible to track them now."

"Do your thing, then."

Zalia stored a mental image of the scene, then began roiling the earth using Natural Matter Alteration until the scene had vanished into the ground. Going off a whim, she pulled some stone from the ground and formed it into a gravestone with the words, "Here lies Councilman Tillman and his retinue."

She didn't even know any of the other people's names.

"There's nothing else to see here."

They turned and took flight again, leaving the fresh patch of earth behind.

When they returned to the capital, Faian was waiting for them. Zalia gave her as many details as she could, even going so far as to send the mental image she had stored when asked. Without more information about the Astar who had done this or any kind of lead towards them, there wasn't really anything they could do.

Zalia watched as, with spirits low, the council all reconvened in the chamber to continue their talks with this new event hanging over their heads. She had a feeling that the amount of arguing would be lessened now that the council members had a better idea of the dangers they faced, not only to the nation but to them personally.

She left, taking up Faian's offer of freedom from the talks. Without anything else to do until it was over, she found the rest of her family, and they left the castle grounds at the top of the hill, making their way down into the city proper.

They wandered for a while, the scene of the massacre weighing heavily on Zalia's mind.

The implications of being at war with the Astar weighed on her too, the realisation that soon enough, they very well might be deep within the kind of death, pain, and misery that had come with the last war. She tried to steel her mind and push past those thoughts, but they always came back around.

While not worried about herself in the coming conflict, she *was* worried about her family. It wouldn't take much for one of the young ones to be killed, and it wouldn't take much more for Aylie or Ember to be killed either. While they were higher rank, they were still vulnerable to something like a Gold rank Astar ambush. They might stand a chance against such an attack altogether as Boreal, Ember, and herself were all quite strong Silver rankers, but it would not end up well for them otherwise.

Eventually, a message came to her mind from one of the telepaths that the council kept. They made their way back up the hill to the castle there and reentered the grounds to find Faian.

"Well?" Ember asked once they found her.

"Proceedings were much quicker once they learnt of Councilman Tillman's fate. The members protesting against the war were a little more compliant once they realised what was at stake. We nailed down some details and have decided that we don't want to take any other actions for now. We will wait on the Morning's Shade to bring us more intel."

Zalia felt restless, ready to act. "And us? What are we supposed to do?"

"You? Well, if you are still willing to listen to what I have to say in this regard, then please, stay home, keep your town safe, and do some research into further protections against the Astar. We'll contact you if there is a task we need that we think only you can do, but for now, it is best that you don't cause any more . . . warnings from the Astar."

The words made Zalia flinch like she had been struck. The scene flashed through her mind as she realised, yes, it had most likely been her actions that had caused Councilman Tillman's death.

She nodded, not having the will to argue against what Faian had said, nor the grounds upon which to form an argument. It had been her actions that had put her family in danger, and the death of Councilman Tillman was the result of her freeing them. She couldn't be held responsible for the actions of the Astar, but she *had* been the one to kick that particular nest.

"I assure you that I won't be doing anything like that again. I think I've learnt to be a little more wary of the Astar after everything that's happened. I let my anger at what they were doing to the people of Endaria get the better of me, but I should have realised that the very people that were treating us like cattle wouldn't allow the cattle to fight back without responding."

Faian looked at her, eyes flicking back and forth as she inspected Zalia's. Then she sighed.

"It's not entirely your fault. This was bound to happen sooner or later. Who's to say we would be more prepared for this fight further down the line than we are now. The Astar might have just picked us off one by one until we weren't able to fight at all. We are stronger for the number of people you freed, at least. The past is the past, we need to look to the future now."

"That we do. I'm sorry, Faian, and thank you. I'll be ready when you need me."

She received only a nod in response, and with a quick ritual, Zalia and her family took to the skies.

They coasted out of the city and towards home. Concerned at the anger she could feel coming from Ember, Zalia sent a thought. *"Are you alright?"*

Ember looked over at her. *"I'm fine."*

Zalia exhaled deeply into the rushing wind. *"You forget I can feel what you feel. What is it?"*

There was no response for a moment.

"I just feel like she put the blame for the Astar's actions solely at your feet. That isn't fair, considering that they already *covered Endaria in demons without provocation. You aren't to blame for this, the Astar are. It's their . . . greed, or xenophobia, that is the cause of this. Whatever reason they have for doing what they do."*

Zalia thought on that and found that while Ember was right, she still could have handled the situation much better. What if she had spent some months working with the council on protections against the Astar instead of rushing off to collect information, only to get some of her family captured and have to start a war to free them? Endaria could be much better prepared, each city protected against the Astar's particular form of attack. Instead, they would have to play catch-up. Though, they did have years to prepare for this.

Still deep in thought, Zalia didn't respond yet as her mind turned to what would come next. It would be a tense few days, weeks, or months until the fighting started for real.

"You're right, but I'm not blameless. It's as she said, though, what's done is done. I'm not worried about being blamed. We must find a way to protect Aylie and the little ones. They might not like it, but their safety comes first."

She caught Ember's eyes and received a nod. They were in agreement in that.

As they flew towards Nature's Reclaim, Zalia heard a voice, Ro's voice, in her mind.

"We must talk."

CHAPTER FORTY-SEVEN

Exile

Zalia

Zalia stood in front of her house as Ro grew from the plants around her, with vines drooping from trees and sprouting wings, and thick trunk legs pushing out from the earth between. Soon, Ro stood at his full height before her.

"Alright, what is it? And why weren't you at the council meeting?"

His voice came to her mind again, no words spoken aloud.

"I have been contacted by an Astar wishing to meet you."

Zalia froze, staring. *"And why the hell would I do that?"*

Ro's form shrank until he fit through the door into her house, stepping past her and finding a nice place to perch before her ever-burning fire. Zalia followed him in.

"You know of the Astar exiles, I saw the slave you freed inform you of them."

She sat down heavily on the couch there, mind racing. *"Yes, but why would they want to speak to me?"*

Ro sat for a time, his deep black eyes unreadable. *"The Astar are not cold, calculating, and egotistical by nature, Zalia. It is their society that forms them this way by exiling any who would show emotion, particularly empathy, towards anyone or anything. It is their monarch that makes these rules, pushes them to fight amongst themselves in a scramble for power. It appears a group of those exiles saw what you did in freeing those slaves and wants to meet you, perhaps even work with you."*

"I don't know, Ro, I don't think I can trust any Astar. It feels wrong."

Ember came in and sat next to Zalia. "Alright, what are you two secretly talking about now? Remember, you promised Faian you wouldn't make any more trouble, Zalia."

Zalia nodded absently, still considering. "Apparently, a group of the exile

Astar saw what we did and wants to meet me, perhaps work with me . . . towards what, Ro?"

"They wish to overthrow the monarch and restore the Astar to be a better people. The memories of the Astar are long, their lives near endless. The Astar that spoke to me told of a time when they helped raise the ones around them, long, long ago. I believe he was ancient, perhaps even older than I."

That surprised Zalia, as surely anyone that was as old as Ro would be Ascendant by now, thus rendering them unable to interfere in the way it appeared they were.

"How did this Astar find you, Nateysta?" Ember asked.

"I used a little bit of my power in helping send Luminescence to you, and they saw this. They are old enough to know of most of the Ascendants that live here and were intrigued by a new one."

"How did they see you?" Zalia asked, actually interested in how that could be accomplished.

"There are ways."

Zalia rolled her eyes and saw Ember doing the same. Bloody Ascendants and their mysteriousness.

"Ways that you won't tell us because we aren't old enough or powerful enough to hear or understand them, yet?"

"That is correct."

She sighed. "Alright, fine. We'll have to think and talk about this. I assume you'll be going?"

"Correct. You know how to reach me."

His form withered and crumbled to dust that blew into the fire, burning away. She wondered if that last part was a hint as to how the Astar found him, as she *did*, in fact, know how to reach him. Perhaps they had done something similar.

She felt a tentative hope, a possibility of winning against the Astar. If whoever this Astar was *actually* wanted to help them in their fight, the knowledge Zalia could gain from them would be priceless.

Of course, she would need to talk to Faian about this as soon as possible. She wasn't going to run off and cause more problems without at least letting her know about it first.

As she started thinking about what else she could contribute to their efforts, an idea came to mind.

"We need to free Hidey," she whispered.

Ember turned from the fire to her. "What? Why?"

Thinking about her actions in retrospect, Zalia couldn't help but feel she had been going about this wrong.

"I'm not a spy or some kind of infiltrator. I spend most of my time with plants, not people, and while I might be stealthy, sneaking around a city is an entirely different prospect. Instead, I should have found a way to free Hidey, then had him go and work on getting information."

Ember nodded in agreement.

"Okay, that is true. You do have to remember, though, that while things did go wrong, you also managed to do a lot of good. Just think about all those people that live here now, ones that will contribute not only to the war but to the good health and prosperity of your people."

Zalia grumbled a little, knowing that she was right. "What do you think about meeting this Astar?"

Ember frowned, staring back into the fire. "I don't know, Zals, it seems dangerous. Would you go to meet them alone?"

Zalia nodded. "Yeah, kind of. Ro would be with me, I'm pretty sure he can interfere since the Astar brought him into it, which gives me a bit of comfort. I also have my armour that will stop them from teleporting me away, so . . . I guess it should be alright? Then again, they could be Gold or even Emerald rank."

"That's what I'm afraid of."

Zalia sighed. "I just realised I'll have to fly back to the capital to talk to Faian."

Ember poked her arm. "Just get Aylie to bring you both into a dream tonight, silly."

"Oh yeah."

Ember rolled her eyes, and Zalia knew what she wanted to say. Something about forgetting others can help and contribute to the things that needed doing, or some such.

"Okay, okay, I'll ask her later. For now, though, I want to figure out a way we can free Hidey. I think I've got a plan but it might be a little dangerous."

"Wouldn't be you if it wasn't. Come on then, what is it?"

"Alright," Zalia began, standing to turn and face Ember, "So, Hidey is being controlled by someone who knows his true name, right?"

"Yeah, we think so at least."

Zalia paced back and forth a little. "Well, the way he emphasised what he said, I can't imagine it was anything else. Anyway, the chances are that whoever controls him is an Astar, since that was who Juniper was working with."

"I think that's correct."

Zalia held up one finger. "So we either have to find out his true name so we can counteract those orders, which would probably involve breaking Zayes out of Cormaine." She held up a second finger. "Or, we take Hidey out of his prison, take him somewhere that the Astar will try to ambush us, but lay a trap first, then kill the damn Astar, thus freeing Hidey."

Ember sat up. "Zalia, what if the Astar is higher-ranked?"

Zalia pointed at her. "Good point, but I already thought of that. Hildebrandt. We have to find a way to hide her nearby."

Ember started to look thoughtful, which was good because it meant she had run out of obvious problems with the plan. "Okay, what happens if whoever this Astar is sends someone else to do it? We might kill that Astar, but Hidey still won't be free."

That one made Zalia pause. "Hmm, that's a little harder. We can't really control that, can we? We can't really control if the Astar even makes a play to free him either. Damn."

Ember sat back. "It's still worth a try, though, I guess. Either Hidey is freed from the Astar, or we kill one of their underlings."

Zalia tapped a finger against her leg repetitively, thinking. "We have to convince Hidey that we're moving him and not laying a trap for the Astar, though. As far as we know, they can hear what he hears."

"Like you'll ever be able to lie in a way that he won't see through."

Zalia held a finger up, like she was going to protest, then didn't. "Okay, fair. We need someone who is excellent at lying straight to your face . . ."

She trailed off as she thought of someone. By the expression on Ember's face, she had thought of the same person.

"Indis."

Zalia nodded.

"We don't know where she is, though."

"We don't, but we don't need to. Fortunately for us, the range at which Aylie can bring someone into a dream when familiar with them is quite far."

Ember cursed. "Damn, are we really going to go to her for help?"

"She owes us."

"I know, but I don't know that she'll see it that way."

"We'll just have to see how her removal from office has affected her, then go from there. If she can't or won't help, we'll find someone else."

Ember nodded her agreement, so Zalia moved on.

"Right, so I'll talk to Faian about this and the Astar that wants to meet with me tonight. Then, if she agrees, I'll have Aylie reach out to Indis. I guess we'll have to go find Indis after that."

"Yeah."

Ember didn't look too happy about the thought, and Zalia felt the same. There were quite a few strong emotions between them and Indis. It had been a long time since they spoke properly, though, and things had hopefully settled since.

"What do we do if things go wrong with Hidey?" Ember asked.

"Like what?"

"Well, assuming we do get Indis to help and she does successfully lie to Hidey, what if, say, they send a Diamond rank Astar to get him back?"

Zalia thought about it, realising it was a hole in the plan. "Hmm, that isn't really something we can do anything about, right? Unless . . ."

Something occurred to her, perhaps their only way to fix this issue.

"Ro is able to interfere with the talks with the exiled Astar, and he is the only being in Endaria on our side that would be capable of taking down a Diamond rank Astar. What if we find a way to involve the exiled Astar in this, thus involving Ro as well?"

Ember frowned. "That . . . seems convoluted. It could also lead to problems with the exiled Astar if we use them as bait. The Astar who knows Hidey's true name also might just now show up if they find out about the exiled Astar as well, which might lead to the Astar as a whole finding out that we may be working with them. No, that seems like a bad idea."

After thinking about it, Zalia came to agree with her. It was just a bit too complicated of a plan, one with too much risk for the reward of freeing Hidey.

This put a dent in the wheel the plan had been rolling on, which brought Zalia to a stop.

"Damn."

How could they solve the problem of simply being too weak?

"I've read Hildebrandt's abilities, and I don't think the Astar are actually capable of harming her. I'm not sure anything is really capable of harming her, as long as her mind remains firm. Maybe she would be capable of beating something Diamond rank?"

Ember shrugged. "I don't know. Maybe she could, but that would depend entirely on what the Diamond ranker's abilities are, wouldn't it? It wouldn't be the first time we've seen beings capable of attacking the mind and soul, Aylie being one of those."

"Well, you have a good point there. It's worth the risk, though. I think if the Diamond rankers amongst the Astar were wont to come wreak havoc in Endaria, there wouldn't be anything we could do to stop them either way. There's no point planning everything with the expectation that they will, otherwise we would do nothing other than sit here and wait to die."

"Alright, I can't argue with that. I guess we talk to Faian and see what happens then?"

"Yeah."

With their conversation done, their words turned to simpler things, like what they were eating for dinner. It was nice, thinking of only the little things, because Zalia knew that it wouldn't be long before the mind-altering stress of war was upon them again.

CHAPTER FORTY-EIGHT

To Dream

Zalia

When night came, Zalia tried to fall asleep. She had slept just a week and a half ago, so getting her body into the space where it would do so again was hard, but Aylie helped. Her control over the dreaming world allowed her to guide Zalia into the dream they had prepared.

She found herself drifting off and allowed sleep to take her. As soon as she did, her eyes opened to see an endless, blank mist stretching into the distance. Shapes began to take form amongst the mist, rocks, hills, and grass. She walked forwards and into a beautiful rolling landscape of green, glittering stars shining brightly above. Turning around, she found Faian standing there, looking confused.

The dreams made by Aylie weren't like other dreams. Normally, they were foggy and odd, with illogical jumps and events. Aylie's dreams felt like reality, an experience so vivid you questioned whether you were in a dream at all, or if you had only just woken up.

"Hello, Faian."

Faian's eyes finally focused on her. "Zalia? What's happening?"

"Aylie has brought you into a dream with me so that I may talk to you."

Faian looked simultaneously confused and annoyed. "Why, may I ask, have you done that?"

Zalia walked around a bit, always pleasantly surprised by the lifelikeness of Aylie's dreams. They hadn't always been this way, she was just so good at it now.

"Ro has informed me that an Astar exile wants to talk to me and is even interested in working with us against the Astar monarch."

Faian froze and then immediately began pacing. "Damn it, Zalia, you really know how to throw a twist in a woman's day . . . night. What do I even say to that?" Then she pointed accusingly at Zalia. "You told me you weren't going to make any more trouble."

Folding her arms, Zalia stood her ground. "I didn't, Nateysta came to me with this. I can't exactly tell an Ascendant what to do."

Faian threw her hands up. "Alright, I'll think about it. I'm not so blind I can't see the possible advantages of an alliance with a rebellious Astar. There's a lot we could learn from them. Is that all? I'd rather my sleep be restful."

Zalia tapped a finger against her arm. "No."

"Oh for—What now?"

"We have a plan to free Hidey."

She outlined the plan for Faian, going over everything she and Ember had gone over but in a quicker, more concise way.

Faian listened attentively, despite her annoyed expression. Zalia couldn't help but wonder if she had interrupted a nice dream.

When she was done, Faian reacted a lot more positively than she expected.

"The plan sounds good. You can contact Indis, I'd rather know where she is and what she's up to, anyway, but don't do anything more than that until I've had a chance to talk to the council about it. Is that all?"

Zalia nodded, and Aylie released Faian from the dream. She faded away slowly, melding into the background until it was like she hadn't been there in the first place.

Zalia had to wait a few minutes as Aylie tried to find Indis, the dream shifting and roiling in a terrible, hallucinatory way. She had to close her eyes to stop the motion sickness, yet could still feel the strange feeling of movement through her other senses.

It eventually stopped, a feeling of intrinsic solidity passing over the dream. She wondered what these feelings were connected to in what was happening within the dream. In reality, was the roiling, shifting feeling the movement of the space through the astral?

The thought of reality—which meant something so, so different to her now than it did just five or six years ago—being involved in the dreamscape made her chuckle quietly to herself.

The small smile quickly left her face as the faint outline of a person resolved into Lady Leyra Indis.

Indis looked around in confusion, opening and closing her hand a few times, twisting it around to inspect it. Then she saw Zalia standing there, and the confusion in her expression deepened. "What a weird dream," she murmured, looking away again and walking over to a tree, running her hand down the rough bark.

Zalia waited a moment, wondering what Indis would do.

Indis leaned down and picked a flower, smelling it and frowning again. Zalia had to agree that she found Aylie's dreams wonderfully realistic.

Indis finally turned to Zalia. "Why are *you* here?"

"Aylie has made this dream and brought us both into it so that I can talk to you."

Looking closer, Zalia was surprised to find that Indis looked a little . . . rough. The woman usually held herself to high standards and, even when travelling, barely had a fleck of dirt on her when it could be avoided. Zalia had almost been convinced that she had developed a passive ability that kept herself clean.

Now though, that illusion was broken. While Aylie was able to draw people into dreams, she couldn't control how they appeared there. This meant that the bags under Indis's eyes and the drawn-out look of exhaustion mixed with ruffled hair and worn clothes were all real. Indis had definitely been through some shit.

Though, Zalia supposed it was to be expected when the people Indis had worked towards helping her entire life rejected her.

A passing look of worry came over Indis's face at Zalia's words, though it was quickly masked behind her signature look of superiority, the one Zalia remembered so well from their times together. A little bit of the old Indis was still in there then.

"And why, exactly, do you want to talk to me?"

Zalia searched her expression, trying to see through the mask she'd put up. Why was it that she always did this? "I know we've had our differences, but I need your help to free Hidey."

Indis waited, looking unimpressed.

With a sigh, Zalia continued. "We have a plan to free him, but we need someone who can convincingly lie to his face about something. Obviously, I'll never be able to do that, but I think you, of all people, could pull it off."

Anger broke Indis's mask. "Right, so you've brought me here just to insult me. Real grown-up of you, Zalia."

Zalia frowned. "What? No. We need—"

"I heard you the first time. Why should I help Hidey?"

This wasn't going how Zalia had expected at all.

"Because he can and will help the people of Endaria, surely that's something you can appreciate?"

Indis scoffed. "The people. The damned people of Endaria. They can go to Cormaine for all I care."

Zalia almost recoiled at the venom in her words. "You don't mean that, I know you don't. Look, I understand that you're hurt about not being voted in, Indis, but—"

"Do you!? Do you really!?" Indis yelled. She continued quietly, "Do you know what it's like to be rejected by your own people, the ones you've laboured and destroyed yourself for? Do you really understand that, Zalia?"

Zalia was silent, speechless at the tears rolling down Indis's cheeks.

"No, I didn't think so."

In that moment, Zalia realised that Indis knew that she'd been doing things that were . . . wrong, all in the name of her people. She'd known and done them anyway, through some twisted sense of morality that the result of her actions warranted them in the first place.

Zalia knew what her childhood and early life had been like and thought that, perhaps, Indis just didn't know how to do things any other way.

"So will you not help? War has been called against the Astar for their actions, and we need every bit of power we can get. Hidey would be invaluable to us right now, and while I could find someone else to do this, I would much prefer someone I know would succeed."

Indis basically snarled at her. "I will not help you. The people of Endaria decided that they would be better off without me, so be it."

At that, the dream began fading. Zalia met Indis's eyes and held them, searching deep within and finding a terrible loneliness there. As Zalia's eyes opened to the real world, she didn't feel anger or disappointment, instead finding herself sad. It was an emotion she was surprised to feel about Indis, yet it was the right one. There was no way to describe Indis's life up to this point other than tragic.

Zalia sighed as she got up, stretching to relieve the tension in her muscles. They were step one into their plan and things had already gone very wrong. Without Indis, they would have to find someone else to lie to Hidey. Or, perhaps, lying to him wasn't necessary. Could she find a way to draw out the Astar without tricking them?

Ro had called them egotistical and had stated that their cold and calculating manner was not natural, but driven by their society. That meant that those emotions were bottled up and put away. What if . . . what if she could taunt them into a fight?

She would have to wait for Faian's go-ahead, but it might be possible.

It would be many hours until the others woke up, so Zalia went to Aylie, who would still be awake. She hadn't yet developed the ability to use her dream powers on others when she was asleep herself, if that was even possible.

She found Aylie sitting casually, one knee up to her chest, on one of the large trunks that wrapped around their house from the Ancient of Life that grew above.

"Hey," Zalia called up.

Aylie looked down and gave a wave.

Zalia climbed up with ease, her powerful body able to lift weights far greater than her own.

"I assume you heard everything?"

Aylie nodded.

"Puts a bit of a hitch in my plan."

Aylie nodded again.

"Are you alright?"

Aylie shrugged.

Zalia brought her into a gentle hug, not saying another word. Sometimes it was better to get someone talking. Other times, though, it was best to let them find their words on their own. Zalia felt this was one of those times.

They sat there under the stars, wind pulling at their clothes and hair as the heat from the day dissipated into the night.

More than a few times, Aylie opened her mouth as if to say something, then stopped. Still, Zalia waited. She stared at the sky, drawing lines between stars to create constellations of her own. The sky here held different stars than the ones from her own world, and as such, the constellations she was used to weren't here. That saddened her a bit sometimes. Her world might have been terrible in many ways, yet the stars had always been the same, without care for the small happenings on a planet far away. They had reminded her that while it might seem that the world was ending sometimes, it didn't really mean anything to the universe as a whole. To some, that was a horrifying thought. To Zalia, it was comforting.

"I did something that I think might be bad, back with the Astar."

Zalia snapped out of her reverie, pulling away just enough to look at Aylie. "What do you mean?"

"When I was out of my body, part of the mist, I was trying to talk to you for so long. Everything felt . . . fuzzy and thinking was hard. I pushed and pushed, and a message appeared saying that I had broken the protective barrier between my body and soul. I could talk to you after that."

Zalia frowned. This is what she had been hiding? It explained why the dream she had crafted had felt so much more *solid*.

"That is strange, for sure, but I don't think it's something bad. Why do you feel that it is?"

"I—I don't know. I've just felt different since it happened. I'm scared."

Zalia pulled her in close again as Aylie's voice cracked, hugging her tight and giving her a kiss on the head.

"We'll figure it out together, alright? You don't need to be scared."

Aylie started to cry. She had grown so tall and so strong that Zalia sometimes forgot that Aylie was still young, a teenager. It was a hard time in life, even without magic.

"Oh, darling, it'll be alright. We'll figure it out."

She held Aylie as the night passed by, each hint of Aylie's pain and fear breaking her heart. How she wished she could just take that all away.

CHAPTER FORTY-NINE

Astralbound

Zalia

When morning came and the rest of her family awoke, Zalia knew that Aylie would still be in bed and might be for some time. She was a little troubled by what Aylie had said and was starting to worry about its meaning as well. What did it mean that the protective barrier between her body and soul had been broken?

After thinking about it all night while everyone was asleep and Boreal was out doing who knew what, Zalia had become convinced that it did affect the dreamscape Aylie created. It had been so much more real and solid this time. It had been a long time since Zalia had been in one so she'd assumed it was a result of practice.

Why Zalia was worried, she could not say for certain.

The only effects of the change that she had noticed so far were the dream and the other odd *something* that she had noticed about Aylie a few days back. One of those things was good while the other wasn't meaningful at all, which left no reason to be concerned. The way her body and soul existed in the world had fundamentally changed, for better or worse.

Everyone was going about their day after a large breakfast. Zalia hadn't told Ember what Aylie had shared with her just yet; she would ask Aylie if it was okay for her to. While she most certainly shared everything with Ember, this secret wasn't hers.

Boreal had come back for breakfast only to take her children and leave afterwards. Had it been a few years ago, Zalia would have been sure she was up to some mischief, but her once young feline friend had grown up, becoming more serious and grounded.

Lumin was with Aylie, asleep at the foot of her bed. He was much too large to fit on the bed anymore, and Zalia had a feeling he wouldn't fit in the house much longer, knowing how large his previous incarnation had been. That was an issue for later, however, one that probably wouldn't take much to fix considering the fluid state of their home. It would adjust the height of its rooms and doors to accommodate Lumin.

With Boreal out, Lumin and Aylie asleep, and Ember busy for the day ensuring that the people they had freed from the Astar had been given places to live, as well as food and water, Zalia had to make her own plans. She would have gone with Ember, but she wanted to do something for Aylie.

There were a few things that Zalia had in common with Aylie and those were a love of high-up, open spaces, and a dislike of people. Not a dislike of the people themselves—they were just more comfortable without others around, free from the sounds, smells, and sights of people going about their days. It wasn't the fault of people, rather a preference on Zalia and Aylie's behalf. Ember was very different, with a love and care for people that had drawn Zalia to her in the first place. It had been the trip the two of them had taken around the city of Endelbyrn, going from farm to town to farm, healing and helping wherever they could that had made Zalia truly like Ember. It was perhaps Zalia's tendency to help people in need despite her dislike of being around them that had caused Ember to return the feelings.

That was why Ember was out helping the people they had freed, while Zalia was planning to make a retreat in the town, just for Aylie.

The Ancient of Life formed a canopy that spanned over and across the centre half of the town, its thick branches and massive trunk supporting the weight of countless leaves that allowed beams of light to shine on the town below. Zalia flew up to the top of the tree, where its trunk finally grew thin. Thin relative to the rest of the tree, at least. There, with two branches as supports, Zalia began her work.

The Ancient of Life wasn't like the other two ancients. Wisdom and War were both animals: a crow and a plains cat. You could talk to them and receive answers, both having an active part to play in the day-to-day life of the people and animals that lived in the city. The Ancient of Life instead spoke with the plants that lived in the city.

If she focused, Zalia could hear them talking, not in voices but by some form of magic. It wasn't magic like Zalia had, but a type that all plants shared. She had felt it, even helped create it, but didn't have control over it like the Ancient of Life did. It made the plants in the city act as one being, working with each other to form a strong ecosystem. It was the Ancient of Life that oversaw this ecosystem, ensuring that the trees lining the main roads of the town bore fruit, that the grass growing between the cobblestones thrived yet did not overtake everything, that the vines climbing the buildings supported the structures instead of slowly breaking them apart. It was the work of the three ancients together that allowed so much life, and so many plants, animals, and people to thrive together rather than slowly destroy each other.

Up amongst the branches, Zalia used her mental communication to talk to the tree, telling it of what she needed. She could have just used Healing Presence and Natural Matter Alteration to create what she wanted, but found it better to ask the tree to change of its own accord.

When it was done creating what she asked for, Zalia spent some time walking about, planting a few choice herbs and making slight alterations. She tried her best to keep it as uncluttered as possible, wanting the space to remain open.

When she was done, she flew back down to their house below and waited. It had been a few hours yet Aylie was still asleep. They had stayed up talking quite late the night before.

When Aylie finally awoke, Zalia waited for her to eat breakfast before showing her what she had made.

They stood in Aylie's room as Zalia pulled a small ritual from her vault. She had prepared this beforehand, creating the correct ritual on a little wooden plate that could be moved. After placing it in the corner of Aylie's room, Zalia activated it and gestured for Aylie to step through.

Zalia followed her through to the platform high above the sounds and smells of the town below. It was a round section of rough but flat bark ten metres across. She had planted the portal at one edge, now linked to Aylie's bedroom below. In the centre of the space were two seats like trunks with soft leaves forming a comfortable place to sit. There were small trees around the platform, along with railings at the edges. All of it had a pattern of translucent Soulroot planted throughout, forming an active ritual. The ritual wasn't something that would be felt immediately, but the longer Zalia stayed in the space, the more she felt . . . connected.

"What is all this?" Aylie asked in a whisper.

They could see incredibly far from this high up, the lands around them visible far into the distance.

"I told you that I'd help you work through this soul thing last night and I meant it. I thought I'd make a place for us to do that, just you and me."

Aylie was staring at the Soulroot like she had started to feel what it was doing.

Zalia went and sat on one of the stumps, crossed her legs, and waited. Aylie sat opposite her, then closed her eyes.

This would be the hard part.

Making this place had been easy, a simple and clear way of showing that she meant her words. Aylie had gone through changes, but figuring out what that meant was another thing entirely, and Zalia had *no* idea where to start.

Souls were not her specialty, and Aylie probably knew a lot more about them than she did. She knew that they didn't exist on the astral normally, as one of

Aylie's abilities made it so that part of hers existed there. If part of Zalia's also did, then she would be able to do some of the things Aylie could. So, she supposed Aylie might not know more about it than Zalia did, considering it was the astral, the realm of thought that Aylie had experience working with.

So where *did* the soul normally exist?

The obvious answer was in the body, as she knew it could be damaged by some abilities or the overuse of mana and passives. Aylie could even heal souls with the once-per-day use active that her Healing Presence had developed. Whether that was right or not, though, she didn't know.

"Alright, Aylie. I was able to feel that something about you has changed, but does it feel different to you?"

Aylie nodded.

"Okay, describe that feeling for me."

Aylie hesitated, then started speaking. "It's like . . . there used to be three parts of me, my body, my mind, and my soul. Now it feels like there's only two, my mind and . . . my soul and body aren't two different things anymore."

She saw Aylie shiver, her eyes still closed.

"Alright. How about the part of your soul that is still in the astral, can you still feel that?"

Aylie nodded.

"And you can touch the astral still?"

Aylie nodded again.

So it doesn't stop her abilities from working at least.

Then Aylie frowned. "I can feel it better now, though, it's almost as if I can . . ."

Aylie reached her hand forward and pulled on . . . something. It was like she grabbed an invisible curtain and pulled it over her body—her body that vanished as she did so.

Zalia jumped up in alarm, staring at where Aylie had been. "Aylie!?" she called.

There was no response.

She looked around but couldn't feel or see anything. Then she felt a touch on her mind, like someone had brushed her thoughts with a hand. It was her turn to shiver.

Used to the action of mental communication through her magic, Zalia tried to open her mind to Aylie's touch, and words flowed in.

"I'm still here, Zalia."

The thoughts entering her mind had a sense of panic but also excitement to them. Where previously it had just been Aylie's soul that was sent to the astral by the Astar, it was now her entire body that went there.

"Can you get back?"

"I don't know how!"

This time, the sense of panic was much greater.

"Don't worry, we'll find a way. Hold on, I'll get Lumin up here, they might be able to help."

"Alright."

The thought was wavering, the fear obvious.

Zalia sent a thought down to Lumin, who responded immediately, appearing out of the portal moments later.

"I saw that thought . . ." Aylie said.

"Alright, Aylie, can you see Lumin?"

"I can."

They knew that Lumin had a way of solidifying things on the astral from their time back in the mists, and Zalia was hoping that it would help now.

"Alright, Aylie, try to grab onto the same thing you did before. Pull it open and step through."

There was a moment of nothing before Aylie appeared again, as if she had pulled the curtain of the world back and stepped through.

Aylie stared at her for just a moment before laughing, almost manically. "Oh, gods. I was in the astral. Entirely."

Zalia put a hand to her head, looking up and letting out a sigh of relief. "Please don't do that again for the moment."

Aylie nodded in agreement. "I don't plan to, don't worry."

They both sat back down and Zalia found she felt exhausted. Too much emotional turmoil. "What was it like?" she found herself asking.

Aylie looked thoughtful. ". . . Different, this time. When the Astar separated my body and soul, it was like a piece of me had been ripped away. This time it was like my whole being was finally in the same place for the first time ever."

Zalia shook her head in amazement. "What did you do? *How* did you do it?"

"A part of me is still there, I just . . . stepped over to it. Then there was nothing left of me here so I couldn't step back. Lumin let me feel the barrier, though, so I just did the same thing I did the first time and came back. I think . . . I think I might have been able to do this before, when I gained the ability to touch the astral, I just only figured it out. I *think* that I'll be able to do it without Lumin here, with practice. Now that I know what to do."

Zalia hugged Aylie close. "You are amazing."

CHAPTER FIFTY

Overconfidence

Zalia

Zalia and Aylie had spent a good portion of that day practicing going into and out of the astral, with Lumin there just in case. There might have been some dangers involved in going there, but they hadn't found any as of yet. Zalia wondered if there was anything that lived there natively, some kind of creature that lived off thoughts, perhaps?

Either way, she had made Aylie promise not to go back until she had spoken to Ro about it. Hopefully, the Ascendant would have some kind of insight into the place.

She had also told Ember about what was happening, with Aylie's permission, of course, and other than concerns for Aylie's safety, Ember was on board with helping her figure out the changes. Leaving it unattended could lead to a dangerous outcome. It was better she understood what she was capable of than accidentally do something that got her hurt or killed.

Done with practicing for the day, Zalia was looking into setting up a portal to the capital. It would be extremely helpful not only with the things that she was trying to do, but it would also set up a path for trade that was worlds above the current caravans going from city to city.

First though, she would need to find a way to condense the size of the ritual required for the portal. There just wasn't enough space in the town for another huge ritual. There *must* be a way to do it, she knew this because the Astar did.

Stored in her vault was a memory of the dormant rituals that the Astar created, and she focused on it, solidly centring the image in her mind. Without an understanding of the Astar ritual runes, it was hard for her to figure out how they worked, though. None of the people freed from the Astar town knew about them either, it had been one of the first things she'd asked them once they'd been on the road back to Endaria. Studying Astar runes just hadn't been on their list of priorities as mindless bodies forced to do labour.

She gave up on it, after a while, deciding that it just wasn't going to happen. Not from the memory, at least.

That night, she realised that she would have to go back to the capital. Again.

It wasn't just that she was awaiting the decision of the council on her plans, it was the fact that Hidey was kept there. It made her sad every time she remembered the dark, blank cell that Hidey had been living in for the past years, sealed away in a tiny cube. He deserved better than that, for what he had been through and what he had managed to do for Endaria despite his situation.

As often happened, thinking about Hidey dragged her mind to the topic of Zayes. It occurred to her that she knew what had imprisoned him in Cormaine. The Astar had done it, she was sure of that. Who else was capable of sending a powerful person to another world, who else was working with the demons that resided there? It was Hidey's bond with Zayes that had given him sentience and sapience in the first place, and it was possible that Zayes's death would have removed those things from him. It was her only idea for why the man was still alive.

It also occurred to her that the very bond that Zayes and Hidey held might be the thing that allowed them to get back to Cormaine when the time came. Aylie had been able to send a portal from Ember to Zalia through their bond after all.

Already having everything she needed for a trip to the capital, she bid her family farewell and began the flight. She could fly indefinitely and at a much faster pace than she could with the whole family there, meaning the trip would be much shorter. It would still be an annoyingly long time, though.

Ember had voiced concerns about Zalia leaving the relative safety of the town with its anti-teleportation magic active, but out of everyone, she was now the second least likely in Endaria to fall to an Astar ambush, after Hildebrandt, of course. Zalia was also insistent that they needed to take a front foot in this, both because it was caused by them *and* the feeling she had that if they allowed the Astar to have their way, the powerful would be slowly stripped away until Endaria was nothing but people of Bronze rank and below.

It was for this reason that she flew quickly, pushed by winds that she controlled and made weightless by an easy Zephyr ritual.

Perhaps an hour out from the capital, an Astar appeared before her with twin swords at the ready.

Zalia was ready, half expecting something like this to happen, and reacted immediately. Her armour already on, she activated Fight or Flight, and the speed at which she perceived things slowed down. She could feel where the sword in the Astar's left hand would strike her and twisted to avoid it, a powerful beat of her wings changing the course of her flight just enough that once the blade had passed her by, she was able to deliver a high-speed armoured boot to the Astar's face.

She felt something crunch satisfyingly upon impact, orienting herself as the Astar went flying back. Without hesitation, however, the Astar was right next to her again, a sword swinging at her.

Fight or Flight saved her again as she summoned her own sword just in time to block the Astar, letting their strike slide down the length of her blade, held hilt up, point diagonally down and angled left towards the ground. The parry gave her a burst of speed that she used to bring her sword around in a strike, blade glowing a bright blue, towards the Astar's neck on the right side.

The Astar's second sword came up to deflect her strike, but she surprised them by allowing her sword to disappear, a bow replacing it at her side. Instead of her intended strike, she continued the momentum past the Astar's angled blade to punch it squarely in the face, blood from her previous hit to its face coating her gauntlet.

The Astar was thrown away from her again, but this time arrows flew after them. Unfortunately, her enemy was Gold rank and well trained.

Her first arrow was struck aside and the next dodged due to the Astar teleporting straight up next to her again.

Taking a gamble, Zalia teleported away from the Astar as it did so, hoping that there would be a cooldown on the ability.

The gamble paid off as Zalia finally bought herself some space. She began a ritual, combining Zephyr, Water Lily, Flame-root, and Manifest into a powerful combination.

Seeing what she was doing, the Astar floated towards her as fast as it could, which thankfully wasn't very. It appeared that while the Astar were powerful spacial mages, they weren't very quick with their flight.

As the ritual neared completion, the Astar used its aura like a weapon. The force came crashing down on her, ripping Healing Presence aside and striking at her soul. She gasped, barely maintaining the ritual as pain seared through her. The only reason she was able to was due to her experiences under the clutches of the Astar who had used a demon to torture her.

The ritual activated, a storm that ripped at the Astar manifesting around her. The Astar continued its attacks on her soul until a second ritual, one made from Soulroot and Dodge-vine, snapped into place. This one protected her from the attacks against her soul.

There was a momentary pause in the fight as the Astar considered its next action. It continued to deflect her arrows with ease before teleporting to her again. With Fight or Flight gone, Zalia didn't react in time, her sword appearing in her hand just as a strike hit perfectly between armour plates and took her arm off at the elbow. She let out a pained scream but had to ignore it as she caught the arm, activated Protection of the Wilds, and pressed the arm back against the stump. The burst of healing allowed it to knit itself back on, the shield from Protection of the Wilds blocking the two strikes that followed the first.

The ability was enhanced with Zephyr, further fueling the storm whipping around her that tore at the Astar. It had burns and cuts across its body and wasn't looking great, considering the difference of rank in the fight.

Things turned in Zalia's favour even further when the shield broke under the Astar's onslaught. A bright flash of light struck the Astar, blasting a small hole through its lower abdomen.

At that moment, Zalia saw shock on the Astar's face. It obviously hadn't expected her to put up this much of a fight, let alone injure it substantially.

Zalia prepared herself for it to attack again, but the Astar simply vanished.

She looked around wildly, expecting it to have gone behind her to attack, yet it wasn't there. Her heart beat as she spun around again, expecting a surprise attack at any moment. A headache built, and she realised that she was running out of mana. She had to drop both other rituals, only able to maintain flight due to it no longer requiring mana.

Still worried about where the Astar had gone, but not planning to stick around for it to come back with more of its kind, she continued her flight towards the capital as quickly as she could. Concern came down the bond between herself and Ember, so she sent a comforting wave back, a sign that she was alright. Ember would have felt the pain and stress that she had experienced during the fight.

She was looking over her shoulder the rest of the flight there, feeling paranoid without someone to watch her back. This was the second time a Gold rank Astar had shown up near the city and she had a feeling that it was a trend that would continue. She would have to get the portals between the cities working sooner rather than later.

When she arrived at the city, four guards met her in the sky this time. It appeared they had increased their security.

They allowed her through and she went straight to the keep.

A guard there showed her to Faian's room upon arrival, and Zalia stepped in, thanking him for his help.

"Zalia, you're here again already."

It was a statement, not a question. Zalia came to the capital very rarely.

"To grace you with my chaotic presence, of course," Zalia replied somewhat sarcastically, taking a seat.

Faian tensed and Zalia held her hands up.

"No, I didn't do anything or start anything. I did get attacked by that Gold rank Astar on the way here, though."

Faian relaxed. "Did you . . .?"

"No, didn't manage to kill it. The Astar kind of ran away."

Faian arched an eyebrow. "You made a Gold rank Astar run away."

Zalia shrugged. "Their magic is strong, their auras even more so, but if you have a good way to counter both of those things, then they are quite weak, physically. Even the ones that are trained with weapons aren't particularly strong."

Zalia had to ignore the slight ache in her elbow, well aware that the fight could have gone very, very differently for her. One wrong move would have been death for her, where the Astar had much more room for error.

"I see. And why are you here so soon, might I ask?"

Zalia rubbed at her elbow. "Ah, right. Yeah, Indis has completely refused to help so I have had to make a revision in the plan. I think I'm going to have to annoy the Astar that controls Hidey into fighting me. Kind of, um, play with its ego and insult it so much that it has to."

Faian put her face in her hands, voice muffled through them. "Zalia, that is a terrible plan. Not to mention *dangerous*."

Zalia tapped the desk between them. "It's not as bad as you might think. From my experience, the Astar are quite sure of their own abilities and have paid for that mistake more than a few times. A group of them attacked me and the large number of Silver rank people I freed, and they paid horribly for that. The two Astar that captured me played with me instead of just killing me outright, paying for it when Hildebrandt arrived. Now this Gold rank Astar wasn't able to kill me because I don't think it expected me to fight back as well as I did. If it had gone all out to start with, it might have actually got me. Instead, it wanted to play with its food and its food kicked it in the mouth. Not that they have mouths."

Faian looked back up. "Alright, I see your point but *why* do you think this means insulting the Astar is going to draw it out?"

Zalia locked eyes with her. "Because if I insult this overconfident asshole, they are going to want me dead more than they already do."

CHAPTER FIFTY-ONE

Transport

Zalia

Zalia and Faian stood in the dark room that served as Hidey's prison. It was surprising to Zalia that Faian had allowed her to come here to mock the Astar in front of him so easily. She was also surprised that Faian had the authority to allow it without first speaking with the council, unless they had already agreed to grant Faian control over this.

It had taken a little bit of brainstorming before they had decided on the best course of action, and Faian had insisted that she be here for it. Hildebrandt had agreed to help when they went outside the city to bait out the holder of Hidey's true name.

"Hey, Hidey, how are things?" Zalia started.

"A little cramped."

Zalia snorted in amusement. He still had his sense of humour intact, it seemed. "I see that. I've come with some good news for you. We'll be able to let you out soon."

The surprise and hope in his voice was evident. *"You will? How?"*

Faian stepped up. "Zalia has found someone who will be able to discern your true name, and we shall be transporting you there to be done with this shortly. We will be able to trust that you are with us once that is done."

Zalia waited, her body relaxed but tense in her mind. This was the single lie that they would need to tell, the single thing that it was important for Hidey to believe and the reason Faian had come. Zalia wouldn't have been able to tell it without giving everything away, but Faian had a little more practice than she did.

"I see. When will we be leaving for this person, then?"

Faian smiled. "We know better than to tell you that."

Hoping it had worked, Zalia interrupted to begin her part. "Though, I did want to talk to you about the Astar a little. I've been surprised recently to discover that they are all quite weak. Even those who are trained to fight are barely able to hold their own without their teleportation magic."

Hidey remained impassive, but Zalia could only tell that the cube-like shade was such by the lack of verbal reaction.

"*Not much is known about the Astar.*"

"Perhaps not previously, but I've been learning and I'm thoroughly unimpressed."

"*You should take care in your words, Zalia.*"

Zalia started. The way he emphasised the word was as if he were not only warning her to be careful with her words, but to take care in what she was doing as well. "Don't worry Hidey, I'm not scared of the Astar."

"*You should, perhaps, reconsider.*"

Zalia shook her head. "After everything I've been through, both at their hands and those of the demons, I don't have space in my mind for that. They will feel what I have felt."

With that, she left.

Faian came with her and once they reached the surface once more, Zalia turned to her.

"Was that too much?"

Faian shrugged. "It was a little dramatic but if they're as egotistical as you say, it should anger them a little. I would think they are already angry at you for the destruction you wrought in their town and the people you freed from their grasp."

Zalia nodded her agreement. She really did suck at being believable. "Well, I think he didn't catch on to your lie, at least. I'm not the greatest at telling, but it sounded like he might have been worried for us."

"I caught that as well, though whether it was because he caught on to what we were doing and was trying to warn us, or because he thinks we are unprepared for an attack, I don't know."

"Nothing left other than to go ahead with it then, hey?"

Faian nodded.

"When should we do it?" Zalia asked.

"Immediately. I don't want to give them time to break Hidey out before we take this out of the city, if they would do such a thing. Go and get Hildebrandt, I shall organise transport for Hidey."

Zalia gave an affirmative nod and ran off through the city towards Hildebrandt's house. They were near the castle that loomed over the rest of the capital, and so Hildebrandt's house was close. It only took her a few minutes to reach her destination, and upon arriving, she knocked politely on the door.

Hildebrandt answered it promptly.

"Zalia, how are you? Would you like to come in?"

Zalia shook her head. "Don't have time, we're starting the transport of Hidey right now. Faian's idea, not mine. You ready to go?"

Hildebrandt's armour, shield, and large mace appeared. "Always."

They ran down the slight incline to where Hidey was hidden and waited. Faian wasn't there, but a few soldiers joined them after their arrival. Ten minutes later, another group of soldiers came jogging down, bringing their numbers from five to twelve. Two of these soldiers were Silver rank with the rest being Bronze.

Trailing the final group of soldiers was a large covered cart being pulled by an animal Zalia didn't recognise. It was extremely muscled like a bison, but in place of horns it had clumps of earth that floated about its head. Recognising the earth magic for what it was, Zalia also noticed that its steps landed with more weight than they should have, as if each step was a mini earthquake.

They were sure to be noticed now.

Faian was walking alongside the cart with another sat in the seat meant for the driver. Strangely, the man directing the bison-like creature wasn't doing so via whip or reins, but communicated with the creature by manipulating the earth that floated around its head. She watched as he pulled back on the earth very slightly and the animal slowed to a stop.

Moving from the side of the cart, Faian gestured to the two Silver rank soldiers, and Hildebrandt then made her way down into Hidey's prison. There wasn't a building attached to the underground room, just a door made from steel surrounded by even more steel. The grounds around them were unoccupied and bound by a fence with only a single gate.

It was only a moment before the four came back up, with Faian gingerly holding the black cube that held Hidey. Zalia hadn't ever asked where they had gotten the item and realised she probably should have. Something like that could be useful in the future if she ever came up against shades or similar enemies. It was more than likely to happen when they went back to Cormaine.

One of the soldiers opened up the back of the cart for Faian and she stepped up into it, placing the cube on a small pedestal inside. She locked it in with a cage and then jumped back out.

"Alright, we're set to go then. I unfortunately don't think we can bring any more people than this, and even then I wouldn't want to put any more soldiers in danger. This is the least we can bring without it being suspicious. Hildebrandt, you'll wait within the cart itself, as it has some protections against perception of different types."

Hildebrandt nodded her agreement and hopped inside.

"I can add some rituals of my own to hide the inside of the cart if you'd like?" Zalia suggested.

Faian agreed, so Zalia cast two different rituals, one to protect against normal sight and another to protect against more magical means. They were both quite basic rituals and thus easy to maintain without loss of much mana.

"Excellent. I'll have you two at the rear, four on each side, and Zalia and you two at the front." Faian pointed in turn as she spoke, with the two Silver soldiers at the back. The general sat up next to the driver of the cart, settling in for the long drive.

Zalia went to her place as told, summoning her armour and bow which floated next to her. It was strange never firing the bow herself anymore as it took a life of its own. Stranger still was how she didn't see it as unusual at all. Had it been years ago, when she first arrived in Endaria, the sight would have caused her to think she was crazy.

They made their way out of the city and onto the road between the capital and Nature's Reclaim. Their hope was that they would be attacked between the two cities by whomever knew Hidey's true name. Zalia just had to hope that the Astar who did know the name hadn't shared it with many others. She didn't know the Astar society that well but knew enough to know that it was unlikely one of them would share an advantage like that with the others, especially if they were of high rank themselves.

So much of the plan relied on luck, on being lucky enough for the Astar to show themself, on being lucky that the Astar hadn't shared the name, on being lucky enough that Hildebrandt could defeat them.

Zalia wasn't concerned about that half, as even a Diamond rank Astar would have a very hard time killing Hildebrandt. She also had a trick that would stop that same Astar from killing any of the rest of them.

Was the plan reckless? Perhaps. That said, it would be a huge win to start off the war if it worked. A potential kill of a high-rank Astar, and Hidey would be freed from his constant servitude. Who knew what information the shade held already.

Many hours later, they were still trundling along the road as Zalia thought of the Gold rank Astar that had tried to kill her. It was unlikely that the few wounds she had managed to inflict on them had killed them. If it had been a normal person, perhaps, but not a Gold ranker.

It was even harder to kill anything of Emerald rank. Zalia had only seen Hildebrandt injured once, when she herself had shot her with an arrow that had sunk only the smallest amount into Hildebrandt's shoulder. That had only happened because Hildebrandt had allowed it, holding back all her passives during the practice. If she hadn't, Hildebrandt's retaliation passive would have turned Zalia to dust.

The body became quite strange the higher rank you became, and Zalia had started to notice the changes in herself as well. The body mattered less and less, able to recover from more injury. How could you die when your entire body could regenerate in a matter of seconds?

The answer, obviously, was damage to the soul that existed within the body. This, it appeared, was how fights were fought at higher ranks. Ascendants were the epitome of this, those who had reached a point that bodies no longer mattered, with attacks being inflicted on the soul that were then reflected in the bodies created.

Hildebrandt was quickly reaching that point of existence, with her abilities able to affect the soul, whether it be her incredible recovery or her Godly Strike.

Zalia was hoping that she and her family would be able to reach that point as people became considerably harder to kill. There were only a few more ranks to go for herself, Boreal, and Ember, with Aylie quickly catching up, and the young ones not far behind that. Zalia expected them to reach Bronze rank soon, with Aylie not far to go until Silver. Boreal was also very quickly approaching Gold, ahead of Zalia by a good margin.

It had reached a point where the increased speed of her ranking up due to gaining magic so late in life had caught up, and the slowing of her ranking up due to having three classes instead of two was becoming evident. Ember would also reach Gold before her, and perhaps even Aylie would catch up sometime down the line, reaching Emerald before Zalia did.

She was shaken from her thoughts at Faian's yelled alarm. Everyone around her burst into movement, and she followed suit, looking up to see not one but three Astar.

CHAPTER FIFTY-TWO

Fight for the Oppressed

Zalia

The cart behind Zalia vaporised as Hildebrandt shot up into the sky with a powerful jump. Only one of the Astar vanished from where it hovered, appearing again closer to the ground.

At the peak of her jump, now at the same height as the Astar, Hildebrandt activated an ability.

This was an ability Zalia had not yet seen, but had read when shown by Hildebrandt. It was called Defend the Kingdom and as she activated it, a large, golden dome covered Hildebrandt and the Astar, and a floor appeared underneath them, locking the three inside.

Zalia had caught a peek at the rank of the two Astar still in the sky, and worry filled her at having not one but two Emerald rank Astar to fight. It wasn't an impossible fight for Hildebrandt, but Zalia was concerned for her all the same.

The dome was powerful against the Astar in that it was nearly indestructible, even by Hildebrandt's standards, and blocked anything except allies from entering or leaving its area, lasting for an entire day. Every time something struck the dome it would trigger Backlash, a powerful retribution ability, meaning even attacks that missed Hildebrandt would still cause the Astar to be struck.

Zalia had to change her focus from the fight above to watch the Astar down with the rest of them. She swore it was the Gold rank Astar that she had fought before, and it was now healed and ready to fight again. It hadn't yet been a day since her first fight with the Gold ranker, and so Protection of the Wilds wasn't available yet. Fortunately, she wouldn't need the ability, as she had three other Silver rankers with her.

Faian called for the Bronze soldiers to retreat and make a formation around the cart, and the earth mage that had been driving it got to work building a dome of their own. Metal flowed from the ground, building up and around to form an ever-thickening barrier between the Bronze rank soldiers and the fight far above their power. They were there to ensure no Astar would teleport in and steal Hidey while the rest of them fought.

The Gold rank Astar was waiting, having learnt to be wary of Zalia, who now had allies, so she flew up to start the fight herself.

Arrows flew from her bow as Zalia began a ritual. It was a curse effect that would hold the Gold rank Astar from teleporting. Not about to allow Zalia to cast her rituals without retaliation, the Astar deflected an arrow before appearing next to her, ready to strike.

Barely a few metres in the air and ready for the attack, Zalia shot backwards as the soldiers below jumped to grab the Astar. They dragged it down from the air with their weight as Zalia's ritual activated, a slight warping of the air the only apparent sign of it working. The soldiers slammed the Astar into the ground, but it got to its feet quickly with a lithe movement, dodging out of the way of the soldiers' blades.

The Astar had to ignore Zalia for the moment as it fought the two soldiers, its dual swords flashing in the light as it defended itself. It even managed to deflect Zalia's arrows all the while.

Faian stood back from the fight, radiating an aura that made Zalia feel energised and ready for battle. Her mana was recharging faster than the ritual could use it because of this, so she started casting a few more.

Purple flames covered the Astar, a sizzling sound coming from its skin. It looked straight up at her as she did this, and with a small flash of light, both of her rituals were dispelled.

Hildebrandt

Hildebrandt stood her ground as she waited for the Astar to make the first move. It would be a hard fight, she knew, and one that would take a very long time. She only hoped that it wouldn't outlast the lifespan of her dome.

One of the two Astar held a massive two-handed sword, while the other wielded two daggers, one coated in a blue light, while the other seemed to pull the light of the world into itself. She was wary of the daggers, sure that whatever was creating these effects on them would be nasty to deal with. The greatsword was another matter entirely, something she was better equipped to deal with.

She hefted her shield towards her enemy, watching as the aura from Stand Your Ground spread towards them, almost as if the air were alight. The effects of her shield and armour would be important in this fight, as she had no doubt that her body would be pummelled and very possibly destroyed at one point or another.

Defender's Immutable Shield (Heirloom) - Deeply bonded Gold rank.
Tin - This shield cannot be broken by any normal means. In addition, the wielder takes slightly less damage from all sources.
Iron - Damage is mitigated by the shield, whether it be blocked or reduced, and instead heals the wielder.
Bronze - You may ignore all magic effects for five minutes. This ability has a twenty-four hour cooldown.
Silver - When Backlash is triggered by blocking with this shield, the effect is further increased.
Gold - When you would otherwise die, you are instead healed to a healthy state. This effect is negated only if you die by a weapon impaling you.
Defender's Godly Armour (Heirloom) - Deeply bonded Gold rank.
Tin - The material of the armour is magically strengthened.
Iron - When standing your ground, you and the armour take less damage.
Bronze - The strength of the effects this armour provides scale based on how outnumbered you are in a fight.
Silver - Your Resilience and Vitality increase based on how damaged the armour is.
Gold - If the armour is ever damaged beyond use while you are wearing it, your skin becomes like the armour until it is repaired, gaining all abilities and effects it would otherwise provide.

The Astar with the greatsword moved in first, appearing before her, already swinging. The sword impacted her shield, but instead of throwing her off balance, she remained unaffected while the Astar was blasted backwards. Backlash triggered twice as always, empowered by Godly Strike, which attacked the very soul of the Astar. It slammed into the side of the dome, and Hildebrandt followed up with Explosive Force, blasting it into the dome wall again as it bounced off.

The explosion reached the other Astar as well, yet the dagger-wielding foe went translucent, the wave passing over it without harm.

The Astar that had just been slammed into the dome not once but twice, affected by four instances of Backlash, two from hitting her and two from surviving Explosive Force, stood up and rolled their shoulder. If the creature had a mouth, Hildebrandt had no doubt it would be twisted into a grin.

Zalia

Zalia had to throw herself backwards as the Astar appeared before her, one of the swords missing her by a hair as she fell. She tried to kick at the hand holding the sword to disarm it as she went but was dodged.

As she landed on her back with a painful impact, the Astar came down with her, twin swords held in preparation to impale her. Zalia rolled out of the way, but one of the soldiers was already there, blocking the swords with the heater shield he wielded. He was pushed into a fighting retreat as Zalia got to her feet and the other soldier joined, spear flashing in at opportune times.

A kick sent the shield-wearer flying, and the Astar got within the spear soldier's reach with a quick teleport. The soldier tried to ward the Astar off with the haft of the spear but only managed to block one of the swords as the other sheared through his armour and left a gaping slash from shoulder to hip. She stumbled backwards, gasping in pain, while Zalia jumped in to help with her own sword at the ready.

Zalia activated Fight or Flight, the slowing of time to her perception and increase of speed helping her to match, then outmatch the Astar. For a moment she pushed the Astar into a retreat while Healing Presence healed the wounded soldier behind. The man with the shield was up already, dashing in slow motion to help her.

Fortunately, Fight or Flight also told Zalia where strikes would hit her. She dodged one blade by twisting her body, stepping back with her right foot. The second blade would have hit her left shoulder had she not parried it, using that burst of speed and power to swing her own sword in a glowing arc at the Astar's own shoulder in a counterattack.

Instead of making contact, her strike was avoided by the use of teleportation. She felt where the sword would hit her, a jab right between her shoulder blades. The feeling disappeared as suddenly as it had appeared, and she turned to see the shield-wielding soldier had managed to change the direction of his charge and shield bash the Astar in the face.

Fight or Flight ran out at that moment, but Zalia didn't need it as the Astar went stumbling. Now healed, the spear soldier helped her ally, and together they pushed the Astar's stumble into further desperation, twin blades fending off the soldiers' strikes with blinding speed.

Having had her rituals dispelled once already, Zalia instead began casting an anti-teleportation ritual on the area they were fighting in, hoping that the Astar wouldn't be able to dispel it in that way again if it weren't a curse on its body.

Nearby, Faian was sweating as she continued to funnel strength, energy, and mana into Zalia and the other two soldiers.

Her sword now turned to her bow, Zalia realised the Astar was constantly speeding up as they began to block each strike with further ease than the one before. The occasional arrow from her bow joined the chaos as she continued to cast her ritual and the Astar failed to block one of them, catching the arrow in the shoulder instead. The impact knocked its block off balance, and the spear soldier managed to impale it through the side of its abdomen.

Acting quicker than she thought should have been possible for the Astar's rank, it cut through the haft of the spear with a powerful strike, leaving the tip still buried in its body. The shield wielder tried to continue the momentum of their advantage, but the Astar managed to disarm his sword with a quick, twisting parry that sent the blade flying away.

Without missing a beat, the soldier pulled out a belt dagger as the spear wielder pulled out a side sword.

Zalia's ritual activated as arrows continued to fly, and seeing that Faian was about to run out of mana to give, she cast Nature's Wrath.

Vines grabbed the Astar's legs as five elementals made of stone ripped themselves from the ground. The two soldiers stepped back to take a moment to calm themselves as the elementals began attacking the Astar with pummelling strikes. It couldn't block them all and was soon stumbling about trying to keep its feet, the vines easily tearing away as it was struck over and over.

Unfortunately, the stone elementals were only Bronze rank and couldn't inflict much damage on the Gold ranker. The rest of Nature's Wrath under Zalia's control, however, very much could.

Fire rained down from the sky, spinning into a whirling tornado filled with flame. She threw spikes of stone into the mix, aiming them so that they would impale the Astar that had disappeared into the whirlwind. The Astar hadn't teleported from within the tornado's eye; she could still barely see it hunkered down in the middle, withstanding the bashing, impaling, and scorching she delivered upon it.

Then she noticed the *power* building within the Astar's hands as her attacks continued. With a powerful punch, it hit the ground and everything exploded.

CHAPTER FIFTY-THREE

Mutual Destruction

Zalia

Zalia woke up mid-flight. She was arcing through the air with a torn body, tears, scrapes, and pieces missing from her torso. They healed quickly, the remnants of her armour beginning to repair at a similar rate.

She landed, rolling a few metres before coming to a stop with a groan. Her bow was still firing arrows from overhead, and the ringing in her ears faded as they healed. Healing Presence was similarly healing the others as well. Faian had it best, having been far from the point of impact, while the shield soldier was pretty torn up but okay. The spear wielder had it the worst, having been as close as Zalia but without heirloom armour to protect him. Zalia could feel that her anti-death had triggered on the woman and that her five earth elementals were no more.

The anti-teleportation ritual was still in effect; she had somehow kept it going through her temporary unconsciousness. That was good, because it meant that as she groggily got to her feet, the Astar was only sprinting towards her, not already at her side, stabbing her with its swords.

Her bow turned into her blade once more as she prepared herself, casting a ritual that would help further protect her. With her mana thankfully high because of Faian's ability, Zalia inspected the Astar for wounds.

It wasn't looking great either, with scorch marks, slashes, and holes through its body. Even as she watched, however, she could see them healing over. Much slower than her own healing but still quick enough to keep it moving. The Astar was so quick now, reaching her within moments, swords swinging. It must have had abilities like Larel; the longer the fight continued the stronger it became.

She activated Fight or Flight, only just off cooldown, and met its swords with her own.

They were evenly matched, for the moment, as she stepped to the right around a jab, deflecting with her blade as she did to throw the arm off balance. Her right hand came up, and the Astar's other sword scraped down the remnants of her armour there, hitting the ground to her right. With increased speed and a glowing power within the sword, Zalia swung with her left hand at the Astar's arm. It had already managed to pull that arm from the deflection, however, and parried her own strike.

Zalia instead kicked at the Astar's legs but the Astar intercepted with its shin, which was guarded by a strange power she only now just saw. It had a similar power across its body, small places that were unharmed by Nature's Wrath.

With her leg kicked aside, she used Mobility to instead push against the air in front of herself and jump directly backwards, coming to a stumbling stop as Fight or Flight ran out.

Then the spear-wielding soldier was there, now with only a side sword, having healed faster because of the anti-death measure. She struck at the Astar's turned back, managing a slash down the side of its spine. The Astar spun in place, disarming and then stabbing the soldier through the throat. Blood spurted as the soldier went down, gurgling.

Zalia yelled and struck out with her own sword, managing to impale the Astar through the chest, her blade leaving a wound that glowed with burning light. She could feel Healing Presence healing the soldier on the ground even as she choked and realised that the wound would not kill the woman. Zalia just had to keep the Astar distracted.

Without Fight or Flight, however, she was far outmatched by the still increased speed and strength of the Astar. It was slowed considerably by its wounds, but not enough.

Zalia avoided having her head chopped off by a thread, managing to push the blade aside just enough to continue living. She received a sword through the gut for her efforts, the Astar's blade punching through her armour. Attached to Zalia by the blade, the Astar came with her as she teleported next to the soldier with the shield who had recovered enough to rejoin the fight. He had another sword, Faian's she realised, and grimly set to taking the Astar's attention off Zalia as her wound recovered.

Faian joined the fight as well, though she wasn't nearly as skilled with the sword as the rest of them, her powers mostly resting in the empowerment and leadership of an army.

The three of them managed to hold the Astar off as the spearwoman got back to her feet, one hand holding her sword and the other her throat. She looked scared, more wary of the Astar than ever.

There was a moment's pause in the battle as they surrounded the Astar. Zalia's anti-teleportation was still active, its effects only applied to teleportation that wasn't her own, and so the Astar could not escape. It could have flown up, yet it looked confident.

Zalia struck but had her sword deflected. The other three took the moment to attack as the Astar was distracted, but it bent backwards under the spearwoman's swing, twisting as it did to avoid the shieldman's jab and stabbed its other sword through Faian's leg, receiving a dagger slammed through the chest for the stab.

That turned out to be a bad trade for the Astar, as Faian's leg quickly healed, though the dagger was left behind in its chest as Faian stumbled back.

Zalia continued the attack but found every move she made was blocked or dodged. They continued until the shieldman had his sword arm severed. He gained Zalia's respect as he continued to fight without the arm, moving forward with his shield raised to present a threat to the Astar. Zalia managed to get a slash down the Astar's leg in return, with the Astar now having more than a few glowing wounds that refused to heal.

Most of the damage done by Nature's Wrath was healed by now, however, though it seemed as if the Astar's healing had slowed significantly.

Faian backed off, without a weapon, to retrieve the charred top of the spearwoman's spear. In that time however, the Astar managed to disarm the spearwoman once more. This time, it took off her head.

Zalia growled with frustration as the woman died but continued her attacks. She pushed for any advantage, struggling to get any hit in that she could. The Astar's confidence had grown at the kill and it now pushed hard, mostly ignoring the shieldman. It had one of its swords knocked out of its hands for the mistake, but the shieldman received a whipping backhand that knocked him out.

With the Astar's sole attention now on her, Zalia struggled to hold her ground. She only had to worry about the one sword now, however, so she had a slightly easier time of things.

Still, she retreated step by step, reaching the edge of the anti-teleportation ritual. Gritting her teeth, she held her ground and something clicked, a notification appearing and instantly vanishing in front of her. She didn't need to read what it said, though, as her bow appeared next to her. With sword still in hand, she knew that the heirloom must have ranked up, as she had both forms active at once. Steeling herself, she pushed back into the fight.

Hildebrandt

Within the dome, Hildebrandt had to ignore the continuing fight she knew was going on outside even as she felt an explosion so large that it reached her despite being inside. The two Astar before her were too skilled to allow her mind to be distracted.

The greatsword wielder struck at her again but twisted the blade so it missed when she presented her shield towards it. The Astar had been learning to only strike her when it would hit anything other than her shield, and her armour now had dents in its surface that represented that.

She had avoided being struck by the daggers so far but had to give a good portion of her attention towards that Astar to avoid it, allowing the greatsword wielder to get in hit after hit, each denting her armour further.

It was obvious what their play was in this fight. Keep her locked down with the threat of a dagger in the back while the greatsword wielder smashed her armour apart. Once that was done, they would have an easier time killing her. They couldn't have known that when her armour was destroyed, her *skin* took on its properties.

She swung three times in quick succession, each strike throwing a bolt of energy that slammed into the greatsword wielder. The Astar arced with pain as her strikes inflicted damage on its soul, something not so easily healed as the body.

The Astar wielding two daggers appeared behind her, but she was ready for it; they had already tried something similar a few times. A quick step of her foot and a twist of her upper torso allowed her to bring the shield up to block the dagger that was going for her spine, angled in such a way that it would slip between helmet and breastplate.

The triggered Backlash threw her attacker across the dome but as before, the Astar became translucent, slowing to a stop before reaching the wall.

Hildebrandt growled in frustration, uncertain of how to deal with the duo. Her attacks hurt them, that much was obvious, but they could also wait her out, as their recovery was enough to counteract the damage dealt by her aura and Backlash triggers. If things continued in this manner, she would lose the fight . . . eventually.

She hefted her mace, considering doing something stupid.

> **Mutual Destruction, Warrior's Mace (Heirloom) - Deeply bonded Emerald Rank.**
>
> **Tin - This mace hits with extra force.**
>
> **Iron - Godly Strike (Previously Strike) is empowered when used through this mace.**
>
> **Bronze - The damage this mace inflicts through physical attacks and Godly Strike (Previously Strike) is increased based on how injured you are.**
>
> **Silver - The Bronze effect of this mace is now also increased based on how damaged Defender's Godly Armour is.**
>
> **Gold - Mutual Destruction. You may temporarily lose all bonuses to Vitality, Resilience, and recovery related to Health and Mana from all sources. Each bonus lost in this way provides an equal boost to both Dexterity and Strength. When this effect runs out, you lose all bonuses gained by the effect but do not regain your bonuses to Vitality, Resilience, and recovery related to Health and Mana until seven days have passed.**
>
> **Emerald - The Gold rank effect of this weapon now also increases all

> **damage dealt by you by an amount proportional to bonuses lost during its use.**

Yeah, she was going to do something stupid.

She activated the Gold rank effect of her mace and felt all the stacked bonuses to her defences from armour, shield, and numerous abilities and passives fade away. Strength flooded her body, which now reacted so quickly that her mind could not keep up.

The two Astar noticed something was wrong immediately. The burning aura flooding from her suddenly intensified, its damage multiplying to many times over what it had just been. The Astars' skin began to melt off, though their natural recovery dealt with most of the damage.

Unfortunately for them, the aura was more of an ability for weaker foes.

She triggered Explosive Force on the greatsword-wielding Astar, and a deafening explosion filled the dome. Hildebrandt remained in place thanks to Stand Your Ground, but the Astar became a bloodstain on the wall.

The dagger-wielding Astar stabbed her in the back, having become translucent during her attack. She felt a coursing pain ink its way through her body, but the Backlash that hit the Astar was well worth it. It caused the Astar's body to explode in a gory mess, leaving nothing but the stumps of two legs there.

Their bodies being destroyed didn't mean they were dead, however.

As the first Astar began to grow back from the bloodstain on the wall, the second began growing back from the stumps that remained of it. Hildebrandt didn't give it a chance.

Her body burned with a fiery pain as she slammed her mace into the soul of the Astar that remained there, hit after hit, each empowered by Godly Strike. She could see the panic in the soul of the Astar as her empowered attacks burnt away its soul, piece by piece.

The other Astar finally managed to free itself and came after her, swinging. The strike landed, cutting her from shoulder to hip, all the way through.

She ignored the wound as that Astar blew up as well. Her body just managed to hold itself together as she pounded on the soul of the second Astar over and over and over.

With a final impact, the Astar's soul dissipated. The heirlooms belonging to the Astar dropped to the ground, two daggers and an amulet.

She turned to the other Astar with a wicked grin wracked with pain. There was nothing to stop her relentless assault as she attacked the soul of the second Astar, each strike filled with power. She didn't know how long it had been when that soul died too.

The grin never left her face, even as darkness pulled over her vision once the effects of the ability ran out. As she lost consciousness, the last sensation she felt was that of falling through the sky.

CHAPTER FIFTY-FOUR

Hidden Pain

Zalia

Zalia blocked the sword swinging towards her body in a two-handed grip with her own, bracer held to blade for extra support. Even with that, she was knocked stumbling by the two-handed strike from the Gold rank Astar.

As she stumbled, however, her bow shot an arrow that hit the Astar in the shoulder, punching it back as well.

Righting herself, Zalia prepared for another round with her opponent, yet they both paused as the giant dome in the sky behind and above them vanished. Zalia's heart beat wildly, worry and fear flashing through her mind. Why had the dome disappeared? Was Hildebrandt dead? Had she lost to the Astar?

She risked a look up and over her shoulder as her bow shot at the Astar again, but all she saw was a single humanoid body falling from the sky. It could have been anyone with the brief glance she allowed herself.

The Astar was obviously expecting its allies to come finish her and the others off as it waited lazily with its sword idly blocking the arrows from her bow. Seeing the Silver rank soldier that fought with her sneaking up behind the Astar, Zalia engaged again.

She struck, a solid overhead strike angled from the Astar's right shoulder to left hip. Her opponent hovered backwards gracefully, deflecting her strike for good measure. That gave her bow the good opportunity to shoot the Astar in the leg.

That made the usually expressionless Astar's face, its face that had no mouth or nose, twist in an expression of . . . annoyance?

She was tired, exhausted from the long fight, even though her body was in perfect condition and constantly healed by her ability.

An impact sounded from behind, a body hitting the floor. Zalia ignored it, continuing her attack. She tried for a one-handed jab towards the Astar, knowing it would be blocked or dodged again. As the Astar moved to do exactly that, she dropped the sword and jumped at it. The Astar deflected the arrow that came from her bow, ready for it this time, but didn't manage to avoid her as she grabbed onto it and punched it in the face repeatedly. With one hand holding its sword arm and the other punching, she couldn't avoid the Astar's other arm that shoved at her.

She stumbled back but managed to keep hold of the sword arm, which she used as leverage to pull on the Astar as she kicked it in the chest.

At the same time she did that, a sword came through at the very point she kicked, impaling her foot to the Astar's chest.

She groaned in pain as she stumbled and then fell backwards without support, and unable to bring her foot down to catch her, she dragged the Astar with her.

Zalia could see the surprise on the soldier's face as he realised what had happened, but she let go of the Astar's sword arm to summon her own and throw it to the soldier. He caught her sword as she grabbed onto the Astar again, managing to free her foot and hold it for just a moment.

The soldier stepped forward and jammed her sword through the struggling Astar again. Her bow shot it too, leaving yet another glowing wound in its body. She continued to hold the struggling enemy as her bow and the soldier shot and stabbed the weakening Astar over and over. Eventually, the struggles stopped.

Zalia lay on the floor, utterly exhausted as her final wounds healed. The soldier had accidentally stabbed her a few times and the burns left by her sword were painful and took much, much longer to heal. It brought her a kind of understanding, a realisation of what her sword and bow were doing to her enemies. That wasn't an understanding she ever thought she would have, and it was one she definitely didn't need.

She got up after a few minutes, realising that she needed to go check out the body that had fallen from the sky.

It was Hildebrandt, lying unconscious on the ground with a large, two-handed sword next to her. Her own heirlooms were nowhere to be seen and neither were the two Emerald rank Astar. Zalia checked her pulse and found her very much still alive. She wasn't even wounded, at least not on the outside.

Searching around for a bit, she also found two daggers and an amulet, all three items heirlooms along with the greatsword. She stored those away in her vault, planning to give them back to Hildebrandt when she came to.

Except she never did.

Zalia waited next to the woman for nearly an hour while the soldiers mourned the woman who had died killing the Gold rank Astar. Still, Hildebrandt did not wake.

Healing Presence was flowing through her, but Zalia's magic didn't heal the soul like Aylie's could. She had a feeling that was what Hildebrandt needed right now.

Faian came over to check on Hildebrandt, obviously as concerned as Zalia was. Not only was she Endaria's only Emerald ranker, she was also a good friend.

"Why won't she wake?"

Zalia looked up. "Damage to her soul, I think. I don't know what she did up there to kill both Astar like that, but whatever it was has drained her. I think they must have attacked her with some kind of soul-destroying attacks as well."

Zalia had received damage to her own soul before, through overuse of passives mostly, and it had never done something like this to her. Whatever had happened up there must have been truly damaging in a way that what she had experienced wasn't. That didn't surprise her, considering the speed with which Hildebrandt had taken out not one but two Emerald rank beings. It wasn't an easy feat, despite her rank.

Faian nodded, accepting Zalia's words. "Alright, bring her to the remains of the cart, we need to get moving."

With that, Faian walked off to organise the rest of the soldiers. The Bronze rank soldiers that had been with the cart, protected by a stone dome, were all unharmed—no one had tried to sneak into the cart to steal Hidey while the rest of them fought. That was fortunate, as a single extra Gold rank Astar would have killed them all with ease.

All things considered, this had been a great victory for them. Two Emerald rank and one Gold rank Astar dead in a single fight. It would increase their chances greatly in the war, assuming there were a limited number of Emerald rank Astar.

Zalia was a little confused as to why these Astar hadn't been out and about, destroying towns and killing people. The power of these few they had just killed would have been enough to cripple their entire population, perhaps even end the Endarians as a race. Most towns would be wiped off the map in minutes by beings such as these.

She tried to pick up Hildebrandt to bring her to the cart, but failed. With a frown, she put her armour on for the extra strength it provided and lifted again. She managed to lift the woman just a bit before dropping her to the ground again.

Damn, she was heavy.

After another failed attempt, she had to call over the other Silver rank soldier to help her. As he leant down to pick up Hildebrandt's legs while Zalia lifted her by the shoulders, she caught his eyes.

"Thanks."

He shrugged, exhaling sharply with the effort of lifting Hildebrandt. "Only following orders."

"It takes a lot more than following orders to go up against something of higher rank like you did today."

He paused, then replied, "For my son. We lost his mother in the invasion, and now I fight so that he can have a future free from fear. I know it might be selfish, endangering myself like I do, but someone has to fight this battle. I know my mother will look after him if I die."

Zalia found herself nodding, strangely understanding. "I've got a daughter, of a kind. Saved her from the demons after her whole family was killed. I sometimes wish she didn't get involved in all this but she has her own past to pay the Astar back for."

"Pay them back for? For what?"

It was Zalia's turn to pause. "I guess it's not widely known yet. The Astar are the ones who brought the demons to Endaria. They've been treating us as cattle, culling the population and providing challenges so that we'll . . ."

It struck Zalia suddenly, the explanation to her earlier question. Of course the Astar weren't going about destroying towns, they weren't trying to wipe them out. They were cultivating Endaria to grow stronger so that they might use them as slaves. What better way to wipe out the weak amongst their number than send the demons. The average rank within Endaria was significantly higher now than it had been, though their numbers were reduced. They probably didn't see this as a war at all, more like a herd trying to escape its pen.

"So that we'll what?" the soldier asked.

"So that we'll grow in rank."

He frowned. "What would they want to do that for?"

Zalia shook her head. "I'm sure the council will make an announcement about it all when they're ready."

They finally got Hildebrandt to the cart and managed to get her onto it. The little pedestal that held Hidey was still intact.

"*Can you let me out of here now?*" he asked.

Zalia rolled her eyes.

"*You know we can't do that yet, we have to make sure one of these Astar was among the ones with your true name.*"

"What's your name?" she asked the soldier.

"Heston. You're Zalia, right? I remember seeing you fight on the battlefield before the capital, in the air."

Zalia nodded. "Yeah, I remember that battle. Those were some terrible days."

Heston nodded his agreement to that. "Aye, that they were."

He moved off to report to Faian, and Zalia turned back to the Hidey cube.

"*Though, I would love to be able to let you out right now, if I could.*"

She received the mental version of a huff of annoyance from the cube.

"*And how are you going to make sure that was the one who knew my true name? It was the one with the daggers, by the way.*"

Zalia paused for a moment, realising it was a good point. *"Well, there were things you haven't been able to tell me. What was Zayes's last mission before retirement, the one that ended with him being imprisoned in Cormaine?"*

There was silence, and for a moment Zalia feared that they hadn't caught the real holder of Hidey's true name.

"I don't like thinking of that time. I will, though, just to prove this to you."

Silence again. Zalia waited patiently, understanding it must be hard for him.

"It was my fault, in a way, that he was captured. That Astar with the daggers, it caught me a few months before Zayes was meant to retire from the Morning's Shade and leave it to the administration of the others. It tortured me, in ways that I cannot describe to you, but understand that there are things that can be done to a soul that should not be. It was in this way that it found my true name and in this way that it made me betray Zayes. I led him into a trap through pretence that I had something important to show him. He trusted me implicitly, you see, because of the nature of our bond. He didn't know that I had been captured, however. He didn't know I was being used."

Zalia could feel the pain in his voice, the obvious frustration at being unable to act to save his friend. *"I see. I believe you, Hidey, but it isn't up to me to free you unfortunately. Faian and the council will have to decide that. It's them you'll have to convince. I'll speak for your side in that meeting when it comes."*

Hidey didn't reply, and she understood his continued frustration with his situation. He couldn't be free still, despite his mind being freed from the Astar. They had to make sure, and Zalia wasn't going to act rashly in freeing him. She had already done enough damage in the recent past with her rushed decisions.

With Hildebrandt on the cart and the soldiers organised, they started towards the capital. Zalia stopped them straight away, however.

"Wait, Faian, we should go to Nature's Reclaim."

Faian turned to her, confused. "What, why?"

"Because my daughter can help heal Hildebrandt. She is the only person I know of who can provide healing for the soul."

Faian considered, then agreed. They were halfway between the two cities, but she realised it was more important to have their Emerald ranker up and about than anything else at that moment.

With the decision made, they continued on their journey to Nature's Reclaim. Home.

CHAPTER FIFTY-FIVE

Delayed

Zalia

Zalia ran in front of the cart as they arrived at the gates to Nature's Reclaim. On the wall above stood four of the new Silver rankers in the city, while the gate proper remained closed. Seeing it was her, a man above called down the other side and after a moment, they swung open.

She couldn't help but notice that the gates had a change made to them, swirls of a runic language she didn't understand marked into the timber that glowed a very dim white. Was it another change that came as a result of freeing people from the Astar?

As they entered, a crow landed on a nearby post, staring at them with a cocked head. Zalia turned to Faian. "Plan on staying for a day or two?"

The woman hesitated, then looked at her exhausted soldiers. "One night, then we'll be off to the capital. I'll need to talk to Hidey and inform the council on what happened."

Zalia nodded, then walked up to the crow waiting for her. "Find temporary housing for these soldiers, preferably together and near my own home. I'll have Hildebrandt and Faian as my guests personally." She paused, then added, "And Heston."

As she spoke, she sent images of each person mentioned to the crow. It flapped off with a single affirmative *caw*.

Some of the soldiers whispered amongst themselves, likely questioning why she was talking to a crow. A minute later, those whispers had stopped as the group was led away by a waist-high, round, four-legged creature with a long snout.

Zalia led Heston and Faian, who drove the cart with Hildebrandt on it, to her own home.

When they arrived, a little fenced off area with a covered barn section grew out of the grass nearby. The grass grew longer and thicker as well. Zalia helped Faian unhitch the animal that pulled the cart, two wheel stops growing to hold the cart in place, and directed the animal into the fenced off area where it feasted upon the luscious grass.

All three of them struggled to get Hildebrandt inside and into a new room that the house had changed to create. It was small with only a single bed surrounded by a couple seats. The space reminded Zalia of a hospital room, though it was missing all the machinery that such a room would usually hold.

She also showed Faian and Heston the two rooms that had appeared adjacent to Hildebrandt's before wandering away to find the rest of her family.

Ember wasn't there, she knew that much from their bond. She was most likely out ensuring all of the people they had freed were okay. Boreal and her children were also out in the city and a slight questioning down their bond had Boreal informing her they were spending time with the Ancient of War, Boreal's partner and her children's father.

Aylie and Lumin were in the house, though, so Zalia brought them down to see Hildebrandt.

"Well? What can you see?"

Aylie was staring intently at Hildebrandt, focused not on the woman's physical state but that of her soul. Her Spiritual Connection ability allowed her to see damage that was done to a soul, while the Bronze rank of her Healing Presence could heal that damage. Zalia's didn't do that, instead preventing the death of herself or a nearby ally once a day.

"It is damaged alright. There is some sort of . . . I don't know how to describe it. It's like there is an infection in her soul, a blue power riddling it. I can see a cut as well, from her shoulder to hip. There are many scars across the surface as well, perhaps wounds that have healed slightly."

Zalia was tense and she could see Faian was similarly worried. "The blue power, can you heal it?"

Aylie shrugged.

"Let's find out?"

She activated the ability she had that healed the soul and watched closely. Instead of watching Hildebrandt, Zalia watched Aylie intently, trying to discern what she was seeing from her expression. It wasn't anything good.

"The cut healed, as did the scars. The blue power, whatever it is, did not. It's strange . . . I feel like I could touch i—"

Zalia grabbed Aylie's hand as she reached out to touch it. "Don't do that."

Aylie pulled her hand back, abashed. "Right."

Zalia didn't want to see what power that could take out an Emerald ranker would do to a Bronze one.

"So, what do we do?" Faian asked.

Zalia shrugged. "I don't know."

They both looked at Aylie but she looked just as lost.

All of them glanced at Hildebrandt as she twitched slightly.

Zalia pulled out some Soulroot and Frozen Heart. "It can't hurt," she said by way of explanation to Faian's curious look.

Faian gestured as if to say, "Go ahead."

So Zalia did.

Using the pieces of plant as seeds, she prepared a living ritual using the two herbs and once done, activated it. She felt some effects of the healing herself, less of the warm, comforting presence that normal healing gave, but rather, a soothing coolness. Not one she felt in her body, but instead in her soul, as strange as that was to experience.

Between the two types of healing, Hildebrandt twitched a little more. It was like she was in pain or . . . fighting something?

"I don't know what else we can do to help her. I think it's up to her own body to fight whatever this is off."

Faian sighed and sat back in her chair. "Nothing to be done then?"

Aylie nodded at the same time Zalia did.

Faian pushed herself up out of her chair with obvious effort. "I'd best check up on my soldiers, where did you house them?"

Zalia gestured to a vine that grew out of the wall. "Follow that, it'll lead you to them."

With an odd look at Zalia, Faian followed the vine as it continued to grow down the hallway and out the front door towards where the soldiers were, and Faian walked past it, the sections behind her disintegrated.

Zalia put a hand on Aylie's knee to get her attention. "I'm just going to go find Ember and tell her how it went, alright?"

Aylie nodded, still focused on Hildebrandt.

Zalia stood and made to move, pausing on her way out. "Oh, and see if there is anything Lumin can do, would you?"

Aylie didn't reply but Zalia knew she would do as asked.

Going out into town, Zalia breathed in the fresh air to settle her mind. Ember was in the eastern section of town in a small grouping of houses that were the homes of the Silver rankers. The Ancient of Wisdom had put them all together in hopes that they could bond and help each other through their experiences. Solidarity could be a powerful tool in the healing of a group.

Zalia started towards that section of town, watching the people that walked by as she did so. As the . . . leader or creator of Nature's Reclaim, she felt a responsibility for the people that lived here. She wanted them to feel both safe and happy in their lives and did a good job at that for the most part, or so she thought.

The ever-present healing that permeated the town was an important piece in that, as it meant everyone in the town was always healthy. No sickness spread, people's pains and injuries healed, albeit slowly. The effect was somewhat dampened when spread across such a large number of beings.

By the expressions and body postures of the people she walked by, Zalia felt that the general mood of the town was good. It wasn't as high as years prior, as news of the coming war and events had been spread by the Ancient of Wisdom. It wasn't Zalia's place to hide anything from them, and neither would she want to. It was important that everyone was ready.

She found Ember sitting with a small group of people, only four others, at a bench in one of the town's parks. Ember said something, gesturing grandly overhead and one of the men at the table laughed. Zalia couldn't help but smile at the sight of her partner doing what she did best; help people heal.

"Got a moment?"

Ember turned towards her at the words then said a quick farewell to the others at the table before coming over to Zalia. "Hey, Zals, how did it go?"

She knew that Ember would have felt the same things Zalia had during the fight and so would have a basic understanding already. They still enjoyed speaking to each other, however, rather than relying on the bond between them for all communication.

"Good, we managed to kill two Emerald Astar and one Gold. Hildebrandt isn't in a good way, though."

Ember immediately began walking towards their home, the conversation continuing at the table they left behind. "What's happened?"

Zalia shrugged. "There is some kind of power left over from her fight that is holding her down. It's something attacking her soul that we can't really do anything about at the moment."

"Shit . . ."

"Yeah."

They walked in silence for a minute, before Zalia realised she hadn't ever checked her heirloom weapon's rank up. "My sword and bow ranked up to Silver as well."

Druidic Armaments, Blessed by Starlight (Blessed Heirloom) - Deeply bonded Silver rank.

Tin - The blade and arrows of your armaments are kept magically sharp and remain so permanently. Arrows fired from the bow have a powerful seeking effect.

Iron - Both blade and arrows fired from the bow gain the Starlit effect. Additionally, drawing the string of the bow without an arrow will create a starlight arrow already nocked.

Bronze - Parrying an attack or firing an arrow from the bow will infuse your next strike with a powerful cosmic force. In addition, it will also

> **make you invisible and slightly faster for a short duration.**
> **Silver - Druidic Blade and Druidic Bow have fused into Druidic Armaments, combining and enhancing both items' effects and allowing for both to be wielded at once.**
> **Seeking Effect - Arrows will adjust in flight to hit vulnerable spots, such as joints in armour or scales, and avoid other natural defences such as bone.**
> **Starlit - Affected weapon passes through non-magical armour and applies Light from Within.**
> **Light from Within - Affected target takes a small amount of damage over time as starlight glows from within.**

Zalia was surprised to find that the heirloom had become a single item again. It had started off as just the bow, then split into two but now fused back to one; a single more powerful item.

She shared the description with Ember who murmured in appreciation. The effects of her heirlooms at reaching Silver were showing themselves to be considerably stronger than prior ones, as expected.

The Bronze effect applying to both blade and bow was incredibly powerful. Since parrying would make her invisible to her opponent, it would allow her to strike with enhanced speed and significantly more power, with each arrow fired giving the same benefits.

About to reach home, they were stopped by a crow that landed on a fence in front of them. As it alit on the fence, Zalia heard a commotion coming from the north.

"North gate!" the crow yelled at her, its speech croaky and broken.

Zalia and Ember immediately started sprinting towards the north gate. After a few moments, Zalia's flight ritual activated on Ember and they flew up over the crowds of people either running towards or away from the gate.

They arrived to chaos. There was a group of townspeople, wearing armour and wielding weapons, surrounding something Zalia couldn't see. On the opposite side of the gate was a dead Astar with a spear of sand impaling it straight through the chest. There was blood all around them.

Landing, Zalia and Ember pushed through the crowd, some people moving aside as they were recognised. There was red blood here, the owner of which was sat propped up against the open gate, having fallen there.

The man had a sword sticking out of his gut, the source of the blood. Looking around, Zalia realised that there were a number of people who looked ragged and dirty, their appearance telling stories of a long journey.

Zalia looked down at the bloodied man again and found she recognised him: Matthias, leader of the Morning's Shade.

CHAPTER FIFTY-SIX

What Hides in the Storm

Lady Indis

Indis stared down at her hands. The trees, snow, and ice around her didn't register to her mind as she inspected the roughened, calloused hands. It was still strange seeing anything other than soft, smooth skin there.

She grabbed a bunch of her hair and pulled it around to the front, hacking at the long threads until it was cut short. The damn stuff was just getting much too inconvenient. She discarded the hair, throwing it to the side as she continued trudging through the snow.

It was quite peaceful out here, any sound dampened and all signs of life hidden by the snow. For this reason, she was beginning to understand why Zalia had enjoyed living out here by herself for so long. Of course, had it been a few months prior, Indis would have *hated* being out here away from her people.

My people.

She huffed in derision at the thought. Her people indeed.

Things were different now, her point of view changed by recent events. She wanted nothing to do with *people* anymore. *People* had betrayed her, throwing her out to the figurative wolves after everything she had done for them. Disposed of her after the years of her life she had spent fending for them, giving of herself for them.

A chittering sound came from her left, and Indis spun, blasting the noise with a bolt of lightning from the sky. The crack of thunder broke the serene peace of the snow-laden land and she watched the charred remains of a bird fall the last few feet from a tree that was now splintered itself.

She slowly lowered her hands, staring at the dead bird. Even this beautiful, natural place. She ruined even this.

When she'd arrived in the north, she had gone to see if Zen would take her in. Even Zen, young, naive, innocent Zen hadn't wanted her there. He hadn't said that outright, of course, but she could tell from his actions that her presence bothered him. So she had left.

Where do I belong?

The question continued to bother her. It had ever since the day of the vote. Where was home?

Another crack of thunder shook the sky and Indis looked up to see that a storm was brewing. Had she done that?

Either way, she needed to find shelter. But where?

Snow began to fall from the sky, slowly at first. It fell down thicker as Indis pushed through the already deep snow towards who knew what. A cave, perhaps, or a hollow of some sort.

The cold didn't bother her usually, the time she had spent in the north prior lending her enough levels in Cold Resistance that the normal climate of the north couldn't harm her. This cold was different, somehow. She felt chilled to the bone and began to shiver violently. Lightning arced across her body as she used it to warm herself, a strange but effective use of the ability.

Her struggle was only made worse as time passed. Lightning struck again to her left, a tree exploding at its impact. She ducked by instinct as a piece of wood shot by her face, impaling another tree to her right. Snow fell so thickly now that she struggled to see more than a few metres in each direction. Where had this storm come from?

There was a sound of a wingbeat, far away. Then another.

Indis shuddered and pushed through the snow with increased desperation. The wingbeats continued, growing louder and louder. She didn't know what was making the sound but she didn't want to find out.

She spotted a small icy cave entrance, just ahead. Only a few more metres. Then she felt a sharp pain in her foot as she stepped on something, followed by a slight burning sensation like poison.

A shadow fell across her as the beating of wings threw the wind into a cyclone. She had to hunker down, so close to the cave, lest the wind rip her away. Staring upwards, she could only see a form so massive it blocked out the sun, and the glitter of scales as lightning exploded from the creature's body. Snow whipped around her as another wingbeat blasted the land. She cringed down even further, trying to retreat into the snow around her even as it was pushed away by the beating of the massive creature's wings.

A hand grabbed her and she reactively arced lightning across her body. She heard a grunt of pain even as the hand continued to pull, dragging her out of the storm and into the cave. The hand let go as she whipped around to fight, preparing a lightning strike for whoever dared grab her like that.

She wasn't prepared for what she saw.

It was a man, tall but not extremely so, with lanky limbs and a pair of goggles over his eyes. He wore a shirt and shorts with nothing on his feet but pieces of wood strapped by leather. The man had the appearance of someone heading for the beach during summer, not someone in the cold, snowy north.

> **? - Bronze rank.**

"W-who the fuck are you!?"

He stood there with his hands raised, the right one slightly scorched, obviously not in the market for another blast of lightning. "Hey, wait, I just saw you were there. I didn't mean to surprise you."

Indis narrowed her eyes, glaring at him until he backed up another step.

She could barely hear him over the wingbeats that continued outside, though they now faded into the distance.

He gestured further into the cave saying something about tea, pulled up the goggles, then backed up and turned to walk the way he had pointed.

The storm outside was weakening, apparently a localised effect around whatever that creature had been, so she could have left then and there. Something about the man drew her in, however. Perhaps it was the loneliness she felt, or the fact that he had invited her in rather than turn her away, as so many others had. Whatever it was, she warily followed him in.

There was a faint smell to the cave, like it had once been the home of some creature, and the ice that coated the walls had a slight magical sensation to it. She inched forward, limping slightly as her foot healed, the tiny bit of poison already dealt with.

Poking her head around the final corner, she found the man crouched down next to a smokeless fire that had a pot of tea heating above it. The cold of the unnatural storm was fading from her bones, but the warmth of the fire called to her all the same. She hesitantly joined the man by the fire, crouching down but not sitting. If he decided to attack, she would be prepared. She wore her battle robes still, an heirloom passed down through generations within her family.

> **Lightning Mage's Battle Robes (Heirloom) - Bonded Gold rank.**
> **Tin - Slightly increase damage and slightly decrease mana use of all lightning-based abilities.**
> **Iron - Foes struck by your lightning have their resistance to lightning reduced. This effect stacks.**
> **Bronze - Lightning-based abilities become exponentially stronger the longer you channel them.**
> **Silver - Lightning controlled by you becomes more directed, changing course to jump from enemy to enemy, rather than be attracted to the**

> **ground or other inanimate objects. Additionally, your magic cannot be dispelled or subdued.**
> **Gold - Lightning controlled by you that strikes enemies stays for longer, arcing across their body for a time before fading. Additionally, you are immune to all lightning damage.**

She had worn the robes from a very young age, as she had been gifted the Gold rank heirloom by her father.

The man across from her watched her as warily as she watched him, perhaps wondering if she was going to blast again.

"My name is Hedion," the man offered.

She paused, uncertain, then decided to introduce herself. "I'm La . . . Leyra."

She almost introduced herself as Lady Indis, but that wasn't really her anymore, was it? Without title, lands, or even the remainders of a family left to her, could she really call herself nobility?

If he noticed her hesitation, he didn't comment on it.

"Leyra, nice to meet you. Might I ask you what you're doing out here?"

"I could ask you the same thing."

He shrugged. "Fair enough. I come out here regularly to collect different herbs and alchemical components that can only be found here."

She saw no lie in the words and trusted her own instinct in that regard. It was true that there were particular items that could only be found here, and she had even collected some of them herself the last time she had been here with Zalia, Ember, and Zen.

"I'm looking for something."

He tilted his head just slightly. "What for? I might be able to help."

Myself, she thought. "I'd rather not say."

He shrugged, indifferent. "Alright, want some tea?"

She stared at it. "What's in it?"

He looked down, then back up, obviously realising she was suspicious of it.

"A particular herb that grows a bit further north than most like to travel. When brewed like this it has long-lasting warming effects on the body."

He poured a cup and held it out to her.

"You first," she said.

He shrugged again, then drank a bit before proffering it to her once more.

Leyra accepted the cup but waited, holding it and allowing the warmth of the drink to seep into her unshielded hands. "What was that thing out there?" she found herself asking.

The man, Hedion, looked towards where the cave arced up and around to the surface. "I don't fully know. I've never seen anything like it."

Leyra hadn't either. She had a feeling that it was a creature like that which had stopped the Endarians from spreading their borders further north, with similar reasons to the south. Sometimes, she wondered just how big the world was, how much of it they would never see.

She looked back at him, trying to decide if the tea was poisoned and he just had a resistance to it. Why would that be the case, though? It wasn't like he had been here brewing poisonous tea in the expectation of finding someone else out here. She took a sip.

It was good, relatively tasteless, but she could feel the spreading warmth radiate through her body immediately. It was comforting

"It's quite dangerous out here," Hedion said.

Leyra shrugged. "So?"

He hesitated a moment. "Well, if you are looking for something, maybe I can help you? If you'd be up for helping me out a little along the way as well. There are a few creatures here that I'd rather not fight on my own."

She thought about it for a moment. While the thought of being alone out here with a complete stranger was not a good one, he seemed . . . harmless. In fact, she was entirely sure that she could defeat the man in a fight if it came to it.

Besides, what else was she doing?

Maybe she could find a place to belong here, away from the people she had once sacrificed herself for, who had then rejected her.

"Alright, I'll give it a go."

CHAPTER FIFTY-SEVEN

Free At Last

Zalia

Zalia jumped forward, inspecting Matthias with a discerning eye. Apart from the sword in his gut, he seemed to be in good health. She crouched down, met his eyes, and once acknowledged, pulled the sword out, throwing it with a clatter behind her.

The double-layered healing of her Grove and Healing Presence grew new skin over the wound in moments.

"Matthias!? Where have you been?"

He looked up, exhaustion obvious. "Zalia?"

She nodded.

Matthias had vanished long ago after the huge ritual had brought demons to Endaria. He had once been one of three leaders of the Morning's Shade and also happened to be Gold rank, specialising in sand manipulation magic.

"What has happened to Et's Way?" he asked.

She started, hearing the name of the town that she had replaced so long ago.

"This is Nature's Reclaim now, and I'm the appointed lady of the town. A lot has changed since you disappeared."

He started getting to his feet and she helped him up. Ember shooed the curious townspeople away, though they still waited around at a distance.

Matthias's eyes went distant.

"I feel like I've been in a dream," he whispered.

Zalia thought she knew what had happened. "The Astar had you?"

His eyes focused back on her. "Yes, you know about that?"

She looked at the other people who had apparently arrived with him, similarly exhausted. They all wore the same simple clothes that the Astar gave to their mindless slaves.

"Yeah, me and my family were the ones that freed you and the others from them."

"That was you!? In the sky, summoning lightning?"

Zalia nodded.

Then, strangely, the man teared up and *gave her a hug*.

How odd.

She returned the hug, patting him on the back a bit awkwardly. "Thank you."

"I'm sorry I couldn't get you out with the others, we didn't have time to wait any longer."

He shook his head, breaking the hug. "I understand. How many did you save?"

"Around one hundred and thirty. Would have been more if the Astar hadn't chased us the whole way."

Matthias shuddered. "We were thirty, originally. They just wouldn't let us go."

Zalia looked around at the six remaining, including Matthias. It must have been a torturous journey. They wouldn't have had anti-teleportation and had apparently not had any craftsmen amongst their number. She knew that they hadn't gotten all of the slaves out, she just hadn't imagined that Matthias had been amongst that group.

"It's good to see you alive, Matthias. We're in need of you now more than ever."

He looked at her. "In need? Why?"

She shook her head. "A lot has changed since you left. Come, you and yours are welcome in Nature's Reclaim. We'll see you looked after, and we can talk once you've slept. You all look exhausted."

Matthias turned to the other members of his group who all looked just as exhausted and dirty as he did. "That sounds good."

She saw a tension leave his body. They had spent the past weeks hunted and on the run, she knew how that felt.

Zalia gestured to the few guards nearby and pointed at the body. "Burn that, please, I'd rather not have even a dead Astar here."

They moved to do as she asked while she led Matthias away from the gates and towards her home. She had a feeling that he would be surprised to find Hildebrandt there and even more so to learn of the state that she was in.

A lot had changed in the past four odd years, which was about the time he had been enslaved for. He probably didn't even know about the war, perhaps even the invasion, depending on how early he had been taken.

When they arrived, Zalia showed Matthias to Hildebrandt's room, where he rushed over to check on her. Zalia had told him the short version of the story, enough that he wouldn't be surprised to find her there.

While he did that, Zalia pulled out the heirloom items that had dropped from the dome with Hildebrandt. They were hers by right, to do with as she wished.

> **Twin Daggers, Starfire and Void (Heirloom) - Emerald rank.**
> **Phasing Amulet (Heirloom) - Emerald rank.**
> **Warrior's Greatsword, That Which Cleaves (Heirloom) - Emerald rank.**

She wasn't particularly surprised to find that the daggers were technically one heirloom and personally didn't have much use for them. The Phasing Amulet might have been something she was interested in though.

Matthias shook Hildebrandt's shoulders gently.

"She won't wake, we've tried various types of healing she just . . . won't wake. I think it was this dagger that stabbed her." Zalia held the dagger, Starfire, out to him and he took it, inspecting the weapon.

Then, she began to tell him of everything he had missed.

She started with the invasion, describing the horrors she witnessed and what they had to do to clean out the demons. Then came the few years of peace, the small discoveries she made about the Astar during and after the invasion that led to the realisation that the Astar were stealing people, something he knew of intimately. Finally, she got to the more recent events, which she went into with more detail. What she had done to free the slaves, himself included, how the council of Endaria had reacted and their current official state of war with the Astar.

He took it all in stride, still holding the dagger carefully so as to not scratch himself with it.

"So much lost time . . ."

Zalia waited, unsure what to say.

"Is there nothing you can do for Hildebrandt?"

Zalia shook her head slowly. "No, not that we know of. For now it's up to her to fight it off, though Aylie and I will continue to do what we can."

Then she realised that she hadn't really gone over why Hidey was imprisoned or what the purpose of the fight with the Emerald Astar had been. That was fine, Hidey could explain what had happened to him now.

"Hidey is here too."

She saw a faint smile on his face at the nickname and it occurred to her that this was a very different man than the one she had met previously. That man had been stern and intrinsically disappointed in everything and everyone around him. This Matthias seemed . . . normal.

"Can I see him?" Matthias asked.

"Sure, yeah."

They left Hildebrandt there and Zalia quickly checked in on Heston on the way out of the house. He was fast asleep, loud snores muffled by the vine-leaf coated walls.

It didn't take long to reach the place that the Ancient of Wisdom had given to the soldiers temporarily; it was a house large enough for them all to sleep comfortably for the time being. She went inside to find most of them asleep or nearing sleep, with Faian nowhere to be found.

Zalia gently prodded one of the awake soldiers and got directions to Faian. She was out in the back of the house in a small fenced garden, holding Hidey's cube.

The conversation Faian and Hidey were having fell to silence as Zalia and Matthias pushed out into the backyard.

Matthias stormed forward and grabbed the cube from Faian. "How *could* you," he hissed at it.

Zalia raised a hand. "He wasn't actu—"

"We trusted you, we *relied* on you. And you betrayed us." Matthias dropped the cube to the ground, then stomped away.

Zalia stood there as he pushed past her, dumbfounded. He had seemed like he wanted to see Hidey because he missed him, not because he wanted to yell at him.

"So he made it back then, I see," Faian commented.

Zalia barely registered the words. She had mentioned to Matthias that Hidey was being controlled, though she hadn't said by whom. Couldn't he see that it wasn't Hidey's fault?

"Can you let him out yet?"

Faian smiled, leaning down to pick the cube Hidey was stuck in back up. "I was actually just about to do just that."

Zalia felt a spike of excitement. Hidey would be free at last!

She knew it hadn't been easy on the shade, spending years trapped in the tiny cube. In a way, it was similar to what Matthias had been through, yet quite the opposite. Where Matthias had his mind dulled and trapped while his body remained free, Hidey had his body trapped while his mind remained free. Two similar yet somehow very different experiences.

Faian held the cube up near to her mouth and whispered something into it. A sharp crack resounded from the cube and smoke began to leak from it. The smoke slowly took form, growing in size until Hidey stood before them, whole once more.

Zalia moved forward and dragged him into a hug. "Welcome back."

He let out a long sigh of relief, hugging her back before stretching luxuriously. His hands pulled open and closed over and over, almost of their own accord. "*It feels so good to be free once more, not just of body but of mind.*"

And Zalia realised she had been wrong in her thoughts. Hidey *had* indeed been mentally imprisoned as well, in a different way, yet at the hands of the Astar as well.

Hidey looked over her shoulder towards where Matthias had stormed off. "*I should speak to him.*"

Zalia shook her head. "Eventually, but first, you should see Hildebrandt. She went through a lot to get you out of that cube, and is still going through it now. It wouldn't have been possible without her."

"*You're right, of course. Will you show me the way?*"

"Of course."

She did, however, meet Faian's eyes, receiving a nod of approval. There was a warning there, though, a silent message to be careful still. They were ninety-nine percent sure Hidey was free, yet it would be best to remain wary for now.

Still, it was hard to feel down as she watched Hidey take a single step, smiling all the while.

CHAPTER FIFTY-EIGHT

Hidden Injury

Zalia

Zalia sat in the corner of Hildebrandt's healing room while Hidey floated by her side. She kept an eye on him out of the corner of her eye as she spoke with Boreal.

The Ancient of War was there too, pretending that Boreal was the only reason for his presence. Despite the casual appearance, Zalia could tell there was some tension in his body. This was the first real possible internal threat they'd had in Nature's Reclaim, and it was the Ancient of War's responsibility to ensure nothing bad happened. Zalia didn't expect the ancient to deal with it himself, however, as Hidey was Gold rank. She was pretty sure he was, at least, though not certain of it, considering she still couldn't discern his true rank using her abilities. Even if she could, she wouldn't be able to trust what she saw, anyway. Who knew if it was possible to show a lower rank than was reality?

"We're going to have to go meet that Astar who wants to talk with us soon," Zalia thought to Boreal.

"They're not very tasty," Boreal explained.

Zalia rolled her eyes, a faint smile pulling at her expression. *"I would rather hope to never find that out for myself, so I'll believe you."*

Boreal huffed out a breath, obviously disappointed with Zalia's priorities. *"Always talking, never eating. I guess I can hold back. Only because they're not tasty, though."*

"Will the Ancient of War be alright to look after the young ones? I don't think they should come on this particular mission."

Boreal bumped her shoulder into the large cat standing next to her: the Ancient of War, her partner. She purred at some unheard mental response. *"Yes, though, he says Aylie is not so little anymore."*

Zalia shook her head. "*I'd like Aylie to come with us—she is able to see things that the rest of us can't. Besides, I think she might be able to escape most dangers by entering the astral anyway.*"

Zalia saw the ancient tense, and she looked over to Hidey standing over the small table, holding the three heirlooms Hildebrandt had won off the Astar. He was staring at the daggers, particularly focused on the one called Starfire.

"Something wrong?"

Hidey looked up at her. "*No, just . . .*" His form fuzzed a bit, like he was shivering. "*I've some bad memories of these daggers.*"

The fear and pain in his voice made Zalia shiver too. "I'm sorry to ask you to dredge up those memories further, but is there anything you know of that we can do to help Hildebrandt?"

Hidey thought for a moment before shaking his head. "*She fights a battle in her soul, her own strength against that of the starfire. Normally, she wouldn't struggle so much against even an Emerald rank heirloom like this, but I believe she must have used an ability linked to her mace. Both Matthias and I have warned her many times against using it, and I know of only one other time that she has. If she survives a week from the time of the battle, I have no doubts that she will pull through quickly. It's surviving that week that I am worried about.*"

Zalia frowned, looking down at Hildebrandt. She had once shared the descriptions of her abilities with Zalia, barring that of her heirloom items. How, exactly, they made Hildebrandt so vulnerable, Zalia couldn't imagine. Hildebrandt's defensive capabilities were such that killing her normally would take someone tough enough to withstand Backlash, all while putting out enough damage to kill her at the same time. Evidently, not even two Emerald rank Astar were capable of that.

"How do we help her during this week, then?"

Hidey shrugged. "*I am no healer, Zalia. You would know better than I.*"

Zalia stared at Hildebrandt, unhappy. She had been hoping Hidey could help in this. Fortunately, there was one more source of information that she might be able to get some answers out of. When she had left Cormaine, the dying collective had given her the sum of their vast and ancient memory. While most of it was undoubtedly important memories of the past, a good few bits were memories of a divined future. The real future strayed further from the memories each time she used them to learn something, as the act of changing history that was yet to occur made what was beyond more uncertain.

Mentally telling Boreal and the Ancient of War to keep an eye on Hidey, Zalia went up to Aylie's room and went through the portal there that led to the top of the Ancient of Life. Constructed amongst the boughs of the tree was a place of spiritual connection, a comfortable platform that Zalia had created for Aylie to learn the extent of her abilities.

Preparing herself for the mental pain and soul strain that came with accessing the collective's memories, Zalia reached into the Ethereal Vault Gauntlet and opened the door between memory and mind.

As always, flashes of memory from the collective and from her own mind pushed to the front of her consciousness. An image of Cormaine as it had been came first: deep, cool, and calm intertwined rivers flowing around islands covered in beautiful wildlife and the homes of the Bathar. It was followed by an image from Zalia's own childhood, a room filled with stone pews and a lectern at its end, behind which stood a large cross. A stab of pain pulsed through her body before the image moved on to yet more scenes of Cormaine and Endaria as they had been.

The memories came to the present, Hildebrandt lying on the bed overlooked by Hidey and the Ancient of War, but with Zalia and Boreal nowhere to be seen. Aylie kneeling in a place filled only with clouds and a huge star before her that pulsed with a blue light, veins extending from the star into the far distance. An expression of pain filled her face as she struggled against an unseen foe.

The present passed by, and though Zalia tried to stop the memories there, sure she had just seen a possible solution to their problem, more followed. She saw herself standing in a huge underground space filled with the jagged, alien architecture of the Astar, a city that spanned the horizon. Then she was in Cormaine, surrounded once more by the dark spirits that filled the sky there, yet no longer in the seemingly endless caves that she had been in before.

She finally cut off the memories, doubling over with a gasp, hands to her head, as a migraine pulsed pain through her mind.

Congratulations! Ethereal Vault Gauntlet has ranked up from Bronze to Silver due to your regular accessing of a complex memory.
Ethereal Vault Gauntlet (Heirloom) - Bonded Silver rank.
Tin - You may tear open space to access an ethereal vault. The ethereal vault is a limited extradimensional space that you may enter and store objects within.
Iron - You gain the power to store and retrieve information within the ethereal vault. By concentrating on a specific topic, memory, or piece of knowledge while wearing the gauntlet, you can mentally "record" it into the gauntlet's vault. This information is then stored in an abstract, ethereal form, like a shimmering light. When needed, you can access the gauntlet to "read" the stored information, allowing you to quickly recall facts, details, or instructions you have previously recorded.
Bronze - Your control over the ethereal vault extradimensional space becomes more refined. You gain the ability to manipulate the spacial dimensions within the vault, allowing you to efficiently organise and stack stored items without regard to their physical sizes. This ability enables you to store a larger quantity of objects within the same limited space.

Silver - The deep connection between your Druid Groves and the Ethereal Vault Gauntlet allows you to form permanent portals to your vault attached to each Grove. These portals are different in that only those with permission may enter, and they will remain even if another portal is created elsewhere, allowing easy access to your Groves at any time. Additionally, your vault is now a permanent space, allowing you to close it with people and objects still within the vault but outside its storage spaces.

It took her a minute to recover from the physical pain as Healing Presence worked to counter the mental strain. She knew that the feeling of fatigue in her soul would dissipate soon too, though it would take more time.

The memories of the past didn't disturb her so much as the ones of her possible future did. To know that she would go to the Astar city *and* Cormaine once more did not bring her comfort. She hadn't seen any of her friends or family in either image, which was disconcerting.

She had gotten what she wanted, however. The image of Aylie kneeling before the blue sun was the answer.

Aylie had seen that the struggle Hildebrandt was going through was within her soul, not her body. While the soul did not exist in the astral—normally, at least—it *was* more accessible from there. It was also a place that Aylie could go.

It would be easier to help Hildebrandt from there, to help her fight the strange power off. Zalia would just have to avoid the situation the image had shown her: Aylie by herself, kneeling and in pain.

Before attempting to deal with that, however, her attention was dragged to the vault gauntlet's rank up. With the Silver rank of Mobility, she had gained the ability to mark a place that she could teleport to at will, with a long cooldown. This was a bit different.

Limited only to her two Groves, it was a bit more restrictive in its uses, but the ability to go home from anywhere without any cooldown simply by opening her vault portal helped her feel just a bit safer doing what she would have to do. She wished she'd had the ability when going to the Astar town for the first time, as rescuing the slaves there would have been so much easier.

After reading through that particular notification a few times, she read through the short list of level ups for skills that she hadn't checked in a very long time. Knowing that she wasn't close to any skill rank-ups, she hadn't been too pressed to keep an eye on them.

Congratulations! Kill Shot has reached Silver 6.
Congratulations! Hunter's Mark has reached Silver 6.
Congratulations! Fight or Flight has reached Silver 6.
Congratulations! Survivalist and associated skills have gained two levels, reaching Silver 10.

> **Congratulations! Hunter class has reached Silver 6.**
> **Congratulations! Natural Matter Alteration has reached Silver 9.**
> **Congratulations! Druid Grove has reached Silver 11.**
> **Congratulations! Herbal Magic has reached Silver 12.**
> **Congratulations! Nature's Wrath has gained two levels, reaching Silver 8.**
> **Congratulations! Protection of the Wilds has gained three levels, reaching Silver 8.**
> **Congratulations! Healing Presence has reached Silver 12.**
> **Congratulations! Druid Class has gained three levels, reaching Silver 8.**
> **Congratulations! Mobility has reached Silver 11.**

With all of that out of the way, Zalia opened up her vault to have a look.

The inside was relatively unchanged, though the walls that were decorated with imagery of her bonds with Ember, Boreal, and her two other heirlooms now included imagery of the three ancients as well. The only other change in the space was two semi-transparent portals that were next to each other at the end of the space.

She could see the front of her house as seen from the portal hub in Nature's Reclaim. While the only portal that had previously been there was one that led to the Grove in the desert, the slightly sideways view from this portal told her that a second had joined it there. The other portal in the vault gave a view into the desert Grove, showing the portal hub there.

Zalia opened the portal leading to Nature's Reclaim and stepped through. She turned around and closed the portal again, seeing that it was present there, yet she was unable to look through it to the vault while it was closed. Good.

Feeling more confident about meeting the rebel Astar now that she had a way of getting not only herself but her family out of there, Zalia went to find Aylie and Ember.

CHAPTER FIFTY-NINE

With Certainty

Zalia

When Zalia found Ember and Aylie, they were sitting together upstairs talking about their experiences as souls separated from their bodies at the hands of the Astar. She waited a while as they spoke before eventually interrupting them.

"Hey, could you two come downstairs in . . . ten minutes once I've brought Faian over?"

Receiving two nods in return, Zalia also sent a mental message to Boreal asking the same.

She walked off to find Faian as well, knowing that the Ancient of War was still watching Hidey. They needed to talk about what would happen next, in regards to her meeting with the rebel Astar, what Hidey should or could be allowed to see and do, *and* whether or not Aylie could enter the astral to try and help heal Hildebrandt. The more she thought about it, the less she liked the idea of letting Aylie in there with some very dangerous Emerald rank magic.

Additionally, while they were relatively sure that Hidey was freed from the Astar's influence, there wasn't *really* any way to be certain. They would just have to trust him and hope that it didn't backfire. That was Zalia's feeling anyway, though she knew she too often trusted much too easily.

Faian was easy to find; she was looking after her soldiers, ensuring they were fed and organising for supplies to be gathered for the trip back to the capital. Zalia knew they wouldn't be staying long.

Though a tiny bit annoyed at being disturbed from her organising, Faian agreed to come with Zalia and they both went back to her house, where Hidey, Boreal, the Ancient of War, Aylie, Ember, and Heston were waiting. Matthias was still out somewhere in the city, but Zalia knew he could care for himself and would come back if he needed anything. She wasn't worried about him causing any trouble.

With everyone now in a bigger room that had constructed itself during the time it took Zalia to walk from the soldiers' housing back to her home for the meeting, she started it off.

"Alright, I think the first thing we should discuss is how much, exactly, we can trust Hidey with."

Hidey stared at her and she raised her hands defensively.

"Look, it's nothing personal but you *know* that we aren't entirely sure of your freedom from the Astar's influence."

Hidey didn't argue, though Ember looked like she might before Faian chipped in.

"Until the council has come to a final decision on this, we should not explain too much to the Hidden. As such, if this meeting will be a sensitive conversation, as I believe it will be, I would prefer if Heston and whoever you choose, Zalia, would accompany him out of the house until we are finished."

Ember looked as if she was going to argue again, but Hidey agreed.

"I shall go along, perhaps I can find Matthias and speak to him."

Zalia gestured to the Ancient of War, who was only there to keep an eye on Hidey anyways, and he and Heston followed Hidey out of the room. She felt bad, of course, but was more than happy to leave the decision of how and when to trust Hidey to the council.

"Alright, the thing I mainly wanted to talk about was meeting the Astar rebel. I've got an easy way for me and anyone that comes with us to escape, *and* Nateysta will be there with us without bounds on what he is allowed to do. All I really need is permission to do it from you, Faian."

Well, she didn't *need* permission and would probably go and meet this Astar even without Faian's allowance, but since she lived in Endarian lands and had been given a chunk of said lands as her own, it was best to get along with the country's ruling council.

Faian met Zalia's eyes and held them for a while, considering what could go wrong with Zalia's plan. "Alright, fine. I feel that it is a little rushed but trust that you know what you're doing."

"I do. From what Nateysta has told me, this Astar has willingly chosen to meet under his power. If it is a trick to gain information or even harm me, it will go very poorly for them." Zalia waited for anyone else to speak up but she knew that Ember, Aylie, and Boreal were in agreement with her. "Last thing then, I might have learned of a way to help Hildebrandt."

"What? How?" asked Ember, ever the healer.

"I looked into the memories of prophecy gifted to me by the collective as they died and saw Aylie alone in a blank place, kneeling before a blue sun with fiery veins extending into the distance. I do not wish the image itself to come to pass, but it told me what we have to do."

Everyone looked confused as to what it meant, except for Aylie, of course.

With Aylie's permission, Zalia had told Ember about Aylie's new ability to step into the astral, but she wasn't about to tell everyone unless Aylie agreed. Seeing that Aylie understood, Zalia gestured to her to explain.

Ember realised what the memory meant as Aylie started speaking.

"It means we have to enter the astral to help Hildebrandt fight off the fire that continues to burn within her soul."

Ember was already shaking her head. "No, not happening. Those are prophecies, Zalia. If we let Aylie go in there then the image you saw will come to pass."

"And what if it comes to pass by us not going in with her? What if she ends up trying it by herself?"

This was, in Zalia's mind, what was wrong with prophecy and visions of the future. There were too many different ways of interpreting them.

"How do you know this will help?" Faian asked, obviously sceptical. "And how do you plan on getting into the astral in the first place?"

It was obvious to Zalia that Aylie didn't want to tell Faian about her ability.

"We have a way, maybe. The only reason I've brought it up now is to ask you to look into whether you have any healers amongst the population of the capital who are able to help with something like this. I wouldn't want to go in there without others to help."

Faian shrugged. "I'll ask around but I doubt many would want to go once I explain what it is they'll be doing. Fight off an Emerald rank curse by going into the astral? Oh, and someone has had a prophecy that only one person even makes it so far as the centre of this thing? Don't forget that the vision might mean anyone that goes in with Aylie won't make it."

"Just have a look, we might not even go ahead with it, depending," Zalia said. "Hidey said that Hildebrandt should be fine if she makes it a week. If it's looking like she will, then it won't be a problem. We're going to have to have a talk about whether it's a risk worth taking either way as well."

She met Ember's eyes at that, a promise that she wouldn't do anything without talking about it properly first. Ember was bound to give her a stern word or two for bringing it up without doing that beforehand, but she wanted to let Faian know what was going on. It was, after all, important to Endaria's continued existence that Hildebrandt make a full recovery as quickly as possible.

"I will make a return to the capital soon. Assuming you meet with this Astar over the next few days, you should come to the capital as soon as possible afterwards to transport any healers I might find here. If you decide not to go forward with this plan to enter the astral in order to help Hildebrandt, I would like to know as soon as possible." With that, Faian stood up and left.

Ember's eyes tracked Faian out of the room, then turned to Zalia.

"I know, I know," Zalia sighed. "Should've talked to you about it first."

Ember nodded. "Yes, but we can talk about that later. You know, the first time we talked about meeting the rebel Astar you said you'd want to go alone, but I couldn't help but notice you say 'me and anyone that comes with us' just earlier."

Zalia pursed her lips. "I think you, Boreal, and Aylie should come with. Not only does Aylie now have an easy method of escaping if she needs, but she is able to see things that we can't, which might be important. Plus, Ro will be there, and with full use of his abilities, so the chances of this being some kind of trick are very low. The more I think about it, the more certain I am that you should all come along, if you want."

Ember nodded in agreement. "You know I'll always come with you."

Zalia heard the hidden meaning in the words. An offer made many years ago of escaping into the wilds, somewhere they could live free from all the politics and nonsense that happened within Endaria. It was a tempting notion to her still, though as usual the feeling of responsibility deep within her won out. "Great, we'll get ready to leave for the meeting tomorrow maybe, then? I'll have to ask Ro where it is first, though."

"Tomorrow is good, with the soldiers leaving in the morning I shouldn't have much to do."

With that, Ember left to go about the rest of her day. Boreal stayed with Zalia, obviously without anything to do.

It was strangely quiet in the house at that moment, with the guests gone. After a short pause to think, Zalia realised that it wasn't the lack of guests that was causing the peace, but the lack of five particular kittens.

"Where are your children?"

"*Completing their test.*"

The two of them left the house, idly making their way towards the temple dedicated to Ro at Zalia's lead.

"Test?"

"*Mmm, they are to bring to me a Bronze rank kill with a weight greater than their combined weight.*"

Zalia cocked an eyebrow. "Oddly specific, why?"

"*They will reach Bronze rank soon,*" Boreal sent proudly, "*and I wish for them to work together just a bit better as a team.*"

"You don't think it's a little dangerous for them?"

Boreal huffed a dismissive breath. "*Not at all, we took down Bronze rank animals plenty of times, did we not?*"

Zalia frowned. "Yes, but I distinctly remember them being dangerous fights each time."

"*I don't.*"

Zalia rolled her eyes.

Catching the expression, Boreal bumped her shoulder into Zalia, a movement that would have knocked her off her feet had she been less dexterous. "*I'm serious, even if any of us were injured, we were often healed up before anything bad could happen. Besides, I remember you telling me about those beasts you cleared from near Juniper's farm when you were such a low rank. If you can manage that, they can manage one Bronze between them.*"

Zalia held her hands up in defeat. "Alright, Mother Boreal, I'm sure you're right. I'm going to go and talk with Ro, want to join me?"

Boreal said nothing, but continued to follow anyway. Both that action and the bond let Zalia know that she was in.

When they arrived at Ro's temple, it was to a scene of slight chaos as they saw Boreal's five kittens dragging a number of bodies through the streets, more than just the one that Boreal had expected.

CHAPTER SIXTY

Meetings

Zalia

Zalia watched Frost, who was using a bed of ice to assist her, drag her kill over to drop at Boreal's feet. The other young cats all dropped their own prizes in the pile shortly after, each staring up at Boreal in turn. By the looks of it, they had chosen to bring back a Bronze rank creature of a weight greater than their combined weight *each*.

While some of the nearby townspeople looked surprised, slightly amused or amazed, others were looking a little disturbed. Zalia decided to take matters into her own hands and opened her vault, moving quickly to store the bodies inside.

She could feel the pure pride radiating from Boreal through their bond and could see the equally strong emotion within the five young cats' auras. Zalia shook her head in a mixed feeling of amusement and dismay. How was she going to deal with the five of them?

As kittens, they had been a collective menace. As young cats, they were the same except with a much higher capacity for destruction. That capacity would only grow as they did, and though it might be helpful during times of war, it might become a problem if they didn't settle down as Boreal had. She could only hope.

Zalia only noticed then that Frost and Breeze had ranked up to Bronze, with the other three just behind. They would similarly reach Bronze in the coming days, and the timing couldn't have been better. She had hoped that Aylie would reach Silver before things with the Astar kicked off fully, but with her rank already accelerated far past what someone her age should be, things had slowed down in that department.

Leaving Boreal to praise her children, Zalia waved away the crowd and stepped into the temple of Nateysta. She could have tried to commune with him outside of the temple but enjoyed the feeling of peace and safety that came with entering its boundaries.

"*Nateysta, I wish to speak with you.*"

She pushed the thoughts out from her mind towards the stone and wood of the temple, strongly focused on the altar in particular.

A small vine grew from the side of the altar, creeping along the floor towards her. It thickened quickly before sprouting a fruit like an orange that increased in size dramatically over the course of a minute. The peel of the fruit shed to reveal Nateysta, Ro, in his usual plant-crow form.

"*Zalia.*"

"*Why do you always arrive so dramatically?*"

She kept the words as a thought so as to not disturb the others at prayer around her, though Ro had done that pretty thoroughly by himself. The worship of Nateysta had become a full-fledged religion in Nature's Reclaim, which was only half Zalia's fault.

"*A god must awe his followers from time to time.*"

It was hard to argue with that, and who was Zalia to refute? She didn't have any experience as a god after all.

"*If you say so, Ro. Look, I think we're ready to meet the exiled Astar. Do you think you could make it happen? Soon, if possible.*"

Ro leaned down, the tip of his petrified wooden beak turning to the side so that one of his deep black, beady eyes could stare right into Zalia's.

Despite the years of experience Zalia had interacting with many different Ascendants, some friendly, some hostile, a creeping shiver went down her back. Staring into the ancient eye of Nateysta gave her a feeling of a power stretching forever across the horizon, powerful and unknowable.

"*I can do this, but know that once this meeting happens, there will be no rest until the end of this conflict.*"

"*I had a feeling. We're ready, but there is one thing I need to be sure of first. You can protect the others if they come with us, right?*"

Ro replied with a simple nod before standing back upright. "*Good. The Astar has been waiting patiently for your answer. Bring everyone who will be attending to the front of your house, and I will transport everyone to a meeting place of my choice.*"

Before Zalia could get in a goodbye, Ro's avatar had disintegrated, the pile of dust blown out the door by a cool wind.

Knowing that Ro could probably still hear her in the temple, she muttered a goodbye anyways before leaving.

Outside the temple, Boreal and the young ones were still clumped together, though the crowd of other people and animals had dispersed. Zalia hadn't inspected the bodies she had stored just yet but hoped that Boreal had the sense to send the young cats on this trial somewhere outside of the Grove's influence.

"*Boreal, come on.*"

Zalia walked back towards the house, and Boreal popped out of the cat puddle to follow, her children trotting after in a mess of fur.

They made their way back to the house and found Aylie and Lumin making preparations for the meeting. She took after Zalia a bit in that way, always wanting to be prepared for whatever situations they might encounter. Though, thinking about it, Aylie could have developed the trait more as a result of the events of the past few years, rather than taking after Zalia.

"Hey, where's Ember?" Zalia asked, not feeling her within the bounds of the house.

Aylie looked up from her little pile of supplies ranging from dried and preserved foods to useful tools, including, Zalia saw, an anti-teleportation bracelet that she had given to Aylie.

"Oh, she went out to find the Ancient of War and let him know that he would be in charge while we're gone."

Zalia nodded to herself, ticking that off her mental list and adding "thank Ember" to it.

With that being dealt with, she only had a few things left to handle. Lumin and Aylie would be fine without a doubt and Boreal had wandered off to do her own preparations which likely consisted of finding the young cats something to do while the rest of them were gone. Zalia just had to think about what she needed now.

A plan for dealing with the Astar monarch had been slowly forming in her mind ever since hearing about the rebellious Astar. Ro had told her that the Astar monarch had the aspect of the Astar themselves as their godly realm, which she hoped would work to their favour.

In her vault, Zalia had an artifact created by a high-ranked inventor called Et. She had gotten the artifact, which was called a 'constructed heirloom,' by freeing Scour, the god of the desert, from it. The heirloom could be used to trap a god by drawing it in within a place of concentrated power related to its aspect. For Ro, that would be one of his temples, and she hoped that the rebel Astar would know of a place that would function as the same thing for the Astar monarch so she could draw them in and trap them with it.

That was the basis of her plan, and though many if's and how's still remained to be ironed out, she hoped it would be a good enough base to build on.

Finding herself still leaning in the doorway of Aylie's room, staring at nothing, with Aylie watching her curiously, she pushed off the doorframe.

"Well, it seems we're really doing this thing."

Aylie nodded. "Yeah, is there anything you wanted me to do while we're talking with this Astar?"

"Actually yes. I want you to try and read the Astar like you can read others. The ability might not work the same on Astar, if at all. Oh, also, if you think they're able to sense your poking whatsoever, stop. I don't want to endanger the meeting if possible."

"Easy enough."

Zalia turned to leave. "Oh, and Aylie, if it does come to a fight, take yourself to the astral straight away. I don't want you getting hurt."

She saw a small spark of defiance in Aylie's expression before it faded away to agreement. Unsure whether she should be concerned about that, Zalia left to her own room. There she opened the portal to her vault and hopped in, comforted as always by the calming, serene aura within.

While Nature's Reclaim had the same healing power covering it that the vault had, it had grown somewhat . . . distant ever since the town had been occupied by others. It felt more neutral, belonging less to her than to the town, whereas the one in the vault was still very much in tune with her.

She hadn't cleaned out the shelves of the vault in . . . well, since she had gotten the thing. There hadn't been any need since the shelves were mostly empty still, despite the five new bodies now stored in them. Strangely, there was still the body of an Astar in there too. Thankfully, everything on the shelves was kept frozen in time which would make disposing of all the bodies much easier.

The Astar body was the first to go, burnt to ash that she mixed with water and buried in the herb garden at the back of the vault. She left the bodies of the animals slain by Boreal's children in case they wanted them back. There were quite a few pieces of junk from her time in Cormaine, including a sword, maps, memories, and the ritual that Juniper used to bring them there. She left all of that to one corner of the vault shelves.

The God-trap and Et's journal on the machine were both at the front of the vault, the trap having repaired itself after Zalia destroyed it to free Scour. Near the front she also kept fresh food and water for the rest of her family, should they need it, along with a supply of Ember and Aylie's favourite snack, a chocolate-covered candy made by a baker near the eastern gate of the town. Though, as far as Zalia could tell, they didn't have cocoa in Endaria, so the 'chocolate' was slightly different than what she was used to from her own world.

Happy with the amount of food, water, and herbs she had stored in the vault, she left and made her way to the living room.

Since preparations for their meeting with the Astar were mostly already taken care of, Zalia looked to the second to last thing on her mental list. She had been thinking of making a gift for Ember but had been having a hard time figuring out what it should be.

She spent some time using her abilities to form different shapes out of wood, a delicate ring, a circlet designed with the imagery of flames in mind to match her armour, and various other pieces of jewellery. Nothing felt quite right.

All of these things she was able to make with a simple thought, no effort required to perform the creation. While the thought was there, it didn't feel like enough.

Her thoughts were interrupted by Ember poking her head in the doorway.

"We're all ready."

Zalia jumped, storing the circlet in her hands before Ember saw it. More time had passed than she realised. "Alright, let's do this."

She got up and followed Ember out to the front of the house; Boreal and Aylie were already there. Boreal was wearing her heirloom armour and frozen circlet proudly, ready as she always was for battle, her children waiting in the doorway to the house. Aylie had a backpack filled with supplies and her staff held in hand, the anti-teleportation bracelet firmly on her wrist.

Ember was wearing her own armour, though the trail of fire it usually left was turned off at that moment, thankfully.

Zalia gave Ember a kiss and a murmured "thank you," ticking that last item off her mental list.

With a thought sent out to the world, Nateysta arrived. "Ready?"

Zalia nodded, and with a rush of power tinged with the aura of nature, they were taken away.

CHAPTER SIXTY-ONE

The Astar Rebellion

Zalia

Zalia had only been transported by Nateysta's power once before, the day she had returned from Cormaine to Endaria. As the land around them whipped by, so fast she couldn't discern any details, memories of Delphi came back to the forefront of her mind.

It had been a long time since she had thought about them and the collective, though their combined knowledge and memories of the past, present, and future were stored away safely in her vault.

She reached out a hand to touch the side of the bubble of power surrounding her, feeling a perfect smooth shell. Outside the transparent bubble, the only visible forms in the blur were the rest of her family in their own bubbles, similarly looking around in awe.

Even her sight of them vanished as they plummeted down to the ground, then through it. The earth opened up to swallow them before closing up behind them. She could feel them slowly decelerate before bursting out into a cavern deep, deep underground and landing.

The massive cavern was lit by numerous green, glowing crystals that grew from the stone of the floor, walls, and ceiling, which was supported by thick pillars of stone. There were small, many-legged, soft-shelled creatures wandering about the place, the biggest of them barely reaching Zalia's knees. The strange crabs were tending to a type of vine that grew over everything, creating soft foliage underfoot and drooping masses from above that, combined with the pillars and glowing crystals, created a space filled with cast shadows.

Aylie and Ember both pulled closer to Zalia, while Boreal dashed away to investigate the nearest crab creature. She sniffed at the thing as it stared up at her with curiosity and raised one paw before Nateysta appeared, growing from the bud of a vine.

"Do not touch them, Boreal. This is not a place created with predators such as you, and you will respect it."

Boreal did something that Zalia could rarely get her to do and listened, stepping carefully back towards Zalia while a slowly growing group of crabs followed her, their footsteps sounding with soft *tick, tick, tick*s across the floor.

Nateysta turned and walked away, heading towards the far end of the cave down a gentle slope.

"What is this place?" Zalia asked, a little awed.

The slope led to a big pool of water, perfectly still and lit from within by the same green crystals as the rest of the cavern. Their path wound around the side of it to a small clearing where there sat a giant throne of wood covered in bark like the trunk of a tree. Growing over it were hundreds of different plants, some of which Zalia recognised but most unknown to her.

"It is a place of pure, unadulterated nature, one without predators. It is a place of me and of peace."

Nateysta stepped over to the throne, growing in size to fit to its size before perching on it. The plants all over it grew up the trunks that were his legs even as they grew to meld into the throne, making them seem as one. The way he stood there without even a twitch of movement gave the appearance of a statue that Zalia struggled to see past, even though she knew better.

There was a splitting sound from further back in the cave where they had come from, and two more bubbles of Nateysta's energy dropped through the ceiling, depositing an Astar each. Zalia watched them carefully as they observed their surroundings and, strangely, walked down the same path to the throne. Zalia was so used to the Astar floating or even teleporting everywhere that the sight of them actually using their legs was a little disconcerting.

Zalia and her family stepped to one side of the clearing as the two Astar took the other, each of them looking at each other warily.

? - Diamond rank.
? - Diamond rank.

A shudder went down Zalia's body at seeing both Astar were Diamond rank, though Nateysta could deal with both with ease. Neither group spoke for a long time, with Nateysta the first to break the silence.

"I will make this clear, if it wasn't already, to all of you. There will be no violence nor anger here. Any to break the sanctity of this place will be expelled."

"I wouldn't dream of it, Ro."

The Astar both gave Zalia an odd look at the nickname, but each bowed deeply to Nateysta in acknowledgement of his words.

Each of the Astar was much different than Zalia's experience with the rest of their kind. Where the Astar were usually uniform in their apparel, wearing clothes in dull greys and blues that matched their skin and runes, with long hair that reached past their feet, these ones were very different.

They both wore clothes that included colours of blue, green, and brown, matching a more earthy appearance than their otherworldly kin. The runes inscribed in their skin were also varying in their colour, rather than a uniform light blue. They wore bracelets, earrings, and necklaces, each piece crafted with gold and deep, rich brown wood.

The most disconcerting part of their appearance was the twinkle of emotion in their eyes, the expression on their faces. Though it put off the idea of what an Astar was in her mind, it was also strangely comforting to know that these two were so different to their kin. All in all, they looked more like spirits of nature than alien creatures, even their auras blended into the environment rather than the staying as the hard bubble Astar usually maintained.

Zalia could see them inspecting her much in the same way she was inspecting them, feeling the gentle but polite touch of aura against her own even as she did the same to them.

A reverberating voice, much like Nateysta's, deep and gravelly, resounded through the air.

"To begin, I extend an apology from my people to yours for the actions of our more . . . violent kin."

Then, shocking Zalia even more, the two Astar put their hands together as if in prayer and kneeled, bowing their heads. She looked over at Nateysta, who remained stone-still, before gauging her family's reactions.

With the others looking just as shocked as she felt, Zalia moved towards the Astar. They raised fervently anxious looks towards her as she approached, and it occurred to Zalia that they might be just as, if not more, in need of an alliance.

Feeling a hint of goodwill towards the Astar at the show of humility, she held out a hand to help both Astar up, though neither needed it.

"There is no need to apologise for the actions of your kin if you had no hand in deciding their course. You are of their blood, but it is they who must answer for what they have done."

Despite having heard one of them speak, Zalia hadn't been able to discern which of the two it was. She listened closer as they spoke again, yet couldn't discern from which of their auras the words came.

"And they will."

The Astar each took one of her hands and stood. Zalia took a step back so as not to be towered over by the tall Astar.

"You may call me Zalia, how can we address both of you?"

Watching Zalia put her hand to her chest as she introduced herself, both Astar copied the action.

"I am Het'jel."

Zalia looked at them both, waiting for a second name before realising she wouldn't get one. It was a stark reminder that despite being at war with the Astar, they knew next to nothing about them.

"You are both Het'jel?" She undoubtedly massacred the pronunciation of the name, unable to put the meaning behind the word that the Astar did using their odd aura speech.

"We two are one."

Zalia looked back at Ember, who shrugged. "Alright, then. Let's begin then, shall we? I have many questions and am hoping you have answers for them."

A feeling of affirmation came through the auras of Het'jel, and Nateysta's head tilted ever so slightly. Chairs grew from the ground, two for the Astar and three for Zalia, Ember, and Aylie. A small padded pedestal grew for Boreal so that she had somewhere to sit too.

As Zalia took her seat, a small table grew from the space between them, separating the two sides, with Nateysta at the head of the table.

"I guess the first question I have for you is what are you looking to get from us?"

"I shall need to provide context to answer this question."

Het'jel waited and Zalia nodded for them to go ahead.

"As I'm sure the venerable Nateysta has informed you, I am part of a rebellious faction of the Astar. Each Astar amongst our number has different reasons for being part of this rebellion, but there is one thing that ties us together. That thing is our common dislike for the course that the monarch takes for our people. They lead the Astar down a path of weakness and of hate. Many of our number grow complacent and lazy, lacking the motivation to strive for strength, and their own mixture of complacency and sense of superiority is what causes them to strike out against your people. They see your people fight and grow stronger by the day, just as we do, and it is this strength we see in you that has led us to reach out."

Zalia frowned. "You say that the Astar have grown complacent, yet there are many powerful members amongst them. We had to fight two of them at Emerald rank just days earlier."

The two as one, Het'jel, both shook their heads. "Things are not as they appear. The loss of Ven'kal has had a large impact on the strength of the Astar. In truth, Ven'kal was one of two of Emerald amongst the Astar number. We know of only one of Mythical and one of Diamond. There is also the monarch, of course."

"When you say one, do you mean the two bodies as one, just as you are?"

Het'jel cocked their heads. "You do not know of the duality then?"

Zalia shook her head. "The duality?"

"Each Astar is born with two bodies. We are two minds and two bodies, thinking and acting as one. It is this very nature of our people that has caused the monarch to go astray. One of two became Ascendant while the other remains Mythical. A disconnect has formed between the two, causing them to be disconnected not only in body but in mind. I warned them not to follow this course, yet they would not listen. Now I must fight to have them removed, lest their condition ruin the Astar people forever."

Zalia sat up straight to reply, yet it was Ember who got there first.

"Wait, you knew the monarch before they ascended?"

There was a sad expression in Het'jel's eyes as they replied. "Things were not always as they are now. The monarch thought that allowing only one of two to become Ascendent would give them the power to ignore the rules that encompass the others of that rank, and it did. They did not foresee the problems of the mind that would come with it, they cannot see them even now. Only I and a few others who can see from outside their minds have seen the changes."

Everyone turned to Nateysta as he spoke. "I understand now. An Ascendant locked to the physical plane not by an avatar but by the other half of their soul. That would indeed warp their minds."

Het'jel nodded their heads. "Yes, venerable one." Then they turned back to Zalia. "Now, to answer your question. We look to you and yours to assist us in removing the monarch. Not only would this solve our issue and allow the Astar people to thrive again, but I believe it will fix yours as well. With the monarch gone, the Astar will no longer follow their decrees out of fear. There will be civil war as those who have profited from the monarch's ways fight those who have suffered from it, but that is not an issue that your people need worry about. If anything, it will give you reprieve from Astar focus and allow your people to recover and grow stronger."

Zalia sat back heavily in her seat, breathing out deeply. "I must admit, I'm tempted by the offer. It won't be up to me to make the final decision on this but I have a feeling the council will be tempted too. How do you plan on actually removing the monarch? Do your people have the strength to fight against all the high-ranked Astar?"

Het'jel shook their heads. "No, we do not. The rebellion will launch an all-out attack on an edge city, and the monarch will send all the high-ranked Astar to deal with us. It is likely that many of our number will be wiped out during this fight, but it will be worth it if we succeed. With no defenders, I and your strongest will go to fight the monarch and remove them from power. It is a gamble, but one that our people have considered for a long time. The only reason we have decided it is a good course of action now is we believe you have the strength to assist us in removing the monarch."

Zalia stared at the Astar, mind turning. Could she really trust Het'jel? Nateysta seemed to think so, yet she wasn't sure how well he knew how to read people.

"What makes you think we have the strength?"

"You managed to kill Ven'kal, did you not? You must have some amongst you who are powerful enough to stand up to the monarch, having achieved that feat."

Zalia tapped her leg a little nervously as she glanced at Aylie. "Well, you *could* say that."

CHAPTER SIXTY-TWO

To See the Sun

Zalia

One Emerald rank? That is all it took to kill Ven'kal?"

Zalia shrugged. "Yeah, she's pretty strong and a defence specialist. It's almost impossible to kill her, as far as I can tell."

"Perhaps this will be enough. If they can keep the monarch's attention while we deal the damage, victory is possible. It will be a risk still, yet much of the ante will be paid by us, not you."

Zalia turned to Ember who was able to hear the thoughts she sent down their bond. *"Should I tell them about the God-trap?"*

Ember shrugged indecisively. *"They seem trustworthy, but they're still Astar. I'm not sure how far we can trust them at this point."*

Undecided, Zalia held onto the information for now. "What about the second half of the monarch, will they be able to intervene?"

"Yes, though not as directly as they might wish to. While able to act more than one such as Nateysta could, they will not be able to hurt us directly. The battlefield will be changed to disadvantage us greatly, however. We should expect the place of our combat to be infused with the Ascendant power of the monarch quite thoroughly. I doubt Nateysta will be able to do more than keep other possible weaker defenders away. Gold rankers and the like."

Zalia perked up. If they would be fighting in a place directly linked to the Ascendant half of the monarch, all they would have to do is wait for them to manifest an avatar directly before using the God-trap. With the Ascendant half taken care of, the fight would go much easier for Hildebrandt and Het'jel.

"Okay, I think we can manage. This might actually be possible."

Ember leaned forward, resting her arms on the table. "I know you said that once the monarch is removed from power, many of the problems facing Endaria would be dealt with, but I think the council would like to know exactly what your plans are if we do succeed."

Both of Het'jel's heads turned to face Ember as she spoke. "I will take the throne, of course. There will be those who rebel and a war will be fought amongst our own, but we will prevail. If your council would go so far as to formally support us, I believe that many will fear fighting the alliance that managed to take down the monarch. To use the method of control that the monarch uses will be unsavoury, but a widespread change of culture will take time and patience. I might be a tyrant to my people, but I will use the power to ensure that I will be the last."

Zalia turned to Ember and Aylie, then back. "We are not one of mind as you are, Het'jel. Would it be alright if we take a moment to deliberate?"

Het'jel nodded their heads and Zalia, Boreal, Aylie, and Ember all got up. She walked with them back up the path around the lake for a distance before finally speaking.

"Thoughts?"

Aylie was the first to pipe up. "There is something fundamentally different between these Astar and the ones that captured us in the town. That might be a good thing?"

Zalia nodded agreement. "I noticed that too, their auras, right?"

Aylie shook her head, looking thoughtful. "Yes, but no. That is different but there is something about the way their souls interact with their bodies that is different. With the Astar we've interacted with so far, it's almost as if their souls are at a disconnect with their physical bodies, despite being the same thing. Het'jel is different; they feel more connected."

Zalia pondered for a moment as they continued up the gentle slope, making sure not to step on any of the hoard of intrigued crab things walking around. "Might have something to do with how the Astar are made to cut off any and all emotion. In the few minutes we've talked to Het'jel, I've seen sadness, anxiety, concern. You won't find that on the expression of any normal Astar, though it might be a trick to draw us in."

It was Ember's turn to shake her head. "I don't think so. They feel genuine to me."

Zalia turned to her giant feline companion. "Boreal? Any thoughts? . . . And no we won't be taste testing them."

Boreal had looked excited for just a moment, but sullenly drooped her head as Zalia took tasting off the menu. "*If they can kill monarch, yes.*"

"Alright, that's one for it, and I'm leaning that direction too. Aylie? Ember?"

Aylie nodded decisively, while Ember's agreement was a little more subdued.

"We take it to the council and let them decide. This is all assuming Hildebrandt survives, of course, but it does appear promising," Ember said.

Zalia waited a few moments, but no one changed their mind, so they started back to Het'jel and Nateysta. "Decided, then."

They took their places at the table, and Het'jel looked at them keenly.

"Alright, we'll suggest forming an alliance to the council," Zalia said. "Some of them might want to meet with you under similar circumstances to this, if you'd be willing."

"Of course. Nateysta knows where to find us when you are ready."

With that, the table and chairs dissolved even as the spheres of Nateysta's power encompassed them. They were all taken from the cave at speed, the Astar zipping away in a different direction once they reached the surface.

The meeting hadn't taken long and neither had the journey there. Their return to Nature's Reclaim took a similarly short time, and they were back home before they knew it. It had been a long day, not because a lot of time had passed but because a lot had happened all at once. Matthias had returned, Hidey had been freed and they had met with the Astar rebellion. Despite all that, it was still early in the day and there was much to be done.

Nateysta had disappeared the moment they landed safely and Ember soon took his example, letting Zalia know that she would check on Hildebrandt while Zalia told Faian of their meeting. Boreal went off to find her children, obviously excited to talk to them about their hunt earlier that day and Aylie followed along with Zalia.

They went to the housing that had been given to Faian and her soldiers, finding them all but ready to leave for the capital. She went over their conversation with Het'jel in detail, finishing the conversation with a strong recommendation that they agree to the alliance and form a proper plan with the Astar rebellion. Faian kept her eyes on Zalia with an intense gaze, obviously trying to catch every word and emotion that she showed.

Once she was done talking, Faian agreed with her assessment but stated that she wanted to meet with Het'jel, just as Zalia had expected. All of this, however, relied on Hildebrandt's recovery.

Zalia had very specifically not told Het'jel about her injuries. If it turned out that they *were* working for the monarch, she didn't want to tell them that Endaria's only proper defence was currently bedridden. Feeling no strong emotions either way from the bond with Ember, Zalia figured that there had been no change in Hildebrandt's state.

She left the group of soldiers to their tasks and went back home. Just as she expected, Hildebrandt was in the same comatose state with no visible difference. Aylie's gasp of surprise told a different story, however.

"That's really bad," she said, walking up and staring seemingly through Hildebrandt.

"What?" Zalia asked.

"The power," Aylie said, gesturing, "it grew when we were gone. Not by an insignificant amount either."

Ember cursed, staring at Hildebrandt as well. "I can't see that at all. Triage only allows me to see physical wounds while Emotional Soothing shows mental ones. The soul is completely out of my area of expertise."

Zalia put an arm around her gently. "I'm frustrated too. It feels like we should be able to help."

Ember held her back as they watched Hildebrandt's uneven breathing. The same thing was roiling around both of their minds: whether it was worth the risk to enter the astral by Aylie's power and attempt to deal with the magic affliction directly. It was a big risk, should things go bad, and the memories of prophecy left by the collective were quite unhelpful.

"I have to go in there," Aylie murmured.

"Aylie," Ember said as she turned to her. "Don't you dare. Not without talking about it properly first."

"I agree. While I do think we should go in and help, I think we really need to be prepared first," Zalia said.

Aylie's shoulders sagged. "Fine, but you both know that if it gets too bad we'll do it anyway." She left, Zalia and Ember stepping out of her way.

"She's right," Ember murmured.

Zalia pulled her into a proper hug. "Yeah, I know. Hildebrandt is Endaria's main hope, we can't let her die without trying."

Ember let out a deep sigh. "Alright, we better prepare for the worst then, shouldn't we?"

"Yeah, we should. In fact, it might be better to try take this thing on before it grows any stronger."

Ember pulled back and looked at Hildebrandt for a long time. "Yeah."

Zalia watched over Hildebrandt that night, even though she had no way of discerning the state of her soul. Hidey, Faian, and her soldiers left for the capital the next morning with Matthias in tow, having found him the night before. Zalia waved them off before returning to the comatose Hildebrandt to keep watch. Aylie said that the power had grown again overnight and was firm in her belief that it would grow strong enough to kill Hildebrandt before the seven days passed and her massively reduced defence returned to normal.

The next few days were spent in anxious preparation as the power only grew worse. Aylie and Zalia argued often to enter the astral and deal with the power, but Ember refused until the third day.

Zalia had spent much of the interceding time creating an ointment that was a mixture of Soulroot and Dodge-vine. The intended effect of the mixture was to provide extra defence for the soul, something that would help if they did end up going in. While initially intended for that use, she found that applying some to Hildebrandt every few hours helped to slow the growth of the affliction. It wasn't enough, however.

On the morning of the fourth day, Aylie was insistent that they had to act now. Zalia had adaptive protection runes on her armour and had even changed the mobility-increasing ones to be a soul protective–specific one to double down on it. Making any kind of impact on the power at their lower rank might be hard, but it had to be done.

It was decided that Zalia and Aylie would go in, while Ember cared for Hildebrandt in the physical world. With their overlapping auras of Healing Presence, along with all the defensive abilities Zalia had, they hoped to survive. It was Aylie's powers over the astral and soul that they were relying on to combat the power directly.

Both Ember and Boreal embraced them in firm hugs before stepping back. Zalia stared into Ember's eyes as Aylie got closer to Zalia. She reached a hand out and grabbed onto something ethereal and invisible to Zalia's eyes. With a tug, Aylie pulled aside the curtain of reality and draped it over Zalia and herself.

Their vision distorted and twisted, the experience much like that of the dreamscape Aylie could make when it moved. Everything settled once more to a cloudy world with vague shapes hidden in the mist. Before them, a blue sun burnt, tendrils of power stretching into the distance with a few holding firmly onto the shape of a person. Hildebrandt was suspended by the sun, struggling against the bonds that held her yet making no impact on them.

With protections in place, Zalia and Aylie walked towards the distant sun.

CHAPTER SIXTY-THREE

To Kill a Sun You Need a Star

Zalia

The surface of the once-calm blue sun became violent and reactive as Zalia and Aylie walked closer. Zalia prepared herself to react in an instant if the power decided to strike out at Aylie, whom she had told to leave the astral, should she need to use Protection of the Wilds. If it came down to her using that ability, they'd both need to get out as soon as possible.

Hanging below the sun, Hildebrandt watched them approach with warning in her eyes. Zalia tried to reach out with her telepathy but found that the power didn't work. Odd.

They took a few steps closer and one of the tendrils of power floating off into the unseeable distance whipped down to strike them. A wave went through it like a loose rope that had been flicked by a hand, and a central section of the tendril came down with a crash next to them. They managed to jump out of the way of the tendril just in time, the thing thicker than Aylie was tall.

"Hildebrandt!" Zalia yelled.

Hildebrandt didn't respond, but her struggling grew stronger.

Looking over at Aylie, Zalia could tell she was still resolute, and the duo continued forwards.

There was no heat coming from the sun, but there *was* an oppressive aura of some kind. It was a weight on their souls that grew heavier the closer they got.

Now knowing that she needed to watch out for the tendrils, Zalia could see the beginnings of another attack coming from a different one. It wobbled ever so slightly and when the wave of movement returned to the sun, it increased tenfold, the section of tendril flying down towards them.

Zalia tried to teleport at that instant, yet found that Mobility didn't work either. Late to react, Zalia was scraped by the tendril, a burning pain sent down her back. It coursed through her, but the defence of her armour and the ointment, in addition to her natural resilience, allowed her to struggle back to her feet. The pain was considerable but nothing she hadn't dealt with before.

"Are you alright?" Aylie asked with worry.

Zalia nodded, but found that Healing Presence wasn't working. Hers wasn't, yet Aylie's was.

"I thought you said abilities worked in the astral?"

"They do!" Aylie exclaimed.

The burn all down her back was slowly healing up from Aylie's power but nowhere as quick as Zalia's own power would have worked.

"Something is wrong, my abilities won't work, none of them."

Aylie frowned and opened her starlight portal. Moonlight shone down from somewhere above, the radiant light illuminating an oval shape in front of them. A similar beam of light was cutting straight through the sun in front of them to create the other side of the portal next to Hildebrandt.

"Come on, let's get closer. Those tendrils will have a harder time hitting us there."

Zalia looked at the portal sceptically, but stepped through.

The weight pressing down on their souls grew substantially stronger as they arrived near Hildebrandt, the look of warning still in her eyes.

"We're going to get you out, Hildebrandt." Zalia tried summoning her weapons and found that at the least, they still worked. Her sword appeared in hand while her bow floated in the space next to her. They hadn't had a set plan to help Hildebrandt out of her situation, but seeing her strung up by the blue sun's power made their course forwards obvious.

She stepped up and swung at one of the significantly smaller tendrils even as Aylie spoke.

"Zalia, wait—"

Her sword passed straight through harmlessly, and she looked back at Aylie in confusion.

"I don't think you can help here. Only my power works. I think the reason that your vision shows me kneeling before the sun alone is because I'm the only one that can fight this thing. You should leave."

Zalia walked over under the still-growing weight. "What!? You can't be serious, Aylie. I won't leave you here alone. I might not be able to fight, but I can still stand by you."

Aylie looked at her with a sad smile. "Don't worry, Mum, I'll save her."

With that, Aylie pulled the fabric of the world over Zalia, sending her back.

The nauseating feeling of movement mixed with blurred colours came back to Zalia as she was sent away. Her vision swam until the real world came into focus.

"No! Aylie . . ."

Ember turned in alarm at her sudden appearance. "Where is Aylie? Zalia, where. Is. Aylie?"

Zalia dropped her weapons, which faded to a quickly dissipating mist. "She sent me back . . ."

Ember stood sharply. "What? Why?"

Zalia shook her head. "My powers didn't work in the astral, but hers did. I think she sent me back so I wouldn't get hurt."

The burn she had received in the astral wasn't present here in the physical world, yet she could feel the pain on her soul instead. It wasn't dissimilar to the discomfort of overusing passive abilities or mana.

"Your vision was right . . ." Ember whispered.

Zalia moved to hug her close. "She'll make it out."

Aylie

Aylie stared at the space Zalia had just been in, immediately second-guessing herself. Steeling her mind against the doubt, she turned to face the blue sun. It almost felt sentient to Aylie's senses, like a spider with prey in its web staring down at another possible catch. Here, though, Aylie was *not* prey.

She used the Healing Surge of her Healing Presence, multiplying its strength tenfold and giving it the ability to affect the soul. With newfound strength, she pushed back the weight of the sun and tried to encompass Hildebrandt with it. The sun pounced, hundreds of smaller tendrils of power shooting from its surface above to slam into the incorporeal presence of her aura. A struggle between them began, one not of physical strength or finesse, but one of the soul.

The tendrils of power from the blue sun pushing against her aura made the usually invisible bubble into a visible boundary. She struggled, eyes closed and teeth gritted against the sheer force of the power fighting against her. It may have been a semi-mindless chunk of power given purpose in comparison to her very real and very resolute will, but it was Emerald rank.

She staggered forwards, one step, then another. Each foot in front of the last brought her that much closer to Hildebrandt. The barrier that was her aura was crushing inward, forced within a metre of herself in any direction. Sparks of blue and yellow power melted away as the blue sun sacrificed parts of its strength to try and crush her underneath it.

It felt like an eternity before she was able to take another step forward, and even longer for the next. All thought passed from her mind as the strain of maintaining her aura brought her to one knee. She struggled up and took another step, lifting her head and opening an eye to find Hildebrandt in front of her.

The tendrils of power that had been suspending the powerful form of the Emerald rank Hildebrandt had been pushed back by Aylie's advance. The form of Hildebrandt's soul now lay on the ethereal mist that made up the floor in front of Aylie. She fell to one knee again, managing to scrape forward and within reach of the woman. Her other leg buckled, and Aylie found herself kneeling, head bowed, before Hildebrandt.

She reached out and pulled the fabric of the astral over the woman, sending her back to the physical realm.

Even as she did, the strength of her aura finally failed. The minute of tenfold strength had passed and the power of her aura fell with it.

The tendrils from the blue sun flicked angrily, the purpose of the power having been stolen from it. They snaked slowly towards Aylie, and she struggled to lift an arm to take herself from the astral. A tendril latched onto her arm, dragging it up and away from its purpose. Her other arm soon followed, and Aylie found herself being oh so slowly lifted from the ground.

Zalia

Zalia and Ember waited with bated breath as a war waged within the astral. The usually stagnant form of Hildebrandt was thrashing in defiance of the power that sought to destroy her. Knowing that the astral was a space of thought, Zalia pulled out the poultice of Soulroot and dabbed some onto her forehead. Its purpose was to assist someone in entering a more meditative state where they could see into the astral ever so slightly. She handed it to Ember, who did the same.

All of a sudden, Hildebrandt woke with a shocked gasp of breath. Her eyes were wild with the adrenaline of prey hunted by a predator. Ember rushed forwards to check on the woman, but Hildebrandt's eyes locked onto Zalia.

"We have to help her," Ember said.

Zalia nodded, taking the Soulroot poultice from Ember and dabbing some onto Hildebrandt's forehead as well. "This will allow us to enter a meditative state and see slightly into the astral. I understand now why my abilities didn't work there—it's not a place of power but a place of the mind. If we lend our minds to Aylie, she might be able to fight against the blue sun."

They all sat in silence as they descended into the meditative state. Slowly, their vision was overlaid with the misty land with the giant blue sun. It had Aylie in its grasp, pulling her up to replace Hildebrandt. Zalia pushed all of her mind towards lending Aylie power, believing in her, trusting her.

Aylie

Aylie's head drooped as she lifted up, certain that this was the future that Zalia had foreseen, the fate that had awaited her. It had needed to be done, though, for Endaria. Aylie might never have grown strong enough to avenge her parents, slaughtered by the demon invasion, the invasion that had been orchestrated by the Astar, but she knew Zalia would do that for her. She knew that *Hildebrandt* would do that for her.

A trickle of power from somewhere else made its way into Aylie's soul. She knew that power, she had felt it from the day that she had been saved from the demons by Zalia. Her head lifted to stare into the sun in defiance.

It sent more tendrils to raise her as she pulled against its influence, but another tendril of power came to her. She knew the feeling of this power too, the kind, calm sternness of the other woman who had adopted her. With the support of Zalia and Ember behind her, Aylie's feet found the floor once more. She shook off a tendril, finding two more in their place, yet continued the struggle.

Her aura managed to push back all the tendrils entirely, forcing them mere inches from her skin. Teeth gritted with concentration, pure will holding the blue sun at bay, Aylie continued the fight.

Another source of power came to her, this one unfamiliar. It was incredible, stronger than that of Ember, Zalia, and herself put together many times over. She pushed the tendrils back with ease, summoning the staff gifted to her by Zalia.

Holding it in two hands, she raised the staff up to the sky and, with eyes closed, began to channel the power granted to her into the staff. With a flash of light, her eyes opened, glowing white and blue as the stars above. A twinkle in the heavens heralded the doom of the blue sun as a star equal in size descended at speed, trailing a blazing, white fire.

Aylie slammed the butt of her staff into the misty ethereal floor beneath her and the summoned star impacted the blue sun, the collision of the two massive celestial objects sending an explosive ring of blue and white fire spiralling away. The tendrils of the blue sun vanished with the blast, blown away by the sheer force of the two objects.

The surface of the blue sun cracked, then gave way as Aylie's white star slammed straight through into its core. The blue sun exploded from within, the remnants of its power sprayed across the astral as Aylie's star took its place.

She took one hand off the staff and smiled a victorious grin as she pulled the fabric of the astral over herself, transporting back to the physical world.

CHAPTER SIXTY-FOUR

Storm of the North

Zalia

Zalia let out a deep breath as Aylie reappeared, looking unharmed and grinning like a maniac. "Aylie! That was amazing!"

All of them had seen what Aylie had done, calling the star from the sky to obliterate a power that *should* have been so much stronger than her.

"And stupidly risky," Ember added, relief and anger battling on her face.

Aylie stood her ground, making eye contact with Ember. "I'm a higher rank than either of you were when you first started adventuring with the Morning's Shade. I've also had much more training from the both of you in that time, and you both did risky things. Don't think I've forgotten that you both fought a Gold ranked elemental."

Zalia definitely couldn't argue the point, but Ember tried anyway.

"And we were also both much older, with higher-ranked backup *and* teams around us." Relief finally won out on Ember's face as Aylie had the sense to look just a tad sheepish. "I'm glad you're safe, though."

Ember hugged her tightly as Zalia turned to Hildebrandt.

"How are you doing?"

Hildebrandt was shivering, as if cold, despite the fact that she shouldn't be able to be. "I'm . . . I'll be alright."

Zalia helped her sit up against the wall, a thick blanket of soft leaves growing up and over to help warm her. "I won't scold you as I'm not your mother, but it was a risky thing you did to kill those Astar."

Hildebrandt shrugged with a rustle of leaves. "It had to be done. I wasn't going to beat them, otherwise."

Zalia nodded. She knew better than most that sometimes sacrifices had to be made. Despite that, she never wanted it to be others that made those sacrifices. "Well, as it is, you killed them and we were able to free Hidey. You've also got three new heirlooms."

She looked over to where the heirlooms were resting on a side table, and Hildebrandt followed her gaze, frowning.

"I don't really need any more than I have."

Zalia gave her a pat on the shoulder. "Don't worry about that now. Unfortunately, I'm going to have to get you focused on something else."

Zalia began talking, leading Hildebrandt through the events over the days she had been in the coma. Matthias's return brought joy to her face, while the meeting with the Astar rebel Het'jel brought concern and suspicion. Boreal walked in to see what all the fuss was about as Zalia spoke, sitting far from where Ember and Aylie were still talking and staring at Hildebrandt.

When she got to describing the plan, Hildebrandt's expression grew more concerned.

"That's a big risk for someone who just basically told me off for my previous one. I'm not sure I can fight something like that."

Zalia held up a hand. "In my defence, I brought it back to Faian for approval, and she and the council will talk it over before anything is decided. She'll also be meeting with Het'jel to get a feeling for them. Also, since you won't be the one doing damage to the monarch, you won't have to use Mutual Destruction again. The danger to you personally will probably be less than what you've just been through."

That got Hildebrandt looking thoughtful. "True enough, though the abilities of a Mythic ranked enemy who has an Ascendant ally should *not* be underestimated."

Zalia didn't argue the point, turning as Boreal spoke.

"*There is one more we can bring to the fight.*"

Zalia raised an eyebrow. "Oh, you have some mysterious ally that I don't know about?"

Boreal looked down and licked her paw in an innocent manner. "*Maybe.*"

Zalia looked back up at Hildebrandt, giving her a long-suffering expression and exhaling deeply. "Alright, then, who is it?"

Boreal stopped and looked back up. "*The one who gave me my crown.*"

Zalia frowned. "You know you never told us where you got that, right?"

Boreal was silent for a while before finally replying, "*I'll take you to meet them, only you. I made a promise not to reveal them to you until the time was right.*"

Zalia put a hand on her hip, looking Boreal up and down. "You're keeping secrets from me? Where *did* you go for those couple months?"

Zalia *swore* she could see smugness on Boreal's face despite him being unable to form human expressions. Maybe it was just exuded by her aura.

"*Let's go.*" Boreal started to walk out the door.

"Wait just a damn minute, go where?"

"*To the north!*"

Zalia rolled her eyes. "Boreal we can't just walk out and go to the north without saying anything to anyone!"

That finally got Ember and Aylie's attention.

"What? Why are we going to the north?"

Zalia turned an exasperated look to them. "Boreal apparently has some mysterious friend who can help us fight the monarch, and only I'm allowed to go meet them."

Ember gave Boreal a look identical to the one Zalia had just given moments earlier. "Boreal, are you keeping secrets from us?"

Zalia pointed at Boreal as she tried to inch her way out of the door. "You stay there!" She turned back to Ember. "That's what I said! If Boreal has a secret Emerald or Diamond rank friend hidden in her paws, I swear."

Everyone in the room was focused on Boreal now, her ears pointing backwards as if in an attempt to make herself more streamlined for a dash to safety.

It was Aylie who spoke up first. "You *are* keeping something from us, I can see it in your thoughts. Why didn't you tell me about this, you share *all* your secrets with me."

Like swivels on a queue, Ember and Zalia's heads both turned to Aylie.

"*All* her secrets?" Zalia asked.

Aylie paled. "Yeahhhhh."

She extricated herself from Ember and looked like she was about to explain, then disappeared.

Zalia looked at Ember. "I'm going to go with Boreal up north to find this powerful friend of hers. In all seriousness, if they're real and willing to help, I wouldn't say no."

Ember nodded. "Good, we have a bit of time before Hildebrandt is in a state to be fighting again, so we've got the time. Aylie and I are gonna have a nice long chat while you're gone."

Hildebrandt, who had been silently watching the entire ordeal, spoke up. "You're all crazy."

Ember turned to her. "You have no idea. It's Boreal's fault, she was the one that turned insanity into normalcy for all of us."

Zalia nodded her agreement as she left the room. "Yep, allllll Boreal." She put a hand on Boreal's back as she said so, the feline still frozen in the doorway. "Let's go meet your friend, shall we?"

A journey to the north of Endaria from their relatively central home of Nature's Reclaim used to take quite some time to complete. That had been back in the days of low-ranked travel, however. Now at Silver rank, with plenty of abilities that assisted in mobility, such as the Mobility and Flight passives as well as Zalia's many rituals to enhance speed, the journey wouldn't take long at all. It would be cut short even further by her ability to step back through the vault created by her gauntlet and instantly return to either of her Druid Groves.

They decided against bringing Boreal's children, as they would slow travel down considerably, since both Boreal and Zalia were able to go almost indefinitely without sleep due to Zalia's Survivalist passive, the ability shared with Boreal through their bond.

Excited at the sudden and unknown nature of their journey, Zalia applied the ritual of flight to Boreal as they left the house and took to the sky. It reminded her of her early days in Endaria, going wherever at a whim, without responsibility or any purpose other than survival.

Hours turned to days as the distant rolling hills and forests of Endaria flashed by beneath them. Zalia didn't manage to get any more information out of Boreal other than the promise that her friend was indeed real and very capable of helping in their fight against the monarch.

She had no idea where or how Boreal had found a high-ranked ally and befriended them enough within the short span of a couple months to the point that they'd fight a Mythic ranked enemy, but she was absolutely going to get the story out of her when they got back to Nature's Reclaim. Neither she nor Ember had pushed Boreal to tell them about her months away, but it was apparently about time they did.

The grass and green trees of Endaria turned to the snow-laden mountains of the north before long. Directed by Boreal, they flew past the mountain that contained Glemp and his people. Further and further they went, flying at speed for more than a day past the mountain. Zalia began to wonder just how far north Boreal had gone to find whatever ally this was, and *what* this ally was, before a mountain came into sight between two others. Boreal pointed it out and they made their way towards it.

It was large, taller even than Glemp's mountain home. From their low vantage point, Zalia could tell that it ended not in a point but was either flat or caved in on top.

She started to fly up towards it but Boreal interrupted her.

"We land and walk from here."

Zalia frowned. "What, why?"

Boreal didn't answer to Zalia's frustration, flying down to land.

She followed, her curiosity growing by the moment.

They landed amidst the thick powder of snow covering the ground, neither of them bothered by it or the cold it gave off. Pushing through with ease, they made their way up the base of the mountain as it grew steeper and steeper. They needed to clamber up amongst boulders and even climb rock faces at points, but Boreal insisted that they make the journey on foot. Up and up they went until they finally reached the top, the air thin to the point that were they not both capable of surviving with very little air, it might have been a problem.

Atop the mountain was a deep caldera, inside which the snow had fallen and then melted. The water made by that snow was rising up into the sky as steam, though the small amount of steam quickly dissipated into the air.

The cause of the melting snow was a massive, scaled form. With each breath of the giant, winged creature, sparks of lightning jumped to the ground around it, stone shattering and chips flying at its impact. The lightning wasn't what was causing the snow to melt, however. That was caused by the sheer heat coming off the creature.

Seemingly without a second thought, Boreal stepped over the ledge and would have walked right down towards the creature had Zalia not grabbed her by the tail and dragged her back.

"*Boreal!*" she hissed.

Boreal spun as Zalia pulled her back over the ledge, taking her tail out of reach. "*What?*"

Zalia poked her head over the edge, then ducked back as the massive creature let out another deep, rumbling breath. "*What the fuck is that!?*" Her voice was still a whisper, though she switched to telepathy to ensure she didn't wake the beast.

"*My ally! This is Rozestrazix, Storm of the North.*"

Zalia blinked at Boreal, shocked. She didn't know what she had been expecting but it hadn't been what looked to be an *entire damn dragon*.

They both heard the cracking of stone, and Zalia felt a bolt of fear run through her, the feeling deep and primal in a way she hadn't experienced in a long time.

"Reveal yourselves," a deep, thunderous voice commanded.

Boreal hopped over the ledge without further consideration, while Zalia stood, trembling.

"Ahh, young Boreal, it is good to see you again."

Zalia stared at Boreal, then the dragon, as it lowered its head to allow Boreal to bump her head against it.

"What the—"

CHAPTER SIXTY-FIVE

Boreal Always Has Been Cheeky

Zalia

Zalia stared in shock and awe as Boreal companionably butted heads with a dragon in a manner that was much too friendly. How exactly Boreal had made friends with *that* without Zalia finding out, she wouldn't ever know. The dragon before her was massive, blue and white scales glittering in the sunlight even as jolts of lightning sparked across their surface.

"So . . . you're Rozestrazix, then?"

The name felt alien on her tongue, though it flowed easily enough.

"Yes. You are Zalia, Hunter of the North, Druid of the Old Ones, Protector of Nature, and Mother of Beasts. Boreal has told me much of you."

Zalia took a hesitant step over the ridge she had been hiding behind and into the dragon's nest, looking accusatorily at Boreal. She had really jumped her with one hell of a surprise.

"She has, has she? Interesting. How exactly do you two know each other? She has forgone informing me of your existence until very, very recently."

Boreal, in full-out Boreal form, was ignoring both Zalia and Rozestrazix, choosing to explore the sights and smells of the massive nest around them. Zalia almost didn't blame her, as it was quite impressive, though the dragon towering what looked like thirty metres above her was significantly more so.

"I would ask you forgive her this, as it was I that asked her not to reveal my existence to you or any other that she knew."

Zalia nodded hesitantly. "Okay, I'll bite. Why, exactly, did you ask that of her?"

Rozestrazix settled down, the ground trembling beneath their giant form as they curled their tail in a manner that reminded Zalia of a cat. "Please do not bite. The reason I brought Boreal to me in the first place was for business without a time constraint that is irrelevant to other beings."

Zalia, still shaking from first contact with the massive, Mythic ranked being, attempted to appear calm by forming a chair for her to sit on, matching the dragon's demeanour. She was also a little off balance by the dragon's request for her to not bite. That was apparently not a commonly used phrase in its day-to-day conversation.

"Are either of you going to tell me about that business, now that I know of your existence?"

Rozestrazix's tail flicked as they considered, the action sending a blast of wind through the nest. "Perhaps I shall, however it is more important that we discuss the reason I have brought Boreal, and you by extension, here this time around."

Zalia fought off the urge to summon her armour out of instinct. Boreal had brought her here because there was a chance that the dragon would join their fight against the monarch.

"Boreal did tell me that there was perhaps one other that would join our fight. Did you call us here to tell us that you plan to?"

"That is correct."

Zalia tapped at her legs, choosing her words carefully despite the fact that Rozestrazix was completely calm by all measures of the word. "Excuse my bluntness but . . . why? It's not your kingdom, your fight, or your people. Why would you help us?"

The dragon huffed out a light breath, the gentle gesture for its giant form more like a force of nature for Zalia. "It is none of these things for you either, is it? All of those things are irrelevant, however. I am not so unaffected by the actions of the monarch as you assume."

Zalia frowned. "What do you mean?"

Rozestrazix lifted a giant claw, gesturing to the wide landscape laid out before them. "I am the guardian of this place and by extension, your kingdom. I keep these lands safe from the things that would enter it and destroy every living thing here without remorse. I keep the natural order of life safe, much as you do. The actions of the monarch brought beings from out of this world into it, many of whom attempted to enter these lands. To this day I am still rooting out those monstrosities from beneath the ground. The monarch of the Astar has gone too far; they have broken the natural order to bring themselves power at any cost. Due to the strangeness of their existence, the forces that should have already dealt with them cannot, so those of us with the power to do so must step up."

Zalia found herself nodding, the surprisingly logical and thought-out reasoning of the dragon more refreshing to her than water from a stream.

"Alright, I have nothing to argue with there. The council will be more likely to enter into this agreement with the Astar knowing that someone of your strength will be there, I feel, though learning of your existence might scare them."

Rozestrazix blinked slowly, shaking their head gently. "You will not tell them of my existence. The manner in which I shall be joining this fight will not be direct, but much like how the Ascendants of this world act. I shall manifest my power, my strength, and my will through you, Zalia. My main reason for being might be to guard these lands, but both you and Boreal will be given my might for the coming fight so that you might succeed. Be warned, Zalia, that this power will not be nearly enough for you to fight the monarch directly. Instead, it may keep you alive where you might die otherwise."

More than a little confused, Zalia watched Boreal tumble over the edge of the nest, only to pop back over trailing a drift of snow.

"Why do you not want to be revealed to the people of Endaria? Why bring me here if you only plan to channel your power through us, why not just use Boreal instead?"

Rozestrazix laughed, the sound vibrating the very world around them. "You ask many questions, yet by virtue of your asking, you answer them already. Do you not think you wouldn't notice if Boreal became incredibly powerful for the fight to come? You would have discovered my existence after the fight either way. As to why I wish to keep myself secret? Have you not seen with your own eyes what your people do to things they fear? Look how they engaged the Astar, look how they reacted to the invasion that ravaged the kingdom. These people charge blade first towards the things they fear. No, I will remain hidden from them."

Zalia stared at Boreal as she ran around the nest, pouncing on piles of snow and chasing after the flakes that were thrown into the air as a result.

"So . . . why put yourself in Boreal's path? Why reveal yourself to her?"

There was a twinkle in the dragon's eye as they responded. "The question you should ask is why *I* put Boreal in *your* path."

Zalia stared, unsure. "What do you mean? How could you have done that? Were you the one to kill Boreal's real mother?"

The dragon shook their head. "No, I simply helped Boreal live long enough that you would find her." Rozestrazix stood, shaking the ground with the force of their steps. "I am not long for the mortal realm, Zalia. I shall ascend, soon, and leave these lands without protection."

They turned, staring at the playful Boreal who turned in turn to face the dragon.

"Who better to take my place than one who knows deeper than any other the reality of this cold land? One born from it, one who knows the savagery of its nature. I found that you, too, lived in the manner of these lands and hoped that you would be a good guide for Boreal so that one day, she might take my place as the guardian. She is only one of many I have my eye on, yet is the most promising by far."

Rozestrazix took to the sky with beats of their wings so loud that even the dragon's rumbling voice barely sounded above it. "Leave now, you will find my strength flowing in your veins when you need it most."

With that final word, Rozestrazix dove down towards the lands beneath, wings beating as a storm formed above and around them.

Feeling like she had been put through an aeroplane turbine, Zalia turned to look at Boreal, her fur having received a similar treatment to Zalia's hair.

"You have been keeping a damned Mythic dragon from me!?"

Boreal walked up to her, then brushed against her leg as she walked past. *"You're not the only one who can make big, strong friends."*

As Boreal hopped over the ridge back towards their path downwards, Zalia stood stock-still, staring into the far distance.

She felt like someone had tased her.

Ember was *not* going to believe her when she got home. If she could even tell Ember about the dragon.

"Wait, Boreal." Zalia chased after her, catching up in short order. "We can tell Ember and Aylie about this, right?"

Boreal stopped for a second, staring upwards, before replying, *"Yes, but no one else."*

Zalia narrowed her eyes at Boreal. "Do you have some kind of way to communicate with Rozestrazix?"

Boreal avoided eye contact. "You *do*!"

She knew that Boreal was cheeky, she always had been. This, though, was on a whole different level.

Feeling Ember's curiosity through their bond at the wild and chaotic emotions Zalia had accidentally broadcast down it, she called up the entrance to her vault. "Come on Boreal, we better get back. The quick way."

They stepped out of the snow and into the calm, nourishing aura of her vault. With the relaxation she had built up over their long flight across Endaria dashed in one short conversation, the calm was very welcome indeed.

She was able to open up the portal that led back to Nature's Reclaim, making the journey that had taken them days in a few short steps.

Ember was waiting for them both on the front lawn by one of the Ancient of Life's giant trunks. "So? Who is this mysterious ally that Boreal is bringing?"

Zalia held up a hand for patience. "You are not going to believe this. Let's get Aylie and sit down for a chat, Boreal has *a lot* to explain."

Ember raised an eyebrow. "How bad could it be?"

Half an hour later, they were sat in the comfortable, warm living room as Boreal finished up her explanations.

Aylie stared dubiously at her, while Ember was watching Zalia with wide eyes, obviously believing the tall tales more having felt Zalia's emotions.

It took Aylie looking to Zalia for a confirming nod before her dubious disbelief turned to shocked disbelief.

"You're friends with a dragon?" Aylie asked.

Boreal dipped her head.

Zalia nodded.

"Yep, Boreal has been friends with a damn Mythic ranked dragon for who knows how long. Apparently they told her not to reveal its existence which only barely gives her an excuse."

Ember pointed to the crown floating above Boreal's head, one of her heirloom items. "You got that crown from a *dragon*!?"

Boreal had the *audacity* to look smug.

Zalia shook her head, still in disbelief at what she had just experienced. "I mean, they were huge! I could barely believe my eyes. Apparently, they're going to lend Boreal and I their power for the fight so we can measure up to the monarch."

Ember looked between them. "Well, that's actually a relief. I mean, I knew you would insist on joining that fight either way so some extra distance between you and death is a good thing."

Zalia frowned. "What? I wasn't going to fight the monarch. Neither was Boreal."

Ember gave her a flat look. "You say that now, but come time to kill that damned monster and you would be on your feet and out the door, ready to slay evil at a moment's notice. You can't help it!"

Zalia shook her head but didn't argue. There was plenty of evidence that Ember could use to prove her point and not much that Zalia could use to defend herself. In fact, Zalia even lost that argument to herself in her own head.

"Right. Has there been any word from the council?"

Ember nodded. "Yeah, it looks like we're doing this thing. They met Het'jel and were apparently convinced because Nateysta delivered the news yesterday. Give the rebellion a little bit of time to set up the baiting attack on a relatively distant town and this thing is a go."

Zalia took a deep breath, centring herself. Now that it was on, she couldn't lie to herself that she definitely would have gone anyway. It looked like everything had come to this, a final fight against the monarch. If they won, Endaria might finally have the time it needed to recover. If they lost, not only would Zalia and Boreal be dead but so too would Hildebrandt and most likely the majority of the Astar rebellion. There wouldn't be much in the Endarian kingdom or otherwise that would or could stand up to the monarch then.

Better that they won, then.

CHAPTER SIXTY-SIX

Rise Together or Die Trying

Zalia

While they waited for word from Het'jel about the coming fight, Zalia spent as much time as she could with her family.

They were all aware that, despite the power that would be lent them by Rozestrazix, there was a possibility that either Zalia or Boreal would die. Ember agreed that she and Aylie shouldn't join the fight, but they would wait by the portal to Zalia's vault should she need to bring them in for some kind of emergency. Aylie had already proven that in some situations, she was much more capable than almost anyone else due to her power set.

It was nice to relax and spend time with each other, though there was a haze of thoughts spinning around Zalia's head the whole time. A question that kept coming to the front of her mind time and again was about something Rozestrazix had said. They had told Zalia that they defended the northern lands from something, which protected Endaria by extension. She wondered what it was that lived out there beyond the dragon's lands that it had to remain in the north to defend against.

She might have been in this world for many years now but she still barely knew what could be found beyond the borders of Endaria, even less so beyond the lands adjacent. In her own world, she knew what the entire planet looked like because of the power of technology, yet here it was a mystery, unknown to any. It made her wonder if this is what the people of earlier times felt, the reason that they so often left their lands to discover other countries and peoples.

Time passed by quickly, the building tension in Zalia's body reaching a peak when Nateysta finally appeared three days past her return from the north.

"It's time, prepare yourselves."

He waited while Boreal, Zalia, and Hildebrandt, who had recovered from her use of Mutual Destruction, gave a warm farewell to the others. Zalia spent minutes that felt like eternity—yet were still too short—speaking softly to Ember and Aylie before kneeling down to ruffle the fur of Boreal's five children, each of them clustering around her to form a puddle of cats.

Eventually, Nateysta managed to draw the three away from the rest, and they were swept up by his power. Now familiar with the mode of transportation, Zalia leaned back to try to relax while they were dragged across the world. She cocked her head as two more spheres joined them from the direction of the capital, and though a normal person wouldn't have been able to see their occupants, Zalia was easily able to identify Larel in one and Matthias in the other. Larel gave Zalia a little wave and Zalia returned it, raising her arms on either side of her in a questioning gesture. Larel mimicked punching things, and Zalia laughed quietly to herself, while Matthias remained looking forward with a stoic expression.

She wasn't sure how good an idea it was to bring someone so low as Gold rank to fight the monarch, but she wasn't about to make a fuss about it. Not only was she lower-ranked than them but who was she to try to refuse them the chance to fight for their home?

It occurred to her then that almost all of Endaria's power in high-ranked people were in that little group. Hidey would still be back in the capital with Faian, who was herself quite close to Gold rank, but other than that, the closest they would have was Larel's partner, a Gold rank brewer. Zalia wasn't quite sure if he knew how to fight or not, though.

The distance they travelled must have been much further than that of Nateysta's serene cave as they were flying through the sky for maybe half an hour before their trajectory curved towards the ground, sinking into it and continuing downwards. Zalia ruminated about how much of this world apparently lived underground before they burst out into a brightly lit cave filled with the greenery of a forest.

They landed atop a cliff that gave them a sightline of the giant space, their view that of a forest extending into the distance, amongst which many Astar floated. Looking closer, Zalia could see buildings scattered throughout, the construction built in unity with nature rather than the normal Astar towns that reminded her more of the cities of her own world. The sources of light were giant spheres of warm white power that floated around, letting off small discharges of light as if they were miniature suns.

Nateysta, in his medium form, larger than any of the group members but not as massive as the day he had fought the thousand-eyed one, perched amongst the boughs of a nearby tree. Larel came over to embrace Zalia, then Hildebrandt, while Matthias stood to the side staring over the cavern.

"Larel! I didn't know you were coming."

Larel gave a brilliant smile. "I wouldn't have, but that giant tree bird over there said I have a powerset uniquely capable of beating enemies much more powerful than me. He's not wrong, so I decided to come along for the ride."

Zalia caught Hildebrandt staring over at Matthias and she realised that they hadn't seen each other in a long time. She gave the woman a nudge, and Hildebrandt walked over, the two of them speaking in low tones.

"Well, I'll admit I'm glad you're here, though I don't know if it will be safe for you."

Larel snorted. "You, a Silver ranker about to engage in a fight with a Mythic ranker, are telling me that I'm not safe?"

Zalia shrugged, ceding the point. "I have secrets that will help me"—Zalia jerked her head in the direction of Boreal—"and I don't think she can actually die anymore."

Larel raised an eyebrow at her. "I'd love to know how that works some other time. You going to tell us about these secrets you have?"

Zalia pretended to think about it. "I guess we'll find out. First though, I have a feeling our hosts are about to greet us." She pointed towards where two Astar that she recognised were flying towards them.

Het'jel landed, the transition from flight to walking so smooth it might as well have been second nature. They looked at Matthias, who was still admiring the cavern despite his conversation with Hildebrandt.

"It is beautiful, is it not? I remember planting the first seed myself."

Matthias visibly flinched as he realised who had spoken. He had obviously not fully recovered from the trauma of his capture, not that Zalia had expected him to in such a short span of time.

Zalia looked up at the nearest tree, guessing it to be thirty to forty years old. "So you've been here for a while then?"

Matthias took a step back from Het'jel but was ignored as they focused on Zalia.

"The rebellion has had to move many times over the span of its existence, but this is one of the longest lasting homes we have had. It took us a long time to develop the correct magic to allow us to remain hidden from the rest of the Astar."

Zalia nodded her head in sympathy. The Astar did seem to have a knack for finding things. "Well, how go preparations?"

Nateysta shifted ever so slightly in the tree behind them. "I have gathered a few forces of my own to assist in the fight and will bring them when the time comes."

Het'jel looked up at Nateysta, the heads of their two bodies simultaneously bowing in reverence. "And our people are finalising their plans for their attack. We've chosen a strategically important town, one that supplies most of a type of crystal that is often used for magical constructs within the Astar nation. It isn't a place we can hold should the monarch remain living, but if we win against them, then our ability to control what follows will be considerably improved. Additionally, we will take down the portal network in the town the moment reinforcements arrive from the monarch. This should slow them from getting back to help them if they call."

Larel and Boreal both had similar body postures indicating disinterest, each of them more of the kill-first-and-ask-questions-later type of person. Matthias managed to stop staring at Het'jel with suspicion at the mention of the crystals, some of the scholarly interest that Zalia remembered about him surfacing.

"These crystals will be important enough to warrant drawing away a significant force from wherever the monarch is while not drawing the monarch themselves?"

One of the two bodies of Het'jel turned to Matthias, and Zalia could see him visibly steel himself to not turn away.

"I believe so. Unfortunately, the one consistent personality trait of the monarch these days is a unshakable faith in their own strength and everyone and everything else being beneath them. They won't deal with us themself, it's probably one of the reasons we haven't been all hunted down and killed yet. The monarch will tell their subordinates to deal with us and let all those of us beneath them fight each other to the death."

There was sadness in their expression and aura, the same sadness they had expressed when Zalia had met with them more personally. Zalia knew where that came from, as they had been friends with the monarch before they had changed.

Matthias clued into the sadness too, narrowing his eyes in suspicion. "Do you know the monarch?"

The second of Het'jel's bodies turned to face him at the question. "Yes, we were close once. I've known them longer than any of you have been alive, longer than some Ascendants have existed."

Matthias stepped forward, looking a little aggressive. Zalia stood on edge, ready to intervene if she needed to.

"Tell me then, are you going to be able to fight them with everything you have?" he asked. "Can we rely on you to do what needs to be done?"

Some of the sadness in Het'jel's aura turned to anger, and Zalia glanced over at Nateysta to see if he would do anything. He didn't so much as shift.

"Know this, human. I choose to fight and to, with luck, kill my friend. It is not through anger or vengeance but mercy that I kill them, mercy to the person they once were, mercy to those they hurt that they never would have if they were in their right mind. I've looked for decades, centuries, for a way to help them, a way to free their mind from the split state from which they suffer. Short of forcing their second body to ascend, something that is simply not possible, I have found nothing. Do not lecture me on *my* priorities, on *my* dedication to this course of action. I have more invested in our success than you will ever have."

Matthias held the gaze of the body of Het'jel before him, staring deep into their eyes before slowly nodding his acceptance.

Larel sighed, loudly. "Right, if you are done with whatever that was, can we discuss what exactly the plan actually is?"

Everyone in the group of people turned to her.

"What? I really *don't* want to die, so I want to know how we plan on avoiding that happening."

Het'jel walked forward, using a type of spacial magic to carve out a semi-circle from the ground. A set of long steps leading from the outer edge and to the centre slowly lifted from the dirt. At the centre was a throne upon which a small figure sat.

Large pillars rose from all around the circle's edge, each one a work of art in broken and jagged shapes that elicited a shiver down Zalia's spine. From the flat tops of those pillars, beams stretched across to meet above the throne even as a wall rose behind it.

"This is the throne room of the monarch. It is a simple affair, and you will not find much to work with when it comes to a fight. While it may seem small, these stairs stretch for a few hundred metres, and the throne is large enough to fit the monarch's bigger than normal form."

Hildebrandt frowned as she walked around the little model. "How big, exactly? Defending against larger foes can make things difficult."

"The same size as Nateysta currently is," they replied, gesturing to where Nateysta perched in the tree, his form approximately eight metres tall.

"Well, that's going to be annoying."

Zalia nodded her agreement, though she doubted she would end up fighting the monarch. That would depend on how strong Rozestrazix's power made her and Boreal.

"Hildebrandt and I will engage the monarch directly while those of you that are Gold rank and below will be around the perimeter of this battleground to stop anyone from interfering in our fight. The high-ranked amongst the Astar numbers will be off to fight our attack on the border town and will be stuck there for some time, but there will still be those of Gold and Silver rank who are looking to improve their standing in the eyes of the monarch, and they will undoubtedly come to protect them. It is your job to stop their interference. Even though the damage they can do to us will be minimal, any distraction can be potentially fatal."

Larel scratched at the back of her neck. "So . . . that's it, that's the plan?"

"Unfortunately, the monarch has complete control over the structure and earth around this place. It is like a temple to them, completely within their power. It's impossible to tell what they will do with that, but we must adjust to any changes as possible."

Larel had a smile growing ever so slightly on her face. "So what you're saying is, kinda wing it and see what happens?"

"That isn't . . . inaccurate."

Nateysta shifted with the sound of creaking wood, saying, "The forces I have gathered will help maintain this boundary also, in addition to the help they will provide for the attack on the outer town. Zalia, I have seen that you will be given a little bit of assistance as well, from not one but two other powerful beings. It is good that you have managed to find a way to live through this."

Zalia looked over at him with narrowed eyes.

"Ro, have you been spying on me?"

He didn't reply.

"Also, where is Lumin? I know you've got them doing all that Ascendant training stuff but will they be joining us for this fight?"

"They will, if I deem it necessary."

Hildebrandt was looking at Zalia with curiosity. "You've gotten some help from two powerful beings?"

Zalia frowned, realising what Nateysta had actually said. "Well, only one, from what I remember. Hey, Ro, who is the other one?"

He, once again, chose not to reply.

"Enough," Het'jel interrupted. "Each of us will be responsible for our own fates soon. Neither Hildebrandt nor I will be able to take our focus from the monarch long enough to help any of you should you need it, so do not expect it."

Everyone nodded. They had all known that, even without Het'jel saying it. Killing the monarch was the purpose of their mission and it came before everything else.

Before they had left, Zalia and Hildebrandt had spoken with each other about what they would need to do. There were a few key advantages that they were keeping secret, one being the God-trap that Zalia had yet to tell Het'jel about. She didn't know if the Ascendant side of the monarch would choose to appear during the fight but if they did, Zalia was going to try to use the thing on them. Taking that power away from their enemy would greatly increase their chances of actually winning.

The other plan they had in motion was in the case of defeat. Should it get to the point that there was no chance of victory, Zalia would open her vault and get them all out of there. With Hildebrandt to defend their retreat, it should be possible for them to live through this thing one way or the other.

Het'jel broke down the small model in front of them all, and Zalia noticed that many of the rebel Astar in the distance were vanishing through portals.

"The time has come. Today we forge a new alliance between our people, one that will benefit us both," Het'jel said. "We will take the future of the Astar from the depths and show them the stars, even as we pull your drowning kingdom with us."

Hildebrandt hefted her heavy shield, keeping the mace in its loop for now while Larel cracked her neck and knuckles. Sand began to swirl around Matthias even as Het'jel began to create a complex diagram in the air before them. A portal opened and the two bodies of their Astar ally ran through, quickly followed by the others.

Zalia looked to Boreal as ice crackled along her close friend's back, then summoned her own weapons and armour, the ritual runes inscribed on their surfaces granting their power. With trepidation and hope surging through her body, they stepped through.

CHAPTER SIXTY-SEVEN

An End Comes to All Things

Zalia

Zalia was swept away by the familiar swirling colours of long distance tele-portation, the visual mess resolving itself into the massive throne room of the monarch. Larel was already on the way to the far side of the space where she would defend from any enemy that came towards the room. Matthias stayed on this side, gesturing for Zalia and Boreal to take the middle.

The throne room of the monarch sat high above an expansive city filled with Astar, floating about as pinpricks below. The skyscrapers and industrial structures of the city below were strangely at odds with the alien jagged architecture of the Astar, the view of a cityscape familiar to Zalia yet the individual details so very different.

She turned back to face the throne room as Hildebrandt and Het'jel approached the top of the stairs where the throne sat, its imposing form out-stripped by that of the monarch.

The eight-metre-tall form of their enemy stood from the throne as the two approached, their voices emitting from their auras much as Het'jel's did. "Het'jel, have you finally come to give your allegiance to me once more? You should not have brought this *filth* if you did."

Unlike Het'jel, the monarch's voice came from everywhere, the entire hundreds-of-metres long room vibrating with their very essence. Zalia understood what it meant for this place to belong to them, not only physically but the very soul of it.

"I have not, old friend. This is your last chance to give up on your ideas of ruling halfway between Ascension and mortality. Ascend your second body or have it die."

Zalia's heart felt like it was in her throat as the powerful beings confronted each other, the *power* that was exuded by their existence building ever stronger as conflict came closer.

Rage twisted across the monarch's face, before it was immediately schooled into neutrality again.

"I. Will. Have. Your. SOUL."

The words were screamed at such volume that Zalia's eardrums popped, healing back quickly.

As if choreographed, Hildebrandt, Het'jel's two bodies, and the monarch engaged in combat as nothing more than a blur to Zalia's eyes. The massive indestructible dome that was one of Hildebrandt's powers went up, and Zalia took her eyes away from that fight, her attention focusing away and towards the city laid out before them. A few Astar were already flying up towards them from the city below, though they looked to be of Silver rank and below.

The anticipation of a fight built within Zalia's body, and she could see the heavily muscled form of Boreal tensing up beside her.

From above, green orbs of Nateysta's power appeared as animals both familiar and alien were brought down into the Astar city. Those capable of flight were deposited directly in the air, many of them immediately diving down to attack the Astar on the way up.

Others, creatures lithe and bulky, fast and tough, scaled and covered with fur, were deposited along the pillars lining the throne room of the monarch. There were all kinds, ranging from Bronze to Silver to Gold.

An Astar appeared nearby and it was attacked by two animals, one a heavily muscled thing like a bear and the other a sleek fox-like creature. The bear was immediately torn in half by the Astar's spacial powers, but the fox jumped up and clamped onto the Astar's spine, a crunch resounding as it did.

Zalia had to look away, her bow shooting blindingly fast arrows down towards the Astar as her sword flashed at the one that had appeared before her. The Bronze ranked Astar, realising their mistake too late, died instantly by her hand.

It was quickly followed up by another, this one Silver rank and wielding proper weapons. Zalia danced around them, keeping her eye on Boreal as her friend fought a vicious battle against two Bronze and a Silver Astar.

A surge of power flooded through her body, the blessing of Rozestrazix making her feel stronger and faster. The Astar before her was suddenly sluggish and weak and it took her only a few seconds to dismember them, dodging their once quick dagger now easier than breathing.

Another Silver rank Astar appeared before her, and Zalia dodged the sword with a burst of speed upwards. She used the momentum to impale another Astar and threw their body at the Silver ranker. A third Astar tried to capitalise on the distraction of the other two to attack her from behind but found themselves being mauled by Zalia's shadow come to life; one of Boreal's abilities.

With Hunter's Mark on both the Silver rank Astar and the one that had tried to ambush her, Zalia spun and stabbed the quite mauled Astar straight through where she thought its heart might be. She used Kill Shot to do so, and the damage far over what the Astar could take was redirected to the Silver rank one, who had their entire torso blown up by the power.

Using a control over the wind that she hadn't ever experienced before, even when using Nature's Wrath, her bow was enhanced and her speed increased. The arrows that had sometimes been dodged now punched through heads and torsos as they saw fit, while Zalia spun between dozens of low-ranked Astar, taking them apart one after the other.

"What in the world did you just do, Zalia!" Larel called from her right.

Zalia only paused long enough to give a wink that had her laughing, battle mania obvious in Larel's expression as she blew up a group of three with a single punch to the leader.

The fight went smoothly from there. Each Astar that challenged her was quickly cut down without much fuss. She descended into a trance, moving with lethal efficiency, enjoying the obscene power that flowed through her body.

Nearby, Boreal was experiencing the same power, except instead of control over the wind, lightning arced across her body. The dozens of bodies of the Astar she had been fighting lay nearby, some scorched and others torn apart.

Zalia gave her a feral grin, then felt a fundamental change in the ground they were standing on. It felt like the smooth marble floor beneath them had awoken from a deep slumber and, with a grinding sound, moved.

Hildebrandt

Hildebrandt grunted as a force like she'd never felt before crashed into her shield. If it hadn't been for her power to resist knockback, she would have been sent flying into the wall with enough force to break bones.

Het'jel was moving quickly, dodging away from the bullet-fast fists of the monarch with one of their bodies as the other sent spells from afar. A lance of reality-warping power struck the monarch in the chest, but they shrugged off the impact and tried to grab once more at the closer body of Het'jel, missing by a hair's breadth.

Hildebrandt broke Stand Your Ground to dash closer, planting her feet and reactivating the ability just as the monarch punched her. The impact sent a blast of air out, but her shield absorbed most of the impact. Backlash struck back at the monarch at the same moment Hildebrandt's mace impacted, both forces striking at their wrist to little effect.

Het'jel's closer body created an ethereal chain and it snaked out to wrap around the monarch's other arm before latching the other end to the floor. It pulled taut, dragging the massive form of the monarch off balance and pulling their arm to the side.

The other body of Het'jel and Hildebrandt simultaneously took advantage of the off-kilter monarch, Hildebrandt striking with her mace twice before hitting them with Explosive Force as Het'jel cast a lengthier ability that slowly pushed a lance of the same reality-warping power down into the monarch's head. It inched ever down into flesh as the ground around them screamed the monarch's rage.

Another chain wrapped around the monarch's other arm and dragged them to their knees with a loud thud.

"Give up! Your body WILL be leaving this mortal plane, ONE WAY OR ANOTHER."

An ethereal collar locked around the monarch's neck and a chain appeared to drag their head down to hit the floor. The spike of force drilling into their forehead was smashed straight through their skull by the impact. Het'jel summoned another of the lances that began to push through the monarch's spine.

"You are *weak*."

The ground around them shook as the monarch spoke. Their head began to lift from the ground, breaking the chain. The monarch snapped upwards, shattering the chain on their left arm and exploding with an immense force. Het'jel's closer body was thrown away as the flying one weathered the blast better from a distance. Hildebrandt, who had just shaken some of the fear from the start of the fight, sheltered behind her shield.

A punch unlike anything else the monarch had used so far sent Hildebrandt flying, the force so strong that it broke Stand Your Ground. She hit her dome with so much momentum that it sent a crack through the supposedly indestructible surface.

Zalia

Zalia was momentarily shocked as the walls around her began to close in in an attempt to crush her. She flew upwards as the ground shook and barely cleared the walls as they slammed closed behind her.

An explosion rocked the battlefield originating from the dome, and Zalia looked over to see that Hildebrandt's dome had cracked. She stared in disbelief for a moment before her attention was drawn away as one of the beams arching overhead grew a spike that lanced down towards her. She dodged the attack and found herself in the way of a sword strike from a Gold rank Astar.

This wasn't the first time a Gold rank Astar with a sword tried to surprise attack her midair but this time, she was the stronger one.

She dodged easily, flipping in midair to kick the sword out of their hand in an acrobatic move. Her own sword followed in an upwards slash as she finished the flip, cutting a shallow line down their torso as her bow shot them in the leg. The air answered her call and swept the Astar's sword off the edge of the throne room and straight through the head of a Bronze ranker floating up there.

Without missing a beat, the Astar got in close to grapple her, pulling her down towards the high walls that were growing upwards still. She dropped her sword, twisting her head to the side to allow her bow to shoot the wrist of the hand holding her arm. That move freed her left arm to punch the Astar straight in the gut with as much force as she could muster. They let out a wheezing gasp at the impact, and Zalia followed it up by using both her hands to pull their head down into her knee, hearing the crack of bone for her efforts.

Bloody but impassive, the Astar pulled back slightly only to be jumped on from behind by a feral Boreal coated with ice and arcing lightning.

The lightning made the Astar's back arc, revealing their neck for Boreal to bite into. She shook the Astar like a limp doll before ice grew up and over their body, freezing it, only for it to shatter into a million pieces moments later.

Zalia took the moment of reprieve to check on Matthias, barely able to see him through his swirling storm of sand. He had managed to avoid the marble walls by lifting up on a rising tide, then swirled it into a frenzy with which he was savaging dozens of Astar using a death-by-a-thousand-cuts method. Larel, on the other hand, was punching through walls with explosive force, neither Astar nor wall able to get in her way as the low-ranked sycophants were cleared away. Many of the low-ranked ground animals had unfortunately succumbed to the power, but it looked as if they had won this initial flurry of combat.

Boreal and Zalia's attention was drawn away from their allies as another powerful being appeared on the battlefield. They stared up as a Diamond rank Astar came down towards them. They hadn't won their fight just yet, then. Unfortunately, even if they had won their battle, that wouldn't have won the war, and another crack had just formed in Hildebrandt's dome.

Hildebrandt

Hildebrandt dropped heavily to the floor after hitting the side of her dome again. The monarch was using her body like a wrecking ball against her own power, slamming her time and again into its surface until it was cracked all over.

She stood up and activated Stand Your Ground once more. Het'jel tried to chain down an arm but was unsuccessful as the monarch marched towards Hildebrandt. Steeling herself for another strike, Hildebrandt shook off her fear. The only reason she hadn't yet had her body completely destroyed was that the monarch kept hitting her shield, which healed her for as much damage as it blocked. Not that she necessarily needed her body to continue fighting.

Realising it was time, she activated another ability of the shield, making her immune to magical effects for a time. The monarch punched her with another of its powerful attacks but failed to break Stand Your Ground.

Hildebrandt stared up at the face of the monarch, a hole straight through their forehead, as a sneer crossed their face. The monarch wrapped a massive hand around Hildebrandt and picked her up.

"Filth."

She was thrown at speed, the dome cracking once more as she struck it. It was webbed with fine cracks and Hildebrandt feared that it would break soon. When that happened, they would have a hard time stopping the monarch from harming their allies.

Larel

Larel appeared next to Zalia only moments after Matthias did. They stared up at the descending Diamond ranker with dread.

"There weren't supposed to be any in the city," Matthias said.

Larel cracked the knuckles of one hand. "Ifs, whys, whens don't matter now. We do what we have to."

Matthias nodded in agreement. "What are you doing to suddenly be so powerful, is it Nateysta? Can you give us that power too?"

Zalia shook her head, not clarifying any further.

He looked at her but didn't push. "I guess we do our best, then."

With the power given to them, Zalia and Boreal were operating on a level, stat-wise at least, akin to Emerald rank. The two of them might have a chance against the Diamond ranker if their abilities were functioning at that rank too. As it was, most of the strength someone like Hildebrandt had as an *actual* Emerald ranker came from her abilities, not her stats.

Zalia spun her sword around, flying up to meet the Astar in battle.

"You two keep the others at bay, Boreal and I will deal with this."

With her anti-death measure still available, and Boreal having her own as well, they were still within relative safety. If those measures were used, she would need to call up Larel and Matthias to fight with her.

As she rose into the sky to meet the Astar, wings beating and wind swirling around her, sword held to the side, she began to feel the influence of a new power. A deep red glow rose up from within her eyes as words from a long time ago echoed through her mind, sent there not by anyone present in the fight.

"You may take refuge in the heat and stone, but the heat and stone will not rise to fight at your bidding, Druid. Not yet, at least."

It was the words spoken to her by the Spirit of Heat and Stone, the Ascendant that was the creator of Glemp and his people, who she had asked to help them in their war against the demon invasion.

Fire licked its way down her sword and with a battle cry, she burst upward with a sudden increase of speed. Boreal followed her, jumping off quickly created platforms of ice, lightning crackling through the air with her every movement.

The Diamond rank Astar crashed down into her, twin glaive flashing. She deflected the first blade, leaning back to dodge the other side as it came up. She pushed forward to stab the Astar in the chest only to have her sword caught between arm and torso. With a skilled twist, her weapon was ripped from her grasp even as the twin glaives came around to slash her across the chest.

She flapped backwards, giving Boreal room to jump up and latch her powerful jaws on the glaive-wielding arm. Her sword, still aflame, reappeared in her hand as her bow shot powerful, air magic infused arrows towards the Astar. They dodged nimbly, grabbing Boreal by the back of the head and tearing her off their arm.

Zalia used the moment of time to cast Nature's Wrath and compressed a bubble of air and fire down around the Astar, crushing it with the power. A perfectly spherical shield appeared to block her attack, and the five air elementals she had summoned with the ability came to increase the pressure.

The shield exploded under the combined weight of the power, but the Astar was not in it. They had vanished, reappearing behind Zalia to strike. The current power of her mental stats along with her new affinity with the air allowed Zalia to see the strike coming, and she bent completely backwards, dodging the blade meant for her neck.

She turned that backwards flip into a kick that sent the Astar flying through the sky, chased by three arrows, each striking their target. Boreal followed up her attack with a Pounce from behind that froze the Astar in a cage of ice, sending them tumbling down to the ground below. Zalia dove with them as the Astar landed, shattering the ice from their body with the impact. She came down moments later, her sword impaling the Astar point-first, going straight through their torso and into the ground below as her bow shot more arrows into the still form.

Zalia was thrown back by a punch to her chest that had her vision swimming, and the Astar ripped her flaming sword out of its chest and threw it to the side. The sword reappeared in her hand once more, but she didn't use it as she directed earth and plants to appear from the ground and entangle the Astar. Each restraining plant or clump of earth was thrown off easily enough, but the sheer number of them gave enough time for Zalia to summon a ball of lava above the Astar, slamming it down onto them with a ground shuddering impact.

Given a brief reprieve from combat, Zalia watched as Hildebrandt's dome cracked once more, then shattered. The sound was loud, like glass shattering then trickling to the floor.

A powerful aura washed over them all as the forms of the monarch, Hildebrandt, and Het'jel were once again revealed. The monarch was growing further in size, the strength of their presence increasing many times over, and Zalia realised that this is what she had been waiting for. The Ascendant power of the monarch was showing itself in a move to finish the fight.

"Matthias, Larel, take over!"

They reacted instantly, engaging the Astar with Boreal as Zalia dropped down to the ground.

Preoccupied with Boreal's ice encasing them, the Diamond rank Astar wasn't able to stop Zalia as she hit the ground and pulled out the God-trap. She placed it on the ground and with a thought, activated the item. It rose from the ground, the concentric rings spinning faster and faster, but nothing happened.

Zalia stared at it, confused as to how it was meant to work. The diary they had taken from the same place they had found this item said nothing about how to make it work, other than to activate it.

In a flash of blue and white light, Lumin appeared next to her, barking excitedly. The presence of the starlight wolf had a strange effect on the world around them and the monarch suddenly stumbled, then growled.

"*What* is that?" The voice reverberated through the stone but it sounded weak, confused.

A powerful light was drawn out of the monarch's chest, and Het'jel didn't pause, using ethereal chains to tie down the monarch once more. The massive form of the monarch began to shrink in size as the bright light continued to stream from it. The light shaped itself momentarily into the appearance of another Astar, face wracked with pain, anger, and fear before it was sucked into the spinning God-trap.

The battlefield froze for a moment, everyone's eyes locked onto where the monarch's Ascendant power had been stolen from them. The pause of silence broke as the monarch screamed, a pained and broken sound.

Het'jel silenced them.

The chains holding the form of the monarch still dragged them to the floor, more powerful ethereal chains arcing over the body to restrain it even further. A complex circle of runes began to appear in the sky at the beckon of Het'jel's second body, and once complete, blasted a blinding beam of reality-warping power downwards.

The spell continued, more and more of the power annihilating the body of the monarch until the stone of the throne room echoed their last, faint words: *"I will make you pay for this . . ."*

CHAPTER SIXTY-EIGHT

Oathsworn

Zalia

The silence of the throne room was broken by Larel's yell, and Zalia turned to see that the Diamond rank Astar had fled. She looked to Het'jel to see if they would follow but they didn't give chase.

Before her sat the God-trap, the essence of the monarch's Ascended side trapped within.

"What do we do with this?" She looked at Het'jel again.

"I do not know what that is, I have never seen anything of its like." One of their bodies came over to inspect the spinning concentric circles, carefully inspecting it. "This will not hold them forever, though it will do so for a very, very long time."

Knowing what higher-ranked beings usually considered to be a long time, Zalia figured that meant almost forever on the time scale of a mortal like herself.

"We are going to have to find somewhere to hide it then. It's important that the monarch isn't freed by any of their forces while you wrestle for control."

A flash of light and a wash of aura signalled the appearance of Nateysta behind them, in his largest form.

"That will not be necessary."

Another huge figure appeared, a swirling mass of fire and earth mixing to create a core of lava. It was followed by yet another, this one a cloud with strikes of lightning crackling through it. A fourth appeared, a swirling tide of water growing to form an elemental larger than Zalia had seen before. Lastly, there appeared another Ascendant that she recognised. It was Scour, the Desert Storm, his appearance just as his title would suggest. Each of them was an Ascendant of extreme power, their overlapping auras feeling like the weight of the world pressing down. Lumin left Zalia's side to go stand beside them, the wolf's form diminutive in comparison.

"We will deal with this ourselves, now that you have locked them away. Entering into the space of another Ascendant is always a dangerous prospect, even in larger numbers. Now, however, the monarch cannot retaliate."

Nateysta raised his wings, casting a shadow across the throne room as a small tendril of the monarch's power left the God-trap to reside in a sphere of his power. The other Ascendants of nature followed suit, raising arms or directing tendrils of power towards the God-trap, syphoning away little bits of the monarch until the trap was empty.

"Each of us shall guard a piece of them to ensure that they will never rise again."

The awed onlookers had to look away as flashes of multicoloured light signalled the departure of the Ascendant council. Only Nateysta remained, in his smaller form now.

Zalia took the God-trap and stored it away in her vault once more, hoping that she would never have the need to use the item ever again. She looked around at her allies and let out a breath of relief that she had been holding, very literally, since stepping through the portal to the throne room.

Boreal came up to rub against her leg, the loud purrs reverberating through the air. Zalia laughed, so relieved that they had succeeded against the monarch that she couldn't contain her joy. Even the power of Rozestrazix and the Spirit of Heat and Stone leaving her body didn't cut into the pure happiness flowing through her.

Larel came up and gave her a back-crushing hug. "You know, I didn't think that the socially awkward, little low-ranked archer tagging along to help clear a mine of minor elementals would end up here amongst gods and Ascendants, swinging so hard above her weight class too!"

Zalia smiled, extricating herself from the crushing grip. "You're telling me. If you had explained any of this to the me from five or six years ago, I wouldn't have believed a word. In fact, I'd have thought you were a little insane."

Het'jel, Hildebrandt, and Matthias all came over to join the small group.

"This was quite an unusual fight, unique even in the experiences of my long life. Most surprising was the power that I felt coming from you, Zalia. What did you do? While I have you here, where did you find an item capable of trapping an Ascendant?"

All eyes turned to her and Zalia gave her best sly smile. "A girl needs to keep some secrets to herself."

Both the eyes of Het'jel narrowed from starry orbs into suspicious starry orbs. "Are you secretly an Ascendant yourself?"

"What? No, no. Nothing like that. As for the God-trap, that is a little something I found in a temple in the desert with that sandstorm Ascendant we just saw trapped inside it."

Matthias stared at her with wide eyes. "*You* are the one that freed Scour?"

She looked up at the sky where Scour had just been, then back down to Matthias.

"Um, yeah?"

Matthias, in a move that shocked everyone present, went to one knee in front of her.

"What is happening?" she whispered.

"I cannot express my gratitude deeply enough. I have spent a good part of my life searching for Scour, a tradition passed down through generations of my family. The powers I wield come from the teachings of that Ascendant, from times past. Thank you."

Zalia got a hold of Matthias by the shoulders and lifted him to his feet. "Ooookay, none of that. I stumbled across Scour in a long forgotten temple, that's all. Please, it's fine." She tried smiling in a friendly manner. "Besides, helping the old Ascendants of Endaria has kind of become a habit for me."

"To the benefit of us all," Het'jel added.

Zalia turned to them. "Right, what do we do now?"

"Now, you go home. You have all done well in helping us, and I hope that peace can be found between our two peoples. I will not ask that you do more in stabilising my rule as the new leader of the Astar people. but I will let it be known that any and all help will be gladly received."

Zalia turned from Het'jel to Nateysta. "And how about from your side? Is there anything else you feel we should do?"

"I must speak with you before you depart, but the others may go."

Zalia nodded, then opened her vault. She then opened the entrance inside that led to Nature's Reclaim, and Ember and Aylie came sprinting through, looking ready for battle.

"Woah, woah. We're all good. We won and now we're coming home."

Ember stopped mid-charge, staring at her. "Oh."

Zalia gave both her and Aylie hard hugs before gesturing for them to go back. "Wait for me, I'll be through in just a moment, okay?"

Ember nodded, then pulled Aylie back to Nature's Reclaim with her.

Zalia wandered over to Nateysta, walking with him to the edge of the throne room to look out over the Astar city that she thought was their capital.

"This could have gone a lot worse than it did."

"I do not think so. I and the others have been planning for such an outcome, though they have done so for much longer than I."

Zalia considered his words for a long time before speaking again. "The starlight wolf once told me that the Ascendant spirits of nature would not intervene, that they would not act beyond their nature. What changed?"

There was a twinkle of humour in Ro's eyes as he replied, "Tell me Zalia, would you have fought as hard as you did this whole time, or done the things you did, if you had known that the Ascendants of Endaria were working so hard towards this outcome?"

"Probably not, I might have even left Endaria for good somewhere along the way if I had known that the Ascendants were actually working towards fixing the root of the problems facing the kingdom."

"And none would have blamed you for doing so. It is not the duty of an Ascendant to interfere in the mortal world in a manner so direct as what the monarch was doing. Even those who are of the Mythic rank are expected to act in a higher manner than the normal person. Beings of our power have such destructive capabilities that if we were to engage in fights within the mortal realm as others do, the world would nearly be destroyed by the strength brought to bear. You saw a little of this when I fought directly with the thousand-eyed one above the capital, yet that was on a smaller scale than most."

Zalia nodded, understanding a little. "And that was why they all came here to help deal with the monarch?"

Ro nodded. "All of us are hesitant to interact directly with any mortal being, and the monarch had managed to abuse that by the dual nature of their existence. Half in our world, half in yours. None of the others would have interfered directly in the battle against the mortal side, yet when the monarch manifested their Ascendant side to fight, they all began to move to join the fight, even if it cost some of us centuries of recovery to do so."

Zalia frowned, leaning against the pillar next to her as she watched chaos unfolding beneath her. There were animals brought by Nateysta still fighting below, while it appeared that the rebellion had also begun to assault the city. There would be much blood in the future of the Astar people.

"But I used the God-trap."

"Yes, there was no need for them to interfere directly. They like to keep it that way, intervening with the mortal realm in small ways such as blessings or sending their worshippers, elementals, or beasts to perform duties for them. It is like this that we stop what happened to my own world from happening here. You have gathered much goodwill amongst their number with your actions. Much of the work you have done towards this goal has reduced how much they have needed to act."

Zalia nodded, understanding. "That all makes some sense now, at least. Are you still planning on going to reclaim your world?"

"Yes. The thousand-eyed ones and their ilk have no qualms about interfering directly in the mortal realm. In fact, none of them are even from a world like you would understand it. We will need many Ascendants to remove their grasp on Cormaine."

The happiness from defeating the monarch had been slowly seeping from Zalia's body, but the rest of it left as she realised where Ro was taking the conversation.

"I promised to help you retake your world, when the time came. The Endarian people owe you as much as well."

Ro didn't reply for a while, staring out at the city with her.

"Yes, I will call on you all to help me retake my own world. The Ascendants here also owe me for my help in stopping the monarch, and they have each given me promises of assistance when the time comes. Do not worry, though, Zalia. The time *will* come that I call on you, but I wish for you and your people to regain strength and grow beyond your current capabilities before that time comes. Go, be with your family. Rest, but do not idle. You must be ready when the time comes."

With that, Ro vanished.

The omen echoing in her mind, Zalia returned through the vault portal to her home, finding the love and peace of her family waiting. Despite their relaxing presence and the beautiful sights of the home and family Zalia had made, Ro's words did not leave her mind. She had a feeling that they wouldn't until the day he came to find her.

About the Author

Leif Roder is the author of the Hunting and Herbalism series, originally released on Royal Road. They studied both aeronautics and software engineering before quitting university and moving abroad, where they began writing books on their phone while on the bus on the way to work. This eventually turned into a full-time career as an author. Now, they write all kinds of fiction, from fantasy to sci-fi with a sprinkling of magic to short stories about cats. They also enjoy a little wall climbing and archery as a treat. Roder lives in New Zealand.

RESPAWN YOUR CURIOSITY

follow us on our socials

podiumentertainment.com

@podiumentertainment

/podiumentertainment

@podium_ent

@podiumentertainment